The A. Meredith Walters novel that started it all . . .

FIND YOU IN THE DARK

Picked for the "What to Read After *Hopeless*" List
by *Maryse's Book Blog*

"Emotional, turbulent, and honest."

—*Heroes and Heartbreakers*

"I can't recommend A. Meredith Walters's books enough. . . . You don't leave her books behind after the story has ended. These are the kinds of books you carry with you."

—*In the Best Worlds*

"There is no question that A. Meredith Walters is one of my favorite authors. She always writes her stories so that we can relate to the characters; they jump out of the books and into our hearts each and every time. Her books have deep meaning to them but are also sweet and sassy with some sexy to steam up the pages."

—*Book Addict Mumma*

"Brilliant, amazing, gut-wrenching."

—*Shh Mom's Reading*

"One wildly bumpy ride. . . . Emotional doesn't even begin to cover it. The feelings were so raw and vivid that it seemed so real. . . . This is one story that I plan to follow to the end. It's going to be me and my tissue box all the way."

—*The Bookish Brunette*

ALSO BY A. MEREDITH WALTERS

Find You in the Dark

Light in the Shadows

lead me not

A. MEREDITH WALTERS

GALLERY BOOKS

NEW YORK   LONDON   TORONTO   SYDNEY   NEW DELHI

*For everyone who is lost
and hopes to be found . . .*

G

Gallery Books
A Division of Simon & Schuster, Inc.
1230 Avenue of the Americas
New York, NY 10020

First Gallery Books trade paperback edition August 2014

GALLERY BOOKS and colophon are registered trademarks of Simon & Schuster, Inc.

For information about special discounts for bulk purchases, please contact Simon & Schuster Special Sales at 1-866-506-1949 or business@simonandschuster.com.

The Simon & Schuster Speakers Bureau can bring authors to your live event. For more information or to book an event, contact the Simon & Schuster Speakers Bureau at 1-866-248-3049 or visit our website at www.simonspeakers.com.

Cover photograph © Jan Scholz

Manufactured in the United States of America

10 9 8 7 6 5 4 3 2 1

ISBN 978-1-4767-7414-5
ISBN 978-1-4767-7415-2 (ebook)

prologue

maxx

*j*ust *this once,* I swore as I felt the needle kiss my skin. I grimaced as the sharp tip slid beneath the surface and connected with the waiting vein. The prick of pain bothered me. The sensation made me feel sick to my stomach.

Given how eager I was for the release, it was almost comical how squeamish I was when it came to the methods I had chosen to get my fix.

I don't want this.

If only it were true. Too bad want and need were two entirely different things.

Sure, I didn't *want* this. But my body sure as hell *needed* it. My veins burned as I unloaded the drug into my body. I picked at the skin around my nails, waiting for the high.

I had never gone to this extreme before. I had always kept myself perilously close to the edge without actually going over.

But this was different.

I was different.

And the need to drown out the chaos in my head outweighed

the inherent fear I felt of the needle that now hung limply between my fingers.

I was a goddamned mess. I sat there, squatting in the stall of the nastiest public toilet I had ever been in, when I could be *out there*, doing anything else but this.

What the fuck was wrong with me?

My phone buzzed in my pocket, but I didn't bother to look at who was calling me. Because I already knew it would be *her.*

Aubrey.

In a moment of stupidity I had called her. I had let my obsession with her rule me. Now she was worried.

I wish she would stop fucking worrying.

Christ, now I felt guilty. Because I *should* feel guilty for what I was doing to her.

I fisted my hand over my heart, ready for the pain that resided there to go away. I checked the time on my watch. Five minutes.

Five freaking minutes already. It felt like five fucking years.

Any second and I would forget about all of this.

My phone buzzed again, and this time I pulled it out and stared at the screen. Aubrey's name flashed bright in the dimness.

Like a beacon.

Or my salvation.

Before I was too blissed out on the high to care, I felt the fear.

A deep-in-my-bones sort of panic that not even the smack could erase. It all had to do with *her.*

Aubrey.

And the consequences of my selfish choices on the two of us.

In my sudden clarity, I wished to God I could take it back—the moment when I had let the shameful taste of oblivion mean more than the peace I had found in her arms. I wanted to suck the poison from my veins and go back to those minutes before I had thrown my life away for a chance at drug-induced nirvana.

Because *she* was my nirvana. My quiet in the storm. And what

I felt for *her* was a hell of lot more real than anything I could experience at the sharp end of a needle or through the chalky taste of pills in my throat.

But it was too late, and soon I wouldn't care about any of it. And for the first time I hated it. I hated the high. I hated the relief. I hated *me*.

And then, finally, my limbs became heavy. My heartbeat began to slow. My mind, which was just a second ago debating whether to let her save me, clouded in a haze.

Who needed salvation when I had . . . *this*?

My phone buzzed again, and in a fit of anger, I threw it against the bathroom stall and watched with an encroaching indifference as the pieces fell to the floor.

My eyelids drooped, and my knees buckled. I slid down the wall to sit on the piss-stained floor as the air around me vibrated from the bass of the music playing in the club just beyond the door.

My mouth hung open, and all I felt was the euphoria. I fell to my side and pressed my cheek into the filth, pieces of my phone cutting my face.

Guilt. Fear. Panic. Even love . . . it was all gone.

All I had was . . . *this*.

And for now, that was enough.

chapter
one

"Here are the dates and times for the addiction support group on campus. We coordinate with the local substance-abuse treatment center in facilitating the twelve-week program. The BS in psychology program here at LU requires fifty volunteer hours in a certified program to ensure your eligibility for graduation." Dr. Lowell held out the list, and I took it with a smile.

Dr. Lowell smiled back. She was a small woman with short brown hair and serious eyes behind wire-rimmed glasses. She exuded a no-nonsense persona, which is why I gravitated toward her so easily in my early days at Longwood University. I had craved her rigid demeanor to counterbalance the tailspin in my head.

"Aubrey, I know this will be tough for you, but I think it's extremely courageous and downright awe-inspiring the way you're using your history to help others. The group will be lucky to have you."

I blushed at the compliment and tucked the paper into my bag. Compliments had always made me uncomfortable because I knew, without a doubt, that I didn't deserve them.

"Thanks, Dr. Lowell. I'll have a look at the times and check my schedule. I'll let you know what days I can sit in." I got to my feet and slung my bag over my shoulder. Dr. Lowell came from around her desk and followed me to her office door.

"I've already let Kristie know you'll be assisting with the group. I'll e-mail you her contact details; that way you can communicate with her directly," she said, holding the door open for me. "Now, this will be a lot more than you simply sitting in the group and listening while taking notes. You're going to be an active facilitator. You'll be working with Kristie in preparing for the sessions. She'll want you to lead discussions. Do you think you're up for it?"

It was an understandable question. Despite the fact that I currently had a 4.0 GPA and worked my butt off to maintain my scholarship at LU, Dr. Lowell was one of the few people on campus who was aware of my sordid and overly depressing history.

She was also the only person who didn't allow me any excuses because of it. And for that, I appreciated her more than she could ever know. So her question didn't piss me off the way it would have coming from someone else.

"I'm totally up for it, Dr. Lowell," I said, injecting as much confidence as I could muster into my voice. Maybe if Dr. Lowell believed me, I could believe myself.

Dr. Lowell's smile was a bit thin, and I was almost certain the tiny woman was a mind reader—that she somehow saw into my head and bore witness to my floundering confidence.

Because it was one thing to study the psychological effects of substance abuse. I could recite the textbooks inside and out. I could connect the dots from A to B. I could read the case studies and pretend that those people didn't exist.

It was something else entirely to sit in a circle and hear their stories firsthand, to listen to strangers spill their guts as they shared how close they had come to losing it all. I knew that would make it all so very, very real.

And all that realness was a scary thing for a mind still reeling from a three-year-old trauma.

"Have a good evening, Aubrey," Dr. Lowell said as I walked down the hallway of the psychology building. When I got outside and started my walk through the quad, it was already getting dark. The January air was cold, and I could smell snow.

My phone chirped in my back pocket, and I fished it out, finding a text from my roommate, Renee Alston. The vague words on the screen left an uncomfortable knot in the pit of my stomach.

Heading out. See you tomorrow.

I thought about texting her back, demanding details. Once upon a time Renee had been the ultimate fun girl. She had been the first to blast her music and get crazy drunk.

She used to be my complete opposite in every possible way. The wild girl with the heart of gold. The total extrovert who was the life of the party. Beautiful bombshell with guys falling at her feet. Taking full advantage of her long red hair and killer curves, she worked a room and enjoyed every moment.

But that was before Devon Keeton had entered the picture.

I squeezed the phone tightly in my fist and forced myself to put it back in my pocket. Responding to the text in any way would only further alienate the shadow girl who wore my best friend's clothing.

At one time, our friendship had started to heal the snarly tangles of my wounded psyche. I had opened myself up to Renee in a way I never thought I'd be able to open up again.

So feeling like I was losing something I had come to depend on made me anxious and sometimes bitter.

And more than a little angry.

The campus was surprisingly busy for a Friday evening. Usually the place became a ghost town by four o'clock. The college was small, so most weekend entertainment happened away from the manicured lawns and perfectly pristine brick buildings.

I shoved my hands deeper into my pockets and hunched my shoulders, feeling the cold. I was making some outrageous and rowdy weekend plans in my head that included digging out the rest of my winter sweaters and categorizing them by textile and color. Watch out, world, Aubrey Duncan was getting her cleaning on!

I noticed a group of people standing in front of the brick wall that ran along the north edge of the campus. The students gathered there were pointing, and there was a definite excitement as they stared at something that had grabbed their attention.

My curiosity got the better of me, and I made my way over to the crowd. Shouldering my way through the group, I was confused by what I saw—more particularly, by why it was creating such a reaction.

I tilted my head, trying to make out the detailed picture that had been spray-painted onto the brick. A massive hand was holding a grip of figures meant to be people. Some were screaming, some appeared to be laughing, and others were falling to the ground, a mass of flailing limbs, as they jumped from the grasping, God-like fingers. The picture had been painted in vivid reds and oranges, and the people were outlined in thick bands of black.

Beneath the picture in sweeping block letters was the word *Compulsion* followed by a series of numbers.

It was definitely impressive, for graffiti. I just couldn't understand why people were staring at it as though it held the meaning of the freaking universe.

I turned to the two girls standing beside me. They were talking in excited whispers, pointing at the painting. "I don't get it," I said blandly, arching an eyebrow.

The girl closer to me looked shocked. "X did this," she replied, as though that would explain everything.

"X?" I asked, feeling like I had missed an important lesson on college cultural relevance. From the way the two girls were staring at me, I might as well have a damned *L* tattooed on my forehead.

Look at me! I'm the loser who has no appreciation for spray paint on a wall!

"Uh, yeah," the second girl said, over-enunciating her words as though she was talking to a total idiot. Apparently, I was the idiot in this situation.

"He leaves these pictures for everyone to find. You know, to help people find where Compulsion will be over the weekend. You can tell it was him. See the line of tiny *X*s in the drawing along the back of the hand," girl number one answered, with just enough nastiness to make me want to slap her.

But again, my curiosity got the better of me, and I overlooked her huge case of bitchitis. "What the hell is Compulsion?" I asked, throwing a little of my own bitchiness into the question.

"Are you kidding? Have you been living under a rock for the last decade?" a guy snorted from behind me. Bitch One and Bitch Two snickered, and I gave them a look that was meant to shut them up but only prompted simultaneous eye rolling.

I looked over my shoulder and tried my look of death on my newest ridiculer. The guy had the sense to take a step back and drop his sneer.

"Uh, it's just that Compulsion is the biggest underground club in the state. Finding the location in the painting is part of the mystery. It's like a real-life urban legend," the guy explained.

I looked back at the picture, clearly not seeing what I was supposed to. I wished I could share in everyone's enthusiasm. Their anticipation was tangible.

The girls pulled out their cell phones and started punching the numbers into their GPS. As people figured out the super-mysterious location, there were shrieks and whoops of excitement.

Normally I didn't think too much about how much I had missed in my single-minded focus to become Aubrey Duncan, super student.

But right now, surrounded by people who clearly had way more excitement in their lives than I did, I felt like I had forgotten about some necessary steps in the whole growing-up-and-experiencing-life thing.

Ugh, this was too deep for a Friday night. There were reruns of *Judge Judy* on the TiVo calling my name.

"Good luck," I told the less-than-friendly group before pushing my way back through the crowd.

I headed off campus and walked the two blocks to my empty apartment. The loneliness that greeted me was more pronounced than it had ever been before.

And for the first time in years, I hated it.

chapter
two

aubrey

Normally organizing, categorizing, and putting things in their place was all I needed to go to my warm, happy place. Forget mood stabilizers. If I was depressed, just give me a dustrag and sixty minutes to declutter. Sure, my room looked like something out of OCD-R-Us, but it was that small semblance of control that helped me get through the day.

Renee, back when we could talk about more than whether it was T-shirt or sweater weather, would tease me about having my shoes lined up in perfect rows. She used to fuck with my almost obsessive need to have my desk laid out in completely symmetrical piles. My pens and highlighters, an exact number of each, were sitting just so in my green Longwood University mug. My laptop was placed at an exact midpoint between my Texas Instruments graphic calculator and my leather-bound daily planner.

Okay, so maybe I took the whole neat and tidy thing a bit too far. But I liked knowing where things were. I liked knowing what to expect when I walked into my room. Surprises sucked. Being blindsided, whether in a good or a bad way, put me on edge, and it didn't take a PhD to figure out why.

Too much of my past had been dictated by things beyond my control. One tiny twist of fate, and I had been catapulted into a scary oblivion that I was still trying to claw my way out of.

But if there was one thing Aubrey Duncan did well, it was surviving. Whatever it cost me, I put one foot in front of the other and kept on walking. There wasn't any other option for me.

"You really need to get in the habit of locking your front door. What if I was a robber here to swipe all of your *90210* DVDs," a voice called, startling me out of my mission to get the dust bunnies out from underneath my bed.

I slithered out from under the mattress on my stomach and peered up at the good-looking guy with the dark brown hair who was dominating the doorway.

"I keep those under lock and key, Brooks, you know better than that," I answered, blowing my hair out of my face and wiping a grubby hand across my forehead. I was pretty sure I looked like something pulled out of a ditch. Fortunately for me, Brooks Hamlin wasn't someone I felt the need to impress.

"Shit, you're cleaning your room again? Aubrey, this is bordering on clinical, you know." Brooks shook his head, his green eyes sparkling in amusement.

I smirked as I got to my feet. "Is that your professional diagnosis?" I asked, wiping my hands down the front of his perfectly pressed shirt. Brooks made a face and playfully pushed me away.

Brooks and I were both in the counseling program, though Brooks was a year older and set to graduate in just a few months. Back at the beginning of our acquaintance, I had made the mistake of sleeping with him. More than once.

Brooks was cute and smart and everything I should have looked for in a guy. He checked each and every box. We started dating a couple years ago after we'd shared an Abnormal Psychology class. I was the wide-eyed, freaked-out freshman; he had been the more confident and suave sophomore. But mostly, our relationship was the result of my pathetic need to connect. And I had been convinced that opening my legs was the perfect solution for my emotional isolation. I had been lonely.

A date here and there had eventually progressed to frequent fucking. But then feelings got involved. More specifically, Brooks's feelings, and the whole thing had gotten entirely too messy. I liked Brooks, truly I did, but my heart hadn't been in it the way his had been. The truth of it was that it wasn't just Brooks. Because my heart was *never* in it . . . with anybody. It was as though the organ was permanently disengaged from the rest of my body.

So I had ended it as gently as I was able to. Brooks had taken it well; kudos to the healthy male ego. And we had, surprisingly, become close friends in the aftermath. I still caught him looking at my boobs more often than I would have liked, but I chose to ignore it.

Brooks handed me a slim paper bag. I peered inside and grinned. "Why, Brooks, are you planning to get me drunk?" I teased, heading out into the hallway, closing my bedroom door behind me.

Brooks chuckled. "Nah, just figured you'd want to break up your wild and crazy evening of alphabetizing the soup cans in the pantry."

I pulled two glasses out of the cabinet and unscrewed the bottle of vodka. Brooks found a carton of orange juice in the refrigerator and set it on the counter. I mixed our drinks while he found a bag of potato chips and dumped them into a bowl.

"I hadn't gotten that far yet," I admitted, following my friend out into the tiny living room. The space was cramped, yet homey. It held a worn-to-the-point-of-ugliness love seat and armchair and a circular coffee table. There was just enough room to walk between the furniture on your way into the kitchen without smacking your knees.

Sure, the couch smelled like feet and the table had mismatched legs, but I held each and every piece in an affectionate regard. Renee had called our interior design "Goodwill chic." I liked it because it was mine. Just *mine*.

"Is Renee out?" Brooks asked, making himself comfortable in the armchair before reaching for his drink. I curled my legs beneath me on the couch and sipped at my cocktail.

"Well, she's not hiding in the closet," I joked, making a face as the alcohol hit my tongue. Way too much vodka, not enough orange juice. Shit, if I wasn't careful I'd be falling on the floor after three sips.

"Is she with Captain Douche?" Brooks asked, making me snort.

"Where else would she be?" I responded, knowing I sounded annoyed.

"What's with that guy? He seems like the sort to tear the wings off butterflies for fun. What does she see in him?" Brooks asked around a mouthful of sour-cream-and-onion chips.

That, really, was the question of the hour, though if I thought back far enough, I could sort of understand how it had happened. When Renee had first started dating Devon, even I had been taken in by his boy-next-door good looks and good ol' southern appeal, though I thought he had laid it on a little thick. His Texas drawl was like melted butter in his mouth. He had the "aww shucks" charm down to a science. It had seemed kind of sexy at the time, and his unruly red hair and brown eyes could be construed as attractive.

As the saying goes, looks can be deceiving. And I had most certainly been deceived.

"Maybe it's love," I said, with a hefty dose of sarcasm. I took another drink of my screwdriver and made a face. "Gah, this is gross," I said and put it down on the coffee table.

Brooks shook his head and dumped the contents of my glass into his. "Love, my ass, more like he's got her cock-whipped," he remarked, making me cringe.

"Dude, I don't need to think about Devon or his cock. Yuck." I shuddered.

Brooks picked up the remote and started flipping through the channels until he found a NASCAR race. "You come to my apartment with shitty alcohol, and now you're expecting me to sit through hours of cars driving in circles? I don't think so," I announced, lunging for the remote.

Brooks tossed it in my direction. "Fine, but I'm vetoing the rerun of *Deuce Bigalow* that I know is playing right now," he warned, and I pouted good-naturedly.

"You have no appreciation for Rob Schneider," I protested.

"I just find it extremely disturbing that you can recite all of the dialogue," Brooks countered.

Grumbling under my breath, I finally settled on a cooking show featuring an overly angry Brit. Brooks decided that we weren't allowed to speak unless it was with horrible English accents, which led me to show him my really bad imitation of Judi Dench.

I was just starting to enjoy my evening when my phone rang. I grabbed it and looked at the number, not recognizing it.

"Hello?" I said after answering. The noise on the other end was deafening.

"Hello?" I said again.

"Aubrey!" someone yelled into the phone. I looked over at Brooks, who was watching me questioningly.

"Yeah, who is this? I can't hear you."

"It's Renee. I need you to come and get me." Renee's voice wobbled, and I could barely hear her over the commotion.

"Where are you? What's going on?" I demanded.

"I need you to come and get me now! Please!" she begged, and I could tell she was wigging out.

"Where's Devon?" I asked, trying to make sense of what was going on.

"Just please, Aubrey. Devon fucking left me here, and I don't know anyone." Renee's voice rose into near hysterics.

"Okay, okay. Tell me where you are," I commanded her with my patented Aubrey Duncan composed calm.

"I'm at Compulsion. You know, the club?" she yelled, and I wanted to groan in exasperation.

"Yeah, I know what Compulsion is," I replied, not adding that my knowledge was only a few hours old.

"It's in a warehouse down near the river. I don't know the exact address, and it was dark when we got here. Just please come and get me," Renee pleaded, and I knew she was crying.

"Okay, I'm on my way. Can I call you on this number if I need to? Where's your phone?" I asked, already on my feet and grabbing my keys.

"No, some guy gave me this phone to use. I don't know him or anything. I'll wait for you inside. Just hurry." And then the line went dead.

"Fucking Renee," I growled in frustration. Brooks followed me to the door.

"I'm coming with you," he said, grabbing hold of my arm.

I shook him off. "No, you stay here," I started, but Brooks cut me off.

"No way, Aubrey. Compulsion is hard-core. You wouldn't survive ten minutes! I might as well stick a sign on your ass with the words *fresh meat*. Hell if I'm letting you go by yourself. Why is Renee there?" he asked.

I shrugged my shoulders angrily. "I doubt it was her idea. This has Devon I'm-a-cocksucker Keeton written all over it. God, he left her there, Brooks! What a jackass!" I seethed. It was a lot easier to feel angry than to admit how freaked out I was, how one phone call could trigger a memory I had buried under a mountain of repression.

My mind threatened to relive *that night*. The frantic late-night call. The gut-wrenching fear. The moment when my entire life changed.

Only I had learned my lesson, and this time I wouldn't ignore the person who needed me.

It wasn't until Brooks and I were headed down the road that he made an obvious observation. "Do we even know where this place is?" he asked, and I could have laughed at the ridiculousness of it all.

And finally I did laugh, almost maniacally. Just because it was all so damned absurd. Here I was, rushing off to play *save Renee from her shitty choices*, and I didn't even know where the heck I was going.

"Not really," I admitted once I had settled down.

"Okay," Brooks let out slowly, giving me his you-are-a-crazy-person look. I sure hoped his future patients were never on the receiving end of that particular expression. It could make anyone question their mental health.

"She said she was by the river at a warehouse. Considering I didn't know a thing about Compulsion until a few hours ago, I'm completely useless right now," I said, not bothering to hide my irritation.

"Huh, sounds like it's down on Third Street," Brooks offered, earning him a surprised look from me.

"Didn't know you were so familiar with the stab-'em-and-leave-'em side of town. Makes me wonder what you get up to in your spare time," I remarked dryly.

Brooks rolled his eyes. "I'm not allergic to social situations like you are, Aubrey," was his only explanation. Huh. It made me wonder how much there was to my good buddy Brooks that I wasn't aware of.

The farther we drove into the city, the more obvious it became that we weren't in Kansas anymore. This was a rough side of town. The stay-inside-or-you're-going-to-get-shanked part of the city.

Longwood University was only ten blocks away, but it might as well be on another planet.

The streets were lined with run-down houses. Cars were up on cinder blocks, and there were more than a few burned-out street-lights. Teenagers hung out on the street corners, and the shadows seemed to hold all sorts of unsavory things that I didn't want to examine too closely. I was experiencing a full-on case of the "icks."

I pulled into a parking lot and turned off the car. Brooks opened the door and got out, but I sat there, staring out the window, not sure I wanted to leave the nice, warm safety of my car. Shit, we were going to get shot. I just knew it! Why hadn't I thought to bring the bottle of pepper spray that sat, unused, on my dresser? Idiot!

When I got my hands on Renee I was pretty sure I'd wrap them around her scrawny neck and squeeze. Really, really hard.

Brooks leaned down and braced himself in the open doorway. "You coming or not?" he asked, looking amused. I gave him the middle finger, but finally, ever so slowly, I joined him. I pulled my knitted, woolen cap down over my hair and shoved my hands into my pockets to ward off the cold.

"Someone is going to steal my car, I just know it. I'm seriously gonna kill Renee and her ass of a boyfriend," I said in a harsh whis-per, stealing a look at the abandoned warehouses and dilapidated buildings around us. A group of thugged-out guys walked down the sidewalk, and I seriously contemplated jumping back in my car and heading home, leaving Renee and her bad decision making on her own.

But damned if my loyalty and annoying sense of friendship didn't get in the way of my survival instincts.

"So, any clue as to where this place is?" I asked Brooks, hunch-ing my shoulders as I shivered.

Brooks shrugged and pointed down the street toward the river. "I'd say we head that way. Renee said it was by the river, right?" he asked, and I could only nod. No need to point out the obvious fact that wandering aimlessly around Murderville didn't seem like the smartest plan of action.

We walked quickly, heading toward the water. I wrinkled my nose at the stench of fish and sewage. Trash and unimaginably gross stuff littered the ground, and I tried to suppress the vomit rising in the back of my throat.

"Hear that?" Brooks asked, breaking the eerie silence.

"Hear what?" I muttered around the clattering of my teeth. Jeesh, I was freezing.

Brooks cupped his hand around his ear and then grabbed my hand, pulling me down the street. "I can hear music. It's this way," he said, clearly more excited by this twisted game of hide-and-seek than I was.

"There it is," Brooks called out, yanking on my arm. Bass so loud it shook my insides served as our guide. Following the music, we crossed the street to join a line that curled around the side of an old warehouse. Compulsion was obviously the place to be on a weekend.

"You know, this club is a total legend. It's been around since the nineties and changes locations every week. I've talked to a few people who have been here, but never had the balls to come myself. But I've always wanted to," Brooks said low enough not to be overheard by the people around us.

Everything I knew about the underground club scene came from watching the news and the occasional crappy reality TV show. And it had all seemed so sensationalized, from drug deals, to users ODing in the bathrooms, to people getting beaten up outside. As out-there as the stories sounded, I knew this stuff really happened. I wasn't stupid or ignorant, by any means. I was more than aware of life's dark and scary underbelly. But I was not the type of person to search for it. I didn't get some sick sort of adrenaline jolt from living *life on the edge*.

Give me a cup of chai tea and some new episodes of *The Vampire Diaries* and I was a happy gal.

But as we waited, I strangely found myself understanding the appeal of it. It was hard to deny the intoxicating feel of anticipation in the air as Brooks and I waited in line to be admitted inside. Everyone was hopped up on some bizarre energy as though we were waiting to be led into paradise. Or purgatory.

I scoped out the people ahead of us in the line: a group of girls who couldn't be any older than sixteen. Even I knew you had to be eighteen to get in, but this group looked way too young to be here. They were giggling and bouncing on their feet. One girl helped her friend apply a thick coat of black lipstick while the other girls adjusted their gothed-out clothes.

Something about them reminded me of Jayme. My little sister had always been the first to jump headfirst into a situation she shouldn't be in. These girls weren't much older than Jayme had been.

Shaking my head, I snapped myself out of that particular train of thought and looked over at Brooks standing beside me. He seemed to be feeding on the high of the crowd. I squeezed his arm. "You know we're just here to grab Renee and get out, right? I'm not trying to hang out or anything," I told him, making sure we were on the same page.

Brooks nodded. "Yeah, no, that's cool. It's just I've always wanted to check this place out. It's kind of awesome, right?" he enthused, grinning.

Uh, *awesome* wasn't exactly the word I'd use to describe it . . . at all.

I didn't bother to respond and instead waited impatiently as we slowly made our way to the front door. When we were finally standing at the entrance, I knew instantly that our chances of being let inside were slim to none. I had noticed people getting turned away and others being allowed admittance. I had been trying to figure out how the scary biker-looking guys at the door were determining who would be granted access and who would be denied. But once we were in front of the doormen and given a disdainful once-over I figured it out pretty quickly.

Brooks and I stood out like virgins at an orgy. It didn't take a genius to see that the two of us were so far out of our comfort zone that we'd have to hitchhike back.

"Get out of here," the bouncer said, with barely a look in our direction. He had a close-shaved head covered in some sort of elaborate tattoo as well as inch-round gauges in his ears. He also sported a rather fierce-looking spike pierced through the bridge of his nose. His goatee was styled into a point and dyed a bright red. Another spike poked out from below his lip. This dude was seriously edgy, and my jeans, cotton long-sleeved grungy jacket ensemble, and Brooks's blazer and plaid button-down made it more than obvious that we most definitely didn't belong.

"Wait a second, please. We're just here to pick up our friend. She's inside," I said, stupidly trying to push past him in my agitation. Damn it! What was I going to do?

Scary biker dude pushed me back and scowled. "I said"—he leaned down until he was an inch from my face—"get the fuck out of here." He literally growled when he said it, and it took everything I had not to be cowed under the weight of his glare.

"Come on, man, we'll pay the cover. Double, if you want. We're only gonna be a minute. We just need to find our friend. She called us and she needs a ride," Brooks tried to reason with the guy.

But the bouncer clearly couldn't give a shit whether we were there to get the Queen of England. We weren't getting inside.

The people behind us were becoming antsy and more than a little tired of the holdup. "You heard him, get the hell out of here," a scrawny man said. He was decked out in black leather, looking like an escapee from an S&M club gone bad.

My lips thinned, and my temper started to rise. I was gearing myself up to do battle, if necessary, because there was no way I was leaving without Renee.

Brooks must have recognized the ferocity in my eyes, because he put a hand on my shoulder, squeezing hard, trying to get my attention. I shook him off and leveled scary bouncer dude with my hardest stare.

"Look, buddy, I'm walking inside this door, and you're not going to stop me," I bristled, sounding way more confident than I was actually feeling. In actuality, I was shaking in my Converse sneakers. Bouncer guy didn't seem to mind if I was a girl or not; he was going to physically remove me.

"Let her in, Randy," a voice said from the shadows just inside the door. Randy's face turned a flustered shade of red as he looked over his shoulder at the speaker.

I squinted into the darkness, trying to see who my savior was. All I could make out was the dim outline of a man.

I gripped Brooks's hand and waited to see whether this anonymous man had enough sway to get us in. After a few seconds, the doorman, Randy, turned back to me and took my money. He stamped my hand and waved me inside without another word.

I turned around to wait for Brooks. The bouncer put his beefy arm across Brooks's chest. "Uh-uh. *She* can come in. *You* wait out here," he said firmly.

"She's not going in there by herself," Brooks argued, pushing against the bouncer's arm, but it might as well have been made of stone. Randy, bouncer made of steel, didn't move an inch.

"If you don't get the fuck out of the line, I'm gonna make you move. You hear me?" Randy asked, his voice dipping low, his words dripping with a barely restrained violence.

"I'll be okay, Brooks. Just wait out here for me, all right?" I urged, hoping he wouldn't push the issue. I sort of liked the look of Brooks's teeth *in* his mouth.

Brooks frowned. He wasn't happy. In fact, he was as upset as I had ever seen him. I looked over my shoulder at the dark entrance to the club. The pulsating bass of the music hummed in my head.

I didn't particularly like the thought of going in there by myself, but it wasn't worth Brooks losing a limb to come with me.

"I'll be fine. Renee said she'd be waiting inside," I reasoned.

Brooks started to shake his head when Randy the bouncer, who had clearly had enough, shoved him roughly to the side. Obviously, the decision had been made for me.

"I'll be over there. I'm giving you fifteen minutes, Aubrey, and then I'm coming in after you," Brooks threatened, shooting me a less-than-pleased look.

I pulled the sleeves of my jacket down over my hands nervously and slowly made my way inside. I looked around for the guy who had gotten me inside, but my eyes were barely able to focus in the horrible lighting.

Whoever it was who had saved me from being booted on my ass was nowhere in sight.

I pulled off my hat and shoved it in my pocket, hesitant to move forward. And then, as though I was being pulled forward by an invisible cord, my feet started to move, one in front of the other, until I was standing in the middle of hell.

At least that seemed to be the theme they were going for. Red lights shone through the room, casting everything in an eerie shadow. Barbed wire covered the windows and gave me the feeling of being trapped.

But it was the energy that took hold and threatened to swallow me whole. The music pumped from gigantic speakers suspended from the ceiling, and the floor was a mass of writhing bodies swept away by the beat. The mood in the room was more than just frenetic; it was something I couldn't describe.

It was hot, and the air smelled of something sweet I couldn't place. My heart started to thud in my chest, and my hands started to twitch. I had never seen such total abandon before. The music seemed to hold everyone and everything in its snare; the dancers were helpless against it.

As much as I tried to resist it, I was entranced by the scene in front of me. Compulsion terrified me. It was overwhelming and borderline psychotic. But it also transfixed me in a way that had me questioning my own sanity.

Because suddenly I *wanted* it.

I *craved* it.

I *ached* to lose myself in the oblivion.

That is what this place promised. Sweet and total anarchy. And how easy it would be to hand over my careful control to the frightening and intoxicating world laid out before me.

The thump, thump, thump of the music rattled around in my chest. I could feel the vibration from the speakers buzzing in my ears. The darkness was both smothering and strangely comforting.

I closed my eyes and started to sway on my feet.

And then the moment was over. I was jostled from behind as people pushed past me, pulling me out of my momentary loss of reality.

What was wrong with me? I was here to get Renee, not play irresponsible club kid for the night.

The large, open room was full of people, and it was proving impossible to get through the crowd. I looked around, straining on my tiptoes, trying to find Renee. I elbowed and shoved my way to the outer wall.

I stumbled over something. My hands came out as I fell facefirst onto the ground. My knees collided painfully with the concrete floor. And I lay there, sort of dumbfounded by everyone's total disregard for the pathetic girl sprawled out at their feet.

No one offered to help me up. They simply walked around or, in some cases, *over* me. I tried to get to my feet, but my ankle twisted in protest. I came back down on my knees and suddenly felt like I could cry.

Someone spilled beer down my back at the same time I was knocked sideways. Shit, I was going to be trampled to death. I felt hysteria bubble up in my stomach and overshadow the anger I had felt toward my wayward roommate.

Suddenly a pair of hands gripped me underneath my arms and hoisted me up. I groaned at the pain in my ankle as I steadied myself. A hand pressed into my back, right between my shoulder blades, and pushed me forward.

"Are you okay?" a soft male voice whispered in my ear. I tried to turn to see who was navigating me through the throng, but it was so dark I couldn't make him out.

I nodded, even though it was a lie. I was so *not* okay.

I could feel the heat of the guy's hand through my shirt, imprinting my skin. He was pressed close to me as we moved forward, his front brushing against my back. It was uncomfortably intimate, and if I could have, I would have run far, far away.

"Take a deep breath. You'll be fine," the voice soothed, somehow saying the words I needed to hear.

I found myself complying automatically. The voice floating in my ears through the dark held some sort of strange sway that was hard to resist.

The hand at my back began to move in comforting circles, and I found myself start to relax in spite of my trepidation. It was like the dude pumped Valium through his fingertips. He was *Club Man*, able to calm freaked-out girls with the power of his voice and hands alone! I tried to twist and squint at him again, but I still couldn't make out more than a silhouette.

"*I see thee better—in the dark—I do not need a light,*" the man murmured, his breath stirring the hair at my temple.

Mystery dude was quoting Emily Dickinson? What in the hell? Had I unknowingly dropped down the rabbit hole and not realized it?

And just like that, my calm popped like a soap bubble, and the reality of where I was set in like a hundred-ton weight on my chest.

I was in an underground nightclub trying to find my friend. That was what I needed to focus on.

I didn't know this guy and shouldn't be dropping my guard in a place like this—what the hell was wrong with me?

I tried to push ahead—anything to get some distance from the potential serial killer behind me. But the wall of people made it difficult to move very fast. The hand at my back slipped up to the nape of my neck, fingers curling up into my hair.

My heart was hammering in my chest, and I was scared. I could almost read the headlines now: *Girl killed while trying to locate her selfish jerk of a roommate.*

But then the hand disappeared from my skin, and I was steered toward the bar. I could barely breathe. I was on the cusp of a full-blown panic attack.

"Your friend is over there," came the soft whisper again.

Huh?

I craned my neck and almost passed out with relief at the sight of Renee, perched on a stool, looking shaky and uncomfortable, her eyes darting around nervously.

"Thank you," I said loudly, finally finding enough light to take in the person who'd helped me. He was tall, with broad shoulders; a baseball cap was perched low over his brow, obscuring his face. In the red-tinged light of the club, I couldn't make out a single detail, nothing to identify him. And that was more unsettling than anything else had been up until now.

The inexplicable control this man exerted made itself known again. I was like a fish on a hook, flopping around in vain, hoping to be set free, but at the same time stupidly enjoying the trap.

I wanted to see him. I *needed* to.

The guy leaned in, his lips brushing against my cheek as he spoke. I caught the faint smell of peppermint and smoke.

"You and your friend need to get out of here. This isn't a place for you to be." He brushed my ponytail off my shoulder.

"What?" I asked dumbly. I was having a hard time wrapping my head around the strange turn my night had taken. Why was he helping me? Did I have *easy mark* stamped on my forehead? Or was he a rare breed of Good Samaritan?

I patted the front of my jeans just to make sure I hadn't been pickpocketed. Phone and cash seemed to still be there. That was a relief, I guess. But when I looked up, he was gone.

He had disappeared like he had never been there, a figment of my overactive and overly stressed mind.

I stood rooted to the spot, my ankle throbbing, my head dizzy, my ears ringing. I was shaken.

That man had shaken me. And I wasn't sure if it was fear or excitement that thrummed through my veins.

He was right. I needed to get out of there. I pulled my phone out of my pocket and saw that ten minutes had already passed. If I didn't get Renee outside soon, Brooks was going to go all suicide mission on the bouncer.

"Renee!" I yelled over the music. My roommate and questionable best friend turned in my direction, and her face went slack with relief. She jumped down from the stool and threw her arms around my neck.

"Aubrey, thank you so much for coming to get me," she sobbed into my neck. I hugged the smaller girl and then pulled away.

Renee's eyes were bloodshot; her mascara ran in dark ribbons down her cheeks. Her hair hung in a tangled mess on her back. She wrung her hands together in agitation, and my protective instincts kicked in.

She looked frightened and sad. I wanted to take Devon Keeton by the balls and give them a really painful squeeze. He didn't deserve Renee. Why couldn't she see that?

"Let's go home," I said, wrapping an arm around her trembling shoulders.

Keeping her close, and with a hand out in front of me, I started body-checking people as we made our way to the entrance.

The music had picked up a notch, and the air buzzed with a frenetic energy. It pulled me in and didn't want to let go. A part of me wanted to stay and get lost in it. My feet stopped moving, and I felt inexplicably torn. I needed to leave, but I wanted to stay.

Renee tugged on my arm, and I gave myself a shake. My momentary loss of rational thinking gave way to the more pressing desire to ensure Brooks wasn't making nice with bouncer Randy's meaty fist.

Just as we made it to the door, I felt a tingling along the back of my neck—a sensual awareness that made my hair stand on edge. My mystery man, with his face shadowed, stood just to the side of the exit. I felt his eyes follow my movements, and I couldn't suppress a shiver of apprehension that was oddly enticing.

I tried to meet his eyes, almost desperate to see them. But he turned away, denying me what I sought. I watched with a strange displeasure as he faded into the gloom.

"Aubrey!" I heard a yell coming from outside. Brooks looked anxious, and I knew he was only seconds from bulldozing his way inside.

Holding tight to Renee's hand, I half dragged, half carried her out of the club. We passed Randy, whose scowl could have made a lesser person piss themselves. I was half tackled by a perilously-close-to-losing-it Brooks.

"You gave me gray hair, Aubrey! Gray hair!" Brooks yelled, grabbing me by the shoulders and giving me a little shake.

"Sorry. It took me a while to find Renee," I explained, trying to communicate with my eyes for him to chill out.

Brooks rounded on Renee and gave her his best stern-older-brother expression. "What were you thinking, spending your evening at Hepatitis Central? You need a swift kick in the ass, girl," he lectured, though I knew his harshness had more to do with being worried than anything else.

Renee hung her head sheepishly, and even though I wanted to give her my own lecture, I knew it wouldn't do any good. She was obviously tired and in a state of emotional shutdown.

She didn't need judging. She needed a good night's sleep, and then maybe I could give her the "I told you your boyfriend was a total dickhead" speech.

"Sorry, Brooks," Renee said quietly, and I glared at Brooks, who held his hands up in a placating gesture.

"Okay, it's cool. Let's just get the hell out of here. I sure hope your car still has tires," he muttered as we started to walk away from Compulsion.

As we headed down the street, I couldn't help looking one last time back over my shoulder.

I couldn't decide whether I felt disappointment or relief that the person I was searching for was nowhere in sight.

chapter
three

aubrey

I sucked on the red, angry skin of my thumb, silently cursing the metal chair that lay discarded at my feet. I gave it an annoyed kick before leaning down to pick it up.

"Ouch, did it pinch you?" a kind voice asked. I opened up the chair and set it on its feet in the circle I had created. Kristie Hinkle, the support group facilitator, smiled at me as she pulled the plastic off a sleeve of Styrofoam cups.

Two weeks had passed since Brooks and I had played Batman and Robin on a rescue mission to Compulsion. The disquiet that settled inside me after my experience left me feeling edgy. I couldn't quite put my finger on *why* I was feeling that way. But there was no doubt as to *who* had put it there, even though I had never gotten a look at his face.

Renee had gone straight to bed after we had gotten back to the apartment. When I got up the next morning, she had already left for work. My plans to find out exactly what had gone down at the club were sidelined by my friend's blatant avoidance.

I could tell she was embarrassed. Renee was easy to read. She wore her feelings on her sleeve. And when she became uncomfortable, her MO was to hide away until the dust settled.

I had hoped that Devon abandoning her at the club would have been the wake-up call she needed to make the final break, that it had put the nail in the proverbial coffin of her shitty relationship.

So it was with an almost homicidal frustration that I found Devon the Jackass sitting in our living room the next night acting like he belonged there.

His feet were propped up on the coffee table as he ate a sandwich, crumbs going everywhere. For a moment, I saw red. I gripped my keys in my hand and thought about flinging them at his arrogant, overly large head. You know, right before I kneed him in the junk.

Was this for real? Was Renee really going to allow this guy back into our home after he had left her, by herself, at Compulsion the night before?

I wanted to tell him to get his fucking feet off the furniture. I wanted to scream at Renee to wake up and smell the sucky-boyfriend coffee.

But I didn't, because painful experience had taught me that saying anything would only accomplish the opposite.

Nothing pushed two people together more than a case of Romeo and Juliet syndrome brought on by thinking the whole world was against them.

It was at times like this that the similarities between Renee and my sister were so excruciating that it took my breath away.

I had played the sneering judgmental card once upon a time, and it had cost me dearly. Self-righteous disappointment got me nowhere.

So I had reined in my anger, and I had given my friend a smile, one that she hesitatingly returned, before going to my room to do my homework.

The days passed, and my relationship with Renee came to an

uneasy standstill. She was still with her jerk of a boyfriend, and there still wasn't a whole lot I could do about it.

But for the time being I had to focus my energies elsewhere.

Tonight was the first meeting of the campus substance-abuse support group. I had been reading up on curriculums and methodologies, trying to figure out the best approach for facilitating the sessions. When I couldn't deal with things on an emotional level, it was always easier for me to surround myself with hard facts.

I knew that this would be hard for me, that it had the potential to trigger in me painful memories that perhaps were best left forgotten. But I was bound and determined to do it anyway. I was ultimately responsible for where my life was headed, and this was exactly what I wanted to do with it.

I grimaced at Kristie's question. "They're sneaky little bastards," I said, repositioning the chairs until I was happy with the layout. When I was finished, I joined Kristie at the table and got the muffins and cookies out of the grocery bag on the floor.

Kristie held up her hand to show three fingers covered in Band-Aids. "They got me last week. Those chairs are merciless," she joked. Kristie was in her late thirties and ran the outpatient program at the substance-abuse center in town. She had an unassuming air about her that was both relaxing and inviting. With frizzy black hair and green eyes behind dark-rimmed glasses, she was the epitome of the supportive counselor. I could easily see why people would be comfortable talking to her about their problems. Her demeanor lacked judgment, and her voice was soothing. I instantly liked her. Which was good, considering I would be co-facilitating this group with her for the next twelve weeks.

"Let's have a look at the curriculum materials for the group today. Like I said on the phone when we talked last week, I won't expect you to do much today. Just observe, get to know the group members, get a feel for how these things work. Today serves more as an introduction than anything else. It's a 'get to know you' for everyone. Be prepared for some very resistant individuals, though. Not everyone is here voluntarily, and there's always one or two who have to be an ass," Kristie said, pulling her notebook out of her bag.

I sat down beside her as she began to flip through the pages. "Really? I thought this was a group people came to because they wanted the help," I said in confusion. Kristie chuckled good-naturedly.

"I wish. That would make my job a heck of a lot easier. But no, some of these people have been court-ordered because of drug possession, usually a misdemeanor. Some are first-time offenders; others have been through the system a few times. You always hope they learn something from what you're trying to teach them, but I can't confess to being that naïve," she said, handing me a stack of name tags.

"Wow, that sounds pretty jaded, Kristie," I teased. Kristie snickered.

"I've been doing this group for almost five years. I will always have the hope that I'm making a difference, but I'm only human. And I've seen too many people end up at the bottom to think otherwise. But we keep on trucking. Because giving up isn't an option," she said sagely. I couldn't say anything to that. I understood feeling jaded, but I was determined to feel the hope all the same.

"Do they all go to LU?" I asked. Kristie nodded.

"This group is for students. I facilitate several other groups in town as well. But we keep this one separate and just for the college community. These kids are dealing with issues that are very different from those of the addicts I see in the other meetings. The pressures, the expectations, and the failures of university life go hand in hand with their addiction." I nodded.

Kristie wrote her name on one of the tags and peeled it off. She stuck it to the front of her shirt. I followed suit and then put a name tag and pen on each seat. I had a vague idea of what to expect from the group. Having an addict in the family gave you a front-row seat for that particular brand of fucked-up.

But still . . . I was apprehensive.

And it all had to do with a night three years ago. A desperate phone call in the middle of the night that I had so quickly dismissed as inconsequential. Followed by days of guilt and fear when my fifteen-year-old sister, Jayme, never came home and the realization that her phone call hadn't been so inconsequential after all. Then finally the morning when I had opened the door to find two police officers on our porch. Their sympathetic faces as they told us that Jayme had been found dead in some skeevy alleyway. Cold and alone. It was that moment that everything I had known, my entire world, was flipped on its axis.

I hadn't handled my grief well at first. I had berated and abused myself. My guilt ate me alive. My parents blamed me for not taking care of my little sister. *I* blamed myself for spending so much time on my sanctimonious soapbox that I had been blind to what was really going on.

In the aftermath, my relationship with my parents deteriorated into barely functioning. And I had made it my mission to find a way to fix the pieces inside me that were broken and to live a life that mattered. A part of me was convinced that helping others would in some way help me move on from the devastation of my past.

So I came to Longwood University wanting to escape and to focus on becoming a drug-addiction counselor. It was far enough away from my hometown in North Carolina to feel like I was in another world. Yet it was close enough that it would be impossible for me to ever truly escape what had happened. Because I needed the daily reminder. It was motivation. It's what got me out of bed every goddamned morning.

It made me a fighter.

But it didn't change the fact that I was scared. I worried like hell that I'd never be able to do enough for the people who needed my help. That *I* would never be able to stop the slide once it began. The fear of failure was acute and debilitating.

Kristie made it all seem so easy. I appreciated the way she displayed such competence. She must have sensed my unease because she kindly patted my arm.

"We all have our crosses to bear, Aubrey. Yours led you here. And I know that is a good thing, for you and for the lives you'll make a difference in," she said knowingly. My smile was tight, and I wished I could believe her. But self-doubt was like a mosquito buzzing around my ear. The more I tried to swat it away, the more determined it became to suck me dry.

Before long the group members began to filter into the room. It was a relatively small group. We were expecting only twelve people. I didn't know all of their stories. Kristie had filled me in briefly on the few who had been in the group before. But for the most part, the group would consist of newbies. Four had been court-ordered after being brought up on misdemeanor drug charges. The rest were here voluntarily, which was a bit of a relief. Hopefully that meant they'd be more open and accepting and less combative.

The seats began to fill. There were two girls I recognized from one of the sororities on campus. To say I was shocked to find them in a substance-abuse support group was an understatement, though if there was one thing I had learned in my life, it was that addiction didn't discriminate.

A guy and a girl, obviously a couple, came in behind them. They seemed unsure and more than a little nervous, and a selfish part of me was relieved that I wasn't the only one freaking out.

I needed to do something more than stand by the wall trying to blend in with the scenery. If I wanted Kristie to sign off on my volunteer hours, I had to jump into this experience with both feet. Who cared if I got wet?

I approached the couple with what I hoped was a welcoming smile. The guy seemed very protective of his girlfriend. His arm was around her shoulders, and she was pressed into his side as if he could shield her from everyone else. He had short, cropped dark hair and hoops along the outer shell of his ears. His jeans had holes in the knees, and he wore an old Black Sabbath T-shirt.

His diminutive girlfriend had bright pink hair cut just below her chin. She had a ring through her septum and two studs in her left eyebrow. I could see part of a tattoo on one side of her neck. Despite her kick-ass appearance, she came across as skittish.

"Hi, guys! I'm Aubrey," I said, introducing myself. The girl's eyes darted to me and then away again. I noticed the guy squeeze her shoulders before he turned his attention to me. He didn't smile. His eyes were a dark, chilly brown.

"Hi," he responded shortly, not offering his name. I looked at the girl again, but she had turned her face toward her boyfriend's chest, and I wondered what their story was. They were anything but friendly, and I wished I hadn't approached them at all. But this is what I was here for. They would have to get used to me eventually.

"I'm glad you guys are here. Find a seat. There are drinks and some food on the back table. We'll be starting in about ten minutes," I said, forcing a smile.

The guy watched me closely, his eyes narrowed and suspicious. The girl hadn't moved from the protective shelter of his arm. Something about him reminded me of Devon and thus instilled an instant dislike. Okay, this was going nowhere. Without bothering to attempt to prolong the conversation, I returned to my seat.

Kristie finished handing out a packet of information to the people who had already taken their places and then found her own seat. She glanced up at me as I came to sit down beside her. She looked over at the couple as they finally made their way to the chairs. The guy had moved his arm but was now clutching his girlfriend's hand so tightly it looked as though it hurt.

"I've seen them at the clinic downtown. I know they're two of the court-ordered crew. Don't take their lack of social skills personally. I think they're a pretty rough pair," Kristie said quietly, watching them carefully.

"Yeah, just kind of a sucky start, I guess," I muttered, flipping through the pages of the introductory packet. Kristie chuckled.

"If it didn't suck, I'd start to worry it would be a boring group," she joked. I tried not to stare as the rest of the group entered the room, but it was hard, particularly when I realized I recognized quite a few of the participants, including a frat guy who hung out with Brooks.

There wasn't a whole lot of talking. The room was silent except for the sounds of chairs scraping across the floor as people found their self-designated spots.

Just before group was about to start, the door swung open, and I glanced up at the person who entered.

Instantly the mood in the room changed, and the air crackled with an electric energy. I felt an immediate awareness inside me that was surprising. Because the boy who walked in was beautiful. That was the only word my addled brain could come up with to describe him.

His broad shoulders strained under a shirt that looked as though it had been sculpted to his form. His blond hair fell in haphazard curls around his ears. His almost startling blue eyes were framed by the thickest and blackest lashes I had ever seen. It should be criminal for guys to have eyelashes like that.

His face was lean, and his chin was dimpled in the middle. His lips were stretched in a smirk as he took in the other people in the room. Every single person, male and female alike, focused on his entrance. And he seemed to revel in the effect he had.

There was something in the way he moved that had me frowning. Why did he seem so familiar?

"Welcome! Come have a seat. We were just getting ready to start," Kristie called out to the newcomer, breaking my internal processing. Mr. Hot and Hazardous slowly moved to the last remaining chair, which just so happened to be across from me.

He sank into the cold, hard metal and stretched his legs out in front of him as though he were lounging on a couch and not at a support group meeting. He flashed a brilliant smile in the direction of the girls who sat beside him. They seemed a bit thunderstruck. Not that I blamed them.

His entire demeanor seemed more than a little off. He was a bit too perky for an addiction support group. I continued to frown in his direction, trying to get a read on him. There was something undeniably mesmerizing about him, but there was also something else there that I couldn't quite put my finger on, and it was driving me nuts.

He turned his head and looked at me, and he blinked as though in surprise. His brows furrowed as he studied me as intently as I studied him.

"Okay, then. Everyone, I'm Kristie Hinkle, director of support services at the Community Services Board. And this is Aubrey Duncan. She's a student here at Longwood and will be my co-facilitator for the next twelve weeks." I lifted my hand in an awkward wave.

I was met by twelve pairs of eyes whose owners seemed to take me in and judge me in the span of thirty seconds. Crap, this wasn't going to be easy. Blue Eyes across from me still hadn't looked away from my face, and I was feeling more than a little uncomfortable.

Kristie smiled and gave me a slight nod, letting me know it was my turn to talk. I took a deep breath and looked around the group. "Hi. I'm really excited to be a part of this group. I'm working on my degree in counseling, and I hope my experience can . . . I don't know . . . help you in some way," I said. I wanted to cringe at how pretentious I sounded. They were going to hate me. I just knew it.

Several of the girls rolled their eyes, and their body language immediately told me that I was right; they totally hated me. Maybe I wasn't cut out for this after all.

Kristie recognized my floundering and jumped in. "Some of your faces I know; the rest of you are new. I'd like to take a moment to go around the circle and have you introduce yourselves. Say something about yourself. Why you're here. What you hope to get out of the next twelve weeks. The important thing to remember is that this is a safe place to talk. Anything you say in this room stays in this room. We are all bound by that confidentiality. It is important that you trust each and every person here; otherwise this can't work."

Kristie nodded her head toward a girl I recognized from the front desk of the university's library. The girl looked down at her name tag and pointed at it with a shy smile. "I'm Marissa. I'm a sophomore, and I've struggled with an addiction to Ritalin for almost two years," she said quickly, as though she couldn't get the words out of her mouth fast enough.

Kristie smiled. "We're glad you're here, Marissa," she said sincerely. It continued like that around the circle. There was Kyle, the frat guy. I was surprised to hear that he had been busted for cocaine possession twice and was worried about losing his football scholarship. Looking at him, you'd see an athletic jock who lived for a good time. I would never have suspected he struggled with something like that.

Then there were Lisa and Twyla, the sorority girls, who were best friends but also found themselves addicted to methamphetamines to stay awake so they could get their homework done. There was Josh, who smoked pot so often he was failing most of his classes. Gigi, who liked to dabble in ecstasy on the weekends. Grant and Vince, who liked painkillers. And Lynette, who found herself addicted to Percocet after her knee surgery last year.

Then Kristie turned to the hostile couple, who had become more and more agitated as everyone introduced themselves.

"What about you two? What do the two of you hope to get out of the group?" Kristie asked kindly. The girl looked at her hand, which was still smothered by her boyfriend's larger grasp. She didn't look up, her bright pink hair covering her eyes.

The guy's lips thinned, and he was silent for so long I was

pretty sure he wasn't going to say anything. Then finally he gritted his teeth and said in a barely audible voice, "I'm Evan, and this is April. We just want to put the hours in and get this shit over with."

I looked over at Kristie. Her eyes narrowed imperceptibly, but I noticed it all the same. These two were going to be hard to deal with. Kristie looked at April, who seemed to shrink in on herself. The dynamic between the pair was downright disturbing.

"Do you agree, April? Are you only here to put in the required hours? Or is there something more you're hoping to learn?" The pink-haired girl shook her head. After a few moments, Kristie realized she wasn't going to get anything out of an obviously mute April.

Which left the blond and blue-eyed boy whose name tag on the front of his shirt read "Maxx." Kristie seemed relieved to turn her focus to him. He had sat quietly during the introductions, playing the role of the model group member. He made sure to act interested while the others talked, but I couldn't shake the sense that he really didn't give a shit, that for him this was all a game and he knew what part he had to play.

"Finally, the last member of the group. Why don't you tell us a little bit about why you're here," Kristie said. His grin was deceptively benign, but his eyes revealed a different story altogether. I just wished I knew what that story was.

The other girls in the group were completely transfixed by him. I had read a book once about cult leaders who were able to control a room with a smile or a gesture. They had a charisma about them that made people lay down their lives for them. I had always thought that was ridiculous; no one could be so magnetic that people would happily follow them off the edge of the world if they were asked to.

Looking at Maxx and the way the entire room gravitated toward him, I finally understood it. And the scary thing was that it was obvious he knew the power he had. And he enjoyed it.

Despite my less-than-friendly feelings toward the mysterious boy, I couldn't help my more primal reaction to him. It was easy to fantasize about how his body would feel against mine. He seemed like the type who craved control, and it made me shiver to imagine relinquishing control of my body to him.

My contradictory feelings were also unethical and completely unprofessional. I was here as a facilitator. I was in a position of authority, however tentative, and I shouldn't be lusting after a guy who was here for treatment.

What was wrong with me? This was so out of character that it shocked me.

Maxx looked around the room in a leisurely way, taking his time to make the circle until his gaze finally settled on me. His tongue darted out to wet his bottom lip, and I couldn't help that my eyes fell to his mouth. Fucking hell . . .

A flash of some unidentifiable emotion heated his face. Just as suddenly as it appeared, it was gone, as though it had never been there. His tongue disappeared behind his teeth as he grinned at me, making me wonder if he could read the inappropriate thoughts I was having.

And that pissed me off. *He* pissed me off. Which was irrational. I didn't even *know* him.

My neck flushed bright red under his scrutiny. The strange familiarity I had felt when he arrived only increased the longer he looked at me. When his attention finally shifted away, my breath came out in a noisy rush that embarrassed me.

Kristie gave me a strange look before turning back to Maxx. His lips quirked as though something about all of this amused him. But then, as if he'd flicked a switch, his face smoothed and his eyes became serious. It was like watching someone put on a mask. It was seamless and complete.

"I'm Maxx Demelo," he began, his voice soft and rich. I swallowed around the thick lump in my throat.

That voice. I knew it. But from where?

Maxx lifted his hands in the air, his broad shoulders heaving in a shrug as though he was about to reveal the secrets of his soul. His eyes flicked to me again, and he said with absolute sincerity, "And I came here to be saved."

Was this guy for real?

I looked at the other group members and quickly realized they had all swallowed his Kool-Aid. Kristie seemed to think seriously about his statement as she leaned forward to rest her elbows on her knees.

"That seems like a pretty tall order, don't you think?" she asked him, and I could tell she was as fascinated by Maxx as the rest of us. Everyone, even Evan and April, was fixated on the blond-haired, blue-eyed boy who wore his vulnerability like a badge of honor. It was so at odds with the cocksure, mocking guy who had walked in only fifteen minutes earlier. It was as though he were playing dress-up, trying to decide which character to be.

Maxx crossed his legs at the ankle and rested his hands in his lap. "I don't think so," he said. His eyes drifted my way again, and I felt like a mouse in a snare. I really wished he would stop looking at me.

"I've found my way into hell, and wanting salvation is the only thing that keeps me going." His words were quiet and controlled, and I couldn't tell if he was feeding us all a line or if he meant it.

"I'm ready to be saved. I *need* it, Kristie. So I will do whatever I have to do to get it." He sounded almost angry. Everyone was quiet for a few minutes as if his words had struck a chord deep inside them.

Finally, Kristie blinked as she smiled at the group, shaking off the spell Maxx had created. "Well . . . ," she began, and cleared her throat. "Let's hope you find it," Kristie said, a little too brightly. I watched Maxx and knew without a doubt that he was something dangerous.

He was something primal and unfettered—a force that could take everything and everyone down with him, burning it all in a violent flame. And then afterward he would dance on the ashes.

He was terrifying.

chapter
four

The group was a joke. But if I didn't want to end up in the slammer, I'd have to suck it up and spend the next twelve weeks of my life talking about my fucking feelings. I had been to enough therapy in my twenty-one years to know the score. I knew how to play the part to get me through it.

Share a sob story. Act like you believed the line of bullshit they threw at you. Then get your ass so far on the other side that you never had to think about it again.

But I had been stupid, a little too cocky, and I had gotten myself busted, though I had been lucky and had just sold most of what I had on me that night, leaving only a couple of pills. Possession, not intent to distribute, meant the difference between community service and mandatory counseling as opposed to sitting in a jail cell worrying about getting ass-raped after I dropped the soap in the showers.

So I would become the Maxx who felt guilt and shame, a guy who regretted his decisions, even as I planned how I would do it all over again.

Because choice had been taken from me a long time ago, and there was no place for guilt in the world I lived in.

I had walked into the room on Tuesday evening, expecting it to be the fucking mockery that it was.

What I hadn't been expecting was to see a girl with long blond hair and eyes that had the power to cut through me like a knife. She had knocked me sideways, leaving me scrambling to find my footing.

I was drawn to her. I couldn't help it. Some things were impossible to ignore—and the way my dick twitched in my pants as I stared at her long legs was one of them.

I laid it on thick. I knew how to say and do what was necessary to get what I wanted.

Except I got the distinct impression she wasn't buying what I was selling. And I wasn't sure what the hell I was supposed to do with that. It messed with my head, and it pissed me off.

But it also made me determined.

And whether she realized it or not, her dismissal was all the motivation I needed.

So I watched her watching me, and I figured that maybe this support group thing wouldn't be half bad.

chapter
five

"Are you going to answer that?" Brooks asked from my couch, where he was doing a damned good impersonation of a deadbeat beer guzzler.

My phone vibrated on an endless loop as it danced across my coffee table. We were three hours into our weekly cram session. I was trying to study for my Developmental Psychology quiz, while Brooks made a good show of writing his paper for Behavioral Genetics.

Brooks and I were both pretty intense when it came to our course work, though perhaps at times I put a little more emphasis on the work part than Brooks did.

I had barely registered the fact that my phone had been going off for the past ten minutes. Brooks leaned across the coffee table and snapped his fingers an inch from my nose.

I scowled and batted his hand away. "Stop it!" I grumbled, flipping the page in my textbook, already immersed in language acquisition in children. Riveting stuff.

"Pick it up or turn it off, Aubrey, before I chuck it out the window," Brooks threatened. I gave him an amused smirk, knowing the sound of his bark all too well. Brooks looked fried. His hair stood on end, and his eyes gave him more than a little bit of a harried look.

"Okay, okay. Settle down, boy," I teased, grabbing my phone just before it fell onto the floor.

"Hello?" I said, without bothering to check the caller ID. Stupid Aubrey! I should have known by now to *always* check the caller ID.

"Bre. Finally! I've been trying to call you for over an hour!" my mother chastised into the phone. I instantly cringed. Not only at the sound of my mother's disapproving voice but at her insistence in using *that* nickname.

It was a nickname that should have been buried with the person who had given it to me. But my mom continued to use it, and I knew that had everything to do with the pain it inflicted every time it was uttered.

"Sorry, Mom. My ringer was off. What can I do for you?" I asked, abandoning any semblance of civil small talk and opting for straight to the point.

I hadn't spoken to my parents in four months. We had an understanding to leave each other alone, communicating only when necessary.

I hadn't returned home to North Carolina in over two years. It had stopped being home for me after Jayme died.

"That's ridiculous. What if something had happened? No one would have been able to reach you!" my mother reprimanded, digging that knife just a little deeper. She sounded concerned, but appearances were deceiving.

"Sorry, Mom," I repeated. But an apology would never undo the damage of the last three years.

My mother gave a huff, obviously feeling righteous in her indignation. My mother wore martyrdom well. She was the self-sacrificing matriarch of an ungrateful family.

The whole thing made me sick.

"You need to come home," my mother said without further preamble.

My chest squeezed, and I clenched the phone so tightly in my hand that I started to cut off circulation to my fingers.

I stayed quiet, not trusting myself to speak. I breathed in deeply through my nose. I didn't dare look at Brooks, who I knew was watching me curiously. He had no idea of the emotional land mine I had walked into just by answering the phone. He wasn't privy to the side of my life that I worked hard to hide from.

"Bre! Did you hear me? This is important. I wouldn't bother calling otherwise," she said harshly, cutting me open with the truth of her words.

"Why?" I finally asked, clearing my throat around the huge lump that had formed there.

My mother's annoyed snort was loud in my ear. "Are you serious? Do I really need to remind you of what next weekend is?" she declared hatefully.

The lump dissolved around the flood of my anger. Fuck, no, I hadn't forgotten! Forgetting would *never* be an option for me. She wasn't the only person who had lost Jayme. But my parents acted as though they alone grieved the loss of the fifteen-year-old girl who had disappeared from our lives too soon.

"No, Mom. I didn't forget," I replied through gritted teeth. I wanted to yell and rage at her cold disregard for my feelings. But Aubrey Duncan was a master at containing emotion. I had to be. It was the only way I got by.

"The local teen center is doing a memorial in Jayme Marie's memory, and they want us there. Your father is planning to say something. The newspaper will be there, as well as a local TV crew. The *entire* family should be present for it." My mom's words were final, not allowing any argument.

I was expected to obey, no questions asked.

But I wouldn't.

I *couldn't.*

As much as a part of me wanted to repair the gaping hole in my family, I couldn't return to Marshall Creek. I couldn't go back to the two-story brick house where I had grown up. I couldn't walk past the closed door that would never open again.

No way.

"I can't make it," I said quietly, already bracing myself for the fallout.

"You *can't make it?*" my mother asked angrily.

I shook my head, even though my mother couldn't see me.

"You're telling me that you won't come home for a memorial in memory of your baby sister? You can't take a couple of days out of your life to honor your sister? *You* of all people should understand how important this is! *You* owe this to her!" My mother's voice cracked as it rose to a shrill screech.

I closed my eyes and tried not to let the hatred overtake me. Hatred for my mother, who would never allow me to forget how I had failed Jayme. Hatred for the drugs that had taken my sister before her time. Hatred for the fucking asshole who had given them to her.

And most of all, hatred for myself.

That hatred was a ferocious thing that smoldered in my belly. It was always there. It never went away. And my mother knew just how to stoke it into a full-blown forest fire.

"I have to go, Mom," I said, not bothering to try to explain myself to her, to tell her that returning to Marshall Creek was like ripping a bandage off a wound that was only now starting to heal. There was no point. My mother wouldn't have listened.

And maybe I *was* being selfish. Maybe I should make myself go home. But I just knew it would never accomplish what I would want it to. I wouldn't be able to go there and honor Jayme the way she deserved. Because that memorial was about my parents and their refusal to let go, not the reality of the person my sister had been.

"I can't believe how selfish you are, *Bre*," my mother spat out. The mechanical click indicated she had ended the call.

I dropped the phone back on the coffee table and gathered up my textbooks and notes, shoving them into my backpack.

"What was that about, Aubrey?" Brooks asked, concerned.

"Nothing," I replied shortly, grabbing handfuls of pencils and highlighters and throwing them into the bag.

Brooks's hand gripped my wrist, stilling me. "That didn't seem like nothing. You look like you're about to go throw yourself off a bridge. What the fuck was that about?" he asked firmly.

I gave a humorless laugh. "Sheesh, Brooks, let's hope I never need you to talk me off a ledge. Your suicidal de-escalation techniques suck."

I slung my backpack up on my shoulder and grabbed my keys.

"And you're seriously evading. You're going to be a counselor, Aubrey. You know how important it is to talk about stuff and not bottle it up. That's what leads someone to take an Uzi into a Mc-Donald's. Friends don't let friends become mass shooters," Brooks remarked drolly.

I rolled my eyes. "Why don't you try out the free psychotherapy on someone who needs it," I barked, trying really hard not to take my frustrated bitterness out on him. But he was there, and my hostility was about to go thermonuclear.

"Okay, so a heart-to-heart is out of the question. Just tell me where the hell you're going. You're freaking me out a little here," Brooks said.

I leaned down and gave him a kiss on the cheek. "Stop being such a worrywart. I'm fine. I just forgot that I need to grab a book from the library for my Social Psychology paper that's due in a few weeks. I'll only be an hour or so. You can hang if you want. Renee won't be back until later," I told him, trying to be as nonchalant as possible.

I just needed to get out of there. I needed to walk, clear my head. My mother's accusations bounced around in my mind and threatened to pry the lid off my carefully contained memories.

I had to move. I had to keep busy. My equilibrium demanded it. And sitting and studying with Brooks wouldn't cut it. I required a change of scenery. I had developed carefully constructed coping mechanisms over the years for combating the nastiness that swirled in my head.

"Fine, whatever," Brooks said, grabbing his stuff. I knew he was pissed at me. This wasn't the first time he had tried to climb over my wall. It had been a frequent source of conflict when we were dating. He just didn't understand that no one could get over that massive barrier I had created. He needed to stop trying.

"I'll call you later. Maybe we can grab some dinner," I suggested, offering the only olive branch I could give him. I didn't want him to be upset with me. He was one of my best friends, one of my *only* friends, and even though I couldn't let him in the way he wanted, he was still important to me. And I needed him to know that.

Brooks stiffened, and he turned away from me. "I'll probably be busy," he answered brusquely, heading for the door.

I grabbed his hand before he could leave my apartment. "Brooks, I am who I am. You know that. Don't get angry because I can't be the person you want me to be," I pleaded tiredly.

His shoulders drooped, and he covered my hand with his and gave me a squeeze before leaving.

The emotional exhaustion threatened to undo me. So without another thought to Brooks or my mother, I hurried out of my building and onto the sidewalk. The routine movements of walking the familiar path toward campus did exactly what I needed them to do. I felt the tangled knots loosen and the aching in my heart lessen.

I went to the library, found the book I needed. I purposefully fit all my displaced pieces back to where they were supposed to be. I went into the bathroom and smoothed my hair and fixed my makeup.

Leaving the library, I cut across campus toward the commons. I noticed a couple of guys with buckets of white paint by the wall with the graffiti. I slowed my steps and watched as they took giant rollers and started covering the vibrant colors, drowning them with muting neutrality.

I walked closer, feeling sort of sad to see the Compulsion picture disappear. I stopped and stared at the men as they slowly and systematically erased all signs that the artwork had ever been there.

"Hey, Maxx! Where are those drop cloths? I'm getting paint everywhere," one of the guys called out.

I froze. Maxx? What were the chances?

One of the painters turned to the speaker, and I could see clearly that it was indeed Maxx Demelo. And just because my day couldn't get any worse, I noticed the pile of cloth by my feet.

I thought seriously about running, because that couldn't be any more embarrassing than getting caught standing there staring at him like a moron.

Come on, feet, move!

But some masochistic part of me seemed to enjoy the sense of impending mortification.

Maxx turned around and started to walk in my direction. It was obvious he hadn't noticed me yet. I still had a chance to get away if I wanted to.

But I didn't. Because I sucked like that.

He was dressed in worn jeans and an old gray Longwood University sweatshirt. His blond hair was sweaty and matted to the sides of his face. He had white paint smeared across his forehead.

He looked gorgeous, and he walked like he knew it.

His arrogance was obvious in his every movement, and it annoyed me. I hated his confidence. I hated that he clearly didn't give a shit what anyone thought. I hated that he seemed to possess every characteristic that I wished for myself.

And then he looked up and met my eyes. His lips quirked up into a self-satisfied grin as though my being there fit into some great plan of his.

"Hi, Aubrey," he said, stooping down to pick up the pile of drop cloths.

I thought about ignoring him. But that would be rude. And he was in the support group I was co-facilitating. I was supposed to create rapport—which was difficult when he seemed to bring out this primal instinct to scream at him.

"Hi," I replied shortly. The wind whipped my hair into my face, and I spit strands out of my mouth. Awesome. Way to look cool and collected, Aubrey!

Maxx cocked an eyebrow and regarded me steadily. He didn't say anything. And neither did I. I started to feel uncomfortable under the weight of his scrutiny. Again I was bothered by a niggling sense of déjà vu. I felt like I should know him, though from where, I had no idea.

Maxx's lips were curved in a teasing smile, as though my discomfort amused him. And still he said nothing. He acted as though he had all the time in the world to stand there and make me feel awkward.

Finally I couldn't take it anymore. "So you're painting the wall, huh?" I asked. Just call me Captain Obvious.

Maxx looked over his shoulder. "Yeah, it's part of my community service," he said dismissively.

"Community service?" I asked dumbly. Maxx moved to stand next to me. He pulled out a cigarette and put it between his lips. I tried not to stare as he took a drag and blew out the lungful of smoke.

I hated smoking. I thought it was a disgusting habit. So why did I find it sexy to see Max curl his lips around the end of the cigarette? Ugh!

Maxx flicked ash on the ground and then unleashed a weapon most women would have a hard time resisting.

He smiled.

A full-mouthed curve of his lips lit up his face and made his eyes sparkle. I think I may have forgotten to breathe.

Because damn, he was dazzling.

"You know, being ordered by the court to pick up other people's shit, paint walls, and otherwise make the world a better place," he replied dryly, giving me a wink.

"Well, it's good to know you're taking it seriously," I remarked, watching him as he took another drag from his cigarette before dropping it on the ground and stomping it out.

Maxx shrugged. "It's just I can think of a lot of other things I'd rather be doing," he said.

Was I supposed to find a hidden meaning in his seemingly innocent statement? And why was I second-guessing every nuance in our conversation? It wasn't like me to be so unsure.

"Really," I muttered dryly.

Maxx chuckled and then sobered, his eyes heated and smoldering.

"Definitely," he said quietly, raising an eyebrow, a smirk dancing across his lips.

He looked at me in a way that was both warm and intense, the kind of look that stripped you to the bone and left you shivering.

His eyes were piercing in their directness, and I knew he wasn't fooled by my attempts at sarcasm and nonchalance. My uncomfortable attraction to him, which had begun only a few days before, practically oozed from my pores. It was mortifying.

And I knew I needed to shut this down—for both our sakes. It wasn't appropriate. And he was making me feel . . . disconcerted.

"Well, I think the group is going to be really helpful. I'm sure you'll get a lot out of it," I said lamely, hoping he got the point. It seemed extremely important to remind us both of who I was and what my role was in his life. I needed to reinforce where I belonged. I was a counselor in training, someone whose role was to guide him on a difficult journey.

Nothing more.

Maxx gave me a look that was hard to decipher. "I hope you're right," he said, running a dirty hand across his face, leaving a smudge along the bridge of his nose.

I had to clench my hand into a fist in order to resist the urge to wipe the smudge away. And I knew there was more than my OCD at work here.

His words unsettled me. Was I perceiving a subtext that wasn't there? Or was he purposefully communicating something that I had yet to figure out?

My guess was the latter.

He suddenly dropped his eyes, and I was surprised by the vulnerability that danced across his face.

"I *really* hope you're right," he said softly, and I didn't know whether the comment was for him or for me.

I tilted my head at him, looking at him closely. He seemed lost in thought, and I wondered what had him so consumed.

I couldn't help but be curious about him. He made it impossible not to be. He was obviously a complicated man with a complicated past. I was simultaneously intrigued and annoyed that I was intrigued.

There was a definite line I shouldn't cross. So why after meeting this man once was that boundary so hard for me to remember?

Maxx frowned and opened his mouth, then closed it again. Then he looked at me, and I watched as his face smoothed over and any sign of openness was lost.

"At least I'll like the view." His gaze purposefully raked up and down my body as he raised his eyebrows mockingly. His smile, while trying to be seductive, was hard and brittle. Any softening I had felt was trampled by the overwhelming urge to scream in his face.

His need to fuel my unease seemed forced. As though he were firmly putting us back on ground he was more comfortable with.

"That's not really appropriate," I managed, annoyed by how let down I felt. Because I already missed the elusive, unguarded Maxx that I had glimpsed only seconds ago.

Because *that* Maxx seemed real.

This Maxx was something else entirely.

But who really knew which persona was authentic?

Hell, maybe neither was, and the real Maxx was someone I hadn't met yet.

But one thing was for sure: I couldn't allow myself to *want* to get involved with any side of him. He was in a group I was helping to facilitate. Any relationship we had would need to be strictly professional. I was required to uphold a code of conduct that was as essential as it was required. There wasn't room for gray areas. There was only black and white. Right and wrong.

In-betweens couldn't exist, particularly between me and a man I knew instinctively was trouble—a man who brought with him a whole mess of problems, a man I could only imagine to be the worst kind of disaster.

I hefted my book bag up on my shoulder and shifted on my feet. "I'd better let you get back to painting. Nice seeing you," I said, lying through my teeth. Our encounter had been anything but *nice*.

Confusing was probably more accurate.

Maxx smiled again, and this one was much more natural. He crouched down to the ground and picked a pale purple aster flower from the campus landscaping. He got to his feet and handed it to me. I took it hesitantly, meeting his eyes as I tried to understand his motivation.

"It's just a flower, Aubrey. Don't read anything into it," he scoffed, his eyes laughing at my wariness.

I tilted my chin up, my shoulders stiff, my spine straight as I met Maxx's eyes one final time. "Thanks," I said. I cleared my throat, which had become oddly tight. "I'll see you later."

My heart hammered in my chest as we stood there, staring at each other again. A thousand things seemed to be communicated in his look, if only I was fluent in Maxx.

"Yeah, see ya in group next week," he said, gathering up the drop cloths.

I gave him a small wave and left in the direction opposite the one from which I'd come, forgetting about going to the commons. I just wanted to get back to the sanctuary of my apartment.

It wasn't until I had left campus that I looked down to find the flower crushed in my tightly closed fist. I slowly opened my fingers and let the ruined petals fall to the ground.

chapter
six

aubrey

"devon wants to go back to Compulsion tonight," Renee said, coming into my bedroom. She didn't venture far from the door, standing awkwardly as though unsure she had a right to be there.

At one time, she wouldn't have thought twice about barging in and sitting down on my bed. If I'd complained about having homework to do, she would have thrown a pillow at me and then gone about trying to convince me to get drunk with her.

We would have gone out, and Renee would have gotten wasted. I would have been the DD, but that was all right, because I would have had fun. Because that's how it had been with me and Renee. That was us.

Now she stood in my room as though she had never been there before. She wouldn't make eye contact, and even though her bright red hair was perfectly styled, her makeup was just shy of overdone, and her clothing was clearly thought out and planned. This was *not* the girl who used to invite the entire soccer team back to our apartment for a game of strip poker.

Renee's eyes were dead, her mouth turned down, and she was uncharacteristically . . . blank.

"What?" I asked, narrowing my eyes.

"Devon wants to head over to Compulsion tonight. I thought you might like to come with us. Get out of the house for the evening," Renee suggested with feigned indifference.

No matter how unaffected she tried to act, I knew she was nervous. She did *not* want to go back to the club. Otherwise she'd never have asked me to come along. She would never put Devon and me in a social situation together unless she was completely and totally freaking out.

"Why would you want to go back there?" I asked sharply. I tried to rein in my bewildered accusation. As much as I hated the reason she was asking, I couldn't help but feel a smidgen of hope that her asking at all was a sign that our friendship could be salvaged.

Because I missed Renee Alston. A lot.

Renee's jaw tightened, and her eyes became flinty. "Look, I knew asking you was a lost cause. God forbid your weekend consist of something other than watching *The Vampire Diaries* for the millionth time while Brooks makes his super-witty comments that no one finds funny but him," Renee snapped. I felt a flash of anger.

"Look, if you want me to go anywhere with you and that loser you call a boyfriend, you're going about it the wrong way, sweetheart," I countered sarcastically, allowing myself to unload some of my anger in her direction.

Renee sucked in a breath. "Fuck off, Aubrey," she bit out.

"So this is how it's going to be from now on, I guess. Us barely talking. Me biting my tongue in half instead of telling you what I really think of your fuckhead boyfriend. Both of us ignoring the fact that you've changed. Big-time," I challenged, my voice rising the angrier I became.

Renee's eyes became glassy, and I recognized the tremble of

her bottom lip all too well. Her imminent tears made me feel like shit.

"Forget it," Renee whispered, and left the room before I could say anything else. I pressed the heel of my hands into my eyes and swallowed down the urge to scream. I took a deep breath. Okay, she was being a bitch, but I could have handled it a little better myself. She had tried to reach out in the only way she seemed capable of at the moment, and I had smacked her hand away. And while hanging out with Devon and his idiot friends for the night didn't sound like my idea of a good time, being with Renee in whatever capacity was possible seemed like a positive step forward for us.

I went into the hallway with every intention of making peace.

But just as I was about to call out to her, to accept her invitation, however strange and awkward it had been, I heard the front door open and then shut with a decisive slam.

Not two minutes later, the door opened again, and I hurried to the living room to try to repair the unfortunate situation with Renee.

"I've told you a thousand times to lock that door," Brooks scolded as he headed into the kitchen. He really didn't understand the concept of personal boundaries. Somewhere along the way, my house became his house. My chips became his chips.

My chocolate became his chocolate? Oh, hell no!

I grabbed the bag of Hershey's Kisses from his hands. "There are lines you can't cross, Brooks. Hands off," I warned, putting the bag back in the cabinet.

Brooks looked unfazed as he instead reached for a box of Ritz Crackers and went into the living room.

"I passed Renee in the hallway. She looked as though her ass was on fire. Oh, and she was dressed like a hooch. Let me guess, hot date with her boyfriend, aka I like to kick kittens with steel-toed boots?" Brooks asked, rolling his eyes as I started wiping his cracker crumbs from the couch cushions.

I handed him a paper plate, which he accepted with exaggerated slowness, just to irritate me.

I sat down beside him with a flop. "She went back to Compulsion, can you believe that? And she wanted me to go with her. Sorry, but I just don't see the appeal of worrying about whether you will be knifed in the bathroom for your lip gloss," I muttered.

"Shit! Really? You wanna go?" Brooks asked, perking up.

I leveled him with my version of his patented "are you crazy?" look.

"So we can be humiliated when we're told to go home by the Barbarian Bouncer?"

Brooks tossed the box of crackers onto the coffee table and wiped his hands on his jeans, making me cringe.

"Aubrey, seriously, we should go! Ever since last time I've really wanted to check it out, and you know you want to keep an eye on Renee," he countered.

I started to voice my protests but was rudely cut off by Brooks placing his hand over my mouth.

"Don't you dare deny it! You won't be able to relax tonight for worrying about that flaky roommate of yours. So come on, get dolled up, and let's go get our club on!" I smacked Brooks's hand away and tried in vain to stay irritated with him, which was damned difficult as he started to wiggle his shoulders in a poor imitation of dancing.

"I don't think I have anything in my closet that remotely resembles what a dominatrix would wear. There's no way we'll get inside," I reasoned, hoping he'd drop it while simultaneously hoping he'd wear me down.

Because, damn him, he was right. I wanted to go. Though I wouldn't admit that I had other reasons than just to keep tabs on my friend, that I was actually a teensy bit curious about the world Compulsion offered.

Okay, more than a teensy bit.

Even though I had been in level-ten panic mode during my last visit, something about the music, the atmosphere, the thrilling taste of danger that danced on the end of my tongue, was compelling.

The desire to escape made me anxious. Ever since the phone call with my mother, I had again been held prisoner by memories that I had tried very hard to keep tucked away in my subconscious.

It only took the sound of my mother's voice to blow open the door I kept resolutely shut.

So the idea of letting go, of submerging myself in a world so completely outside my norm, was a lot more enticing than it ever would have been before.

And then there was the mystery man . . .

My decision was made.

"Okay, let's do this," I said suddenly, getting to my feet. I laughed at the wide-mouthed stare I received from Brooks.

I put my hands on my hips and rolled my eyes. "I thought you wanted to go. Come on, help me find something that is sufficiently slutty to get me inside," I taunted, enjoying the shock on my friend's face.

I didn't surprise people very often, but I figured when I did, I might as well make it a doozy.

"Uh . . . okay," Brooks stammered, following me into my bedroom.

Twenty minutes later I was standing in a sea of clothing that was about to make my OCD tendencies go into full-on meltdown.

"When did my penis become a freaking vagina? I'm a guy, Aubrey! A guy! I don't know what the fuck you should wear! I'm all about taking the clothes *off*. Not putting them *on*." Brooks was talking from his perch on my bed, where he had stretched out, watching my one-woman whirling dervish imitation.

I groaned and finally grabbed a jean skirt that I never wore, mostly because I liked keeping the girlie bits covered when I was out in public, and a black, off-the-shoulder sequined top.

Once I was dressed and had zipped up my knee-high black leather boots, I looked at myself in the mirror and wanted to immediately change back into my jeans and sweatshirt. It's not as though I was dressed in anything overly dramatic. It was pretty tame by club standards, but it wasn't *me*.

I had curled my long blond hair and opted to wear more makeup than usual. I just hoped it was enough, because this was just about all the energy I was willing to expend.

Brooks gave me a low whistle when I finished. His eyes raked me from head to toe, focusing a little too intently on my legs. His face was unnaturally flushed, and I started to think that perhaps this was a really bad idea.

I cleared my throat, and Brooks blinked and looked away, seeming embarrassed. "You look nice," he said with a smile as his eyes flicked again over my body.

It was times like then that it was hard to forget that he had seen me naked . . . a lot. Our relationship had surprisingly never been uncomfortable. We had transitioned into easy camaraderie seamlessly. But now I felt a strange sort of tension radiating from him that had everything to do with his overactive hormones.

"Thanks," I mumbled, hurriedly grabbing Renee's black leather jacket. After putting it on, I gave him a quick once-over, noting he had gone home and changed while I was getting dressed.

He had turned in the khakis and button-down shirt for a fitted pair of jeans and a tight gray shirt with some sort of band logo on the front. He had styled his hair into spikes.

I leaned in closer, peering at his face. "Did you put eyeliner on? Seriously?" I snorted.

Brooks's shoulders tensed. "It's about looking the part, Aubrey. Shut up," he responded tersely.

Guy-liner aside, Brooks looked good. Really good. Hopefully *really good* would be enough to get inside the club.

I grabbed my purse and followed Brooks out into the hallway. "Do we know where we're going this time?" I asked as we got into his Honda.

Brooks gave me a grin. "Well, we have to go figure it out," he answered cryptically.

I cocked my eyebrow in his direction. "Care to explain?" I asked, not in the mood for guessing games.

"We've got to go see the picture. Then we can figure out where Compulsion is tonight," he said, sounding giddy. I could tell Brooks was excited. His enthusiasm was contagious. I couldn't help but feel a flutter in my stomach as we made our way to the center of town.

"How do you know where the picture is?" I asked. This really did seem like a lot of trouble just to go to a club. What was with the mystery? Why not just hand out flyers?

"I asked around and was told it's behind the self-service laundry beside the liquor store," Brooks explained.

"Can't we just ask where it is? Why do we have to go to the hassle of finding some crappy piece of graffiti for directions?" I asked, knowing I sounded cranky. But the hurdles we were needing to jump to find the club were deflating my already shaky willingness to go out at all.

Brooks clicked his tongue in disapproval. "Aubrey, this is part of the experience. You need to see the picture, then you can find out where it is. And it's not crappy graffiti. X is an artist, man. His stuff is unbelievable. I've heard people saying that galleries have been trying to locate him for the past year, wanting to sell his work. But no one knows who he is. Or how to find him. It just adds to the mystique, you know?"

I scoffed under my breath. "Why in the hell would a gallery want to sell some squiggles spray-painted on a wall? It's not exactly Monet we're talking about here."

Brooks shook his head. "You have so much to learn, young grasshopper. The urban art movement is huge right now. And X has built a reputation as one of the best. He's only been doing it for the past three years, but if you Google *street art*, his stuff will be up there with Banksy. He's awesome!" he said, as though it made perfect sense.

"How do you know it's a guy? It could be a woman, you know," I pointed out almost belligerently.

Brooks shrugged. "Who knows? Does it matter?"

"And what sort of name is X?" I mocked.

Brooks gave me a look from the corner of his eye and didn't bother to respond. Clearly my lack of appreciation for the mysterious X had lost me a considerable number of cool points.

We pulled down a narrow alleyway between two buildings that ended in a small parking lot. There was a group of people standing beside a Dumpster.

Brooks put his car into park and jumped out. "Come on!" he called out to me, hurrying over to the side of the building. There was a large amount of graffiti—your typical gang tags and names.

But that wasn't what people had flocked here to see.

It was the portrait of a woman on fire that had their attention. It was at least ten feet high and fifteen feet across. It was massive.

"Please explain to me what this has to do with a dance club?" I whispered to Brooks, who had his phone pulled out and was punching numbers into his GPS. He glanced up at me and gave me a distracted smile.

"Not a damned thing, Aubrey," he replied. I frowned and turned back to the picture. The wind had picked up, bringing with it the rancid smell of old garbage. The small parking lot was disgusting. But the crowd of people couldn't care less about their surroundings. We were all here for one thing only . . . to find our way to a club that promised things we couldn't begin to imagine.

I had to admit that the artistry of the graffiti was impressive. I remembered the picture from a few weeks ago, the monstrous hand with people falling from the sky.

That painting had been dark and almost threatening. This one seemed to convey something else entirely.

Longing.

Wanting something you've watched from afar.

Desire.

Blatant, unbridled lust.

Somehow, some way, this smattering of paint on a dirty wall conveyed all of these things. And I knew that Brooks was right. That whoever X was, this person was seriously talented.

The picture depicted the side profile of a woman, her long, golden hair licked by bright red flames as they crawled toward her face. You could see only the outline of her nose and jaw, as she was turned away, looking off into the distance.

The rest of her body was done in dark, bold lines that were almost crude and undefined, until you got to her hand. The hand was painted precisely and almost delicately. The fingers were un-curled, the palm was spread open, and from the hand fell lovely, purple blossoms that reminded me of the aster flowers that grew on campus.

The fire at the girl's feet reached up and seemed to engulf the flowers that were floating to the ground. It was such a contradic-tion—the power of the fire and the placid gentleness of the flow-ers. There was a violent sort of possession in the way the flames seemed to devour the petals that fell from the woman's hand, almost, but not quite, touching her skin, as though they were reaching out for her yet not quite able to reach her. I noticed the characteristic X enmeshed in the red and orange.

A shiver that had nothing to do with the chill in the air raced down my spine.

"I've got it!" Brooks called out, a little too loudly. I jumped with a start, having been so fixated on the painting.

"Come on!" Brooks yelled in my ear, and I gave him a look of annoyance. I noticed others were quickly leaving as well, having gotten what they came for. I glanced back at the picture, feeling strangely sad about leaving it behind.

"Aubrey, it's already late. We need to hurry or the line will be huge!" Brooks urged, pulling me toward his car.

After I was buckled in, I looked again at the picture, wishing I understood the strange twist of emotions I felt when I looked at it. I stared at it until my eyes started to tear over.

Blinking, I looked over at Brooks, who was programming an address into his phone and then setting it down on the center console. I rubbed at my temples, feeling the twinges of a headache coming on.

I felt oddly unsettled, and a part of me wanted to go home and forget about tonight's grand adventure. I felt a sense of foreboding that I couldn't shake, mostly because it was tangled up with an almost euphoric need to let go.

I was a fucking mess.

Clearing my throat, I tried to get my head straight by focusing on my friend, who was practically buzzing with excitement. "How did you get the address?" I asked, knowing that during my free fall into emotional turmoil I had missed a major part of what we were doing there.

Brooks pointed at the picture. "See those numbers painted into the fire at the bottom?" he asked, and I tried to see what he was talking about. And then I saw it. The numbers one and four and then five other numbers intertwined along the base of the flame.

"Yeah, so?" I asked.

"The first two are a street number, the last five the zip code. The stems of the flowers are actually the street name. So you put it into the GPS and voilà, there you have it, the location for Compulsion," he answered, sounding like a little kid revealing a top-secret magic trick.

"Well, isn't that supercreative," I quipped, trying to hide the increasing sense of disquiet unfurling in my belly.

"Just chill out and have fun, Aubrey. Let your hair down for one night," Brooks teased, and I tried not to get defensive at the implied criticism.

"I can have as much fun as the next girl," I argued, and tried not to get annoyed at Brooks's bark of disbelieving laughter.

The rest of the ride continued in silence, and I tried to contain the confusing rush of nerves and excitement that made my heart thud in my chest.

The GPS led us to the outskirts of the city, far away from the lights and bustle of normal, Saturday nightlife. Brooks pulled his car into a field, and I could see people heading off toward a group of trees.

"Let's go," Brooks called out as he got out of the car. I exited the vehicle, walked through the tall grass, and headed for a break in the woods.

It was dark, with the lights of a thousand cell phones and lighters punctuating the air around us. I could hear the thudding of music not too far off in the distance. I stumbled over a tree root, and Brooks had to grab me by the arm so I wouldn't fall. Something about Compulsion clearly had me struggling to stay on my feet.

"There it is!" Brooks yelled into my ear, pointing to a run-down farmhouse that looked as though it had been condemned several decades ago. The building was huge; at one time it was probably a lovely home to a nice family. Now it looked like something straight out of a horror movie.

The windows were either broken or missing glass entirely. The porch was in a crumbled heap at the front. The long line of people wrapped along the side and disappeared around the back of the house.

"Seems like *Texas Chainsaw Massacre* is the theme for the

night," I muttered, zipping the leather jacket up to my chin in an attempt to stay warm.

Once again, we found ourselves waiting in line for our chance to get inside. I wondered if Renee was already there. I recognized a few students from school, but other than that, it was a mass of strangers.

I groaned under my breath as we reached the front of the line and noticed good ol' Randy, my bouncer BFF from our last sojourn to Compulsion. He looked as fierce and unyielding as ever, and I hoped like hell he didn't recognize our sad attempts to fit in as the fake acts that they were.

I was relieved when our obligatory once-over was greeted with a gruff demand for money, followed by a smeared stamp on the back of our hands. And just like that, we were granted access.

Brooks let out a whoop and rustled my hair. "We got in! Awesome!" he enthused, and I tried to smile back. But the deafening boom of the bass and the familiar sensation of anticipation and fear that licked my insides had already taken over.

I had found my escape.

chapter
seven

X

I ran my tongue along my bottom lip, enjoying the numb sensation that filled my mouth. I could still taste the bitterness of the pills in the back of my throat. My eyelids drooped, and my limbs felt heavy.

I fucking loved it.

The music rang in my ears as I pushed through the crowd. I pulled the baseball cap down over my forehead and enjoyed the feel of a hundred bodies pressed against me. The smell of sweat filled my nose, and I wanted to lie back on the floor and let the ground swallow me up.

A girl with bright blue hair and wearing a tight tube dress rubbed up against me, her arms going around my neck. Her lips stretched into an over-enunciated caricature of a smile. She was like a trampy Smurfette with breasts that pushed aggressively into my chest.

Hell, I was game. I'd play along. So I let my hands wander down to her ass. She gave a little squeal as I squeezed.

Yes, I was copping a feel with a random chick, but it felt so damned good. Everything seemed to slow down, the air pulsed, and I wished I could just be like the rest of these crazy fucks enjoying the mood.

But I had shit to do.

Smurfette rubbed against my crotch, and I gripped her skin, feeling like I could sink my fingers into her flesh and disappear. My head was fuzzy, and my mouth felt dry, but I didn't want to move. Ever again.

"You got anything?" the girl whispered in my ear, her tongue darting out to lick the sweat that beaded along my jaw.

I grinned wickedly and pulled her up against my front, thrusting in time to the music. "I've got exactly what you need," I promised, getting off on the gleam of excitement that lit up her pale face.

"How much?" she breathed out, her movements becoming frantic in her enthusiasm.

"Come with me," I said, grabbing her hand and dragging her through the crowd toward the hallway off the dance floor. We were practically running as I found a dark room toward the back of the house.

It was my job to find the spot for Compulsion every month. Call me the location scout or the Master of the Party. Whatever. But it was freaking hard finding a place that was big enough but far enough off the radar that we could get away with playing music way too loud and selling drugs way too blatantly.

This place had been a prize. It had been condemned a couple of months ago and was scheduled to be torn down in a few weeks. Gash, the club organizer, wasn't sure about the safety of the old farmhouse, but he couldn't deny that it was private and just about perfect for a night of barely controlled mayhem.

I had walked through the building several times before tonight, so I knew the layout pretty well. I also knew that where I was leading Smurfette was private enough for what I had in mind.

There weren't any lights. I had to fish out my cell phone and use it as a flashlight while I dug for the baggie in my pocket. I shook out two small blue pills and held them out for the girl.

She practically salivated as she tried to grab them from me. I closed my fist and snatched them away before she could take them.

"Uh-uh," I mocked, wagging my finger in her face. The girl hurriedly pulled a wad of cash out of her pocket and shoved two twenties in my front pocket, her fingers gripping my thigh through my jeans. Looking at her closely, I knew her type well enough, a sad little trust-funder looking for the express train to the dark side.

Lucky for her, I was all too happy to comply.

She opened her mouth, and I dropped the drugs on her tongue. She closed her mouth around my fingers and sucked as she swallowed, her eyes rolling back in her head in ecstasy. "Mmm," she moaned, rubbing her hands down her body, while she deep-throated my digits.

My dick sprung to attention. I was feeling mellow and high as fuck, and right now I just wanted this girl to get on her goddamned knees. Enough with the tease, I wanted the main act.

I pushed her down by her shoulders, making it clear what I wanted. Her knees collided with the filthy floor, but she didn't even notice. She was too fucked-up to care, and I was too much of an asshole to be bothered that she didn't. I should have been disgusted at the way she willingly grappled with my belt buckle. She unsnapped my jeans and pulled down the zipper like a pro.

Hell, I should have been disgusted with myself for what I was expecting her to do. But I had moved past feelings of shame a long-ass time ago.

This was my world. And in this world I took what I wanted, when I wanted it.

The reality I faced on the outside was something else entirely. I didn't have the freedom to call my own shots. I clawed through life with bloodied fingers.

But for right now I was a fucking god.

The girl looked up at me through her blue hair, giving me a glassy-eyed smile. I didn't smile back. Before she could get started, I pulled out a condom. No way was that bitch touching my dick without protection.

When I was done getting ready, I pushed her head down, and she gave me exactly what I wanted.

I didn't touch her. I didn't put my hands in her hair or rub her shoulders. This wasn't about affection. Or even lust. This was entirely about me getting what I wanted. I didn't give a shit about who she was. I wouldn't ask her name or try to find out her favorite fucking color.

I didn't give a shit about any of it. It had been a long time since I allowed myself to care about anyone or anything at all. I just wanted to come in her mouth and then leave. Because it made me feel better. And that was all that mattered.

So I stood there while the bitch sucked me off like it was her job, almost forgetting it was an actual person with her mouth around my cock.

When she was done, she got to her feet and wiped her mouth with the back of her hand. She leaned up on her tiptoes and tried to kiss my mouth, hiking up her skirt as she climbed me like a goddamned tree, as if sucking my dick gave her the fucking right to expect me to put my cock inside her. I had standards.

I shoved her away and removed the condom. I tied it at the end and threw it on the floor at her feet. "Do something with that," I ordered as I zipped up my pants.

Without another word, or a look in her direction, I left the room and headed back to the dance floor.

I felt light as air, the drugs working through my system. I wondered if I closed my eyes whether I would float to the ceiling. I bet I could fly away and never come back. And that was exactly what I wanted.

To go far, far away.

"Yo, X, have you sold all your shit?" I opened my eyes in annoyance, pissed at whoever was interrupting my temporary moment of insane escapism.

"What the fuck do you want?" I snarled at the scrawny dude who stood before me, practically quaking in his crappy knockoff Dr. Martens. This piece of shit was now firmly on my bad side.

The guy grimaced in apology, and I knew he was wondering what I would do. I felt a perverse sort of pleasure at his wariness. I had a reputation for being temperamental and erratic. I didn't give a fuck about those pesky things called consequences.

This was *my* fucking world; I just let them all exist in it.

I should probably note that my drug use came with a hefty dose of narcissism.

"Uh, Marco said you had some . . . you know . . . I just wanted to buy whatever you have," the guy stammered. I didn't know him. But he sure as hell knew me. They all did.

I was a hard guy *not* to know.

Feeling suddenly magnanimous, I pulled out the last of the pills and held them up in front of him. "That'll be double for *you*," I told him pointedly, amused by the flash of anger on his ugly face. What the hell would he do about it? Fight me? Steal my drugs? I didn't think so. He clearly didn't have the balls for that.

I smirked as he handed me eighty dollars and took the two pills in my hand. I folded up the money and put it in my pocket. "Nice doin' business with you," I said dryly, pushing past him and heading toward the bar.

I was on top of the universe. Nothing could bring me down. I was the king of this fucking castle.

And then I saw *her*.

The flash of her blond hair in the strobing lights caught my attention immediately. My eyes honed in on the sight of her—a beacon in my own personal darkness.

She was dressed differently than she had been the last time. Gone were the jeans and T-shirt. Tonight it was all about the short skirt and see-through top, a tantalizing glimpse of what lay beneath.

But it didn't look right. Tonight it was more like she was trying to be something it was so very obvious she wasn't, though I admit that I appreciated the sight of her long legs underneath the short skirt.

It was like seeing a gazelle among lions. She would be eaten alive here. But as I watched her dance, I could tell there was a part of her that wanted to be devoured.

She danced like she wasn't entirely comfortable in her body. There was a hesitancy to her movements that seemed at war with the look of abandon on her face.

And it was a beautiful fucking face.

She seemed to be alone. Just like last time. As though she were waiting for me to swoop in and take her away.

"The usual?" the bartender, Eric, asked me. I barely nodded my head, not wanting to give anyone or anything else my attention.

She swayed to the music, as though willing herself to relax and go with it. She seemed to be begging for me to help her let go.

I smiled to myself, knowing I could help her get to that place she wanted to be.

I could be her white rabbit. She just needed to follow me where I wanted to lead her.

Maybe these thoughts weren't rational. They were bordering on crazy. But they gave me an intoxicating sense of power.

I wanted her.

And I would have her.

I *always* took what I wanted.

But then she wasn't alone anymore. A guy came up to her, and she smiled up into his face, and I watched as she laughed at something he said.

My hands clenched into fists, and I tried to suppress the flush of rage that let loose inside me at the sight of her with someone else. My unreasonable sense of ownership made me see red.

The pair headed to the bar and stood about ten feet away from me. The guy was into her. I prized myself on being able to read people like a fucking book, and this dude's book was a step-by-step instruction manual on how to strike out with a girl who was way out of his league.

He moved in close to her, she took a tiny step back. He put his hand on her arm, she shrugged it off. I grinned at the way she rebuffed his advances each and every time.

The guy ordered them some shots, and I was impressed with the way she slammed them back, though it was obvious she wasn't a drinker. I could tell by the way she grimaced after she swallowed. Her tongue darted out to lick her lips, and I felt a tightening in my groin.

I nursed my own drink as I got my voyeuristic kicks from watching her. The guy, whoever he was, whispered something in her ear and then left her as he headed in the direction of the toilets. Her discomfort kicked up a notch the moment she was alone.

She wore her vulnerability like a neon sign.

I drank some more of my whiskey and turned my attention to the man with a face full of metal and a dead look in his eyes at the end of the bar. I knew the type. I knew what he was thinking. And I knew what he would do if given the chance.

Her friend had yet to come back, so she ordered another drink. The bartender put her beer down on the bar, and she turned away from it to watch the dancers. Full metal jacket took this as an open invitation to play would-be rapist. He subtly dropped a pill I recognized all too well into her open bottle and then slipped back into the crowd.

She didn't see a thing. Given the size of the crowd in the club, her ignorance was both infuriating and understandable. She was in over her head, completely overwhelmed and unaware. She didn't have the street smarts to hang out in a place like this.

In one fluid movement, I was beside her. I made sure that my cap still sat low over my face.

My anonymity was vital.

She reached to grab her beer, but I quickly pulled it out of reach. She blinked up at me in bewilderment with eyes that were a clear and vivid brown, her brows furrowed with irritation.

"Give me my drink," she demanded, trying to sound hard and menacing. She was about as intimidating as a kitten.

Not able to help myself, I reached out and ran a finger down her cheek. She smacked my hand away, and I found myself laughing at her indignation.

"*And all that's best of dark and bright/Meet in her aspect and her eyes*," I quoted, enjoying the confusion on her face. Yeah, I had a thing for Byron. He wrote some dark shit that I appreciated.

The moment would have been uncomfortably cheesy except for the heat in her. I made her hot, I could tell. Yet she hated that I turned her on. She didn't know me. I was a stranger. I knocked her off-balance. But she felt desire nonetheless.

It was a heady sort of power.

"Give me my goddamned drink," she enunciated slowly and angrily.

I leaned over the bar and dropped the full bottle of beer into the trash can. "You're not drinking that," I told her shortly.

She was furious. I grinned in the face of her anger, soaking it in. My veins hummed, and my head felt full. My eyes were heavy, and my feet felt weighted down as if by cement, but nothing could make me leave her.

Not yet.

"Why did you do that?" she asked, and I could see her jaw tightening as she became angrier. I wanted her pissed. I wanted her barely able to hold it together. Because I could tell she wanted that.

She wanted to lose control.

And I felt it was my mission to give that to her.

I leaned in, purposefully close, invading her personal space. It was violating and encroaching, but I wanted to see how far I could push it. I dropped my hand to her waist, to the bare skin below the hem of her shirt. I pressed my fingers into the skin, flattening my palms in order to feel the warmth.

"Don't ever take your eyes off your drink in here," I whispered low in her ear. Her eyes, those incredible deep brown eyes, widened.

She looked up at me, trying to see my face. I ducked my head down, hiding from her penetrating gaze. I knew the lighting would make it difficult for her to see me under the bill of my cap, but I needed to be careful.

I reached up so that my fingers grasped her chin and turned her to face the other side of the bar. "You see that guy over there with his septum pierced and the bad dye job?" I asked, indicating the guy who had slipped her a roofie not ten minutes ago. He was watching us closely, scowling, clearly not appreciating the way I had ruined his plans for the evening.

"Y . . . yeah," she stammered, and I could feel her heartbeat under my thumb. She was nervous, and probably pretty freaked out.

Good.

"He put something in your drink. And then he would have waited," I whispered in her ear. I saw her throat move as she swallowed.

"He would have waited until you went to the bathroom, or gone outside to get some air, and then he would have followed you. You would have been too spaced out from the drug to put up a fight when he dragged you off behind the building," I said. She looked truly scared, and I felt sort of bad. But a girl like this didn't understand the dangers that lurked for her in the shadows.

"And you would have been unconscious while he did whatever he wanted to you," I finished, dropping my hand from her waist and moving away. I adjusted my cap and finished the rest of my drink before pushing the glass toward Eric.

"Guys like that wait all night for an easy mark like you. So if you plan on being here, smarten up. Because there are plenty of predators out there," I told her, suddenly angry. I wasn't sure why I was so mad. But all thoughts of possession, of desire, had been erased by an unfamiliar sense of protectiveness.

The girl frowned and looked at me as closely as she was able to in the dim light. "I remember you. You were the one who helped me find my friend last time." Then she stepped into *my* personal space. *She* violated and encroached. And *I* was the one who took the step back.

"What's your name?" she asked softly, reaching up for my cap, as though she wanted to remove it.

I grabbed her wrist and pulled it away, holding it down at her side. "You should go home. I told you last time: You don't belong in a place like this. I think this just proves it. The mouse doesn't survive long in a room full of cats," I said.

I was starting to feel jittery. I needed another fix, and soon. The drugs had started to work their way out of my system, and I felt my organs screaming to hold it in. My blood and bones were hysterical over the loss.

I was thinking too clearly, and my eyes were too focused. But *she* made me want to see straight.

I didn't understand why. I didn't like the effect she had.

It made me angry.

My night had been consumed by this girl, and there were other things I was supposed to be doing.

She opened her mouth to speak, and I thought about thrusting my tongue between her red lips.

Tasting and conquering.

Making her mouth mine.

But her words and my desires were cut short.

"There was a long-ass line at the bathroom. Sorry that took so long." Her friend returned, and she was momentarily distracted by his appearance. I used that as my chance to disappear into the crowd.

I left her.

I tried to forget.

I tried to resume my night as it had been before I had seen her.

But there was no forgetting. Some people can burrow their way into your head without you realizing it is even happening.

And later on, as I beat the shit out of the guy who had slipped her the drugs, I knew she had burrowed deep.

I just hadn't decided what I would do if she stayed there.

chapter
eight

"You wanna head over to the commons and grab some dinner?" Renee asked, walking into my bedroom.

I looked up from my homework in surprise. Was she talking to me? Was this an actual invite to hang out?

Last weekend at Compulsion had been . . . well . . . interesting.

It was hard for me to decide whether I had truly enjoyed myself or not. The entire experience had been completely surreal.

Being there, pretending to be someone I wasn't, had been liberating in a sense. The need to let go and have fun was a tantalizing temptation, one that for a few moments I had been fully ready to give in to.

But then I had seen *him* again, the stranger wearing the baseball cap. He had swooped in and saved the day as though he had been waiting all night for such a moment.

I had felt like an idiot when he kept me from drinking the drug-laced beer. I prided myself on being hypervigilant when it came to unusual situations. It wasn't like me to leave my drink unguarded.

I wasn't an idiot, but that night I had been all sorts of stupid. I had been reckless and almost endangered myself by my ignorance.

But mystery man made sure that hadn't happened.

I should have been grateful he was there. Instead I had felt supremely irritated that I hadn't been able to take care of myself, and he had basically mocked me for it.

I wasn't the sort of girl who needed rescuing, yet he had done so twice now.

And I still didn't know his name or even what he looked like. And I knew that, without a doubt, that was completely intentional.

When he had touched me, it had been deliberate, as though he was looking for a certain kind of response from me. He knew what he was doing by invading my personal space, and he enjoyed making me uncomfortable.

But then he had disappeared, and I hadn't seen him again for the rest of the night.

I hated to admit that I had spent more time looking for him than I had dancing. I had completely forgotten to look for Renee as well, and it wasn't until Brooks and I were leaving at two in the morning that I realized I hadn't seen her all night.

Brooks had been more than a little drunk, so I had to drive us home. Renee was already home by the time I got back to the apartment. I had seen the light on underneath her door.

But I had been out of sorts and feeling strangely shaky, so I hadn't bothered to find out where she had been. And I hadn't really spoken to her since.

So her sudden appearance in my bedroom caught me by surprise.

"What?" I questioned dumbly.

"We haven't spent any sort of time together lately. I thought we could . . . you know, get some dinner and then maybe rent a movie. It's been a while since we've watched *Dazed and Confused*," she offered, her pale green eyes meeting mine tentatively.

I knew she was trying. She was reaching out. And I wasn't one to smack away what she was offering. It hit me hard in that moment how much I missed my best friend. I suddenly needed the open confidences we used to share.

As much as I loved Brooks, he wasn't Renee.

I closed my Counseling Foundations textbook and gave her a smile. "That sounds great," I said genuinely. Renee seemed relieved that I had accepted her offer so readily. Perhaps I hadn't been as accessible as I thought I had been. Could it be that the state of our deteriorating friendship didn't rest entirely on her shoulders? Perhaps my tendency to shut people out had contributed to the emotional distance between us.

I grabbed my purse, and Renee pulled on her black leather jacket. She jammed her hands in her pockets and pulled out a couple of receipts that I had left behind after wearing it on Saturday.

"Did you borrow my jacket?" she asked me, crumpling the papers and tossing them in the trash.

"Yeah, on Saturday. Hope it's okay," I told her. We had always lived by an open-closet policy since we had moved in together, though perhaps I shouldn't have taken it without permission, given the current state of our friendship.

Renee smiled. "It's okay. You know you're always welcome to my clothes. Anyway, this jacket always looked better on you than on me," she said lightly, and any tension we had been feeling lessened slightly.

"That's true. I can't argue with that logic," I joked, closing our apartment door behind us as we headed down the hallway.

"Where did you go? I thought you planned on staying home on Saturday," she said.

"Brooks and I headed over to Compulsion. I was hoping to see you there, you know, after you suggested it . . . ," I ventured, trying to open up a dialogue between us. I instantly noticed the tightening of her jaw and the stiffening of her shoulders.

"We didn't end up going," she said finally after a few moments.

"Why? What did you do?" I asked, not sure she would answer me, whether she would think I was being intrusive and shut me down. I never knew what my questions would be met with anymore. Long gone were the days of easy conversation. Renee Alston carried a lot of secrets now, and I wasn't sure I'd ever know what they were.

Renee smoothed down her hair, a gesture that usually indicated she was upset about something. I looked at her closely and was startled to see that she looked almost gaunt. How had I not noticed how much weight she'd been losing in the last few months? Her once-vibrant red hair was now the dull color of rust. Her clothes were baggy and seemed ready to fall off her slight frame.

She had always been a curvaceous girl. She was a bit on the short side, coming up only to my shoulders, but with an ass and boobs that put mine to shame. And she had always worked what she had. Now it was as though her clothes were swallowing her up. Her shoulders were drooped, and these days her gaze was always trained at the ground.

"We ended up at a party. Some guy Devon knew," Renee explained, looking at me out of the corner of her eye, most likely watching for a sign of my well-known disapproval of Devon. But I kept my face blank.

"Oh, yeah? How was it?" I asked, walking out onto the sidewalk and waiting for Renee to catch up. The air was cold and had been hinting at snow for weeks now, though I had yet to see a flake. The sky was a flat, slate gray, and I for one didn't miss the sun. I loved the cold.

I remembered the way Jayme and I would wait impatiently for snow. Even if it was futile, given the lack of frozen precipitation we experienced during the winter. She would follow the local weather constantly, hoping for a day off from school. We had developed a strange ritual of doing a dance in the yard as though that would encourage the weather we wanted.

When we were younger, we spent so much of our time to-gether. Jayme had been only two years younger than me, but from an early age, I had felt very protective of her. She had always been shy and insecure, having struggled with body image since she was old enough to worry about that sort of thing.

She just hadn't understood how truly beautiful she was. She had always gone out of her way to make people like her, even if they were the wrong type of people.

Renee stopped walking and turned to me. "We don't have to talk about Devon. I know you don't like him. And actually, I un-derstand why. He hasn't been very nice to you," she stated, and I couldn't help the snort that escaped.

"Or you," I added hesitantly, not sure if I should keep my opin-ions quiet but finding it hard to stifle how I felt.

Renee thinned her lips, and I waited for the argument. It never came. And I was glad I had voiced how I felt without censoring myself.

"Why don't we just go get some dinner," Renee responded shortly, and I knew I had overstepped. It was very clear that she was extending the olive branch only so far, and that I should just take what she was offering and back off.

What was it about an impending train wreck that made it im-possible to look away? That's what Renee's life looked like—a big messy train ride to doom. But as much as I wanted to jump on the tracks and stop it, I knew my intervention would not be appreci-ated. Being Renee's friend of late meant perfecting the art of tongue biting. And I had damn near bitten my tongue in half.

We walked the two blocks to campus in relative silence. It was uncomfortable and forced, and I was wishing I had decided to heat up a pack of ramen noodles instead.

Renee cleared her throat. "So what did you think of Compul-sion? Not really your scene, huh?" she asked in an attempt at teasing.

I tried not to jump to the defensive, to stick my tongue out and stamp my foot in a fit of immaturity while shouting, *It is* so *my scene. What do you know about it?*

But Renee was right. It didn't take a rocket scientist to figure out that a place like Compulsion was typically the last place you'd find straitlaced, in-bed-by-ten-o'clock Aubrey Duncan on a Saturday night.

There was something really annoying about that.

"I was thinking about going back next weekend," I said belligerently, just to see what Renee would say to *that*.

See, I can be as wild and crazy as the next chick.

But it was the truth. I wanted to go back.

I had strangely enjoyed myself. Attempted drugging and possible death by mosh pit aside, it was something I wanted to experience again.

From the look on Renee's face, I might as well have told her I was planning on shaving my head and starting an all-girl pop group. "You're going back? Really? Why?" she asked incredulously.

My thoughts drifted to the man in the baseball cap. He had been insistent that I didn't belong there, that I was the proverbial fish out of water. And now it was obvious that my roommate felt the same way. It made me oppositional and more than a little defiant. Because I was struck by the insane drive to *prove them wrong*.

And something else had become clear to me: being at the club, dancing in the constricting darkness, I felt like I was able to be a person that I couldn't be anywhere else. Someone who was a lot more interesting than watching paint dry. Someone who got a thrill out of more than organizing her sock drawer. An Aubrey who was spontaneous and slightly out of control. An Aubrey who was wild.

That Aubrey was fun.

That Aubrey was *free*.

I gritted my teeth and forced a smile paired with an indifferent shrug. "Why not?" I asked flippantly.

Renee shook her head and followed me into the commons. We got in line for the salad bar, but I had lost my appetite. "You need to be careful in places like that, Aubrey. Sure, they look fun on the surface, but crazy stuff happens there. It's not exactly like going to the mall or something," she responded in that worldly way of hers that never failed to make me feel like an idiot.

I gave her a cheesy grin. "Hey, I remember when the Peach Pit was turned into a nightclub. I've seen what happens when those crazy Beverly Hills kids get their drink and drugs on. I'm so prepared."

Renee laughed.

"Watching *90210* is like a manual for life!" I added. Even though I joked about it, I was slightly annoyed at her insistence that I didn't know what to expect by going to a club like Compulsion. Where had she gotten the idea that I was some silly little shut-in who would be scared of the big bad world?

I knew Renee was just trying to be a good friend. But I didn't appreciate anyone, whether it was a mysterious stranger who made my insides flutter or the girl who up until six months ago had been my very best friend, treating me as though I was incapable of making sound and reasonable decisions.

"That makes me feel so much better," Renee responded dryly. She turned to the salad bar and started dumping lettuce onto her plate. I watched in mock horror at the food she was putting on her tray. I had never understood the concept of eating salad for a meal. It was a starter, not a main course. It just seemed all sorts of wrong, this coming from the girl who consumed coffee and snack cakes like they were major food groups.

If this was how Renee was eating, it was no wonder she was skin and bones. I had a sneaking suspicion that her newfound minimal eating habits had to do with a particular douchy boyfriend and his insistence that she stay skinny. Devon really needed a one-on-one with a baseball bat.

I reached past her and grabbed a slice of chocolate cake and put it on her tray. "Do yourself a favor and ingest some calories," I said before she could argue. I grabbed myself a bottle of water and waited for Renee to swipe her student ID card to pay for her meal.

While I stood there, my eyes drifted around the commons. It was pretty crowded, and there weren't many seats left. If we were stuck sitting with frat guys again, I was going to walk home. A girl could listen to their engrossing discussions about boobs and beer only so many times.

And then I saw him. Standing by the back wall, just to the side of the fire exit, was Maxx Demelo. I hadn't seen him after our run-in on campus. He had missed the last support group meeting but had called Kristie to say he had come down with the flu. His absence in the group had been noticeable, and not just by me. It was like he had left a vacuum in his place. It was hard to believe that one person could influence the entire vibe of a group like that.

Meet Maxx Demelo, future cult leader extraordinaire.

After we had dismissed group for the evening ten minutes early due to zero participation, Kristie had mentioned that members were allowed to miss only a certain number of sessions. I hadn't realized that they were held accountable for their attendance to such a degree.

Having already missed one meeting, Maxx would be able to miss only one more before Kristie would have to report his attendance record to his probation officer. That would come with some hefty consequences, given that his jail time was suspended contingent on his group and counseling participation.

"Are you coming?" Renee asked, nudging my arm with her tray. Startled, I took my eyes from Maxx to follow my roommate to a newly empty table. Thank god, no smelly frat guys.

I sipped on my water while Renee started eating her salad. I watched her as she cut up the lettuce into tiny pieces before putting them in her mouth.

"Does that make it taste any better?" I asked, eyeing her food skeptically. Renee gave me a look that said *Shut up and let me eat.*

In the lull of silence that followed, my eyes flitted across the room again. Maxx continued to stand beside the door, his arms crossed over his chest. He was leaning against the wall and looking relaxed. But even from here I could see the fine tension in his neck and shoulders. His jaw was rigid, and his eyes darted around the room, always moving, always looking.

His blond curls stuck out on top of his head as though he had been running his fingers through his hair. He wore a tattered and worn pair of jeans and a faded blue T-shirt. Without trying, he was still the best-looking person in the room. I hated how some individuals were born with the innate gift of looking awesome without putting forth any effort. It wasn't fair for the rest of us average-looking folks.

He surreptitiously checked the time on his watch and then went back to leaning, ever so casually, against the wall. He kept his head down, purposefully not making eye contact, and it was for that reason alone that I knew he was up to something.

"You sure you don't want anything to eat? You know you'll be hungry as soon as we get back to the apartment," Renee said, interrupting my stalkerish staring.

"I'll be fine," I responded dismissively. Renee's lips pinched together.

I gave her a smile, albeit a forced one. "If I get hungry I'll just raid your stash," I joked, hoping tonight had allowed me to resume my attempts at teasing her.

Renee's lips relaxed, and she smiled back. "I may have gotten you some of those buttered crackers you like. You know, just so you stop eating mine," she added, and I tried not to look shocked. But damn, I hadn't been expecting that.

They may seem like just crackers to you, but for Renee, that was a huge step. And it showed me, more than anything else, that she was trying to repair our broken friendship.

Who knew crackers could fill me with the warm fuzzies?

"Thanks," I told her honestly, and this time my smile was easy and natural and bordering on ecstatic. I didn't quite know what to do with all these olive branches she was tossing my way.

"I'm gonna go grab an apple," she announced, getting to her feet. I leaned back in my chair and chugged the rest of my water. My eyes wandered back over to Maxx, and this time he was standing in front of the exit. He looked around and then quickly opened the door.

What the heck was he up to?

A young boy, probably no more than fifteen, slipped into the commons. Maxx put his hand on his shoulder and leaned down to speak to him. Maxx glanced around the room again before quickly depositing the boy at a table near the back, hidden in a dark corner.

I watched Maxx as he hurried to the dinner line and grabbed two trays, loading them up with food. Not knowing what possessed me, I got to my feet and followed him. I slipped into the line behind him, grabbing a tray, though not putting anything on it.

I really was taking this stalker thing to an extreme this evening.

When Maxx reached the front of the line, he scanned his card. Then he scanned it again. I watched as his mouth formed a thin line and his face flushed red as he swiped his ID card over and over again.

I peeked over his shoulder and read the machine. *Insufficient funds.* Maxx looked back toward the corner table, where he had left the boy. He picked up the trays and started to walk away with them.

The woman working behind the cash register called after him. "You can't take that! You haven't paid for it!" she yelled. Maxx stopped and looked around, realizing he suddenly had the attention of most of the people in the commons.

The smirking look of confidence that he typically wore was replaced by embarrassment and something that looked a lot like panic.

Before the woman could approach him, I stepped in front of her and held out my student ID card. "I'll pay for it," I said shortly, giving her my version of the stink eye. Hey, I could pull off intimidating when I wanted to.

Maxx, realizing I was there and had come to his rescue, looked ready to argue. I shot him a warning look and turned back to the lady, who had a nasty case of psoriasis and was obviously looking to wield what little bit of authority she had in her sorry life.

"You should just go ahead and swipe this. The line is getting pretty huge," I commented dryly, daring her to argue with me.

Bitchy cafeteria lady grabbed my card with an indignant huff and quickly swiped it, practically shoving it back into my hand. "Thank you," I called out sweetly, depositing my still-empty tray back on the stack.

Maxx hadn't waited for me; he was already across the room. It's not like I expected a thank-you or anything, but an acknowledgment of some type would have been nice. Clearly manners were a foreign concept to him.

I followed Maxx back to his table. He couldn't get rid of me that easily. I was more than a little interested in the boy he had snuck into the commons, why he had loaded up the trays with enough food to feed an army, and why he couldn't even look me in the eye after I had stepped in to help him.

I approached the table and could hear the young boy talking to Maxx in an excited voice. "Thanks, man. I'm starving!" he said sincerely. Looking at the frail boy with hollow cheeks and tired eyes, I knew that he meant it. He looked like he hadn't eaten a proper meal in a while.

It was clear that he and Maxx were related in some way. They both had been graced with a head full of thick blond waves and the same blue bedroom eyes. But where Maxx was tall and broad, the younger boy was thin and slight, though it was hard to tell if that had more to do with diet and lifestyle than with genetics.

From the protective way Maxx interacted with him, as well as the clear family resemblance, I figured they were siblings. As I watched them, I recognized that almost-tender nurturing all too well. And I felt a moment of connection with Maxx that made my chest ache from missing my sister.

Maxx slid one full tray to the boy, who attacked the food as though he would never eat again. He smiled down at the younger boy in a way that made him even more attractive, something I hadn't thought possible.

I hung back, blatantly eavesdropping.

"Why aren't you eating at school?" Maxx asked.

The younger boy looked up with those blue eyes that were so much like Maxx's and shook his head. "Uncle David hasn't paid my overdue lunch charges in two months. Sometimes Cory will give me part of his lunch, but I feel, like . . . pathetic asking," the boy said, shoveling mashed potatoes into his mouth.

"What about food at the house? Can't you make yourself a packed lunch?" Maxx asked, becoming more agitated.

The boy wouldn't look at Maxx; he was too focused on filling his mouth with as much food as possible. "Yeah, if I want to bring cat food and beer for lunch," he replied, drinking some of his soda.

Maxx's brow furrowed, and I could tell he was angry. "I gave that asshole enough money to cover whatever you need for months. You're telling me there's no fucking food in the house? And you don't have money to cover lunch at school? Where the fuck did it all go?" Maxx snarled, and the boy shrugged.

"He hasn't been home in over a week. He probably went to

Atlantic City again," the boy said, seeming unconcerned even as his older brother seethed beside him.

Maxx smacked the table with his hand. "That money is for *you*! Not for him to dick around with! I swear, I'm gonna fucking kill that bastard!" Maxx's voice rose, and he looked around to see if he had been overheard. And then his eyes fell on me.

Busted.

Maxx's eyes met mine, and they narrowed in annoyance. Obviously he was *not* happy to see me.

I walked to stand next to the table and smiled down at the boy. I tried not to laugh at the way he was now staring up at me with his mouth hanging open. He had a smear of potatoes on his chin, and I thought about wiping it off. But I didn't want to give the poor thing a heart attack if I touched him.

I turned back to Maxx, who was refusing to make eye contact, his head bowed down as though he found the table really interesting. I stared at the top of his curly head, willing him to look at me, but he was doing a great job of pretending I wasn't there.

"How's it going, Maxx?" I asked, pouring just enough sugar into my voice to be obnoxious.

Maxx's shoulders stiffened, but he still refused to look up. He pushed some peas around on his plate. "Fine, thanks," he said through gritted teeth. I knew without him having to say a word that it irked him that I had paid for their food. I got the distinct impression that Maxx was used to taking care of things and balked at the thought of accepting charity of any sort.

I hadn't meant to make him feel like a charity case. But there was something in the way he had looked as he stood there—his trays full of food to feed his kid brother that he couldn't pay for— that made me want to help him.

But I could tell my help hadn't been wanted or appreciated.

I glanced at the younger boy, who was still staring at me with his mouth slightly agape. "Who's this? Your brother?" I asked, giving the boy a 100-watt smile.

He grinned back and looked over at Maxx, who continued to stare holes into the table. His smile slipped a bit as he recognized his brother's hostile demeanor. He looked from Maxx to me, as though trying to figure out the source of the tension.

"Uh, yeah, I'm Maxx's younger brother, Landon. How do you know Maxx?" he asked, shoveling another mouthful of food into his mouth. Finally, Maxx's eyes met mine and communicated an unspoken plea. His embarrassment and anger faded away, replaced by a request for me to stay silent.

It was obvious Maxx did *not* want Landon to know the particulars of how we knew each other. I could hazard a guess that Landon was completely ignorant of his older brother's more unsavory extracurricular activities.

I cleared my throat. "We have a class together," I lied, smiling at Landon, who beamed at me.

"Oh, yeah? Maxx is ridiculously smart. Like genius smart. You know he's gonna be a doctor. He's the only person in our family to go to college. Dad always said he'd be the one to cure cancer or something," he informed me.

Maxx was clearly this kid's hero—a hero with a drug problem that landed him on probation. He was an angel with one tarnished halo.

"Wow, I didn't know that," I said, glancing at Maxx, who seemed extremely uncomfortable as the focus of our conversation. Gone was the familiar smirking smile. This wasn't a person putting on an act. This was a guy who wanted the floor to open up and swallow him whole. His brother sharing his adulation with me unnerved him.

"But I bet you're just as smart as Maxx, if not smarter," I told the younger boy, who looked ready to burst at the compliment.

"I wish," he enthused, grinning at his older brother, who gave him a pained smile.

I stood there awkwardly for a few moments until it became very obvious that Maxx wasn't going to make any attempts to further the conversation.

"It was nice meeting you, Landon. See you later, Maxx," I said and turned to leave. I was halfway back to my table, when a hand pulled me to a stop.

I looked down at the hand on my sleeve and then up into Maxx's troubled blue eyes. "Thanks for not saying anything to Landon about the group. He doesn't need to hear about that shit," he said gruffly, his apology sounding more like an accusation and, I knew, given begrudgingly.

"You don't need to thank me for that. Maybe you should think about why it bothers you so much if your brother were to find out. Maybe, deep down, you know you're making some seriously shitty choices," I preached. God, I sounded so freaking judgmental. I really should keep my sanctimonious mouth shut.

Clearly, Maxx found my trip to the top of the soapbox as obnoxious as I did. "I don't need to explain my choices to you, Aubrey. You don't know a thing about me." His hand tightened on my arm as he moved closer to me, bending his lips in close to my ear. I shivered as his breath fanned my neck.

Good-bye, pride, it was nice knowing you.

"I'll pay you back. I just haven't gotten around to putting money in my account this month," he explained through clenched teeth, his words hard and clipped.

He was trying to hide his mortification.

I touched the back of his hand. "Don't worry about it," I said softly, which seemed to infuriate Maxx.

"I don't need handouts, Aubrey. I'll pay you back the fucking money," he bit out.

"Fine," I responded shortly, annoyed by his gruff attitude.

"Good," he muttered, and then turned around and walked back to his brother, who was watching us. I forced myself to give

Landon another smile before walking off with more than a little bit of huffiness.

I rejoined Renee at our table. She had already finished her dessert and looked at me expectantly. "Who was that?" she asked, indicating Maxx. Landon was saying something to his brother, but Maxx's eyes were on me, the dark blue unreadable.

I shivered, my heart rate picking up even as I tried to not let him affect me. Our eyes clashed in a silent battle of wills, and I ultimately admitted defeat and looked away.

"Nobody," I answered.

chapter
nine

It was almost time for support group, and I felt like crap. I had been fighting a cold for most of the week, and the last place I wanted to be was in a room full of people who didn't really want to be there.

Kristie had gone out to make copies for an activity we would be doing, and I was straightening the chairs in a circle in the middle of the room. I pulled a tissue out of my pocket and sneezed four times in a row.

"Ugh," I moaned.

"Do I need to start planning the funeral?" I looked up to find Brooks walking through the door.

"What are you doing here? Don't tell me that you've finally admitted that your addiction to gummy worms is ruining your life," I joked.

Brooks grabbed a cookie from the tray Kristie had put out earlier and popped it into his mouth. If there was food around, it would invariably end up in Brooks's mouth. It was a miracle he didn't weigh 800 pounds. I had yet to discover the secret to his trim physique, considering the way he inhaled sweets and carbs. I suspected black magic.

"Nah, I thought I'd just come by and say hello. I have a cram session with a couple other people in my Research Psychology class down the hall in a few minutes. How's the group going?" he asked, taking another cookie.

I sneezed into the tissue again, wishing I could go home and crawl into bed. A heating pad and ten hours of solid sleep sounded as close to heaven as I could imagine. "It's going. I haven't done much. Kristie runs a pretty tight ship, no need for me to mess with the system," I wheezed.

Brooks seemed revolted by my state of deteriorating health. It was a good thing he hadn't decided to go into medicine. His bedside manner sucked. He shoved a box of tissues into my hand and took a very obvious step away from me.

I coughed in his direction, without covering my mouth. Just to be an asshole.

Brooks made a face of complete and total disgust and pulled a bottle of hand sanitizer out of his jacket pocket, squeezing a dollop in his palm and rubbing furiously. Apparently I wasn't the only one with OCD tendencies. I'd remember that the next time he felt the need to make fun of my cleaning regimen.

I knew I looked horrible. I had purposefully avoided the mirror this morning while getting ready to go out, knowing what I would see: Long blond hair, limp and lifeless. Brown eyes, dull and tired. Dark circles and sallow skin. I had a virus, plain and simple, though from that description I could quite possibly be turning into a zombie. I was grossing *myself* out.

Watching the group members start to filter into the room, each looking less than enthused to be there, I realized that the support group was becoming less and less enjoyable. The initial meeting had been promising. Kristie had been optimistic that the group would turn out to be interactive and receptive. But with each group meeting, I knew that even her hopes were fading.

Some members had become more combative and defensive. Others had shut down entirely. Evan and April, the couple in need of some major social skills, were downright nasty.

And then there was Maxx Demelo. I knew Kristie thought he walked on water. You know the saying; if you want to look pretty, hang out with ugly people. And Maxx was doing his damnedest to be the belle of the druggie ball.

He was the only one who made a point of answering questions when they were asked. He volunteered personal information—though whether it was factual might be another story—and he seemed just oh-so-engaged each and every time he came to a meeting.

And while Kristie and I were barely tolerated when we spoke, Maxx Demelo reigned supreme. People listened when he opened his pretty little mouth, no matter what drivel fell out of it.

He was so full of shit.

He was one big ol' pile of fake, and the way he played it up drove me nuts. I had tried to bring up my concerns about Maxx's sincerity to Kristie several weeks ago, and she had blown me off.

"Aubrey, I can tell that Maxx is one hundred percent dedicated to his recovery. He is an example for every single person in the group. I'm so thankful to have someone like him to show the others that there is a light at the end of the tunnel. In fact, I'm thinking about talking to him about providing peer support to some of the more troubled members. I just know he'd help them so much," Kristie gushed, and I had stopped bothering to discuss it. It was useless.

But even while I was regularly overcome with the urge to call Maxx out, I couldn't help but be fascinated by him all the same. It was like watching an actor on stage slip into a character. And honestly, it made me determined to see what really lay beneath his cool and confident exterior.

I had seen how he was with his brother in the commons. I had seen him embarrassed and angry. And some sadistic part of me wanted to see that side of him again.

I attempted to observe him clinically. I had myself almost convinced that he suffered from some sort of personality disorder.

Or maybe I was completely delusional and projecting my own issues onto this poor guy in the group I was supposed to be facilitating.

"God, could they look any more miserable?" Brooks whispered, eyeballing the group members as they made their entrance, taking seats after grabbing their free cup of coffee. Their routines were the same each and every week. Eat a cookie. Drink some coffee. Mumble monosyllabically when asked a question.

This was supposed to be a voluntary group, aside from Evan, April, Kyle, and Maxx, who were court-ordered to attend. Yet the attendance of the others felt forced. In recovery groups, there were usually the one or two who took to their sobriety with the ferocity of a newfound religion.

Not in this group. And I felt like a failure for not figuring out a way to snap everyone out of it. It irked me even more that Maxx alone was the only one to arouse any sort of response from people. In fact, it often felt like he had taken over the group and was the one running it. And Kristie let him.

But the thing about Maxx was that he was a hard man to refuse, and I was learning that there were times when even I didn't want to refuse him. That worried me. A lot.

I turned to Brooks and nodded. "I'm not sure what's going on, but this group is a hard sell. I thought it would be . . ."

"Easy?" Brooks laughed, and I smacked his arm.

"Not easy, just not so difficult," I complained, realizing how silly I sounded. Therapy wasn't supposed to be easy. Groups were going to be a struggle for everyone involved. I had read the case studies, I had devoured the textbooks. I should know this stuff. But I had dreams of walking in and saving the world on my first try. I was an idealistic moron.

Kristie started handing out packets to people as they made their way to their seats. She gave me a pointed look, and I knew that was my cue.

"Okay, you've got to go." I turned Brooks around and pushed him toward the door. Out in the hallway, Brooks chanced a quick hug.

"Knock 'em dead, tiger. I'll come by later with soup and a movie," he promised, making me smile. He really was such a great guy.

"*Twilight*?" I joked, knowing the answer. Brooks tapped my nose with his finger.

"You'd have to be at death's door for me to agree to that one," he stated.

I laughed. He laughed. And then a pointed cough had us both quieting down.

"Has group been canceled or something?" I looked over Brooks's shoulder to see Maxx standing there, hands shoved in his pockets, disheveled blond curls falling over his forehead, and a cold and stony expression on his face.

"Uh, no. Go on in and grab a seat." I indicated for him to walk around me, but he continued to stand there, making no move to head inside the classroom. Brooks looked at me questioningly. It was hard to miss the feral testosterone rolling off Maxx as he stood there and regarded the two of us angrily.

What was his problem?

The three of us stood there, a triangle of silent awkwardness. I couldn't place the emotion that flashed in Maxx's eyes, because everything that came to mind made absolutely no sense. Desire. Longing. Possessiveness. And most strangely, sadness. Maxx looked at me like a man who had lost something.

Oh, come on, Aubrey. This cold is screwing with your brain.

"Call me when you want me to come over. Feel better," Brooks said finally. His suddenly narrowed eyes flitted between Maxx and me as though trying to read the uncomfortable situation we found ourselves in.

"Okay, thanks, Brooks," I said, hoping my friend would get the hint.

Brooks stared at Maxx for a moment longer, and when he looked back at me, his face was a varied mix of emotions. It made me nervous.

But before I could say anything to allay my concerns and Brooks's apparent unease, he mumbled a quick good-bye and walked down the corridor.

I tried to settle the knot that had formed in the pit of my stomach during the difficult exchange, but it was proving tough under the strength of Maxx's gaze.

I eyed Maxx apprehensively. "You can go in, you know," I muttered, not bothering to disguise my irritation.

Maxx ran a hand through his curls and then scrubbed his face. His expression neutralized, and he gave me his trademark careless smile. "After you," he said, sweeping his hand forward, indicating for me to walk ahead of him.

I arched my eyebrow but didn't comment, hurrying inside. I sat down and looked around at the other group members. I attempted to make eye contact and give a smile in greeting to a few of them, but was shut down each time.

My eyes eventually found Maxx's, and I wasn't surprised to receive a blinding grin. I didn't reciprocate and instead turned my attention to Kristie, who was explaining tonight's discussion.

Twenty minutes later, everyone was working in their journals, creating a life map. People had been tasked with identifying both positive and negative experiences that had impacted them in some way. This was meant to lead to a bigger discussion about what had triggered their using. It was a great activity, one that would undoubtedly lead to some great therapeutic interaction in any group but this one. Sadly, I couldn't imagine anyone here taking it very seriously, the way it was intended.

Kristie encouraged me to participate as well. She had told me before group that some elements of personal disclosure from a facilitator can have a powerful impact. She warned me to be careful of what I would expose about myself, but she said that small bits of information could be a great way to create a bond between them and me.

The idea of opening myself at all had always been hard. And it would be absolutely agonizing to do so with this particular group of people.

When the time was up, Kristie started going around the group, asking everyone to share something. Most shared very shallow things, from Marissa getting her first car to Twyla's rejection by her first choice of a university. When Kyle, the frat guy, stated that a negative experience in his life had been the time he got locked out of his dorm room, I sort of lost it.

"Are you kidding me?" I scoffed. Thirteen sets of eyes swung in my direction. Kristie frowned, clearly not appreciating my outburst. She silently reprimanded me for my lack of supportive sensitivity, but I didn't care. I had had it with sitting week after week in a group of people who weren't taking this opportunity seriously.

What I wouldn't give for my sister to have had the chance to sit and learn something in a group like this. Their rigid refusal to absorb any of what Kristie so patiently tried to teach them was frustrating to the point of blinding rage. And Evan and April, with their derisive sneers, tipped me over the edge.

Kyle looked taken aback and blinked in confusion. "Uh, yeah, that day sucked. I had to walk down to campus security, and then I had to wait like two hours for a replacement key. I was late for my chem lab . . ."

I held up my hand and cut him off. "Enough. You know that's total bullshit," I said blandly. Kyle puffed up indignantly, which was a hell of a lot better than his placid disinterest.

"Well, fuck you. What do you know about having a hard life, Miss Barbie Doll?" Evan piped up, his arm squeezing his girlfriend to his side so tightly it was as though he worried she would try to escape—though I wouldn't blame her if she'd tried.

Kristie snapped her fingers, trying to get everyone's attention. "Let's move on to deep-breathing techniques," she said with a fierce perkiness that belied her irritation with my outburst.

"No, Kristie. Let me answer Evan," I spoke up, my eyes meeting his beady dark ones head-on. This guy was used to intimidating others. Well, he could just fuck off.

"I don't think that would be appropriate, Aubrey," Kristie reproached me firmly. I was going to be in trouble for this. But something had to be done. These people didn't respect either of us. They sat there in their self-involved bullshit, thinking they were the only ones with pain. And they didn't understand a god-damned thing about it.

It was time to page Dr. Fucking Phil and call them on their crap.

"I lost my fifteen-year-old sister to a drug overdose three years ago. She was pumped full of heroin by a guy she thought loved her but then left her in an alleyway to choke on her own vomit. Her body wasn't discovered until two days later when the trash guys came to empty the Dumpster she was propped up against," I snapped.

Evan's eyes went wide, and I couldn't help but relish the way he seemed to recoil at my moment of honesty. And then I realized what I had said. Christ, I hadn't meant to say any of that.

I looked around at the group, and everyone's expression was the same. Shock. And pity. Which made me want to hit a wall.

But when I dared to look at Maxx, I didn't see any of those

things on his face. Again, there was an emotion I wasn't sure I was interpreting correctly. Because he looked *relieved*?

Kristie cleared her throat, trying to take control of the group again. Judging from the look of restrained anger on her face, I had screwed up big-time. "I want everyone to take a few minutes and write about one of the events on your life map and why you feel that impacts your addiction," she directed, getting to her feet.

Kristie met my eyes and jerked her head toward the hallway. I sighed and followed her. After she had closed the door to the classroom, she rounded on me. "That was completely and totally inappropriate, Aubrey. I'm in shock right now that you would do something like that. Not only did you belittle a group member and invalidate *his* feelings, but you made the group about *you* and *your* feelings. While disclosure can be beneficial, it most certainly isn't when it's given in a context like this. It has to be about solidifying a connection between counselor and patient. When it's all about you, it's not healthy," she lectured, and I hung my head in shame. She was right. I had overstepped.

"I'm so sorry. I don't know why I did that," I replied.

Kristie shook her head. "I have a good idea why, but this isn't the time or place to get into that. I think it would be best if you left tonight. I'll finish group by myself. And then I think we need to sit down with Dr. Lowell and talk about whether your continued participation in this group as a co-facilitator is suitable," she remarked, sounding nothing like the compassionate and nurturing counselor I knew her to be. Right now she was disappointed and unhappy.

Wow, I had really messed things up.

"I understand," was all I said. I felt horrible, both physically and mentally. I should have gone home and gone to bed and worried about the mess I'd made in the morning. But the thought of possibly running into Renee was less than appealing. I wasn't able to hide my emotions very well, and even though she was on most days still firmly up her own ass, my roommate still read me better than anyone.

I ended up wandering around campus. I felt achy, and I most likely had a fever, but I just couldn't make myself go home. It was late, and very few people were still out. I finally sat down at a bench by the library and stared at a wall that was painted with bright greens and blues. The central image was a figure of a woman walking off a wooden pier into a sea of black sludge, her long blond hair waving behind her as she fell. Her face was nondescript except for her smile. It was as though she was happy to be going to her death.

Well, that was freaking depressing.

I stared harder at the picture, uncomfortable with the odd sense of familiarity I felt. Looking at the woman's graceful yet agonized form, I felt as though I should recognize her.

Bothered by my increasing disquiet, I stood up and walked closer. This was not your typical campus painting of daffodils and laughing students. I had seen this particular kind of art several times before. I leaned in to try to see the details in the poor lighting. And there it was—the tiny patterns on the woman's dress composed of dozens of Xs.

I didn't notice any numbers or words in this picture, though, so I didn't understand what its intent was. It was my understanding that X's paintings held the clues to the location of the club Compulsion. But this picture seemed to have nothing to do with that.

This was a painting created for some other purpose.

"So what do you think?"

I looked over my shoulder to find Maxx standing behind me. I turned back to the picture, not bothering to answer him. The truth was, my outburst in the group had left me feeling raw and vulnerable, and seeing him so soon after making a gigantic ass of myself was embarrassing.

As he came up beside me, the sleeves of our jackets brushed

against each other. Maxx inclined his head toward the painting and asked me again, "Well, what do you think of it?"

I shrugged, not really in the mood for small talk. My pounding head couldn't handle a go-around with the group Romeo. I started to walk away from him when he grabbed hold of my arm.

"Wait, Aubrey. Please." It was that word that did it. *Please.* It was uttered softly and sincerely. And it held me as fast and surely as if he had put his arms around me.

"Thank you for talking about your sister tonight," he said quietly, tugging on my arm so I would face him again. Slowly I complied, looking up into his eyes. All coyness was gone, and I could see only genuine gratitude.

"You don't need to thank me. What I did was wrong. I shouldn't put my shit on you guys. You're there for your own reasons, and they have nothing to do with me and my past," I replied quickly.

Maxx slid his knuckles down my arm and took my hand in his. My fingers were curled into a fist, with his much larger palm surrounding it, protecting it.

"Don't say that. What you said, what you showed me . . . *us* . . . was that you get it. And it made me feel, I don't know . . . connected maybe," he said. I didn't know what to say. I was so tired, both from being sick and from trying so hard to hold it together. Tonight I had cracked. Some of the raging whirlwind inside me had leaked out in the worst possible setting.

But maybe it had *helped.* And that made my failure seem less . . . destructive.

His next words took my burgeoning pink fuzzies and flushed them down the toilet.

"You feel responsible for what happened to your sister, don't you?" he asked, and my immediate reaction was to deny, deny, deny. I didn't know him. I didn't trust him. He had no right to the information he was digging for.

But when I opened my mouth, only the truth came out. "Yes, I do," I responded. Maxx's broad shoulders rose and fell with his deep breath. He seemed to find something in my words that fortified him.

His blue eyes darkened as he looked over my shoulder into the distance. "I understand that, you know? Feeling responsible for someone else and failing miserably," he said with so much pain in his voice that I felt it in my bones.

He continued to hold my hand tight and secure in his, his thumb drawing circles on my skin. I didn't say anything, I knew instinctively that Maxx needed to share something with me, but he needed to do it at his own pace.

The wind blew around us, chilling me, but I didn't move away from him. "My brother expects a lot of me. Landon, you met him," he said, looking down at me, his lips quirking into a tiny smile.

I smiled back. "He seemed like a nice kid," I offered.

"He is. He's a great kid. Better than me, that's for sure," Maxx said tiredly. I didn't respond to that. What could I say? *That's not true, you're a great guy!* Because that would have been a lie. I didn't know whether Maxx deserved that kind of commendation or not.

"He looks up to me. He expects me to be this great and powerful person. To make our lives something better. I just can't do that. It's beyond me to be the sort of guy he needs me to be," Maxx admitted, his voice breaking at the admission.

I was absolutely bewildered by the man who stood with me in the cold January air, his fingers wrapped around mine. He had handed me honesty. I could only do the same. It was only fair. It's what this moment deserved.

"Jayme tried to tell me about her boyfriend, Blake. I wouldn't listen. She wanted me to know what was going on. I ignored her," I let out in the barest whisper.

Maxx's hand squeezed mine. "Jayme was your sister?" he asked, and I nodded, feeling my throat tighten with a suppressed emotion I hadn't allowed myself to feel in a very long time.

I pulled in a shaky breath. "He's the worst kind of evil. Blake. He hooked her on drugs, used her over and over again, and then left her to die. But maybe I'm even worse because I had the chance to save her and I didn't. I was so focused on my own life I didn't see how much she needed me." My voice was a strangled sob.

Maxx pulled me into his chest, his arms coming up to press me close, as though I could burrow inside him and be safe. I curled my arms up underneath me and tried to get my breathing under control. I didn't cry. I never cried. My tears had dried up a long time ago.

But I felt the seams of my world tearing apart as Maxx held me. Something had been altered in the fabric of my universe, and I didn't know what that meant for me or for the man who held me.

I felt Maxx lean down, his breath fanning across my face. And still he said nothing. He just held me tightly against his body, and I thought I might have imagined the tiny kisses along the crown of my head.

But I hadn't imagined how in the space of a few minutes I had calmed down. I could breathe easier, and I was able to unclench my fists.

After what felt like an endless amount of time, he released me. "You should get home," was all he said, his hands returning to the pockets of his jacket. I felt disjointed by the abruptness of our physical separation.

"Yeah, you're right," I agreed, unable to summon up any sort of smile to give him, even though I wanted to. I needed to rest. I was sick and tired, but just then I felt . . . *all right*.

Maxx swallowed; I watched his Adam's apple bob. He wouldn't look at me. He seemed suddenly wary and skittish and ready to be rid of me.

"Good night, Aubrey," he said, turning his back and heading toward the parking lot.

I picked my pride up off the ground and turned to leave, a rush of emotion settling like a thick blanket of unease over my heart.

chapter
ten

maxx

I sifted through the pills in the plastic baggie, my fingers lifting, then dropping them. I wanted one. Just one.

One would be it.

That's all I'd need to feel good.

At least that's what I kept telling myself.

I didn't consider myself an addict, though that was the label the court system wanted to give me.

They said I needed help, an intervention.

What I needed was a new fucking life.

I picked out two pills and set them in my palm.

I stared at them, as if waiting for the mysteries of the fucking universe to be answered.

Come on. You know you want me. We'd have such a good time together, they whispered.

"You know how to make me feel better," I murmured, rubbing the smooth surfaces with my thumb.

Yeah, I was freaking crazy. Talking to my drugs was a sure sign of a serious mental break.

I had homework to do. I was struggling to stay above water. I was so damned close to graduating. I had made it this far. I made sure I did just well enough that I wouldn't flunk out.

I owed it to Landon to try to make something of myself. I owed it to my dead parents, who had thought the boy they left behind was worth something.

The problem was I had lost all taste for the life everyone thought I *should* have.

The only taste I had was for the two tiny pills in my hand.

Never one for prolonging the inevitable, I popped the little pieces of happy in my mouth and crunched them with my teeth before swallowing.

I loved that moment when my arms went slack and my feet sort of disappeared. My mouth hung open, and my eyes drooped. My head stopped buzzing, and I stared at the TV, which wasn't even turned on.

I'm not sure how long I sat there in my shitty apartment, staring at the dark screen, when my phone started ringing.

Ring, ring.

Ring, ring.

I patted the cushion beside me, but the phone wasn't there. My head rolled to the side, and I tried to open my eyes, but they weren't cooperating. My lips stretched into a smile. Damn, I felt awesome.

Ring, ring.

There it was. My phone sat on the coffee table, just by my feet, which were propped up beside it. Maybe my arms could stretch out and I could reach it, because right now they felt abnormally long.

I wished it would stop ringing. It hurt my ears, and I just wanted to lie there and think about nothing. Do nothing. *Be* nothing.

But it wouldn't stop. It kept fucking ringing.

Didn't the person on the other end realize I had more to do than answer the fucking phone?

I hoisted myself up and ever so slowly grabbed at the phone that just wouldn't shut up.

I fumbled with the buttons as though my fingers had forgotten how to work. I laughed at how ridiculous it was.

Finally I connected the call and lifted the phone to my ear.

"Hello?" My voice sounded strange. No, it sounded like I was trying to have a good time. Fuck this fucker who was interrupting it.

"Fucking hell, man, I've been trying to reach you for an hour! Don't you fucking know how to answer a goddamned phone?" the voice yelled into my ear.

I frowned.

"What?" I asked belligerently.

"What? Are you fucking serious? You were supposed to be here two hours ago! Gash is pissed. You know how he fucking gets when he's pissed. Get your ass here now!" the voice roared.

"Is this Marco Polo?" I asked, sounding garbled.

"Are you fucking high again? That's the only reason you'd risk an ass-kicking by calling me that. You're supposed to be selling that shit. Gash is gonna shove it up your ass if you come here fucked-up. You were supposed to have the new location sorted already. It's fucking Thursday, man. Please tell me you've found a place," Marco begged, sounding panicked.

I knew I should probably be panicked too. Gash was not a guy you messed with. Marco was one of the doormen at Compulsion and had been a buddy of mine for a long time. He was also the guy who shaved a bit of extra cash off the intake every Saturday—cash that nicely lined our pockets. Between my drugs and his sticky fingers of stealthiness, we had created a nice little side business that was proving pretty profitable for both of us.

And the truth was I hadn't found a location for the club yet.

There were a couple of promising prospects. An old factory the next town over, a field on the outskirts of the city. But I had been busy. Between school, community service, and making sure Landon was taken care of, I was strapped for time.

But Compulsion was my bread and butter. It was how I made the money to stay at school. It's where I sold the drugs that kept me afloat and put food in my baby brother's mouth. I shouldn't be shitting where I slept.

But I just didn't care—not when I was feeling so fucking awesome.

"It's all good, man. Stop stressing," I slurred, rubbing at my bottom lip. My mouth felt numb. I could barely feel my tongue in my mouth. I stuck my tongue out and poked it with my finger.

I laughed. It was hysterical!

"Damn it! You need to get over here now! You need to tell Gash where we'll be on Saturday. If you don't, he'll staple your balls to your ass," Marco threatened, and I knew he wasn't being dramatic. He was telling the fucking truth.

Gash was one scary dude.

I dropped the phone on the floor. The oxy had really kicked in, and my hands couldn't hold the device anymore. I leaned over and tried to make my fingers pick it up.

Finally I was able to get it back to my ear.

"I'm coming over there," Marco stated, and I snorted.

"Sure, come and get me. I sure as fuck ain't driving," I mumbled, hanging up the phone.

I closed my eyes, hoping I could enjoy the rest of my high in peace. I just needed a few minutes. That was it.

That was all I needed, and then I'd be fine. Perfect, even.

Screw the consequences.

My phone started ringing again, and I thought about ignoring it. It was probably Marco again with some lame-ass threat. He was such a cock blocker.

Again, the stupid thing kept ringing.

"What?" I barked into the phone, my hazy, happy feeling becoming harder to hold on to.

"Maxx?"

I sat up a little straighter and rubbed my face with my hand, trying to clear my head.

"Landon, what's up?" I asked, trying not to sound as messed up as I was. My younger brother had no clue that his hero was such a fuck-up. I had so far managed to keep my arrest and probation a secret, but keeping him in the dark was getting harder all the time.

"Why do you sound so weird? Did I wake you up?" he asked. Even though Landon would turn sixteen in a few months, he acted years younger. Maybe that was my fault. I still treated him like he was a kid.

It made it easier for me to pretend he didn't see me for who I really was.

"Uh yeah, that's cool, though," I lied effortlessly. It was quite a talent, the way I could slip in and out of roles. I could play the good big brother when I needed to. I had so many parts to play, I wasn't entirely sure which one was real.

"Sorry, I can call back later," Landon apologized. I rubbed my eyes, trying to wake myself up. But the drugs were weighing me down, and it was hard to give a shit about anything.

I didn't want to give a shit about anything. It felt too good not to.

"Did you want something?" I asked, sounding like an asshole.

"I just thought you could come over sometime this week and help me fix up the car," Landon said. I was supposed to be helping him fix up Dad's old Mustang for when he got his license. But I hadn't been to my uncle's in over a month.

He sounded so goddamned hopeful. Fuck hope. It was a worthless bitch.

"I don't know," I answered noncommittally. Truth was, I had the time, just not the inclination. I didn't want to put on my smiley face. I hated that fucking face.

Because I didn't have the energy to be that *other* Maxx.

The one with way too much responsibility.

The Maxx that would fail miserably each and every time.

The Maxx I was trying to be didn't fail at anything. He was on top of the goddamned world, and nothing would bring him down. People wanted him. He was the center of the fucked-up universe.

He was a guy who wasn't alone.

"Yeah, I guess you're busy and all. You can't be some hotshot doctor without putting in the work. Hey, maybe Aubrey could help you study or something," Landon teased, attempting some good-natured brotherly ribbing.

His unwavering faith in me made me sick. The mention of Aubrey put me on edge.

What the hell was I playing with her? And more important, was I really playing at all? Because being with her after group earlier in the week hadn't felt like an act.

She had told me about her sister, and it made me . . . *feel*.

My heart had hurt. For her. For her pain.

And I had shared my own pain. My own hurt. Things I spent a lot of time denying even existed.

And for a brief moment, it had been real.

Comforting.

Safe.

I didn't have time in my life for *real*.

It pissed me off.

My mellow high dissipated the angrier I became.

"Look, I gotta go, Landon. I'll try to come by over the weekend," I said quickly. I didn't wait for Landon to say good-bye before I hung up the phone. I didn't want to hear the disappointment in his voice.

I couldn't handle his expectations. The weight of his dependency was like a noose around my neck.

I gripped the phone in my hand and then threw it across the room. Surprisingly, it stayed intact as it fell to the hardwood floor.

I felt like I was suffocating.

I needed numbness.

I needed to escape this shit reality I lived in.

I needed . . . *nothing.*

I picked up the baggie of pills on the coffee table and shook out three 30 mg tablets of oxy.

I heard a pounding on my door, followed by Marco yelling.

I ignored it.

I crushed the pills with the end of my Statistics textbook, swept the powder into my palm, then dropped it into my mouth. The bitter dust tickled the back of my throat and caused a loud coughing fit.

Marco could hear me, so he kept pounding on my door.

Too bad for him, I kept ignoring him.

The moment the drugs hit my system, everything was better . . . calmer.

They never let me down.

The high was my only constant.

When I needed it, it was always there, unconditionally. It didn't need me. It didn't weigh me down with unrealistic expectations. It was the most perfect relationship in my life.

It gave without expecting anything in return.

It was the best friend I had.

chapter
eleven

aubrey

I felt like a kid who had gotten caught by the principal smoking in the bathroom. Dr. Lowell had called me yesterday and asked me to come to her office after classes. I knew what this was about. Kristie had warned me she would be calling my adviser. But in the wake of my strange run-in with Maxx and the insanity of my course load, I had somehow forgotten about how badly I had messed up in support group.

Repression was a glorious thing.

Well, it was time to pay the piper. Face the music. Eat my goddamned words.

"Aubrey, come on in," Dr. Lowell said from the doorway to her office. I picked up my bag and followed her inside. I took a seat in front of her massive desk after she closed the door.

"You know why you're here," Dr. Lowell said without preamble, getting straight to the point. I nodded, my mouth suddenly dry.

"Would you care to explain what happened last week in support group?" my professor asked, sitting down at her desk and folding her hands in front of her. Dr. Lowell was an attractive woman, one of those people who were aging gracefully. Her brown hair, which was only now starting to gray, was cut short and held back with a clip, and her face was wrinkle-free.

And I appreciated that instead of jumping to conclusions, she was looking at me thoughtfully, expecting a good explanation.

"I messed up, Dr. Lowell. I ended up sharing things I shouldn't have in group. I got angry. These people are there to learn ways to change their lives, and they act as if they couldn't be bothered. I guess I was sick of it. But what I did was wrong, and I understand if you think I need to leave the group," I said quietly, ready to take my licks.

Dr. Lowell regarded me intently. She didn't say anything for a long time; the only sound in the silent office was the ticking of the clock on the wall.

She slowly pushed her chair out from behind her desk and got to her feet. She crossed the room and filled her coffee cup from the fancy Keurig she had in the corner.

Why wasn't she saying anything?

Maybe Dr. Lowell was a secret sadist and enjoyed watching her poor, panic-stricken students squirm.

"Would you like a cup, Aubrey?" she asked, holding one out.

I nodded, never able to say no to coffee. I took a sip of the gourmet blend, refusing to allow myself to appreciate the taste when I was most likely going to be seriously reprimanded. But damn, this stuff was tasty.

"I don't want you to leave the group," Dr. Lowell said finally, after I had polished off half of my coffee.

I blinked in surprise. "Really? Because when I spoke to Kristie she seemed to think my presence in the group wouldn't be appropriate anymore," I said.

Dr. Lowell rolled her eyes. Yes, my hard-as-nails professor actually rolled her eyes.

"Kristie is an excellent counselor, but she can be a little rigid sometimes. We're all human, Aubrey. Part of this process is for you to learn your boundaries, to understand the limits in a group dynamic. You will only ever learn those things with hands-on experience. I would be doing you an extreme disservice if I were to remove you from the group. We all make mistakes. That's not to say you didn't act inappropriately. Because you did." She looked at me levelly. "I just don't think you need to be raked over the coals for it."

Dr. Lowell returned to her seat behind her desk. "When I was first out of grad school I had just gotten my license, and I was running a court-mandated anger-management group. All of those attending were known abusers; they had all been convicted of assault, usually on family members. They were a nasty bunch of men. And they treated me like I was a joke. To say I didn't take that too well, particularly since I was a lot more hotheaded in my younger days, is a bit of an understatement." She laughed, and I found myself smiling too.

I just may escape this meeting in one piece. Hallelujah!

"I dumped a glass of water on a group member's head. He apparently hadn't liked what I had to say and had called me the B word." I gaped. I would have done a hell of a lot more than dump water on his head.

"To say my superior was unforgiving was putting it mildly. You have to remember, times were different then, and women were only just starting to be accepted in the workplace. This was the seventies, and while advances had been made in gender equality, it still felt like the stone ages. I was put on professional probation for three months, and I wasn't allowed to facilitate another group until I attended my own anger-management classes."

Dr. Lowell chuckled. "So you see, you're not the only one who has ever had to learn to control her emotions and remember to act professionally."

Dr. Lowell sobered. "Now, we both knew going into this that it would be difficult. It's hard under typical circumstances, but given your personal experiences I knew it would be doubly so. Would it be helpful if you and I were to meet weekly to process how group is going and to assess your participation?" she asked me.

I tried not to be offended. My behavior was what landed me here. But I couldn't help but be insulted. It felt as though she were telling me I was too cracked to be able to function.

"No, I'm sure I'll be fine," I responded stiffly, forcing a smile.

Dr. Lowell nodded. "Well, if at any time you're having trouble, please don't hesitate to come and see me. You know my door is always open. Now, let's talk about where we go from here. Kristie was far from happy when we spoke. And I can't afford to have her questioning this department. The community-services board works closely with the university to assist with the training and volunteer hours for our students. She's going to expect some action to be taken." Dr. Lowell rolled her eyes again, and this time I had to laugh.

Her opinions regarding Kristie Hinkle were pretty clear.

"So I think for the next few weeks, dial it back a bit. Contribute, but don't take over unless she asks you to. I'll explain to Kristie that you and I have talked, and I will have her compile weekly progress notes. I have no doubt that if there are any further issues, you'll hear about it. So will I," Dr. Lowell finished drolly.

"I'm sure," I agreed.

"Okay, then, I think we're finished here. Enjoy the rest of your day," Dr. Lowell said, already turning back to her grading.

I picked up my book bag and slung it over my shoulder, relieved that the meeting was over and I hadn't lost a limb or two. Only my dignity had been dinged.

I had the rest of the day to finish up my research paper for Social Psychology. I headed toward Longwood University's rather impressive library, my steps lighter than they had been when I had left the apartment that morning.

I headed straight for my usual spot, a secluded four-person

table on the second floor. It was hidden behind the horticulture section, not exactly a popular spot for students, so I was rarely disturbed. I unloaded my books and pulled out my baggie of snacks, getting ready for an afternoon of research.

I was making good headway with my paper when I felt a presence in my tiny nook. My pencil froze in midsentence, and I looked up and had to swallow my groan.

"Is this seat taken?" Maxx asked, pulling out the chair opposite me.

"Actually, I usually work here . . . *alone*," I said slowly and clearly, hoping he got the point.

Maxx was either being purposefully obtuse or didn't understand the concept of subtext. I was pretty sure it was the former. He gave me a toothy grin and dropped his bag on the table, knocking over my carefully organized notebooks and highlighters.

I gritted my teeth and moved my things out of his way.

"Whatcha working on?" he asked.

"Shh, keep your voice down. You'll get us kicked out," I scolded, letting him see how annoyed I was to be interrupted.

Maxx held his hands up. "Sorry, I'll leave you to it."

I gave him a curt nod and bowed my head over my book again. I tried to focus on my reading, but with the smell of his aftershave filling my nostrils, I was finding concentrating with Maxx sitting so close pretty much impossible.

When I had written the same sentence three times in a row, I dropped my pen and rubbed my temples.

"Got a headache?" Maxx asked.

"No, just having a hard time *focusing*," I muttered.

"Am I distracting you?" Maxx teased.

I dropped my hands on the table with a bang and cringed. I looked around, hoping the librarian wouldn't toss me out on my ass.

"I sit back here so people won't bother me. I've got a lot of work to do," I pleaded, really hoping he'd get up and leave.

Maxx cocked his head to the side. "I've been trying to place that accent since I first met you. Southwest Virginia?" he asked, not bothering to address my earlier statement. Clearly he was here for the long haul, and I just had to suck it up.

"North Carolina," I corrected before thinking about it.

Shit!

Do not engage, Aubrey! *Do not engage!*

"Ahh, a southern gal," he said, tapping his pencil against his book.

"Mmm-hmm," I said unintelligibly, hoping that would be an end to it.

I should have known better.

"Where in North Carolina?" he asked a second later.

"What is this, drive Aubrey crazy with a million questions?" I barked.

"You're so touchy when you're studying," Maxx said, biting his lower lip to keep from laughing. My eyes were drawn to his mouth, and I found myself staring at the full curve of his lips.

Stop it!

I cleared my throat and started packing up my things. There was no way I'd get anything done with Maxx there. I might as well try studying back at the apartment and hope it was Devon-free.

"Don't leave. I'm sorry, I'll be quiet," Maxx promised. He reached out and put his hand on top of mine, stilling me. "Please." He wielded that word like a weapon. It took the wind out of any and all arguments.

It was annoying.

I settled back in my chair and opened my book up again.

"Fine, but seriously, Maxx, I have a lot to do," I said, shocked at how quickly I had given in.

Maxx nodded and promptly opened up his own books.

I tried to get back to my research paper, but again, I couldn't focus. I looked over at what Maxx was working on and saw that he was looking through an Advanced Corporate Finance textbook.

"I thought you were supposed to cure cancer? How does corporate finance help you become a doctor?" I found myself asking.

Maxx looked up at me, and I couldn't look away. He had a way of looking at me that made me feel like the only person in the world. The only thing that *mattered*. How was he able to do that? He was so damned magnetic; it was like I was being sucked into his force field, or he was a gigantic black hole that could swallow me up.

"I don't see being Dr. Demelo in my future," he responded, his eyes never leaving mine. Did he realize the effect he had on people? I was almost certain that he did, and that was a dangerous power to wield.

It was impossible to read him, and I had always prided myself on my powers of intuition. But when it came to Maxx, I came up disturbingly blank.

"Why not?" I asked, shutting my book. There was no sense in pretending I was going to get any work done. I was in the middle of Maxx 101.

Maxx coughed into his hand and looked away, breaking our connection. "Just not my thing," he answered.

I was prepared to dig—all the way to China, if I had to.

"Well, what's your thing then?" I asked, cradling my chin in my hand as I looked at him. The alcove we were sitting in suddenly felt stiflingly warm and almost claustrophobic. I was wearing a turtleneck, and I wished I had worn something lighter. I was hyperaware of how much I was sweating.

I was sure the sudden heat wave had everything to do with the temperature in the library and absolutely *nothing* to do with the boy who sat across from me.

Maxx smiled a small, secretive grin, and instead of answering, he turned the tables. "What's *your* thing? Counseling, right? Is that about your own issues or do you have some kind of savior complex?"

I sat back, debating whether I should be insulted or not. I couldn't tell whether he was trying to be rude or if it just came naturally. He asked the question with just the right amount of condescension to goad me into defending myself.

"Of course I want to help people. Why else would I be working my ass off like this?" I asked, hating that I had given him exactly what he wanted—information.

"I don't know. I thought it might have something to do with your sister," he suggested, his face showing nothing but kind concern.

How dare he throw that back in my face! I had confided in him in a moment of weakness. I should have known I'd come to regret it. My skin flushed, and I felt myself getting angry. Maxx elicited such passionate feelings in me. Whether they were anger or lust, I felt them strongly and overwhelmingly.

He was dangerous for my constitution.

"It's not appropriate for us to be talking about this," I said coldly, wishing I had left when I had wanted to.

"I'm not trying to be inappropriate. I told you I thought that talking about your sister was an incredibly brave thing to do. I respect that. I respect *you*," Maxx said earnestly.

"I just think that, given what happened to her, it would make you determined to help other people like her. It makes sense. That's all I was trying to say. I'm sorry if my bringing it up upsets you. That was insensitive of me," he said, full of apology.

Okay, so maybe I was overreacting a bit. But talking about Jayme with anyone put me on edge. And the way he had casually slipped it into our conversation left me feeling jangled.

Talking with Maxx was an oddly intimate experience. We might as well be sitting here naked.

Now I was thinking about him naked.

Crap!

"It's fine," I said, surprising myself with the truth of it. I couldn't hold his observation against him because it had been the truth.

"And, yeah, I guess Jayme is why I'm doing this," I admitted, wishing I could staple my mouth shut. Where was my brain's shut-down function when I needed it? Why was I throwing up information about myself to Maxx of all people?

I'm sure it had nothing to do with those incredible eyes that seemed to beg me to give up my secrets.

"It's great that you have something you want to do with your life that means something. There's very little in my own life that I feel that sort of passion about," Maxx said.

"It sounds like you have *something*, though, and that's the place to start," I offered.

Maxx's eyes darkened. They literally smoldered. I had always thought that was trite nonsense best reserved for sappy romance novels. But no, Maxx was doing the whole smoldering thing really well.

"You're right. It's the perfect place to start," he murmured, and my heart fluttered madly in my chest. There was that frustrating innuendo again. It left me unsettled and off-balance.

I got to my feet suddenly, knocking my chair to the floor. The clang echoed in the quiet library.

"I really have to go," I said hurriedly, gathering my things.

Maxx frowned. "Did I say something wrong?" he asked, looking hurt.

"No, not at all. I just have things I need to do." I was making excuses—bad ones. But after my meeting with Dr. Lowell and narrowly avoiding a reprimand, sharing confidences with a group member seemed a surefire way to land myself in a lot of trouble.

"I'll see you next week," I said, hugging my book bag to my chest and trying not to run away.

"Bye, Aubrey," Maxx said, my name soft on his tongue.

chapter
twelve

Maxx had invaded my thoughts, whether I wanted him there or not. I kept replaying our conversations over and over again in my head. I berated myself for the ease with which I had spoken to him. I internally raged against my willingness to share pieces of myself that I had purposefully kept hidden. Most of all, I was puzzled by my uncharacteristic reaction toward someone I didn't know, didn't trust, didn't want privy to the secrets inside me.

So why hadn't I been stronger? Why had I exposed a vulnerability that I had thought I'd lost?

One thing was for sure: I had to learn from my mistakes and remember exactly who Maxx was, and who I was supposed to be.

Regardless of his beautiful blue eyes and sexy smile.

And I would definitely ignore the illogical desire to see him again.

Even if I *was* mesmerized by the man who had snuck his younger brother into the commons so he could eat. Even if I *was* strangely fixated on the person who had plucked a flower out of the cold January ground and given it to me with a smile on his face. And I was entirely too preoccupied with the boy who had shared how scared he was that he would lose himself to the addiction that controlled him.

The obnoxious need to fix him was there. I could feel it. It sat just beneath my staunch resolve, waiting for me to acknowledge that *I* wanted to be the one to bundle him up and take care of him.

Maxx was right. I had a major savior complex.

It was Saturday evening, and I had agreed to go back to Compulsion with Brooks. I hadn't seen him much in the days following the disastrous support group. He had brought me soup and a movie, just as promised, but for the first time I had felt a strange undercurrent between us.

He had been *off*. There was no other word for it. When I had asked him what was wrong, he had said, "Nothing." Which was code for *Something's bugging me, but I'm going to be annoyingly evasive about it just to drive you nuts.*

I hadn't pressed him. I wasn't in the mood to play let's figure out what's crawled up Brooks Hamlin's ass. If he wanted to talk about it, he would.

I knew that he was busy preparing for midterms and was stressed waiting to hear from the grad schools he'd applied to. He had told me enough times that his course load was tough. I had to believe that was the cause for his strange mood.

So why was I being paranoid that it had to do with something else entirely?

This concern, on top of my inexplicable feelings toward Maxx, had me feeling close to a postal meltdown. So I was beyond relieved when Brooks called and made the suggestion that we go back to Compulsion. He had been normal enough, and I had been able to persuade myself that I had been imagining everything.

Renee and I were still engaged in a tentative peace. We had even watched some cheesy sci-fi movie the other night before bed. We had made a silent agreement to avoid the subject of

Devon. Doing so alleviated a lot of the tension that had estab-
lished itself between us over the past six months.

It was only six-thirty. Brooks wouldn't be coming to get me
until ten. I had hours to kill. Renee was out on the couch, studying
for her midterms. I had straightened and re-straightened my
room a good half-dozen times. I had picked out my outfit for the
night, and my reading for my courses was up-to-date. I found
myself bored, and that was unusual. I didn't get bored. I usually
kept myself so busy, boredom wasn't an option. Not knowing
what else to do, I joined Renee in the living room.

A muted image of the Shopping Network flickered in the background, and Led Zeppelin played on the stereo. I flopped down
on the couch and picked up the remote.

Renee glanced up, giving me a distracted smile before returning to her studying. It was nice seeing her focused on something
that wasn't he who shall not be named.

And then, as if the very thought of him summoned his presence, the doorbell chimed. "You expecting company?" I asked
Renee, who shook her head. I got to my feet and started to cross
the room to answer the door when it swung open.

Devon sauntered into the room, his hands holding plastic grocery bags filled with beer; two of his skeevy buddies trailed behind
him. Devon didn't bother to acknowledge me as he walked into
my apartment and dumped the bags on *my* coffee table. His
friends ground mud into the carpet as they walked into the room.

Devon snatched Renee's textbook out of her hands and tossed
it behind the couch. "It's way past study time, baby," he announced, flopping down on the couch beside her and propping
his feet on the table, not even bothering to take off his shoes.

His friends, neither of whom looked as though they had bothered with a shower that day, grabbed stools from the island and
brought them into the living room. Each guy pulled out a bottle of
beer and popped the top, tossing the discarded caps onto the table.

Renee looked flustered and not in the least bit happy to see her boyfriend. But of course she didn't say anything. She let him take over her space, dictate her time, and decide what she would be doing with her Saturday evening.

I stood there, my mouth slightly agape, hardly able to believe the size of the balls this dude had—balls I'd be more than happy to remove with a butter knife.

"Get your feet off the table," I told him, my voice low. Devon barely looked in my direction. At one time I may have understood why Renee turned herself inside out over him. He was good looking in an I-try-really-hard-to-look-this-badass way. But I knew that his attitude, his entire persona, was about as fake as the leather of his jacket.

And despite the image he seemed to try to project, I was becoming all too aware of the person he really was beneath the surface.

Devon Keeton was the type of guy who needed to treat his girlfriend like shit because his dick was ten sizes too small. He was the guy who'd wet his pants if confronted by someone bigger than him but would then turn around and kick a dog, just because he could.

I watched as Devon continued to take over the apartment, his friends opening bags of chips and dumping crumbs on the floor. Renee seemed to shrink in on herself, her eyes becoming hollow.

Maybe it was the sight of my friend losing a part of herself that had me ready to explode. Or maybe it was watching Devon and his friends disrespect our home. Or perhaps it was the increasing amount of food debris collecting on my spotless floors.

Whatever it was, it flipped a switch inside me, and I knew if I stayed there a moment longer, I wouldn't be able to stay silent. I wouldn't be able to mutely watch my best friend be bulldozed by her jerk of a boyfriend.

I looked over at Renee, her eyes staring straight ahead. I felt angry and sad and a deep, gut-wrenching disappointment at her inability to stand up for herself.

I couldn't stomach being there anymore. I grabbed my coat and purse and slammed out of the apartment, the sound of Devon's and his friends' laughter ringing in my ears.

I walked out into the cold winter air and wished I'd remembered to bring my gloves, which I'd left behind in my haste to leave. I shoved my hands into my pockets and hunched my shoulders up to try to shield myself from the wind.

It was already dark, and I wished I were back home, snuggled up in bed instead of outside in the freezing cold, pissed off. This was hibernation weather, and right now that didn't seem like such a bad idea. Between my less-than-professional feelings for Maxx and the fucked-up dynamic between myself and my best friend, the thought of sleeping for a few months sounded extremely appealing.

I found myself walking back toward campus, having no other destination in mind and no other friends to call.

I suppose I could blame Jayme's death for my reluctance to reach out and make new friends, except for Renee and Brooks. Losing her had been traumatic in the worst way possible. But the honest truth was I had never been the sort of person to seek friends. I had a few people I hung out with in high school, but they were the type of friends it had been easy to lose touch with after I had moved away.

Sheesh, this amount of personal reflection was giving me a headache.

"Whoever pissed in your cornflakes had better watch out," a voice called from behind me. I hadn't realized I was already on campus. I was on the sidewalk just behind the library.

As the figure came out of the shadows, I was hit by a déjà vu so strong it had me taking a step back. The wide shoulders, the unrecognizable face. My mind immediately jumped to the guy from Compulsion.

But this wasn't a stranger.

Maxx's swagger was as confident as ever, his smirk firmly in place. He wore an old gray hoodie splattered with paint. His movements were sluggish, and I wondered if he was on something. I hoped not, for his sake. That would land him in the violating-his-probation kind of trouble.

"Did you take a dip in a bucket of paint?" I asked sharply, unable to alter the nasty tone in my voice.

Maxx looked down at his hoodie and shrugged. "Community-service stuff," he explained, and I felt like a bit of an asshole.

"Why so angry, Aubrey? You look ready to kill someone," Maxx observed, leaning against the lamppost, hands in his pockets, looking blasé.

"If you're just going to vomit up more crappy come-ons, please find another girl who's more receptive to your witty personality. I'm honestly not in the mood to fend off your pickup lines," I responded peevishly.

Maxx looked taken aback. He blinked a few times, opening and closing his mouth as though he were trying to think of something to say. I tried to suppress the grin that threatened to give me away.

"What? Nothing to say?" I asked, lobbing my own sarcastic teasing.

Maxx chuckled and rubbed the back of his neck. His smirk transformed into a genuine smile. It lit up his face and took my breath away.

"You wanna hang out?" he asked. It was obvious he hadn't planned on asking me that, and somehow the spontaneity of the offer made it extremely appealing.

"I don't know if that would be appropriate," I stated, trying to regain some common sense, something I was sorely lacking when it came to Maxx Demelo.

Maxx snorted. "What's inappropriate about it? We're not in

group right now. You're a student. I'm a student. We're just two students wanting to hang out. What's the harm?" he asked innocently.

Innocent, my *ass*.

I cocked my eyebrow at him and leveled him with my best who-the-hell-are-you-kidding look. Maxx bit on his bottom lip to keep from laughing. His blue eyes, while red-rimmed and tired, sparkled with excitement.

I couldn't deny that I wanted to spend time with him, that I was intrigued by him. And for some crazy reason, my internal warning bells weren't screaming as loudly as they normally did.

"Come on." Maxx inclined his head in the direction of the sidewalk, lighting up a cigarette as he went.

Fresh out of arguments and more than a little tired of creating them, I fell into step beside him, waving smoke out of my face.

"Do you have to smoke? Some of us have a good relationship with our lungs," I snipped.

Maxx took a last drag and dropped it on the ground. "No smoking. Got it," he said, surprisingly seriously.

"So you're not going to tell me why you're in such a shitty mood?" Maxx asked as we walked.

"Roommate drama," I said.

"Did she steal your Crimson Splash nail polish again?" he joked, and I snorted.

"Do I look like the sort of girl to wage war over makeup?" I scoffed, though I wasn't sure I wanted to know what sort of girl he considered me to be.

"You look like the kind of girl who doesn't take a whole lot of bullshit," Maxx said, bestowing an unexpected compliment. I arched my eyebrow.

"You see right through me, huh?" I replied blandly. Maxx chuckled.

"Never an inch," he said under his breath, though just loud

enough for me to hear him. I couldn't help but smile. There was something about being with him that was both comfortable and unexpected. He kept me on my toes, but there were times when our conversation was as easy and natural as breathing.

The dynamic we fell into seemed to pit anger and distrust against lust and longing. Frustration warred with contentment. Irritation and wariness were at odds with vulnerability and sincerity.

It made being around him exhausting, yet exhilarating at the same time. It was easy to see why people were drawn to him.

When he laughed or spoke, people watched. They hung on. They coveted every tiny bit of him.

He had the potential to decimate everything around him.

Me included.

Maxx pulled me to a stop outside the local movie theater, a building built in the 1940s. I had been inside only a handful of times and had been obsessed about possible mold spores in the bathroom. It had a dank, musty smell that no amount of popcorn and air freshener could get rid of.

Looking up at the marquee, I was both delighted and surprised. They were advertising their Cult Hit Saturday. They were playing a series of lesser-known movies for a fraction of the usual admission price, and one particular movie that was listed had me especially excited.

"You want to go see this?" I asked, jerking my thumb toward the poster of one of my all-time favorite movies, *The Doom Generation*.

"I've been waiting to get you in the dark," Maxx teased, purposefully closing the distance between us. I took an involuntary step back, creating some necessary space.

"*If bullshit were music, you'd be a big brass band*," I quoted. Maxx let out a deep laugh.

"I should have known you'd be a fan," he stated, looking at me with appreciation.

"I love obscure movies. My sister and I went through a phase where we watched *Doom Generation* every weekend," I answered, smiling at the memory of us sitting around quoting dialogue and laughing until we couldn't breathe.

Maxx grinned down at me, and I found myself smiling back at him. And then he did the most peculiar thing. As though without thinking, he lifted his hand and cupped my cheek. His thumb swept up the curve of my face, his blue eyes intense and serious.

"You're beautiful, Aubrey. But when you smile, you're breath-taking," he said softly.

Well, damn. His words were designed to make me melt, and they did, even as I fought hard to resist them. Who was I kidding? What girl wouldn't dissolve into a puddle of girlie drool after a comment like that?

Cleanup on aisle twelve!

He was looking at me with the sort of tender expression that men generally reserve for proms and marriage proposals. It made my insides flutter.

And then he dropped his hand and moved away from me. I stood there, bewildered, my body and heart still buzzing.

Maxx's personality changed so quickly it was hard to keep up. But there were flashes of sincerity, like just now, that made it easy to overlook the times when it was obvious he was trying to be someone else.

Maxx held his hand out for me to take, but I just stared at it dumbly.

"We need to head inside if we don't want to miss the start of the movie," he said, waggling his fingers.

"Okay," I agreed finally, tentatively putting my hand into his outstretched palm. Our fingers laced together, and he gave my hand a small squeeze.

He bought our tickets and popcorn, ignoring my pleas to let me pay my own way. This was beginning to feel too much like a date.

And deep down in the farthest recesses of my heart, I hoped it was. *Stupid, stupid Aubrey!*

When we were seated in the theater, we still had ten minutes to spare before the movie began. We sat in an easy silence, and I was amazed at how I was able to sit beside him and not feel awkward.

It was actually kind of . . . *nice.*

Maxx ate his gummy bears, shooting a smile my way every so often. I watched him out of the corner of my eye as he bit the head off a red gummy bear before popping it in his mouth. He repeated this act of decapitation over and over again as he polished off the box of candy.

"What did those gummy bears ever do to you?" I quipped around a mouthful of popcorn.

Maxx grinned right before ripping the head off the last bear in the box. "They should know better than to be so damned delicious," he answered, licking his lips after swallowing.

I couldn't help but blush at his words.

"I don't know anything about you," I announced without preamble, again shocking myself with how readily I dropped my guard around him, how quickly I began scouting for information.

Maxx cocked his eyebrow. "I wasn't aware you were looking for information."

"Why the mystery, Maxx? You got something to hide?" I asked with a bit more vehemence than I had intended, our relaxed companionship over.

Maxx's eyes darkened. "I'll tell you whatever you want to know, Aubrey. All you have to do is ask," he said firmly. The theater was almost empty. Only a handful of people occupied the seats. But I still worried about being overheard.

I cleared my throat, trying to regain some control over the situation.

"Well, what's your major? Clearly it's not medicine, and it has something to do with corporate finance," I asked like an idiot. Maxx barked out a laugh.

"That's your question? What's my major? Do you want my star sign too?" he joked, and I smacked his arm, giving myself permission to touch him in that casual way.

"Let's start with the small stuff and see where we end up," I volleyed back.

Maxx reached over and stole a handful of my popcorn, tossing a few kernels into his mouth. After he polished off his pilfered snack, he wiped his greasy fingers on his jeans. I tried not to be grossed out by that.

"I'm a business major with a concentration in economics," he said.

"A business major? Really?" I asked in disbelief.

Maxx frowned, clearly annoyed by my incredulity. "Yes, a business major. Why is that so hard to believe? I'm not some dumbass coasting through school," he remarked defensively, his mood turning on a dime once again.

"It's just you're . . . well . . . you . . ."

"Got busted for drugs? Or is it that I'm on probation and have to sit in that fucking room every week talking about my goddamned feelings?" he asked angrily. Great, I had pissed him off— royally, to judge from the way his jaw was ticking.

"I'm not judging," I started to say, but Maxx cut me off.

"The hell you're not," he bit out.

"Look, I'm sorry. I know you're trying to sort yourself out. You're in group. You're doing your community service. I'm not belittling any of that." I tried to backpedal. But if anything, my words seemed to make him even angrier.

"You don't know shit about me or my choices. Or why I've done the things I've done. You don't know *me*, Aubrey," he hissed, his eyes boring holes into mine.

As if possessed by something I didn't entirely understand, I reached out a hand and wrapped it around his clenched fist on the armrest. I leaned in until his face was within an inch of mine.

"But I want to, Maxx," I said softly. And I realized how true that statement was. There was something about Maxx Demelo that made me want to dig, to find out all the good and the bad. But I reminded myself that this probing was overstepping all sorts of boundaries

Maxx's nostrils flared, and he took in a deep breath as though my words were painful for him to hear. He closed his eyes, his brow furrowing. "Please, Aubrey," he murmured.

Though I wasn't sure what his plea was for.

Please, Aubrey, drop it?

Please, Aubrey, I want you to know me?

Please, Aubrey, this is the most mind-numbing conversation of my entire life, so shut up already?

Before I could push for more, the lights went down, and Maxx turned his hand palm up, folding his fingers around mine in the dark.

The heat of his skin enveloped mine, and I couldn't decide if I wanted to pull away or not.

But I didn't. I opened my fist, which had clenched tightly after his initial touch, and threaded my fingers through his. We held hands like high schoolers on our first date. It was innocent and surprisingly sweet.

Soon the intensity gave way to something even more bewildering—contentment, comfort—again with that strange easiness that unfolded like it had always been there. For a girl who didn't get close to people, here I was, tiptoeing into whatever this was without hesitation.

We were laughing and reciting dialogue. Maxx continued to steal my popcorn, and I playfully smacked his hand away. His fingers tightened in mine periodically, as though to remind me that we were still touching.

Please, as if I could forget.

Despite my eyes being trained on the screen, all I could feel, all I could think about, was his skin against mine.

During one of the particularly violent scenes, I turned away, never having been able to stomach it. I trained my eyes on Maxx's shoulder and waited for it to be over. I felt his eyes on me and looked up through my lashes. His mouth was quirked up in a small smile.

"Such a delicate little flower, aren't you?" he teased, his breath stirring the hairs by my ear. I gave a snort and shook my head, our cheeks touching.

Maxx's fingers brushed my hair out of my face, and he leaned in to brush his nose along mine, his lips the barest whisper away. His eyes held mine in the glow of the screen. His hand slid down the side of my neck until he stopped and cupped the back of my head in his strong grip. His other hand came up to cradle the other side of my face, his thumb caressing my jaw.

I licked my lips, my mouth suddenly dry. I should stop this. I should say something. I should back the hell away and put some necessary distance between me and this thing building toward a definite climax.

But there was no acting. No thinking. Just the anticipation.

"I'm going to kiss you, Aubrey," he said softly against my lips. I swallowed around the lump that had formed in my throat.

But I didn't pull away.

I couldn't pull away from him.

The moment his mouth met mine, I tensed up. It was as though the last semblance of rational thought was battling my overworked hormones for supremacy. My brain was trying desperately to stop the rest of me from doing something I couldn't take back.

But then Maxx's tongue skimmed the crease of my mouth, and my lips parted to let him inside.

I had gone under.

He tasted like popcorn, cherry gummy bears, and every decadent, forbidden thing. He tasted like *bad choices*.

I couldn't stop the groan that bubbled up from the back of my throat as he plundered my mouth. He took and he claimed and he made me *his*. I couldn't help but feel a sudden panic as the need to shut down and pull away tried to take over.

But my body ached for this. I wanted him even as I recoiled at the intimacy. My lips slowly began to respond under the pressure of his mouth as my brain was quieted by the sensation of being kissed by Maxx.

This was new to me. The wanting. Under the expert ministrations of Maxx's hands and tongue, I felt any residual hesitation melt away. It was terrifying. It was exhilarating. It was life-altering.

My arms came up, and my fingers wound themselves in the thickness of his curls. His hands continued to hold my face firmly as our mouths slanted again and again.

Our tongues tangled, our teeth knocked together, and I could barely breathe. I could feel the day-old scruff on his face rubbing against my cheeks and chin. I'd have a serious case of beard burn when this was over.

Maxx moaned deep and low, and it rumbled around in my belly, causing me to throb. I leaned farther into him, our chests smashed together over the obstructing armrest. Maxx broke away and glared down at the offending piece of plastic that separated us. Then, without a word, he pulled me over the seat, my legs scraping against it roughly, but I found that I didn't care. I'd worry about bruises later.

I landed haphazardly in his lap, my back digging painfully into the other armrest. My legs were sprawled inelegantly along the row of seats.

Wow, this is so not hot, I thought, trying not to be embarrassed over the days of the week underwear now on display beneath my disheveled skirt. I felt my awkward tension resurface and threaten to ruin the moment. Tiny, anxious voices in the back of my head started questioning exactly what I was doing.

I wiggled into an upright position, fully intending to break away from our passionate embrace. But the pressure of my ass pressing into Maxx's crotch erased my second-guessing.

Maxx moaned again, this time a little louder. I glanced around, worried about the show we were putting on. So far so good, no one was paying us any mind.

I could feel his erection straining under his jeans, and it twisted up my insides. Maxx wrapped his arm around my back and maneuvered me so that I was kneeling, straddling him in the tiny seat, my skirt hiked up over my hips. His hand pressed into my lower back, pushing me against him. His mouth kissed a line up the column of my throat, his tongue flicking against my skin.

"Fuck, you're perfect. So fucking perfect," he murmured as his mouth took hold of mine again.

I ground against the firm ridge inside his jeans, needing some sort of relief from the ache between my legs. We made out and touched for the rest of the movie, but we kept it strictly PG-13. It had both awakened and frustrated me.

We barely noticed when the movie was over and the lights came back on. "Get a room," someone muttered, tossing a handful of popcorn in our direction.

Maxx and I broke away, and I let out a strained laugh. His mouth was swollen, and I'm sure my face was red and raw from his stubble, but it had been worth it. That had been the most potent make-out session I had ever had.

I slithered off his lap and stood up on very wobbly legs, straightening my skirt. Maxx took my hand and led me out of the theater. We didn't look at each other, and I wasn't sure if it was out of embarrassment or an overload of lust.

We stepped out into the cool night air, and I wished I could think of something to say, something to make this moment last or perhaps make it go away. Maxx confused me. He confounded me. He made me question absolutely *everything*.

Maxx stopped abruptly and turned around to face me. He gripped my shoulders and brought his mouth down to mine. He kissed me thoroughly before letting me come up for air.

"Thank you," he said against my lips.

"For what?" I asked shakily.

Maxx smiled against my mouth and didn't answer. Then he backed away, holding on to my hands until they were outstretched between us. Slowly he released my fingers.

"Good night, Aubrey," he murmured, pulling his paint-stained hoodie up over his head and turning away.

"Hope is the thing with feathers—that perches in the soul—and sings the tune without the words—and never stops—at all," Maxx said, his words drifting back to me in the cold, night air.

Why had he just quoted Emily Dickinson?

I stood there, flabbergasted, watching him walk down the sidewalk.

chapter
thirteen

aubrey

for ten minutes I stood outside the movie theater wondering what had just happened. The childishly insecure part of me felt completely and totally rejected.

One minute Maxx had been kissing me; the next he was leaving me alone.

What. The. *Hell?*

If I was hoping to solve some of the mysteries of Maxx Demelo tonight, I was sadly disappointed.

I touched my lips gently with my fingers. My mouth was still bruised and tender, and the cold air stung my sensitive cheeks, rubbed raw by Maxx's scruff. My body was strung tight, my heart felt abused and thrown away, and my head was yelling at me for being such a colossal idiot.

I pulled my phone out of my purse and checked the time. It was only ten o'clock. What kind of guy left the girl he'd been mauling for the last hour without a word? Without an explanation? And without offering to walk her home?

After my shock had worn off, it was quickly replaced with irritation and something akin to rip-his-balls-off rage.

I didn't like being played. I didn't take kindly to being made to look like a jackass. Well, fuck Maxx and all of his kissing awesomeness.

My phone rang, and I looked down to see Brooks's name on the screen.

Crap, I had totally forgotten about our plans.

"Brooks, hey!" I said, walking back in the direction of my apartment.

"Where are you?" he asked, sounding annoyed.

"Uh . . . well . . ." My words trailed off.

"Uh . . . well? That doesn't explain much, Aubrey. I'm at your apartment, but guess who's not here? That would be you. Are you bailing on me?" he asked shortly.

"I'm coming. I just had to run out for a bit. Is Renee still there?" I asked, not wanting to admit where I had been. I was embarrassed, and I felt used.

"Nobody's here. I'm standing in the hallway like a dumb-ass. Your crazy cat-lady neighbor keeps peeking at me through the door. She's freaking me out," he said, dropping his voice into an exaggerated whisper.

I chuckled, though it was a weak impersonation of my normal laugh. "Hang tight, I'll be there in a few minutes," I promised and then hung up.

When I got back to my apartment, Brooks was sitting on the floor outside my door, texting someone. Looking at him, I couldn't understand why he didn't date. He was a good-looking guy who could be doing a lot more with his Saturday night than hanging out with a girl who would never put out for him again.

I wondered, not for the first time, why he limited his social life to hanging out with me. I really hoped the reason wasn't something akin to residual feelings that could never be reciprocated.

"You're finally here! My ass was going numb," Brooks grumbled, getting to his feet as I unlocked the door. I turned on the light and about flipped my shit.

"Whoa. What happened in here? This isn't OCD-compatible," Brooks said, picking up a plundered pretzel bag from the floor. There were empty beer bottles on the coffee table and dishes on the floor by the couch. Trash and discarded food littered the kitchen counters.

"I was gone for three hours! Are you kidding me?" I yelled, slamming the door behind me. I couldn't deal with this crap anymore! This was Devon doing what Devon did best—being a dick.

"I'll clean up. You go get dressed," Brooks offered. I started to argue.

"We'll be here all night if I leave you to do it," he explained, and I knew he was right. I swallowed my need to fix and tidy and went and got changed. I looked in the mirror and cringed. My face was red and splotchy, my lips puffy. I couldn't believe Brooks hadn't interrogated me over my very obvious state of disarray.

After I had changed into a short black dress and my knee-high black boots, I pulled my hair into a high ponytail and darkened my eyes so that they stood out. Not bad for fifteen minutes of prep time.

Brooks had straightened up the best his guy chromosome set was capable of. Seeing the way he had replaced the couch cushions made my eyes twitch, but I appreciated the effort.

He looked up when I came in and appeared relieved to be able to cease his cleaning duties. "Awesome, let's go!" he said, ushering me out the door.

"Do you know where we're going?" I asked, wondering if we'd have to trek through the city to find a mysterious painting to determine our location for the night.

"Yeah, I spoke to some of the guys in my building, and they gave me the address," Brooks said distractedly, hooking his phone up and putting the location into the GPS. I was a little disappointed. I may have been late to the street art appreciation party, but I was now an X fangirl all the way.

We drove through the city until we reached the interstate. "Where the heck are we going?" I asked.

"Apparently the club is in an old textile factory twenty minutes away," he explained, merging onto the darkened highway.

I spoke very little on the drive. My head was too full of other things—those other things being Maxx freaking Demelo. Why had he left so abruptly?

That question burned a hole in my brain and was driving me crazy with a niggling insecurity. My self-esteem had taken a beating, and I didn't like it one bit.

Almost thirty minutes later we were pulling into a large parking lot teeming with cars. The usual crowd of raver kids and emo rejects were milling about, making their way to a dark building in the distance.

And just like every time I approached Compulsion, I felt an instant rush of excitement and anticipation. I was becoming more than a little addicted. It was exhilarating and sort of scary. But it wasn't the type of scary that made me want to run in the opposite direction. Not anymore. It was a scary that I wanted to explore and embrace.

Brooks pulled me toward the huge line, and we took our places. Part of the fun was the people-watching. Compulsion brought out all kinds—from the preppy boys trying their hand at dressing like badasses to the truly freaky. Take the woman wearing pasties and black leather panties—this dominatrix queen held a metal chain attached to a man dressed as a gimp, complete with ball gag.

Brooks discreetly pointed out the group of women, possibly in their thirties, who looked as though they had taken a night off from the coven, with their long, flowing dresses, flower garlands, brightly painted, talon-like fingernails, and necklaces made from what appeared to be human teeth.

We passed the bouncer's keen inspection, and then we were inside. I felt as though the heat and the music were smothering me. It was exactly what I needed.

This time when I ordered my drink, I didn't take my eyes off the beverage. I had learned my lesson. Brooks had gone to dance; I had politely declined, wanting to soak it all in. I also wanted to see if my mystery man would make an appearance.

Finally tired of playing wallflower, I moved into the crowd and started dancing. I had never been a great dancer, but I liked it anyway. Lucky for me, the dancing at Compulsion didn't require a lot of skill. People were bobbing on their feet, glow sticks between their teeth.

I sort of rocked my head from side to side, swinging my hair into my face. My arms rose above my head, and I started to move in time with the thumping bass.

Dancing at Compulsion was a communal experience. Complete strangers pressed against me, and we moved together like one primal beast of sweat and heat. My OCD had taken a backseat to the energy. It was unreal.

A girl with bright purple hair grabbed my hand and looped my arm around her waist. We rocked our hips together, dancing, two people who enjoyed the music, nothing more, nothing less. There was something incredibly freeing about being physically close to so many people who were all here for the same reason.

To escape.

I felt a set of hands on my hips, and without bothering to look behind me, I pulled purple-hair girl into me, and I was dancing in a crazy, debauched sandwich.

It was completely out of character for me, but for once I just went with it. That was the real beauty of Compulsion. It made what was out of the ordinary seem possible.

I loved it. I never wanted to leave.

One song bled into the next without pause. As my dancing

partners changed, I barely registered their faces. I didn't talk to any of them. Words weren't necessary. We weren't here to make friends.

We were there to just *be*.

It could have been minutes later. It could have been hours. But I finally realized how tired and sweaty I was. My legs felt wobbly from all the bouncing and jumping. My hair was plastered to the side of my face, and I was way too warm.

I pulled away from my newest dance partner, a guy with more tattoos than uninked skin. He didn't protest, just turned and started dancing with someone else.

I pushed through the throng and leaned against the back wall, trying to control my breathing. I couldn't see Brooks. I only hoped he was still around somewhere. I couldn't imagine him leaving me behind, but when I pulled my phone out of my pocket I was shocked to see that it was already one-thirty in the morning.

This place seemed to suck you into a void, and before you knew it, you'd lost all sense of time.

A girl wearing barely any clothing came up next to me. "You lookin' for anything?" she asked, yelling into my ear.

"What?" I asked, not understanding what she was asking.

The girl rolled her eyes and pressed a small bag in my hand. I held it up in front of my face and saw that it held a tiny pill. The girl pushed my hand down. "Don't be so obvious about it," she said in irritation.

I tried to hand it back to her with a shake of my head. "I'm not interested in this stuff."

The girl shoved my hand back. "It's a free sample. You want more, you'll have to find it yourself. Don't be a narc; just enjoy the ride," she said, her head bobbing in time to the beat. With a final pointed glance in my direction, she disappeared into the crowd.

I didn't want the drugs. But I didn't know what to do with them, either.

I shook the small plastic bag, wondering what exactly the girl had given me. I was intrigued, despite my better judgment.

I shook the pill onto my palm and stared at it as though it would give me the answer. But I knew one thing: This stuff was bad. I knew this was the kind of crap that had killed my sister.

Yet I was curious.

What was it about being in this place that made me want to indulge in the scary and unknown? It was nuts. It was completely illogical.

And I was smarter than that.

I had to be.

I hastily put the pill back in the baggie and dropped it on the floor, smashing it under my boot.

I felt jittery. The brush with a temptation I didn't entirely understand rattled me, but I felt proud of myself for not giving in.

And then I saw *him*.

The guy with the baseball cap. The one who had stopped me from becoming a rapist's plaything. The man who had prevented me from being trampled to death my first night at the club.

The guy whose face was still a mystery.

He was talking to a man not twelve feet from me. They were partially hidden in a dark corner. Their discussion appeared heated, but it was definitely my faceless guy. I recognized the broad width of his shoulders and the telltale cap pulled low over his eyes.

I started to walk toward him. It was as though I was being pulled toward him.

I watched as he took some money, tucking the wad in his back pocket. I noticed my mystery man put something in the other guy's outstretched palm. The subtle exchange was carried out in less than thirty seconds, but it was obvious what was happening.

My mystery guy was a drug dealer.

Remembering the baggie I had discarded on the floor, I had to wonder if he was the one circulating that shit in the crowd. Considering the steady flow of "customers," it was an easy association to make.

Nice guy, my ass. It was obvious he was like every other predator looking for an easy mark. I was devastated by the new assumption that perhaps our encounters had been nothing more than a chance for him to acquire a new customer. And here I was thinking I was special.

After another guy secured a pocketful of something that clearly made him very happy, a girl took his place and pressed into mystery dude, her breasts brushing his arm. She opened her mouth, and he dropped something onto her tongue. She rolled her head back, her barely concealed breasts popping out of her shirt.

The girl wrapped her arms around mystery guy's neck and rubbed against him provocatively. I couldn't see his eyes, but his mouth was grinning. He put something in his mouth and continued to allow the girl to move against him.

The girl reached up and pulled his cap off, and for the first time I could see his hair. It was blond and curled around his ears in a very familiar way.

I pushed through the crowd, getting closer. And then I stopped, frozen in place.

The guy turned, his hands resting on the girl's hips while she writhed against him. His cap had been discarded on the floor, and I could see his face in the red light that hung above him.

It was Maxx.

Suddenly something dark and ugly unfurled in my belly—something that was possessive and territorial and that pierced with the sting of betrayal.

Only a few hours ago he had been pressed intimately against me. A few hours ago, I thought that we had connected, that I had meant something to him.

But watching him here, in the flickering shadows, wearing the face I recognized but didn't yet understand, I felt like a complete and total idiot. How did I not recognize Maxx in the broad set of the mystery guy's shoulders? How had I missed the soft curls that I had felt with my fingers just a few hours ago?

I watched as he popped another pill in his mouth and then pulled away from the girl, who reached after him. He gave her a less than gentle shove, and she stumbled back, almost losing her balance. He bent down to pick up his cap and set it back on his head. He pulled it low over his eyes, hiding his face again.

But there was no more hiding who he was. He wasn't a mystery. He wasn't a hidden savior.

He was something else entirely.

I desperately tried to ignore the twinge inside me that screamed, *Wait, there has to be more to him than this.*

I backed away, using the mass of bodies as a shield between me and the boy I had briefly allowed inside my carefully constructed walls.

Maxx started to move through the crowd, shouldering people out of his way. I don't know what possessed me, but I began to follow him. I stayed far enough back that he couldn't know he was being shadowed.

My stomach was a twisted knot.

Maxx was stopped frequently, and he would lead people to the outskirts of the dance floor, where he would conduct his "business." It was easy to see that he delighted in his role in this world. He teased the girls who begged for what he had tucked in his pockets. He aggressively stared down the guys who were equally desperate to procure his goods.

And through it all, he walked the room like he owned the place. He was high, not only on the pills he kept tucking under his tongue, but also on his own power.

This place, which had seemed like an escape, now seemed

more like a prison. I felt trapped by the secrets it had revealed—Maxx's secrets.

I had known Maxx was bad news the day he walked into the support group. I knew he had baggage. I knew he had demons. I just thought he was actively fighting them, that he was *trying*.

But as I stalked him through the club, it was clear he wasn't fighting anything. This was a man who gloried in the person he was.

He was a messy, self-destructive, narcissistic person.

My heart ached. My brain felt overloaded, and yet I couldn't make myself turn away from the person he really was.

I had always prided myself on reading people and situations accurately, and my initial impression of Maxx had been a huge neon sign screaming *Uh-oh!* So why hadn't I listened? Why had I ignored that instinct and allowed myself to be swept up in the intoxicating illusion he had created?

Seeing him now, in his element, it was pretty damned clear that the man who had kissed me as though I was the air he breathed was nothing more than the fantasy he wanted me to see. And now all I could do was watch, and revel in my masochistic pain.

It was soon clear that Maxx was loaded. His steps became sluggish and his movements exaggerated, yet his mouth remained fixed in a smug, lazy smile.

He popped another pill into his mouth. Jeesh, how many had he taken? I was starting to worry he'd have an overdose.

But he just continued his arrogant stumbling, colliding with people as he walked. Kept on selling. Kept on being the guy who disgusted me in every possible way. And now I wanted nothing to do with him.

The cold reality of the man I saw weaving through the crowd, selling his drugs and affecting an air of superiority and condescension, crushed that twinge—the one that still felt a connection to the fantasy of Maxx—into smithereens. Those twinges were silly little-girl dreams that could only be destined for a brutal and violent destruction.

There was nothing about *this* Maxx that I understood, even if that twinge was still humming under my skin.

When he turned his face in my direction, the lights flickering madly overhead, I stood rooted to the spot, with people dancing all around me. I wanted him to see me. I wanted to yell *Liar!* into his stupid, gorgeous face. I wanted to scream at him. I wanted to ask why he was doing this. Why he had made me believe a lie. Why he could make me feel a million different things that I had never felt before, only to obliterate them with a truth I desperately wished I hadn't learned.

But he looked past me, his eyes never registering my presence. He didn't expect to see me here, so his drug-addled brain simply didn't see me. And when he turned away, I was both disappointed and relieved.

"There you are! I've been looking for you everywhere! Are you ready to go? It's really late, and I have to be up early for a cram session," Brooks shouted in my ear, grabbing me by the elbow. I turned my eyes away from Maxx to look at my friend. I nodded.

"Sure," I responded, quickly returning my gaze to where Maxx had been standing.

But he was gone.

Disappeared.

And I didn't bother to look for him again.

chapter
fourteen

I was covered in paint. It was in my hair, in the creases of my fingers, splattered on my pants. I dipped a brush into the red paint and smeared it along the brick wall. I was precariously balanced on a ten-foot ladder, my paints propped up on a piece of wood.

It was almost morning, and I should be at home, in bed, not freezing my ass off. I had class in less than four hours. I had shit to do that evening. But I had been out here since one a.m. Because I couldn't sleep. Because all I could think about was *her*.

Aubrey.

We had only spent a few hours together, and I had felt something shift inside me. I had wanted her. I had been drunk on the taste of her. Recognizable lust had blazed between us.

But strangely, it had been more than that. Sitting in the movie theater, laughing and talking to her had been easy and uncomplicated. I couldn't help but relax in Aubrey's company. She had a way about her that was comfortable.

Then she had asked me questions. She made it clear she wanted to know *me*. It had been a long time since anyone had given a damn about the person I am, the man behind the mask that I've created.

Being with Aubrey made me feel, for one perfect moment, that maybe, just maybe, I could be someone else. That I could be someone simple. And that perhaps she'd like me for who I was. Deep down, I could admit I had always craved acceptance, and Aubrey seemed to offer that without conditions.

So I had kissed her. I hadn't been able to stop myself from touching her. I couldn't keep myself from establishing some sort of physical connection with her.

But it had been too much, too soon. I had been overwhelmed. And yeah, I freaked out.

I had left her.

I had run like a coward.

But that hadn't stopped me from thinking about her. From wanting what I had glimpsed in those moments we'd had together, however unrealistic they were.

Now I was filled with a confusing mix of emotions, and I needed to let them out somehow. The only way I could do that was to paint.

Lately, my pictures had been for the club. With those, sure, I still got creative with the message, but they weren't organically *mine*. They belonged to someone else. They were for them, not me.

This picture, these images . . . they were all for me. They said everything that I felt but couldn't say.

I swept my brush into a large arc of red, followed by orange and then purple, a massive sunset. But it wasn't all pussified and pretty. Fuck, no. I didn't paint crap like that.

There were two people holding hands beneath a sky that erupted above them. And from that brilliant, colorful sky rained blood. It flooded everything. And those two people, so content, so happy in each other, would be swept up and carried off by it.

Yeah, it was morbid. No one ever accused me of being Polly Sunshine.

I finished up the sky and slowly made my way down the ladder. I could barely stand. I was much too wasted to be out. I should be facedown in my own drool with the amount of oxy I'd taken tonight.

But when the mood hit, I couldn't deny where it took me. I took the paints and tossed them in the Dumpster. There was no point in lugging them back to my apartment. I didn't have the energy for that, not now that I was finished and the adrenaline rush that had led me here was gone.

I collapsed the ladder and dragged it back to the alleyway where I had found it. I was one for improvising when it came to my art, borrowing or taking whatever I could find to make the picture I saw in my head.

Standing back, I looked at my massive painting under the streetlight as morning tiptoed in. It was huge. It was fucked-up. But goddamn it, it was *me*. And every ounce of longing I felt was all over that fucking wall.

I nodded once, my eyelids starting to droop. I'd better get home before I passed out on the side of the road.

I barely remembered getting there.

✦

I woke up later in the day feeling sick. I was huddled up in my bed, freezing my ass off. I must have forgotten to turn the heat on before I had gone comatose. Every joint, every muscle, ached.

I reached over to my bedside table and felt around for the bag I knew was there. My hand hit the lamp and sent it careening to the floor. The tremors took over, and I could barely pick up the small pill between my trembling fingers.

I pressed it to my lips but dropped it. I patted around the pillows, trying to find my tiny piece of salvation.

After I found it, I put it between my teeth and crushed it

before swallowing, the grit coating my tongue. I lay back, closed my eyes, and waited.

And waited some more.

It was taking too long, so I crushed another pill and swallowed. And waited again.

Still too long.

I took another.

Then finally I could feel it. The gradual slide into numbness. My heart slowed, and I felt like I could finally breathe.

And only then was I able to get out of bed. It was already two o'clock in the afternoon. I had slept through both my morning classes. I had another one in forty minutes, but I just didn't give enough of a shit to make myself go. I needed to get a shower. I reeked. I should probably eat something too. I couldn't remember the last time I had bothered with food. But my stomach didn't feel empty. I was too fucked-up to feel much of anything.

My phone rang. With languid slowness, I picked it up and answered without bothering to look at who was calling.

"Maxx! I got out of school early, do you want to come over and help me with the car?" my brother asked excitedly. I should probably have felt bad for letting him down, but I didn't. Like I said, I didn't feel anything at all.

"Can't, I've got stuff to do," I replied, shuffling into my cramped living room and turning on the crappy television set in the corner. Cool, reruns of *The A-Team* were on. My afternoon was set.

"But you said you'd come over this week," Landon said in a small voice.

"Yeah, when did I say that?" I asked, not really paying attention to the conversation. I made promises and I broke them. What else was new?

"Please, Maxx. David has been asking when you're coming by. I think he needs more money," Landon said, dropping his voice into a whisper.

Typically the mention of my asshole uncle would have set me raging. I hated that fucker. I hated that he used his guardianship of my brother as a noose around my neck. He had it in his head that I would finance his gambling habit just because he gave Landon a place to live. But I had enough habits of my own that needed to be taken care of first. My uncle wanting to play poker wasn't high on my list of priorities.

But I knew if I didn't give him what he wanted, Landon was the one who would suffer. Some days, the guilt of how I was living my life threatened to eat me alive—except for when I was doped up or asleep.

Then life was good.

"Tell him to go fuck himself," I replied, zoning out on the television again.

"What is wrong with you, Maxx? You're never around anymore. I can't ever get you on the phone. You don't come and get me for dinner on Fridays anymore. I had that huge test in biology last week, and you haven't even asked about it. And David is being an even bigger douche than normal. He keeps yelling about how you were supposed to bring this month's money two weeks ago. You promised me you'd make this right, Maxx. You freaking promised!" Landon's voice rose, and I knew he was upset. My brain registered the fact that this should bother me, that I loved my brother and he was my responsibility.

Shit. He *was* my responsibility. I had obligations.

My chest tightened, and I felt panic struggling against the drugs in my system.

I clenched my fist and dug the heel of my hand into my eye socket. I couldn't breathe.

What the hell was my problem? Why was I doing this shit?

But I needed it, so fucking badly. I was tired. I was exhausted. I didn't want to be relied on because I couldn't be anything anyone needed, particularly my sixteen-year-old brother.

"Maxx?" Landon's voice came through the phone. He sounded worried. He should be worried. I was losing my shit.

"Maxx?" he said again.

"I'll be over tomorrow. Tell David I'll bring him the money then. I'll take you to get some new clothes too, all right?" I said finally, after I was able to focus again.

I heard Landon sigh in relief. "Awesome. I'll tell him. See you then," he said, and I hung up the phone and closed my eyes.

The television flickered against my eyelids, and I wasn't nearly high enough to deal with this crap.

I pulled the baggie out of my pocket.

Just one more and it would be better.

That's all it ever took.

Just. One. More.

◆

I had passed out again and slept off most of my high. When I woke up, it was dark out and I was finally hungry. I got up off the couch and made my way into the kitchen. I opened the refrigerator, but there was nothing inside but a bottle of milk that had expired a week ago. Damn, when was the last time I had been to the grocery store?

My stomach rumbled, and I searched the cabinets, finally finding a box of stale crackers. I ate a handful and made my way to the bathroom. Having food in my stomach made me feel a little better, but I was still sluggish and sick.

I thought about the baggie of pills sitting on the coffee table— drugs I'm supposed to be selling or I'll have to answer for it later.

I had to get it together. I had somewhere I needed to be.

I needed to shower and then get my ass over to campus for the support group. It was time to be the other Maxx—confident Maxx, the Maxx others listened to.

I liked that Maxx. He's the one I wished I could be all the time.

The one who was untouchable. I got off on being respected and wanted. I knew the way people looked at me, and I fucking loved it. In the group, at the club, I was a guy that mattered. I was a guy with power and control. I was a guy who knew what he wanted and took it.

The person I was in this apartment when I was alone disgusted me. His insecurity, his self-doubt, his guilt and shame were repulsive. I hated him. I wished I would never have to be him again. But he was always there, waiting to take me down.

In the harsh light of sobriety, he was the pathetic man who looked back at me in the mirror. He was everything I didn't want to be. He was the sum of all of my failures. It's what defined him.

That's not the person I wanted anyone to see, let alone the woman I was becoming dangerously consumed by.

Aubrey.

She made it so easy to pretend that all of those other versions of Maxx didn't exist, that I was just one person, with just one life, that I wasn't hiding a million secrets. I was just a guy who liked a girl who just maybe liked me back.

Being with her, touching her, kissing her, had the power to undo everything. I felt her unraveling me every time we were together. She had a way of making me forget. She was an escape more dangerous than any fucking drug.

I had an addictive personality, and I craved, I desired, I *needed*. Her.

Knowing I'd see her tonight made me move a little faster. I stopped obsessing about the pills on the coffee table, and all I could see, all I could think about, was her long blond hair and the way her lips had tasted.

When I had been with her at the movie theater, I never wanted to leave. I wanted to disappear inside her forever.

But I couldn't handle disappointing her. I was already a failure in every other part of my life. Failing Aubrey had seemed like the worst thing I could do. Despite how drawn I was to her and how easy it would be to fall into normal with her, I couldn't let myself indulge in it.

That wasn't the life I was living.

It wasn't the life I deserved.

So I had left her.

And I had gone straight to the other woman in my life, the one who would never let me go. She was a jealous bitch, and when I was with Aubrey I didn't give her the attention she required.

Addiction was messy. It was consuming.

Addiction whispered in your ear, telling you that she's the only one. She's all you need.

It was easy to not think about Aubrey when I was high.

If addiction was consuming, so was lust. And desire.

Being with Aubrey had the potential to eradicate that other Maxx completely.

But I couldn't let him go. I needed him.

And I was scared that the day would come when I would need Aubrey just as badly.

It would be a fight to the death.

And it was a fight that I didn't think I could win.

chapter
fifteen

aubrey

Maxx was late for support group. I felt his eyes on me as he took his seat, but I refused to look his way. Every time I thought of him, all I could see was last weekend at Compulsion. Him selling drugs. Him taking drugs. Him allowing some slutty chick to rub up against him. Why is it that *that* seemed like the biggest betrayal? I was so stupid.

He is bad news. I had chanted that mantra in my head a thousand times a day since I'd made my unfortunate discovery. I tried really hard not to obsess about how easy it was for me to believe the lies he sold me. Even as I swore I wouldn't fall for his act, that's exactly what I had done.

I wasn't sure if I was more disappointed with Maxx and his inability to be honest and forthright, or with my own gullibility for thinking that, somehow, *I* was the lucky girl who got to see the broken boy beneath the hard exterior. I felt angry and hurt, and I wasn't sure how to cope with it. For someone who had spent a long time bottling up every emotion, feeling something so intensely was crippling.

The image of him hawking his drugs was intricately intertwined with the memory of kissing him. And touching him. And sharing secrets with him that I purposefully had kept deeply buried.

Damn him!

I spoke very little in group, sticking to the agreement I'd made with Dr. Lowell. However, that didn't stop the rest of the group members from watching me like I was going to flip out again at any moment. Most of them seemed almost excited by the possibility.

I made notes and did my best to wear my professional, no-nonsense face. I listened when people were talking, nodding as if their one-word answers were the most profound statements I had ever heard.

Maxx did not get my attention, even though I knew he wanted it. He was his normal charismatic, energy-sucking self. But I wouldn't allow myself to respond to him in any way, not even when he made a rather pointed remark meant for me alone.

"Would anyone like to share something positive from their week?" Kristie asked as a way to start off the group. Of course, no one jumped in to answer. Big surprise.

And, of course, it was Maxx who volunteered first.

"I'd like to share something." Maxx's deep voice seemed to re-verberate in my ears. I kept my eyes firmly on my notebook, making manic little doodles in an attempt to zone him out.

"Great, Maxx," Kristie encouraged, sounding excited as she always did when Maxx took over. And that's what he did. He con-trolled the flow of the discussion. He moved and maneuvered things to fit his purpose.

I had started to overlook his glaringly self-centered agenda when I felt I had a chance at finding something more beneath his narcissistic surface. But that was before I knew exactly who he was.

"I had a date last weekend, with the most amazing and beautiful girl I have ever met," Maxx began, and I felt myself flush. Shit, shit, shit! If anyone found out who that particular girl was, I wouldn't be walking away with a halfhearted warning. I'd have my ass kicked out of the counseling program faster than I could say *poor boundaries.*

"Really? That sounds great," Kristie enthused. Twyla, the sorority girl who sat beside me, made an angry grunt under her breath.

Her friend Lisa leaned over and whispered. "You waited too long, T," she teased. I peeked over at the girls, who both seemed less than thrilled by the news of Maxx's fantastic date.

"We'll see," Twyla whispered back, smirking. I worked hard to rein in the urge to go bitch on her ass. The words *He's mine* blossomed on my lips, and I pinched my mouth closed so I wouldn't snarl them in some sort of animalistic impulse to stake my claim.

A claim I didn't have, nor wanted to have.

I'll just keep telling myself that over and over again, and then just maybe I'll believe it.

"Yeah, we went to see a movie. Kind of lame, I know, but there's something about this girl . . . we have this connection that I've never felt before," he said softly.

I refused to look at him, though I knew he wanted me to. My heart constricted in my chest, and while a part of me did a happy dance, another part of me wanted to scream at him.

His words were nothing more than lip service, and the girlie, giggly part of me was overrun by a self-righteous anger.

I gritted my teeth and doodled more furiously in my notebook.

"That sounds very promising, Maxx. I'm happy you had such a positive experience," Kristie said enthusiastically.

I decided to chance a glance at him. He wasn't looking at me, for once. His attention was on Kristie, and everyone else's was on him. So I took the time to study him, looking for the insincerity that I had convinced myself was there.

But his face was as open and genuine as I had ever seen it. A lump lodged firmly in my throat, and I felt my eyes burn. How could he know what those words meant to me, how much I wanted them to be true?

I looked away before he caught me staring. The rest of the session passed, and I barely registered anything or anyone. I didn't rise to the bait when Evan made a nasty comment about "interfering, self-righteous" people. Nor did I bat an eye when Maxx invariably contradicted him.

I was too focused on my internal struggle over Maxx freaking Demelo. Was he the guy who had looked at me with hope in his eyes? Or was he the man who lorded over a nightclub while he passed out poison? Both were equally frightening.

After support group was over, I helped Kristie clean up and put the chairs away. Clearly, my lack of engagement during group hadn't gone unnoticed. As soon as we were alone, Kristie made it a point to mention it.

"Aubrey, I don't want you to feel scared to speak in group now. You are my co-facilitator; I need you to be involved. There just has to be a boundary between you and them. You have to learn what's okay to say and what should be kept silent. It's a process. That's why you're here," Kristie said, parroting Dr. Lowell's words as we packed up the cups and put them back in the plastic sleeves.

"I guess I just need to find that balance," I admitted, not sure what exactly she wanted me to say.

"You know, this isn't for everyone," Kristie said after a beat. I looked at her in shock, her words cutting me to the quick. It was becoming painfully obvious that I wasn't winning any points with her. I knew she questioned my motivations for being a counselor. I could tell she was beginning to think I didn't have the innate professionalism to manage my personal feelings and keep them separate.

And as more time had gone by, and the more interaction I had with Maxx, I knew, deep down, that Kristie's fears were well founded. I was crossing the line. I was being inappropriate. My feelings for Maxx were beginning to cloud everything.

But that didn't mean I was ready to call it a day. I would fight for the life I wanted with everything I had—even if that meant a hefty dose of denial, denial, denial.

"What do you mean?" I asked hoarsely, trying to keep my voice even, but my emotions were a runaway freight train, and I couldn't stop my lip from quivering as I tried to control my burgeoning tears.

Kristie put her hand on my shoulder in what felt like a condescending gesture. "I just mean that this is a tough field. Not everyone can hack it," she explained and gave me a smile that was too placating to be genuine.

I had thought Kristie was a nice and competent counselor. Competent she may have been, but she was also a tad on the judgmental side. And it was obvious she was being very judgmental about me.

I didn't bother to respond. I grabbed my things, put on my coat, and with a mumbled good night, I left.

"Hey." I started at the sound of the deep voice. Maxx was leaning against the wall, hands in his pockets, a gray beanie pulled down over his hair. My stomach flipped at the sight of him, but my brain wasn't so easily swayed.

I gave him a curt nod and continued walking down the hallway, my shoes clacking against the tile loudly.

"Aubrey, wait," Maxx called out, but I didn't slow down. Maxx was a bomb about to go off. He had destroyed the part of me that thought, however briefly, about throwing caution to the winds. He was a liar. He was a fake. And he was the one person capable of ruining my entire life.

"I've got to get going. I'll talk to you later," I called over my shoulder, picking up my pace. I heard his footsteps speed up, and then his hand was wrapped around my arm, bringing me to a stop.

He pulled me down a dark corridor, his body blocking my exit. Seeing him like this in the shadows, I again felt like such an idiot for not recognizing him sooner.

"Why won't you talk to me?" he demanded, sounding hurt by my dismissal. The guy was a pro. He could play emotions like they were the real deal. Too bad I had no idea whether what he was showing me was sincere.

"What's there to say?" I asked tiredly, trying to push my way past him. Maxx moved to the side, his hands still locked around my upper arms, our chests brushing against each other. Maxx was quite a bit taller than me. It would be so easy to wrap my arms around him and lean in, nestling my head underneath his chin.

My body remembered all too well how it felt to touch him. It yelled at me to stop being so stubborn and to give in. But I wouldn't—not now that I knew the truth.

"I think we have a lot to say to each other. I want to spend more time with you, Aubrey. Please," he pleaded, his voice low and coaxing. His voice was like a sedative. It would be so easy to fall for whatever line he gave me.

I shook my head and tried to take a step back, but Maxx held me firm, not letting me move. "Let me go, Maxx," I said firmly, struggling against his grip.

"Why are you acting like this? I thought last Saturday meant something. It did to me," he murmured, loosening his hands and then dropping them from my arms. His chin dropped, and damned if he couldn't pull off heartbroken with the best of them.

I snorted, causing him to look up at me in surprise. I rolled my eyes and smirked, even as my heart thudded in my chest. "You're good, I'll give you that," I bit out coldly.

Something in Maxx's eyes shattered, then shut down, and he turned away as if he couldn't bear to look at me. "Wow, that hurt," he said quietly, pulling his beanie off and running a hand through his hair.

"If I thought anything you said was the truth, then maybe I'd believe that," I retorted.

Maxx lifted his face, his brows knitted together. "What's that supposed to mean?" he asked, beginning to sound frustrated.

I rolled my eyes again and attempted to back away, but Maxx wasn't having it. He grabbed hold of me again. "Stop moving away from me. I thought you and I had the beginnings of something. What changed? Is it because I left you at the movie theater? Because I get that was a dick move. I just had somewhere I needed to be . . ."

"Like Compulsion?" I asked, cutting him off. Maxx's face instantly went blank.

He affected such a convincing neutral expression that if I hadn't seen him with my own eyes at the club, I would have believed him to be innocent when he asked, "What are you talking about?"

I leaned in and dropped my voice to a whisper, even though we were completely alone in the darkened hallway. "I saw you there. After you left me standing outside the movies. You were at Compulsion, and you weren't selling Girl Scout cookies," I told him, raising my eyebrows, feeling my anger simmer to the surface again.

This time it was Maxx who took a step back. He let go of me as if I had burned him. He folded his hat into his pocket before burying his fingers into his hair and gripping his scalp. "I don't understand what you're saying," he denied, though it was obvious my statement had him panicking.

What a pair we were—both denying everything even when faced with the truth.

I laughed humorlessly. "I was there, Maxx. I saw you selling those tiny little pills that people couldn't get enough of. I also saw you take those same pills, and I know they weren't Tylenol," I accused, crossing my arms over my chest. "I followed you around for a while. I saw it all," I admitted and watched as a multitude of expressions crossed Maxx's face.

Surprise. Anger. Indignation. And then something seemed to break inside of him. He covered his face with his hands and sank down to the floor.

My mouth gaped open, and I didn't quite know what to do. I was not expecting this reaction. I anticipated the denial, a witty comeback about how I was imagining things, or even an arrogant confession. Maybe I even expected an apology. But what I hadn't counted on was Maxx falling apart.

I was horrified with myself that I had led him to this. Where had my sensitivity gone? Where was the woman who wanted to help people? And wasn't Maxx, sitting there, looking lost, a person who needed my support?

I was acting like a scorned girlfriend instead of the counselor I was learning to be. Maxx's addiction had a strong hold on him; that was obvious. But it wasn't the using that bothered me, though that was bad enough.

It was the selling. Pushing that nasty stuff on other people. Sure, he wasn't standing on a street corner selling drugs wrapped in bubblegum wrappers to schoolkids, but in my mind he was taking advantage of people at their most vulnerable, people like my sister.

That's what made me sick.

But mostly, I was pissed because I had started to see the man he was underneath. And it was so much more, so much *better* than the guy who sold drugs to a bunch of strung-out college kids. I took a step toward him, then another, until I was standing over him. He wouldn't look up at me. I didn't know if it was because of shame or guilt, or that he just didn't want me to see exactly what he was. But I already had.

I kneeled down in front of him. "You come into support group every week giving the same sob story. You need *saving*," I said harshly, losing all filter over my thoughts, my emotions taking over. "Who are you trying to fool? Kristie? The other group members? Me?" I asked. "Or maybe yourself. Because you can't like the person you see in the mirror. You can't enjoy selling drugs to support a habit that will ultimately kill you. Wake up, Maxx!" I said, my voice rising.

Maxx's head shot up. "You don't know who I am, Aubrey! You have no fucking clue!" His face was flushed, and his eyes flashed. I had never seen Maxx so worked up, and it was intimidating.

But I wouldn't back down. "Oh, stop it. So you think because you have it rough, that gives you the right to sell that shit? To take everyone down with you? You lie each and every time you come here! You're not trying to get better! You're not looking to get clean! Just be honest with yourself and everyone else," I yelled.

Maxx leaned forward, getting within an inch of my face. "If that's what you really think, if that's who you believe I am, then why the hell are you still here?" he demanded, his face darkening.

I swallowed and got to my feet, putting space between us. But Maxx was on the offensive now.

"You are so fucking naïve, Aubrey. So egocentric. You think you can stand there and pass your fucking judgments. I know that you don't *get* it. That you feel *betrayed*," he bit out. "What you don't understand is that at least when I'm being someone else, when I'm that messed-up guy at the club, then I don't have to be *me*!" he barked.

"And what's so horrible about being Maxx Demelo?" I asked, wanting him to be honest, just for a moment. I was looking for that breakthrough so he could see what was at the root of all of this.

"Because I'm a fucking failure!" he screamed. He scrubbed his hands down over his face and then balled up his fist and hit the wall with a force that made me yelp.

Tears slipped down his face, and he hit the wall again. He covered his face with his arms and yelled, the cry muffled by his sweater. I could feel myself softening toward him; that twinge that only he could give me was starting to replace the anger. I looked around, relieved that we were still alone.

Maxx dropped his hands and stared at me with eyes that were haunted and utterly lost. "I'm a failure," he whispered. "And anyone who expects me to be otherwise will only be disappointed." He looked at me sharply, and his meaning was clear.

Don't expect more from me than this.

"It's nice to feel wanted. To have people need me for something that I can actually give them. I like knowing I can take a pill and none of this matters. I don't feel the guilt. I don't feel the weight of all this *shit*," Maxx growled, pulling at his shirt above his heart.

He narrowed his eyes at me. "So don't talk to me about what you think I should be doing or not doing. Because you don't know a fucking thing about me."

I was at a total loss about what to say. I was no longer standing there as Aubrey, future counselor. I was Aubrey, a young girl trying to save a sad boy I had, against my better judgment, come to care about.

"I can't save myself, Aubrey. I know that. I'm a lost fucking cause." He was so angry. He stalked toward me, grabbing hold of my face, and froze me with the strength of his glare. I couldn't tell if he was pissed at me or himself. Most likely it was a little bit of both.

He shocked me by slamming his mouth to mine with such bruising force that I tasted blood. He pulled away just as suddenly as he had kissed me. He was wild and out of control. He was totally impulsive and unreadable. I wasn't sure what he would do next.

He continued to hold my face tightly between his hands. "I

want you, Aubrey," he said in clear, succinct words. His fingers dug into my skin, and I tried not to wince.

Maxx held me tightly, as if he were worried I'd run away. A conflicting, rational part of me was still contemplating doing just that. I knew better than to get mixed up in whatever Maxx was. He was hands-off in every possible way. But that didn't change the charge I felt around him—or how the destructive, broken man called out to the woman who wanted nothing more than to fix him, to save him, to make his world right again.

"Don't leave me," he whispered, his words making me shiver.

I covered his hands, which held my face, with mine and stared up into eyes that pleaded with me to stay. "You scare me," I told him honestly.

He leaned down and rested his forehead against mine. He took deep, raspy breaths. "I scare myself," he said. I reached up and put my arms around his neck as he dropped his hands to my hips. We breathed in each other, our eyes closing shut, letting the truth of our words hang in the air between us.

"You have to stop, Maxx. You're on probation. If you get caught, you'll go to jail," I reasoned. Maxx nodded, his nose brushing against mine.

"I know. I can't be that guy anymore. But he's hard to let go of. I'm not sure I can do it by myself."

"You're destroying yourself. That stuff killed my sister. It could kill you too," I went on. He didn't deny anything I was saying. He didn't get defensive. He didn't tell me to mind my own business.

He only nodded.

"I need you," he said so softly I barely heard him.

And just like that, he reeled me in. It was almost too easy. But he *needed* me. And I lived for being needed. It was an addiction just as powerful as his. And it had the potential to be just as destructive. I just didn't know yet how much.

"I have to kiss you again. Please," he begged. I was surprised he was asking for my permission, given the way he had attacked my mouth just minutes before. But he seemed to want my consent. It was as though he was letting me know that if I did, this time it would be different. Things between us would change, and there would be no going back.

Maxx opened his eyes, the blue a silent appeal for me to give in. I was powerless against him. I tried to remember the reasons I had for keeping my distance, but with him so close, pleading in that sad, desperate way of his, I couldn't do anything but comply.

I yanked him closer and went up on my tiptoes to reach him. Our lips collided, and his arms came up around me, pressing my body firmly against his. He pushed me back against the wall as his mouth devoured mine. My tongue tangled with his, and my hands gripped his hair, pulling just enough to cause pain.

He groaned into my mouth, and we became frantic. Maxx lifted me up, his hands cupping my ass, and I wrapped my legs around his waist. He rocked his pelvis into me, and I could feel his hardness beneath the layers of his clothing.

Maxx tore his mouth away and started to kiss his way down the column of my throat. I arched into his touch, wanting everything he gave. He moved his hand from my ass to the front of my jacket. He yanked at the zipper, pushing it open. Then he pulled my sweater down, stretching out the neck in his quest for bare skin.

And just as before, I let myself experience the insane feelings Maxx unleashed inside of me, feelings that only he could elicit.

He molded his fingers to my breast, kneading and rubbing. I moaned loudly in the empty corridor, and the sound echoed around us and seemed to drive him on. He shoved my bra away from my aching flesh, his fingers making that first tentative touch. He seemed unsure, but the more I writhed against him, the more confident his movements became, and he took my hard nub between his thumb and forefinger, rubbing it just firmly enough to stoke the fire deep in my belly. I felt the sensation between my legs, and I thrust against him rhythmically, trying to find my release.

"So beautiful," he murmured, before bending his head down to suck my nipple into his mouth.

"Christ," I let out in a rush, my head falling back and hitting the concrete wall behind me. His teeth scraped my hot skin, nibbling and tasting. His tongue swirled around my nipple as his other hand moved to the front of my jeans. Now that he was no longer supporting my weight, my feet hit the floor, and I found that I could barely stand, my knees were shaking so badly.

I wasn't even thinking about where we were or who could see us. All my lust-soaked brain could compute was the way his hand slipped inside my open jeans and ran along the seam of my soaked panties.

Maxx kissed my breast one more time before pulling back to look down at me. Our eyes locked as he slowly pushed aside my underwear to touch my throbbing center. I was a quivering mess. My breasts, still exposed, rose up and down in quick succession as I tried to get control of my breathing.

My lips were aching and swollen. I wanted him to kiss me again, but he didn't. He continued to watch me as he rubbed me slowly and purposefully, the tip of his finger just teasing my opening and then venturing up to press my clit.

"Oh my god," I groaned as he finally slid a finger inside ever so slowly, as though he were savoring the feel of me. I closed my eyes, the sensation almost too much to handle. Maxx ran his other hand through my hair, gripping the back of my head as he started to move his finger in and out of my body. The motion at first was slow and languid, but then the rhythm changed and he pushed in as far as I could take him.

"Look at me, Aubrey," he demanded, his husky voice cracking as he slipped a second finger inside me.

I opened my eyes to look at him and almost shut them again at the naked longing I saw on his face. He was so intense it was painful to look at.

His thumb rubbed my clit as his fingers curved inside me, touching the spot that instantly made me come. I bit down on the scream that threatened to fly out of my mouth.

And then a door slammed at the end of the hallway, and I thought my heart had stopped beating. I shoved Maxx away from me, and he stumbled back in bewilderment.

"Aubrey," he began, his voice hoarse, but I held my hand up to stop him, vehemently shaking my head, hoping like hell he'd keep his mouth shut. I attempted to pull the zipper on my jeans up, but it seemed to be stuck. I hurriedly closed my jacket and pulled it down, covering the evidence of what we had been doing.

Maxx's hair looked exactly like my fingers had been combing through it. His lips were red and swollen, his blue eyes almost black with desire. He looked sexy as hell, and my hormone-laden body wanted him so badly that I was tempted to toss common sense aside in favor of throwing him on the ground and finishing what we had started.

Luckily, common sense prevailed, and I turned away, giving him my back in an attempt to gain some physical and emotional distance. But not before I saw the raw pain on his face at my perceived rejection.

I knew how my actions would be taken. But he didn't understand the ramifications of being caught like this. What it would mean for him and his probation. Or me and my future career. Both would be dead in the water. I had allowed my desire for him to cloud my judgment . . . again. But even now, with my nerves on edge, my fear of being discovered tainting the air, I couldn't stop wanting him.

I wasn't sure I would ever stop.

I wiped my mouth with the back of my hand and reached

down to pick up my bag, willing my heart to calm down, just as Kristie came down the hallway.

She didn't realize Maxx and I were there until she was almost upon us. She startled in surprise to find us practically hidden in the darkened corner of the corridor. Stopping, she frowned and looked from Maxx to me. My hands were clammy, and I hoped like hell I didn't look as guilty as I felt.

"Is everything all right?" she asked Maxx, but she was looking at me. Was that suspicion in her eyes? Did she feel the sexual tension in the air as tangibly as I did?

Maxx cleared his throat. "I was having a hard time after group, Kristie. Aubrey was processing with me before I headed home," he lied effortlessly. He was so convincing.

Kristie's face relaxed. "That's great. I'm glad to see that you're using appropriate coping skills, Maxx," she enthused, patting him on the shoulder.

Words of agreement stuck in my throat. Some of us weren't equipped to deceive as well as others, I supposed. Maxx's eyes met mine, and all signs of his earlier vulnerability were gone. So was the passion. It was like it had never existed at all.

And again I was left wondering which was real.

"I'd better go, it's late," I said when I was finally able to speak. Kristie was still talking to Maxx about resources in the community he could utilize if he needed to. She was completely oblivious to the sexual energy that radiated between us.

Maxx's face was unreadable, his eyes dark and hooded. My heart and body screamed at me not to leave him. But my head said to run.

While I still could.

chapter
sixteen

There was a lot to be said for keeping busy. If you kept yourself focused on trivial things, the more serious stuff began to seem less important.

School and studying did that for me. It put everything in its place and kept me moving forward. There wasn't room in my world for sexy blue eyes and passionate pleas that made me forget everything.

All of this agonizing made me desperately wish that I had someone I could talk to. Someone I could confide in about these conflicting feelings that were wreaking havoc inside me. I missed Renee so much more during this emotional turmoil. I longed for the days when I would have been able to tell her everything.

I felt lonely, even when I was with other people. No one could know the truth of my heart, that it was slowly and surely being given to someone who I was terrified would destroy it.

"I'm thinking of asking Charlotte out," Brooks announced out of nowhere in the middle of our marathon cramming session. I looked up from my notes in surprise. Brooks never really talked to me about girls. It's not as though I would have a problem having this kind of conversation. We were friends. It's what friends did. But we weren't the sort to sit around giggling about dates.

"Who's Charlotte?" I asked, reaching for the bag of pretzels on the coffee table. I was relenting on my "no food in the living room" edict for the time being. Studying required sustenance. And I didn't want to read my notes while sitting in a cramped position in the chairs around the kitchen table.

Brooks stretched out his legs, his feet brushing against mine. I never shied away from touching him. He was my friend. So why did it all feel so . . . strange . . . all of a sudden? Ever since Maxx's show of territorial possession before support group that night, I had felt a shift in my relationship with Brooks, one I couldn't explain or understand, and one that my good friend seemed reluctant to talk about.

"She's in my senior symposium. Blond hair, tits for miles," he explained, looking at me as he took a drink of his beer. He watched me closely. Too closely. What the hell was his problem?

I gave him my most encouraging smile. "Sounds great. I say go for it, buddy," I said, tossing him a pack of Oreos. Brooks caught it in midair.

"Yeah? Well, maybe you could meet her. Tell me what you think," he suggested, still watching me. It was disconcerting, and I didn't like it one bit.

"It's not like you need my approval, Brooks. You like her, ask her out. It's as simple as that," I stated matter-of-factly, hoping to make this conversation less stilted.

Brooks slowly opened the package of cookies and pulled one out. "Well, I'd like to know what you think of her. There's nothing wrong in that, right?" he challenged. What did he want me to say? Why did I get the feeling I wasn't giving him what he wanted to hear?

I shrugged, tightening my ponytail, which had come loose. "Sure, if you want. I'm around all weekend."

Brooks munched on his cookie and seemed to be mulling something over. "Why don't you ever go out, Aubrey? I hope I didn't ruin you for guys forever?" he teased, and I was relieved that he seemed less serious.

I snorted. "Yeah, after you I've started to rethink lesbianism," I joked. The skin around Brooks's eyes tightened, but his lips curved into a smile.

"Now, that would be such a waste," he replied, and I chuckled a bit nervously.

"What's up with that guy from your group? The one in the hall? He seemed kind of weird." And here it was. The topic we had both been avoiding.

I cleared my throat and trained my eyes back on my notebook. "He's just a guy. I don't really know him," I lied. My mind instantly flashed to him and me in the hallway last week. His hand stretching and pressing the most intimate parts of me, the look of wild desire on his face.

I crossed my legs in an effort to stave off the sudden warmth between my thighs at the memory of the foolish, extremely stupid, but mind-blowing things we had done. If I closed my eyes and concentrated, I could still feel his fingers moving inside me, his breath on my neck as I came.

Fuck.

"Really? Because the way he was looking at you was downright . . . proprietary," Brooks said lightly, though I didn't miss the underlying accusation or the flash of potent jealousy.

Fuck. Fuck. Fuck.

"What are you saying?" I asked defensively, not appreciating his insinuation, no matter how truthful it was.

Brooks's eyes shifted away, and he looked ashamed. "Nothing, Aubrey. Forget I brought it up."

I thought about pressing him. I wanted to hear his suspicions, and just maybe I could share what had happened with him. I hated the secrets. I hated the guilt. And most of all I hated the bone-crushing *want* that dampened my will. I needed to talk to someone about this dangerous place I found myself in with Maxx. I worried that I was entirely too close to making the worst mistake of my life.

I must have been experiencing early senility if I thought for one second that Brooks was the person I could confide in. Whatever our friendship was, seeing his face, pinched and unhappy, I knew that confessing my sins where Maxx Demelo was concerned was not wise.

The silence in the room was deafening. Neither of us said anything. You could taste our discomfort, and it was bitter on the tongue.

Brooks let out a noisy sigh. "Aubrey . . . ," he began, but before he could finish his thought, the front door flew open and Renee hurried inside.

Brooks met my eyes in astonishment as we both took in the sight of my roommate. She was huddled in her black leather coat, her red hair matted down the sides of her face. Her head was bowed low as she shuffled into the apartment.

Her shoulders quivered, and I knew she was crying. She didn't say a word as she dropped her purse on the floor and practically ran back to her room. Her door clicked softly as she disappeared behind it.

"What was that about?" Brooks asked, our earlier weirdness gone. I looked down the hallway, knowing that something was most definitely wrong.

"I don't know, but I think I'd better go back there and find out," I told him, getting to my feet, thankful, in a completely selfish way, for Renee's timely entrance, whatever the reason.

Brooks grunted in frustration. "Don't put on the white knight getup just yet. It's probably just another slice of the Devon Keeton bullshit pie. You don't need to get bogged down in that crap," he warned me, and for the first time his dismissal of Renee irked me.

"Well, she's still my friend, and I should check on her. I think you'd better head on out," I said shortly, letting him know by my tone that I didn't appreciate his comment.

Brooks frowned, knowing he'd pissed me off. "Look, Aubrey, I didn't mean anything by what I said. But this is the same ol' rodeo, you know. Don't start thinking you can make this all better for her, because there are some people who don't want the help. The sooner you realize that, the better off you'll be," he said angrily. I had to wonder whether it was Renee we were really talking about.

"Wow, that's so compassionate of you, Brooks. Glad to see you're going into the right profession," I bit out. Brooks's jaw clenched.

"Okay, well, I'll just talk to you later," he said, gathering his stuff. I instantly felt shitty. Whatever had been going on between us earlier didn't change the fact that he had my best interests at heart. Always.

"Wait, Brooks . . . ," I started, but he shook his head.

"Go see what's up. I'll talk to you later," he said, not giving me the chance to make right whatever had gone wrong between us. It felt horrible.

So I did nothing. I let him leave and then turned down the hallway to see about Renee.

I knocked on her door. When she didn't answer, I went on inside. She was curled up in a ball in the center of her bed. She hadn't taken her shoes or her coat off. She looked as though she was trying to disappear inside herself.

In my mind, I flashed back to another time and another person who had been curled up as though she would fall apart if she let go.

I thought about the time I had gone into Jayme's room a few months before she had died. Our rooms were beside each other, and I had heard her coming in hours after her curfew. Mom and Dad had been out of their minds with worry when she hadn't come home at eleven like she was supposed to. They had been after me to go find her, but I had a huge research paper due on Monday, and I had convinced them she was just acting out in a stereotypical teenage rebellion. I had been the good girl. Jayme had been the wild one from the time she started her period.

How easy it had been to dismiss her behavior as *typical*.

I had planned to go into her room and chew her out for worrying our parents. I had been puffed up on self-righteous moral superiority. I didn't make Mom and Dad worry. I did what I was supposed to. Jayme should have been trying to emulate me. She could have learned a thing or two from her straitlaced older sister.

What I had found when I walked into her room had made all my platitudes die on my lips. My fifteen-year-old little sister had been curled up on her bed, much like Renee was now. Her entire body had been shaking with the force of her sobs.

When I had sat down beside her, she had crawled over and put her head in my lap, her long blond hair, so much like mine, tangled in her face. She had been shaking uncontrollably, her cheeks pale and her eyes bloodshot from crying, and from, as I would learn later, the drugs she had taken that night.

I had asked her what was wrong, but she didn't answer. She had only clung to me and cried and cried and cried. And I didn't question her. I hadn't demanded answers. I had only held her until she finally fell asleep. I had then carefully removed her shoes and tucked her under the covers, wiping mascara from her face with my thumb.

The next morning Jayme had acted like nothing had happened. She never mentioned why she had been crying. And I had never asked. I had gotten sidetracked by finishing my paper, and my parents had again threatened to ground her, though they had never followed through. She was their baby. The favorite. They forgave and excused her each and every time.

And then two months later Jayme was dead. And I had never

asked her what made her fall apart that night. Why she had needed me to hold her so badly. And I hated myself every single day for not finding out. Because maybe I could have helped her.

I made the vow then to never make that mistake again.

I went immediately to Renee's side and got up on the bed next to her. I pulled my friend into my arms. She resisted at first, holding herself away from me, but I wouldn't give up.

And finally, she gave in and fell into me, her head in my lap just as Jayme's had been all those years ago. I found myself repeating actions that were oh so familiar: smoothing her hair away from her face and just letting her cry.

This time, though, I didn't stay quiet. I wouldn't pretend that my friend wasn't detonating right in front of me.

"What happened, Renee?" I asked quietly once she had calmed down. Renee rolled her head away from me, covering her face with her thick red hair.

"Please, just tell me what's wrong," I pleaded gently. Renee slowly sat up, her head bowed, hair obscuring her face.

"I've been so stupid," she whispered, her voice breaking as she began to cry again. She pushed her hair back and looked at me almost defiantly. I bit back on a gasp as I looked at her.

Her skin was red and splotchy from crying, but that wasn't what made me recoil in horror. It was the sight of the purple bruise ringing her eye. Her upper lip was busted and crusted over from where it had been cut open.

I covered my mouth with my hand, trying not to scream in rage at the sight of her pretty but now horribly mangled face. There was no need for me to ask who had done this. The savage grief in her eyes was all the confirmation I needed.

I was going to kill Devon Keeton.

"What happened?" I ground out.

Renee shook her head, her hair falling back to conceal her from view. "He was just so angry. I've never seen him so angry. I didn't do *anything*!" Her voice rose in hysteria, and I reached out to hug her. She relented easily this time, not fighting my efforts to comfort her.

I rubbed her back slowly, gently. "I know you didn't," I murmured, all the while plotting a hundred ways to turn her shithead boyfriend into a paraplegic.

"Why do I let him do this to me?" she sobbed into my shoulder, and I couldn't stop myself from pulling back.

"Has he done this before, Renee?" I asked, my words clipped and hard.

Renee's eyes darted in panic as she read the violence in my tone. "Just once," she said in a rush, and I closed my eyes at the flush of my anger. God, I was really going to hurt that bastard.

I hugged her again and let her cry herself out. And when she finally settled down, we lay on her bed the way we used to do, staring at the ceiling while we talked about the things that were the hardest for us to say.

I let Renee do most of the talking, and I listened. And most of all I was *there*. I couldn't help but think of Jayme and how many times I had turned my back because I had other things going on. I had my life—school, a few friends, homework, and college prep. I had my world. And I had been blind to my baby sister, who had just started high school, floundering as she tried to find her place in the big sea of teenage acceptance.

Renee told me about Devon's anger and jealousy, the way he had lost it in the bar when she talked to a guy from her Econ class, punching him in the face and dragging Renee outside by her arm.

Devon had taken her around the side of the building, where it was dark, and screamed at her, accusing her of cheating. He had smacked her in the face and then punched her in the chest. He told her she was ugly and stupid, that she was lucky he even looked at her, that no one would ever want her but him. And then, ignoring her staunch denials, he had threatened to do worse if she ever looked at that guy again. He had laughed when she begged him to stop. He had become furious at her tears.

"I can't see him ever again, Aubrey. Ever!" she cried, covering her battered face with her hands.

I held her as she began crying again, my mind distracted from my own rage by memories of my sister.

◆

"He loves me, Bre. He doesn't want me to even look at another guy. He says he'll die without me," Jayme said, desperate for me to understand.

I had walked in earlier to find my sister and her boyfriend, Blake Fields, in her room fighting. He had her against the wall, his hands pinning her as he yelled in her face. Jayme had been crying, and Blake had only yelled louder. The idiot was lucky it was me and not my dad who walked in while he had his hands on Jayme like that.

I had interrupted and told Blake to leave. When he looked at me, I knew instantly he was on something. His eyes were glazed and bloodshot. I barely noticed that my sister's eyes were also glassy and unfocused. How had I been so blind?

He hadn't put up a fight. He hadn't bothered to say another word to Jayme before he left.

My sister had been furious, her behavior erratic. She had told me emphatically to mind my own business. And I had already started to dismiss the earlier scene as teenage drama, something that I had thankfully opted out of as I grew up.

I waved my hand in dismissal, rolling my eyes at her dramatics. "That's ridiculous, Jay. What kind of nut job says something like that?" I asked, condescension dripping in my voice. What did Jayme know about love? She had just turned fifteen. She was a freshman in high school. She didn't know the first thing about real relationships.

This guy she was dating, Blake, was a junior and had just trans-ferred from another school. I hadn't taken a whole lot of notice of him. He was nondescript in that trying-too-hard-to-be-unique-but-I'm-actually-just-like-everyone-else way. He subscribed to the emo thing a little too religiously. With the black, side-swept hair that fell over his eyes and the skinny jeans and guy-liner, he looked like he had stepped out of the pages of Teen Angst Magazine.

I had seen the people this Blake dude had chosen to hang out with, and it was common knowledge they were the druggie crowd. But they seemed more interested in playing the part of hardcore fringies than actually walking the walk. I didn't take them seri-ously.

Nobody did.

Jayme crossed her arms over her barely there chest and glow-ered at me. She was only just now starting to develop boobs. She had been complaining for years about how flat she was and her ass being like a piece of cardboard. My sister was a late bloomer, and she was fixated on it. Her lack of curves seemed to hit her self-confidence hard. She would say she was ugly, that no boy would ever look at her. So when Blake showed interest, she had been sucked in by his compliments and attention.

She didn't see him for what he really was—a pathetic bully who preyed on girls like Jayme. And she didn't see herself as Mom, Dad, and I did—as a beautiful young girl with her life ahead of her.

She only saw what Blake wanted her to see. She became the girl he wanted. She followed in his dark footsteps eagerly.

"I love him, Aubrey. We're going to be together forever," she said with the passion of inexperience. I rolled my eyes again, not believ-ing her in the slightest.

"What's the rush, Jay? Why can't you just date around and see who you like? Why does it have to be all blood and guts?" I asked, wishing she'd shut up already so I could get back to my reading. I had a mountain of homework to get through, and the longer she

stood there talking about her stupid boyfriend, the less time I had to get it finished.

"He's the only one who gets me. You just don't understand," she wailed, stomping out of my room and slamming the door. I honestly didn't understand her constant need to rush things, why she had to jump in with both feet before she had even learned to swim. But Jayme had always been in a hurry to live. In a hurry to love.

In a hurry to die.

I hadn't seen the way Jayme had slowly started to change every tiny thing about herself. Eventually she stopped talking to me altogether. We became strangers living in the same house as she pulled further and further away from her family and into the world of Blake Fields and his friends.

And I hadn't noticed she had gone anywhere until it was too late.

Until the night Jayme Marie Duncan never came home.

Until she was found asphyxiated on her own vomit in an alleyway outside a notorious druggie hangout, overdosed on drugs I pretended she didn't take.

I noticed then. When it didn't matter anymore.

◆

"Just take it one day at a time," I whispered to Renee as she started to drift off to sleep, exhausted from crying her soul out.

Renee nodded, her eyes drooping shut. "Thanks, Aubrey," she muttered before falling asleep.

I lay there a long time afterward, staring at the ceiling and thinking about all the ways my life had gone wrong, and how now, when I thought I was finally getting it right, I was poised to screw up all over again.

I wondered what Maxx was doing. Was he out up to something nefarious and shady? Was he stoned out of his mind, overdosing in a gutter?

I thought about him selling drugs to those people in the club, and how smug and entitled he had seemed. I hated that man.

But then my mind switched gears, and I thought about Maxx telling me about his brother and worrying that he'd fail him. I couldn't ignore the pull of him and the way he made me want to help him. How easy it would be to fall down the hole with him.

I rolled onto my side and stared at the bruised face of my friend. She and Jayme were all mixed up in my head. And they were twisted with the memory of Maxx when I confronted him about Compulsion. The way he had split himself open when he realized I had seen him. He had been devastated.

He had broken.

And goddamn it, I wanted to gather up all those pieces and put them in my pocket. I wanted to make sure he could put himself back together again.

I would never be able to turn away from Renee.

And I couldn't turn my back on Maxx.

chapter
seventeen

I had been up most of the night with Renee while she alternated between crying and screaming into her pillow. Her phone had started ringing around midnight. At first, we ignored Devon's persistent calling. But around the fifth time, I turned it off, and Renee didn't argue. Her red, swollen face had been set with grim acceptance.

When I got up the next morning for my lecture, I checked on Renee and was glad to see she was still asleep. I had convinced her to skip classes today and rest. She was worried about running into Devon and embarrassed for people to see her face.

I assured her the bruises could be covered up and the swelling in her lip would be gone by morning. Renee had seemed mollified by that and had finally stopped fretting about it.

After her initial admission about Devon's abusive behavior, she had stopped talking about him altogether. She stated she wasn't ready to hash out everything, and I begrudgingly backed off.

Stepping out into the crisp air, I took a deep breath, letting it fill my lungs. I wrapped my coat a little tighter around myself and started walking down the street. I noticed a bunch of painters heading around the back of my apartment building.

I overheard several of them grumbling about "fucking kids and their stupid graffiti." Curious, I followed them and came to a quick stop. I tilted my head back and took in the gigantic painting along the back wall of my building.

"What the hell?" I mumbled to myself. It was amazing. Absolutely stunning. But it was also extremely disturbing.

Because someone had painted a beautiful sky raining . . . *blood*? There were two people, a man and a woman, each with bright blond hair, holding hands, walking along what looked like a macabre version of the yellow brick road into a stormy sea while the gorgeous clouds above their heads unleashed a torrent of blood around them.

The ground was a mass of interconnected *X*s, giving away the artist's identity. I should have known. The style was one of a kind.

But why had the mysterious street artist painted *this* on the back of my building? Because again, this clearly had nothing to do with Compulsion. This was a painting meant to say something else entirely.

The painters were putting up their ladders and opening up tins of white paint. They were getting ready to cover it up. And the thought of them destroying it made me feel panicky inside.

"Wait!" I called out just as a middle-aged man with a potbelly and a bald spot swiped his paintbrush over the blissfully happy couple in the picture. He looked over his shoulder at me in irritation.

"Do you have to paint over it?" I asked, realizing how ridiculous I sounded.

"Look, lady, the landlord hired us to fix this shit. Not our call. So why don't you let us get to work," another guy said, dipping his brush in the pot and bringing it up to the wall, smearing white over the vivid colors.

I didn't say another word. I backed up and watched as the painters slowly eradicated the beauty X had clearly spent a lot of time creating. I felt as though I were witnessing a murder. It seemed a crime to undo something so beautiful as though it had never been there at all.

Feeling strangely sad, I forced myself to walk away, unable to stand there another moment while the men so callously covered up the picture.

Normally, I would meet Brooks for a coffee before my first class on Friday morning. But he hadn't responded to my multiple texts. So I made my way to the coffee shop just off campus by myself.

I hated feeling lonely, and this morning I felt it acutely. I hated feeling that there was something going on with Brooks and that he was purposefully keeping his distance. I was going to have to confront it head-on eventually, but with everything that was happening right now, I selfishly didn't feel like expending the energy the situation required.

I got my caramel latte and a muffin and sat down at my usual table by the window. I pulled out my notes in case there was a pop quiz and took a small sip of my hot beverage. I spent some time people-watching.

It was then that I saw a familiar set of broad shoulders and a head covered in a gray beanie coming into the coffee shop.

I thought hard about slinking down in my seat to avoid being seen, but then I thought better of it. Why should I hide? There was nothing wrong with him seeing me, even if just the sight of him caused me to flush to the tip of my toes at the memory of our encounter in the hallway.

As if sensing me there, Maxx's eyes met mine. I raised my hand in a halfhearted wave, wiggling my fingers.

He smiled that smile that lit up his face.

He is so coming over here, I thought to myself as I waited on pins and needles for him to get his coffee and make the trek to my table.

"Is this seat taken?" he asked, his eyes dancing at our inside joke. But unlike the time he had asked that question in the library, I offered the chair—not without hesitation, but with a lot less of it. I couldn't help that I still had misgivings about being seen with him. My lips tingled and my heart smacked against my rib cage, but I felt an undeniable wariness.

Maxx pulled off his beanie and dropped it on the table. He picked up his mug and blew off the steam before taking a sip. I sat there, staring at him, my tongue tied up in knots.

"So, thanks for leaving me stuck with Kristie, by the way," he joked, taking another sip.

I laughed nervously, cutting my muffin up into small pieces. "Yeah, sorry," I muttered.

"Sorry? I'll leave you to talk about 'solidifying your support systems' for an hour and see how you feel." He was being relaxed, teasing me with a twinkle in his eyes.

He looked happy.

It took me aback for a moment. I wasn't used to seeing him this way. I had grown accustomed to the tortured brokenness hidden behind an overly confident exterior.

But today Maxx was laid-back, as though by acting casual, he was trying to make me forget how he had fallen apart. How he had shown me a side of himself that was scared and unguarded.

This time when I laughed, it was real. "That sucks. She *can* go on a bit," I conceded.

"You think?" Maxx scoffed, reaching across the table and snatching a handful of my crumbled muffin.

"What is it with you and stealing my food?" I asked as he chewed.

"It just tastes better when it's yours." And there it was. The sexual innuendo I had been waiting for. But it didn't irritate me the way it once would have. Instead, it set my skin on fire.

Two girls passed by our table, and I noticed the way they glanced down at Maxx and flashed their best flirty eyes at him. But his eyes never left my face.

I squirmed at being the center of his intense attention. "So, about Tuesday," he began.

I held up my hand, stopping him. "Do we really need to talk about it?" I asked, mildly mortified to be talking about our encounter in the middle of a coffee shop, where anyone could hear us.

Maxx's face darkened, but then it cleared. "I was just wondering when we could do it again?" he asked, and I jumped at the touch of his hand, reaching under the table to touch my thigh.

"Um . . . ," I stuttered.

His fingers traced lazy circles on my jeans, inching slowly upward. I covered his hand with my own, pinning his palm to my leg.

Maxx chuckled and removed his hand. "Well, I'm game whenever you are," he stated breezily, as though talking about the weather. I got the impression that my lack of response had hurt him. And being the person that he was, he covered up the hurt with unaffected seductiveness.

Before I could respond, Maxx got to his feet and pulled his beanie on. His hand briefly touched my shoulder before he gave me a smile and left. The entire exchange had lasted five minutes, and I was left confused and annoyingly turned on.

That boy was bad for the heart.

✦

I wanted to see him again. Even though I knew I should ignore the urge, I didn't. Who was this girl with such a lack of impulse control?

I pulled my car into the parking lot of the abandoned department store where Compulsion was happening tonight. My legs wanted to run toward the booming music, but my nerves held me back.

Now that I was here, I wasn't entirely sure what I had been thinking. The Maxx Demelo who belonged here wasn't necessarily the man who belonged with me. He scared me. He terrified me. He fascinated me.

I tucked my cell phone into my purse and looped it around my arm, securing it close to my body. My heart thudded in my chest almost in time to the bass, which I could hear bleeding into the night air.

I headed toward the line of people who waited just as they waited every single time Compulsion came alive—wanting their chance, hoping they were enough to be given it.

I approached the front of the line and watched as more and more people were turned away. I never understood why some were allowed inside and others were told to leave. There didn't seem to be any rationale to it. Randy, the scary doorman, always seemed to relish the tiny bit of power he had as the gatekeeper.

But after that first night, when Brooks and I had been turned away, I hadn't had a problem. I know I would never look the part. I still didn't fit in with the people who came here, but it was as though I had a magic pass that I wasn't aware of.

Again, I stood in front of Randy and the other bouncer. He gave me a cursory once-over and then held out his hand for my money, which I put in his outstretched palm. He grabbed my wrist and roughly turned my hand over, pressing the stamp on my skin.

Just as I moved toward the door, I noticed another group being told to go home. The girls, dressed to the nines and way more clubbed-out than I was, started throwing a fit.

One girl wearing a dress cut so low that her boobs were in serious danger of flopping out pointed at me while curling her lip. "Why does that bitch get in and we don't? She's a total waste!"

I flushed in embarrassment at the unwanted attention I was receiving from the people in line. They all seemed to be judging me. And clearly I was coming up short. Pardon me if I didn't dress for the goth and metal crowd.

Randy gave the girl and her friends a nasty glare. "Get the fuck out of here. Some people belong here. Others don't. *You* don't," he growled. I knew the look he was giving them. It was the same one Brooks and I had received that first night. I shuddered, almost feeling sorry for them.

Boobs girl huffed and puffed in indignation, pushing her obviously surgically enhanced chest out for optimum effect before stomping off with her friends in tow.

The other bouncer, whom I had never bothered to pay attention to before, turned to look at me. I was still lingering just in front of the door, and he gave me a pointed look to get moving.

"The fun's in there, baby. Though I'm sure I can find something for you to do out here if you're interested." He grinned and then licked his lips. He was cute in a rough-and-tumble sort of way, with a buzzed head and a face full of metal. I knew, without a doubt, that I couldn't handle this guy's idea of *fun*.

I hurried inside the club, followed by the bouncer's laughter. The club was as it always was—dark and oppressive, but with an energy that couldn't be described.

I wanted to dance. I wanted to get wild. It's what people came here for. How easy it was to forget who I was and why I was there. The appeal of it was never lost on me. But I wanted to find Maxx. I had to talk to him here, on his turf.

I started pushing through the crowd, trying to search the shadowed faces for the one I recognized. It was like looking for a needle in a haystack. I remembered how hard it had been for me to find Renee, and I had been able to do so only with Maxx's help.

Maybe if I stood by the bar, he'd find me. He always had before. I ordered a beer and leaned against the wall, watching, waiting. I was nervous. Actually, I was a mess. I hadn't thought this search-and-rescue mission through.

What did I hope to accomplish by tracking Maxx down at the club? I really had some unrealistic, no-way-in-hell ideas when it came to Maxx Demelo. I could admit that I was already succumbing to the daydream in which I was *that* girl, the one he would change for.

But I blamed him entirely for making me feel that way. Because he made me think that I *was* that girl, that he was counting on me to pull him out of the chaos he found himself in.

I didn't even begin to understand exactly what demons he was facing, the struggles he dealt with on a daily basis. I was given glimpses of a tortured soul barely treading water.

Or was that my overly dramatic mind looking for the person who needed me to save him?

Who fucking knew? Maxx had screwed royally with my head.

I wasn't even trying to be subtle as I perused the room, seeking him out. I inadvertently caught the attention of a few less than savory individuals, but I straightened my spine and quickly turned away, hoping the obvious rebuff would be enough to dissuade them.

And then I found the person I *didn't* want to find.

Brooks was out on the dance floor with a girl I vaguely recognized. Brooks was a really bad dancer, as in shouldn't-be-out-in-public-with-moves-like-that bad. But this was a place where style and technique didn't matter, which was lucky for him, because he looked like he was in the throes of a full-on body spasm.

The girl he was with was cute in an unassuming way. She had blond hair that was very similar to my shade and style. She had clearly done a Google search on club attire and had gone for the most extreme example she could find. She was decked out in head-to-toe black leather. She had a flickering glow stick between her teeth, and she bobbed her head around in awkward, jerky movements. She belonged here about as much as I did.

I ducked behind a couple dry-humping beside me, hoping to hide from a possible Brooks run-in. That was absolutely the last thing I needed.

I was so busy making sure that Brooks and Catwoman didn't see me that I didn't realize *he* was behind me until I felt a hand curl around my waist.

"What are you doing here?" Maxx asked, his breath fanning across my cheek. My heart thumped in an uneven tempo in my chest, and I had the urge to lean back into his touch. The heat of him seared my back, and every nerve and synapse in my body tingled in anticipation.

I turned around to face him and realized immediately what a bad idea coming to Compulsion was.

Maxx was stoned out of his mind. I couldn't see his eyes beneath the bill of his cap, but he swayed on his feet, and his lips stretched in an exaggerated smile that was anything but normal.

"Is Red Riding Hood looking for her wolf?" He smirked, and his words were deadened and slurred. The bartender brought him a drink, though I hadn't seen Maxx order one. He picked up his cocktail and took a long swig.

I shook my head, infuriated with myself for being so naïve. And I was angry as hell with him for being wasted. This wasn't a man looking for any sort of salvation. This was a man enjoying his trip to hell.

Maxx's fingers dug into the exposed skin at the hem of my shirt. I could feel the pinch of his nails as he squeezed. He leaned in close to me, until we were breathing each other's air.

"I'll eat you up, little girl. Would you like that?" His voice was rough and hoarse, as though he had been screaming. He was being strange. I had yet to meet this particular incarnation of

Maxx's personality—the strung-out egomaniac. And I could tell right away that I didn't like this version one bit.

I pulled out of his grasp and took a step backward, knocking into a girl behind me.

"Watch it," she yelled, elbowing me in the back. I stumbled forward, and Maxx caught me. My chest collided with his, and for just a moment I felt him relax. His arms came around me, and he cradled me to his body. The seconds passed as we stood there with Maxx wrapped around me.

He leaned down to press his cheek into my hair, and I felt something drain out of him. His shoulders drooped and his knees bent, but his arms tightened their grip. "Aubrey," he murmured into my ear, and I could feel the cold tip of his nose glide along the side of my neck.

Maxx sagged into me, and I staggered under his weight. "Maxx!" I yelled into his ear, trying to pull back. He stumbled toward the wall and leaned heavily against it. I reached up and yanked his cap off his head. His pupils were so dilated that his eyes looked black. Even in the horrible lighting, I could see there was something very, very wrong with him.

"What did you take?" I raised my voice loud enough for him to hear me over the pounding bass. Maxx rolled his head from side to side but didn't answer.

I grabbed the front of his T-shirt and gave him a shake. "Maxx, goddamn it, what the hell did you take?" I screamed into his face. He pushed my hands away with fumbling fingers.

"Back the fuck off, Aubrey. Just leave," he growled. After a few minutes, he pushed himself off the wall and lumbered through the crowd. I took off after him, shoving and nudging people as I followed him. People attempted to stop him, and he was less than civil in brushing them off.

I was scared. Maxx's movements were sluggish and unsteady. He seemed to have a hard time staying upright. There was no way I would let him out of my sight.

Maxx headed toward the back of the old department store and had almost made it to the exit when a guy who looked a lot like scary Randy, the doorman, grabbed him. He sported a green Mohawk and some sort of tattoo beneath his right eye. He was big and beefy, looking as though he ate kittens for breakfast. And he appeared to be extremely pissed off. At Maxx.

Shit. What the hell was going on?

Mr. Mohawk yanked Maxx through a door at the back of the room. I hurried to follow him, not thinking beyond the fact that some scary-looking dude had taken him. Any thoughts about my own safety had flown out the window.

I pushed open the door, which led to a dimly lit hallway. I could see a sign that read "Staff Only" beside a door that was starting to close.

I practically ran so I could catch it before it shut. I used my shoulder to shove it open and slipped inside. I could hear shouting. I followed the noise to a fire exit. The thump, thump, thump of the music made it impossible to hear the words being screamed. People were angry, bordering on homicidal.

I opened the door a crack and peered outside. It was so dark, I could barely see a thing. But a car had been pulled around the back of the building, and its headlights shone on a scene I wish I could forget.

Maxx stumbled precariously on his feet while two guys, including serial-killer-Mohawk-man, beat the ever-living shit out of him. I shoved my fist into my mouth to smother the scream that bubbled up in my throat.

Maxx wasn't moving. He didn't put up a fight. He just lay there as their feet connected with his body over and over again. Mr. Mohawk lifted Maxx up and screamed something into his face. I couldn't hear a thing over the reverb.

Mohawk punched Maxx in the jaw and sent him sprawling. Maxx moaned in the dirt, and even in the darkness I could see an excessive amount of blood. I felt sick. I thought I'd throw up all over myself. I didn't know what to do. I was terrified.

But I couldn't just stand there and watch Maxx be beaten to death. I pushed the door open harder than I meant to. It slammed against the wall, sounding like a gunshot in the night.

The two guys pounding Maxx turned to me in unison, and my blood froze in my veins. These were some cold-assed dudes. Crap, they were going to kill me! I was a witness to their assault; they'd have to get rid of me!

I looked down at Maxx on the ground. He wasn't moving, and I could see that his eyes were closed. I needed to see if he was still breathing.

Tentatively, I walked down the metal staircase off the fire exit and held my hands up. "I just want to see if he's all right," I said placidly. I spoke slowly and carefully, making sure to keep my movements steady.

The man standing beside the guy with the Mohawk cocked his head and regarded me. I couldn't get a read on his face. He was older, maybe in his forties. He had thick, dark hair that could only be dyed. It was too thick and too black to be real. He wasn't remotely attractive. In fact, he was the scariest thing I had ever seen.

"You know him?" he asked, jerking his head toward Maxx's prostrate form. His voice was gruff, like that of someone who had been smoking a pack of Marlboros a day since he was twelve. It was the voice of nightmares and bogeymen. Why the hell was he hurting Maxx?

What messed-up, *Sopranos*-like shit was Maxx involved in?

"He's a friend," I said, enunciating my words. I was such a moron. Why didn't I just hand my life over in a pretty little box for him to stomp on? I could almost imagine him thinking of all the ways he could dispose of my body. I wasn't very big, so it probably wouldn't be too hard.

Scary Marlboro Man snorted. "You need to do a better job

choosing your friends, sweetheart." He laughed as though Maxx weren't bleeding out at his feet.

"Is he okay?" I couldn't help asking. I stopped moving, not wanting to get too close to either of the men.

Mohawk shrugged his shoulders. "Fuck if I know," he mumbled, lighting a cigarette and leaning against the car.

Marlboro Man put his hands in his jacket pockets and looked me up and down. It was extremely unpleasant. I felt violated by his gaze, as though he were raping me with his eyes.

"If you're his friend, get him out of here. And tell the piece of shit to get his priorities in order. That was his last warning." He got into the car with Mohawk, and they backed up the car and left.

Without the headlights, everything went pitch-black. I could barely see Maxx, who still hadn't moved. I fell to my knees beside his body and shook him.

"Maxx! Are you okay?" I yelled, as though he were deaf. Maxx moaned and rolled his head. I shook him again. "Maxx! Wake up!" I was feeling mildly hysterical. This was not how I had pictured my evening going.

The movie inside my head had me finding Maxx and talking him into leaving with me. We would go back to my apartment, where we would have this amazing heart-to-heart. Maxx would break down and share all of his deep, dark secrets. He would tell me I was the only one who could help him. I would vow to stand by his side. And then we would have the most fantastic sex of our lives.

I was absolutely delusional.

Maxx finally came to. He said something, but it didn't make much sense. It was garbled and confused. After a while, I was able to get him to his feet. Not only was Maxx fucked-up, but he was severely injured, making walking an arduous task. I was thinking a trip to the ER was in our future.

I draped his arm around my shoulders and propped him as he struggled to get to his feet. "I can't carry you. You're going to have to walk to my car," I said firmly.

"Okay," was all Maxx said. I wasn't sure he realized who I was or what had happened, he was so out of it. Instead of going back through the club, we slowly made our way around the side of the old department store toward the front.

It took what felt like an hour to get him there. I had to stop frequently to rest. Maxx was a big guy, and he wasn't helping me much. I had to yell at him periodically when he seemed in danger of passing out.

Once we were in the light of the streetlamps, I was able to get a good look at him. One side of his face was bruised and swollen. His left eye was already shut. His upper lip was split and bleeding. His white T-shirt was stained with dirt and blood. He looked like hell.

"Maxx!" someone yelled. I didn't stop, afraid that whoever it was would want to finish what the two goons had started.

"Stop!" the voice called out. I heard footsteps running behind me and turned to see one of the doormen. Not biker Randy, but the other one, the one who had flirted with me when I had arrived.

"Fuck, what happened to him?" he asked, immediately taking Maxx's other arm to help me.

"Thanks," I said sincerely. We were moving much faster now that I had assistance. The doorman wasn't overly big, but he was strong. He handled Maxx easily.

"He was beat up," I explained, not sure why I was telling this guy anything, only that he was helping, and right now that was enough for me.

"Gash," the doorman said under his breath.

"Huh?" I asked, my foot catching on a rock, making me stumble. Maxx moaned as I collided into him.

"I've got him, you can drop his arm," the doorman told me. I did as he said, relieved to be free of Maxx's deadweight. Maxx looked horrible. He was trying to open his eyes, but he wasn't having much luck. The left one was swollen shut, and the right one was glazed and unfocused.

"Can you get him home?" the doorman asked me. I nodded, wrapping my arms around my middle. I was shaking uncontrollably, and my heart was hammering in my chest. I was close to having a meltdown.

"Where's your car?" the doorman asked me, sounding frustrated and out of breath from carrying Maxx's six-foot frame.

I pointed to the far back corner of the parking lot. The doorman hoisted Maxx up so he could get a better grip and jerked his head impatiently. "Lead the way. Our boy isn't light," he complained through gritted teeth.

"What's your name?" I asked him, tired of referring to him as "the doorman" in my head.

"Marco," he answered tersely.

"I'm Aubrey," I told him, though he hadn't asked for my name. I felt that given our current circumstances, we should be on a first-name basis.

Marco didn't make any comment, and I got the impression he honestly didn't care who I was.

I hurried ahead of him to my car and unlocked the passenger-side door. Marco heaved Maxx onto the seat and positioned his head so that it was upright. Maxx's eyes squinted open. I wasn't sure he knew who either Marco or I was. He mumbled something unintelligible under his breath and then closed his eyes again.

Marco muttered a string of curses and then started patting Maxx's pockets.

"What are you doing?" I asked, not liking how rough he was being. Maxx was clearly about to lose any semblance of consciousness. Marco ignored me and pulled out a plastic baggie from Maxx's jean pocket.

He held it up to the light, his mouth tightening and his eyes narrowed. It was empty. Marco dropped the bag on the floor of my car, and I had to stop myself from demanding that he pick it up and dispose of it properly. My OCD didn't recognize the crazy situation I found myself in. All it saw was trash where it shouldn't be.

Marco pulled a wad of cash out of the same pocket and started counting it.

"Wait a minute! Isn't that Maxx's?" I asked in dismay. Was Marco going to rob Maxx right in front of me? What kind of fucked-up world was I in?

Marco lifted his lip contemptuously and didn't bother to look at me as he said, "You need to mind your own business, pretty girl."

He finished counting the money and made a noise of disgust before shoving it back into Maxx's pocket. He gripped Maxx's chin and then slapped him across the face. I let out a pathetic squeak of alarm.

"Stop it! He's hurt!" I protested, my horror giving me a voice when I should have probably stayed quiet.

Marco ignored me and smacked Maxx again. Maxx tried to open his eyes and weakly pushed Marco's hand from his face. "Leave me the fuck alone," he slurred. At least that's what I thought he said. The words were strung together, and I couldn't be entirely sure. But given the way Maxx was struggling against Marco's grip, I could only assume that was the general message.

Marco gave Maxx a hard shake. "Where's the rest of the money?" he growled.

Maxx pressed himself into the back of the seat and shook his head limply. "That's all of it, man," he argued.

Marco dropped his hand from Maxx's chin and looked down at him with repugnance. "Fucking junkie," he bit out, spitting in the dirt by my car.

I slowly got into the driver's seat, not making any sudden movements. Maxx's breathing was shallow, and he seemed to be struggling to stay awake. He moaned and brought a hand up to his bruised face. "Ouch," he said softly.

"Should I take him to a hospital?" I asked dumbly. I didn't know what the hell I was supposed to do.

Marco curled his lip again. "Don't bother. He'll live. Though he might wish he hadn't if Gash decides to finish what he started."

I had no idea who Gash was. I didn't know what Marco was referring to. I just wanted to get Maxx out of there. I was feeling the beginning of a panic attack rearing its ugly head.

Marco slammed the passenger door, and I rolled the window down. "Just get him home. And tell him I'll be by to see him in a few days and that he'd better have one hell of an excuse," Marco said, his words an obvious threat.

I didn't bother to comment. I didn't know what was going on, and right now finding out wasn't my priority. Getting Maxx out of here in one piece was.

"I don't even know where he lives," I said.

"He lives in an apartment above the Quikki Mart downtown. Now get him out of here. Now!" Marco barked, and I jumped.

"Okay, okay. Keep your pants on," I muttered loud enough for Marco to hear me. He cocked his eyebrow at my statement, and his lips twitched. If I hadn't known any better, I might have thought he found me amusing. Marco banged the top of my car before walking off.

"Aubrey! Is everything okay?"

Oh god, just kill me now!

Brooks and Catwoman were standing beside my driver's-side door. Brooks peered down at me, his brows furrowed. His eyes flicked to Maxx, whose lucidity was questionable.

Brooks's mouth pinched into a line, and his eyes narrowed. "What are you doing with *him*?" he spat out, clearly unhappy with finding me with Maxx.

Unfortunately for my friend, I didn't have time for long-winded explanations. "I'm just giving him a lift," I said, shrugging a shoulder and hoping my excuse would be good enough.

Maxx chose that moment to regain consciousness. He rolled his head and looked at me. He seemed confused by my being there, but then his battered face brightened as his glazed eye focused on me.

"Aubrey, baby," he slurred, reaching over to drop his hand on my thigh.

"What the fuck, Aubrey? Isn't this the guy in your group?" Brooks asked, pointedly looking at Maxx's fingers, which were tracing a line up underneath my skirt. Shit.

I tossed Maxx's hand away, and he chuckled before closing his one good eye again.

"It's nothing," I started to say, but Brooks held up his hand.

"Do you understand what could happen here? He's fucking loaded, Aubrey! And you're hanging out with him like this? Inappropriate doesn't even begin to cover what *this* is," Brooks preached, climbing up on that big ol' soapbox he was becoming so fond of.

I wasn't in the mood for a lecture, least of all from Brooks. Maxx started making a gurgling sound in his throat, and I was worried he was going to puke in my car.

"We can talk later. I've got to go," I said in a rush. Brooks leaned into my open window and dropped his voice to a whisper. He was invading my personal space in a way I had never seen him do before. I leaned away, feeling uncomfortable. I looked over his shoulder at his date, who seemed less than thrilled by Brooks's blatant show of male ownership of me. I didn't blame her, and in truth I felt bad for her.

"Don't do this, Aubrey. This is illogical and irrational and completely beneath you. Don't be so stupid," he said firmly, as if calling me stupid was the magic ticket to get me to listen.

He clearly didn't know me at all.

"Get away from my car if you don't want me to drive over your foot," I warned, revving my engine to emphasize my point.

Brooks glared at me. I glared at him. We were in the middle of a silent showdown. Then Maxx started to heave, and Brooks jerked back from my car. I leaned over Maxx and opened the passenger-side door, pushing his head outside just in time for him to throw up.

"Ew, Brooks. Let's go," the girl in the catsuit whined. I didn't bother to look at either of them. I was too busy rubbing Maxx's back as he puked his guts out.

I could tell Brooks was hesitating, but finally both he and leather girl walked away. Maxx finally finished mangling his guts and flopped back in the seat with a moan. I got out of the car and hurried around to close his door, careful to avoid the puddle of vomit in the gravel. I felt bile rising in my throat but was able to keep it down.

I watched Maxx for a few minutes, making sure he wasn't going to be sick again. When I was sure he wasn't, I got back in the car and pulled out of the parking lot.

The drive to Maxx's apartment was silent except for the occasional groan. I pulled up in front of the Quikki Mart and hurried around to get Maxx. He was coming around somewhat and was able to get out of the car on his own.

"Come on, Maxx. Let's get you inside," I cajoled, trying to get him to move, but he was so stoned that stumbling was the best he could do.

"I just want to sit outside for a bit," he said, weaving his way around the side of the convenience store and sitting down heavily on a wooden staircase. He leaned his head against the side of the building and brought his hand up to his face. He didn't seem to be feeling a lot of pain, which was good, because he'd be feeling it in the morning.

"My face feels weird. What's wrong with it?" he asked, still slurring. I pulled his hand away from his wounds and held it between mine.

"You just need to get inside and get some sleep," I said soothingly, hoping to convince him to get to his feet. Maxx shook his head.

"I want to stay out here. Just for a while," he said and then squeezed my hand. "Don't tell Landon. Mom and Dad would be so pissed at me. I keep screwing everything up. Don't tell Landon," he mumbled, his chin hitting his chest.

I gave him a shake, afraid he'd pass out. It was freezing, and I was starting to shiver uncontrollably. Maxx's skin that wasn't discolored and bleeding was ashen and pale. I needed to get him inside.

"Come on, up on your feet," I urged, pulling on his arm. Maxx complained, but after a few moments I was able to get him to climb the stairs to his door.

"Where are your keys?" I asked. Maxx smirked, though it was a sad impersonation of his normal arrogant smile. The split lip made it hard to take his attempts at seductiveness seriously.

"You'll have to get 'em yourself," he garbled. I was glad to know that, even high as a kite, he was still capable of being a jerk.

I rolled my eyes and stuck my hand in his pockets, feeling around for his keys. Maxx chuckled and swayed on his feet, finally using the wall to brace himself. I pulled his key ring out of his back pocket and then went through the process of finding the right one to unlock the door.

After several unsuccessful attempts, I got it open and forced Maxx inside. He was laughing and rambling incoherently. I flipped on the light and deposited him on the threadbare couch that sat in the living room.

Maxx fell onto his side and stayed that way. A cut on his forehead had come open, and he was bleeding onto the fabric beneath his cheek.

"Do you have a first-aid kit?" I asked him. But he was past hearing me, so I started searching for something to clean him up with.

Maxx's apartment was sparse, and what few furnishings he had were old and used. There was a distinct lack of anything personal in his home, and I found that rather sad. It was the space of a man who cared nothing about his surroundings. The neglect and dis-array gave off a quiet sense of despair.

The bathroom was down the hallway, and I was happy to see that at least he kept it clean. I found some Band-Aids and antisep-tic cream in the medicine cabinet.

And then because I couldn't help myself, I opened the only other door in the hallway. I turned on the light and knew right away that this was Maxx's room. The bed was unmade, and there were clothes on the floor. I saw some schoolbooks and an old desktop computer on a table by the window.

I found a clean shirt in his dresser, and then, just because I felt like being a snoop, I started to dig around in the piles of clothing. I found two empty prescription bottles and a ridiculous number of plastic baggies.

Then, in the back of the bottom drawer, I found a folded-up photograph. Pulling it out, I saw that it was a picture of a family. It was one of those generic portrait-gallery shots with the cheesy blue background and awkward posing. A woman with fair, wavy hair sat on a stool in front of a tall man who rested a hand on her shoulder. A young boy with a head full of blond curls stood by the woman's side, and in her lap was a baby, no more than six months old.

I knew without a doubt that these were Maxx's parents. I stud-ied the picture, thinking that maybe this would reveal something about the man who lay passed out in the living room. Maybe I could figure out who he was and why he did the things he did.

I heard a bang from the living room and hurriedly shoved the picture back into the drawer. I gathered the items I had gone searching for and closed the bedroom door behind me.

Maxx was sitting up and rubbing his shin. "You all right?" I asked, sitting down beside him.

"Fucking coffee table," he muttered, turning to me with a wobbly smile on his face. I held up the Band-Aids.

"Let me clean you up," I said. Maxx didn't say anything, simply closed his eyes and let me do what I needed to do. I wiped off the blood and covered the cut with a bandage. I cleaned out the scrapes on his palms, which he must have gotten when he was beaten to the ground.

"Who were those men who beat you up?" I asked, not sure I'd get any sort of answer in the state he was in.

So I was surprised when he answered me. "That was Gash. He runs the club. I guess he's pissed at me," he snorted as though it were a joke.

"I'd say," I mused quietly. When Maxx didn't volunteer any further information, I tried prodding him a little more.

"Why's he pissed at you?"

Maxx gave an exaggerated shrug, his head starting to droop.

"Don't tell Landon," he mumbled again.

"Don't tell him what?" I asked as I finished my task.

Maxx pried his good eye open and turned to look at me. He grabbed my hands and squeezed them so tightly I winced. "About me. Never about me," he whispered.

Maxx shook his head and let out a sob. "They would be so disappointed in me," he cried, gripping his hair in his hands as he became more and more agitated.

I put my hand on his arm. "Who would be disappointed?"

Maxx's chest heaved, his eyes still closed. "They wanted me to be some great doctor. Something special." He shook his head violently. "Look at me!" He grabbed the front of his shirt and pulled at it, ripping the fabric. He was getting really worked up.

Maxx put his hand first in one pocket and then the other. "Where are they?" he asked, getting unsteadily to his feet and digging farther into his pockets.

"Where are what?" I asked, bewildered by the sudden change in his mood.

"I need them!" he yelled, pushing past me and lumbering into the kitchen, where he started taking things out of the cabinets and throwing them on the floor. When he didn't find what he was looking for there, he let out a howl and practically ran down the hallway to his bedroom.

I followed him at a distance. I thought about trying to stop him, but a desire for self-preservation held me back.

He ripped his room apart, dumping clothes on the floor. He gathered the empty baggies and ripped them apart.

"Where are they?" His scream was desperate. He tipped over his bedside table and fell to his knees, looking through the stuff that had fallen out. He picked up a bottle and shook it. It rattled, and the look of euphoria that replaced the hopelessness on his face made me cold. I knew exactly what he had been looking for.

"No, Maxx! You don't need that," I cried, falling down beside him and trying to pry the bottle from his hands. Maxx yanked it away from me and scooted backward on his knees. He popped the top off, and before I could do anything, he dropped the white pill into his mouth.

He crunched it between his teeth. His mouth went slack, and he leaned back against the wall.

"Maxx," I said with bone-weary regret. Maxx looked at me, his normally beautiful lips stretching into a lazy smile that was all too familiar. I used to think that smile was sexy and mysterious. Now it was just sad and pathetic. Now I knew exactly why he smiled that way.

I hated that smile.

I hated how happy he seemed.

I hated how easily he gave in, not even bothering to put up a fight.

This was how he lived his life—from one high to the next, bad choice after bad choice, followed by catastrophic consequences that he cared nothing about, not now anyway.

Maybe in the morning, when he wasn't fucked-up and could possibly think more rationally, he'd care.

I brought my knees up to my chest and leaned my cheek against my leg, exhausted and angry. But I was also resolute.

Maxx licked his lips, his eyes drooping shut. He put a hand through his blond curls and then let his arm fall limply beside him. His head bobbed from side to side as though he was making sure he could still move it.

I found myself watching the rise and fall of his chest, scared that if I stopped looking, even for a moment, it would cease to move, that he would slip away quietly, without me realizing it.

Before I had the chance to fight for him. Because obviously he didn't have the will to fight for himself.

This man wasn't a casual user. He was slowly being eaten alive. It was like watching a car driving full speed toward a brick wall. The sinking feeling of helplessness I remembered all too well made me momentarily immobile.

I would fail him.

I would lose him, just as I had lost Jayme.

I was a fool to think I could make a difference for anybody.

I looked around the trashed room and sighed. I should leave him to this miserable cycle he lived in. I didn't need to be mixed up in all of this. Brooks was right. My being here was inappropriate. The boundaries were already blurred.

And what would it matter anyway?

Maxx reached out and took my hand. "Stay," he whispered. I shook my head. I couldn't stay. Not after everything I'd seen. There was no place for me in his world.

"Please, Aubrey. Stay with me," he pleaded. I turned back to him. His pupils were dilated, and I wasn't sure if it was just the drugs or whether he had a concussion. I should have taken him to the hospital. He may have had broken bones. But I had allowed my good sense to be drowned out by the need to care for him. To do it all *myself*.

As if I had something to prove by making things right, all on my own.

I was scared to leave him in the state he was in. But I was scared to stay, knowing that if I did, that was *it*. I had stepped over that invisible line. And once I had done so, there was no turning back. It would be too late.

I stared down at Maxx, and he looked so young and vulnerable, his face devoid of its characteristic calculation and seductive allure. He seemed . . . innocent.

I wouldn't leave him. I couldn't walk out his door and pretend that this boy didn't matter to me.

Already, he had become something important. Something I should never have allowed him to be. But that didn't change the fact that he *was*.

I opened my mouth to agree to stay, but Maxx's eyes were closed and his mouth drooped open. I found a blanket and draped it over him.

Then I lay down on the bed, wrapping my coat around myself, and watched him while he slept, each rise and fall of his chest binding me to him in a way that frightened me with its totality.

There was no leaving him.

I had made my choice.

I just hoped it was the right one.

chapter
eighteen

My chest felt tight, and my head screamed in agony. Every joint, every limb, ached and burned. It hurt to move. It hurt to breathe. I felt sick to my stomach, and bile rose up in the back of my throat.

I was going to puke.

I tried to lift my head, but even that small movement set off a wave of nausea that quickened the vomit rising up my throat.

I rolled onto my side and retched. And then I retched again. And just for good measure I retched some more.

I moaned, rolling onto my side. I had the sense to know I was on my bedroom floor, though how I had gotten here was a good question. Everything after I had arrived at Compulsion last night was a complete blank.

There were flashes here and there of things I think I'd prefer to forget.

I tried to hoist myself up onto the bed, but instead I started to dry heave. My face and the back of my neck were slick with sweat. The acrid smell of my puke filled my nostrils, and I started to shudder with the need to spew again.

"Jeesh," I heard someone mutter, followed by a pair of cool hands on my upper arms as they pulled me back onto the bed. I recognized the voice, though my fuzzy mind couldn't connect the dots.

I tried to open my eyes but found only one of them was working. Shit, why couldn't I get my fucking eye open?

I started panicking. I slowly patted my face and hissed in pain as my fingers made contact with very raw flesh.

Christ, I was going to be sick again.

"Hold on," the voice urged. There was no holding on to anything. I opened my mouth to throw up, but nothing came up. My stomach was officially empty. But that didn't stop my body from attempting to bring up my stomach lining.

I was shaking uncontrollably, and those cold, soft hands touched my face. I think I moaned at how good it felt. *Don't stop touching me.*

"I'm not going anywhere," the voice soothed. And for the brief second before I passed out again, I felt comforted. And it made the free fall into blackness that much sweeter.

✦

"Fuck," I groaned. I tried to sit up, but my body wouldn't cooperate. My limbs felt weighed down, and the tips of my extremities were on fire. I felt like I was simultaneously boiling alive and freezing to death.

My teeth chattered and my head pounded. My stomach was sore and clenched, ready to expel whatever might be left inside me out onto my bedroom floor.

I thought I was dying.

No, I *knew* I was dying.

I knew this horrible feeling all too well.

I didn't want to die.

I wanted to live.

I wanted to feel good again.

"Please," I begged, not sure anyone was around to hear my pathetic pleas. I vaguely remembered hands and words spoken in my ear before I blacked out. But I didn't give a fucking shit about any of that.

"Give me my fucking pills," I growled, trying to sit up again, though more forcefully this time. My fingers curled into claws as I reached for my bedside table and the bottle I knew I kept there.

"Maxx, lie down. You need to rest," the voice said softly.

The room was dark. I couldn't see who the voice belonged to. I didn't *care* who it belonged to.

"Give me my fucking pills, now!" I screamed. The voice would give me what the fuck I wanted or I would fucking kill it!

I lunged for the drawer, my body not working properly. My arms felt useless, my hands weak and feeble. I slapped at the top of the table, knocking off my lamp, not flinching as glass shattered on the floor.

"Maxx, it's okay," the voice soothed. I was going to kill that voice! I hated that voice! It was keeping me from the only thing that could make me feel better!

"I will stab you in the goddamned throat if you don't give me my fucking pills!" I swore, lunging in the direction of the voice.

"Maxx," the voice cried out, sounding sad.

My body was on fire. My movements made me sick. I leaned over the side of my bed as more stomach acid surged up my throat and out of my mouth, dribbling down my chin.

"Please," I sobbed between full heaves.

The voice didn't say anything. But hands held me as I shook and trembled.

I pushed the hands away. "Please, just give them to me!" I begged, falling onto my side. I tried to bring my knees up to my chest, but I thought I would be snapped in half. I felt as if I were being flayed alive.

"Please!" I screamed. And the voice cooed something in my ear. And the hands rubbed my back. And all I could do was cry and cry and cry. I cried for the thing I needed but the voice wouldn't give me.

And then everything went mercifully black again.

✦

"You need to drink something."

I stirred as the soft voice whispered into my ear. A strong hand gripped the back of my neck, pulling me up. My greedy lips touched the edge of a glass, and cool liquid reached my tongue.

At first my throat convulsed, and my stomach threatened to throw the liquid back up. The glass disappeared while I gasped for breath and tried to control my body's painful revolt.

When I was able to keep from upchucking, the glass was placed at my lips again, and this time I drank more water. My mouth was painfully dry, and my tongue stuck to my lips.

"That's enough for now," the voice murmured as the glass was taken away from me. My mouth gaped like a fish's, desperate for more.

Hands pushed me back down onto the bed, soft fingers caressing my face. I grabbed the hand and held it firmly, the small fingers crushed in my much larger ones.

"Stop it, you're hurting me," the voice gasped, and my eye flew open, still only the one, and I stared up in horror at the beautiful face that hovered over me with a pained expression.

I dropped Aubrey's hand and tried to sit up but found that even that simple action was beyond me. I had zero energy. Moving my head was about all the effort I could expend at the moment. Hell, even blinking was enough to make me want to take a nap.

Everywhere ached and hurt like I had been run over by a Mack truck. My head beat with the constant throb of ten thousand tiny needles burrowing their way into my skull. My stomach felt as though someone had taken it apart, twisted it up, and shoved it back inside my body.

All in all, I felt like a dead man's asshole.

And the last person I wanted to see me like this was Aubrey Duncan.

"What the fuck are you doing here?" I asked harshly, not even attempting to be nice about it. I was way past niceties. The confident guy she was used to seeing was gone. That guy had died a swift and apparently very painful death.

I wasn't sure why Aubrey was there. I sure as hell didn't know how she'd found my apartment. I just knew that I wanted her to leave me to my misery.

If Aubrey was insulted by my less-than-stellar manners, she didn't show it. She went about straightening my blankets and tucking them around me like I was some five-year-old who only needed a kiss and a cuddle to feel better.

"You should try to eat something," she said, getting to her feet. I noticed that her clothes were creased and looked as though she had been wearing them for a while.

Crap, what the hell had happened?

My head was a fuzzy mess. I couldn't remember anything.

Before Aubrey could move away from me, I grabbed her wrist, bringing her up short. "Why are you here?" I asked harshly, wishing I didn't sound like such an ass.

"I couldn't leave you the way you were," she answered simply, giving me a bland look.

I shook my head and instantly regretted it as the needles pierced my head again. "What happened?" I asked, opting to try a different angle.

Aubrey sighed and tugged at her blond ponytail, which was half falling down around her shoulders. She looked tired. And sad? Could that be right?

But she looked fucking gorgeous. She always looked that way. And she needed to leave.

"You need to get out of here," I said, forcing my weak body to sit up. Aubrey looked as though she wanted to push me back down, but she didn't move. She leveled me with an even look.

"I'm not going anywhere," she said shortly.

For the first time, I looked around my room and was startled by the state of it. "What the hell happened in here?" I was asking that a lot.

Aubrey snorted. "You were what happened. You don't remember, do you?" she asked softly, her face wearing an expression that I hated. Pity. And sympathy and every other fucking emotion that was totally and completely useless to me.

I didn't need her pity, or her lectures.

"Seriously, Aubrey, get the fuck out. I don't want you here," I gritted out, swinging my legs around to rest on the floor. The cold air hit my bare legs, and I realized I was wearing only a pair of boxers.

Fuck me, did Aubrey undress me? Normally the thought of Aubrey taking my clothes off would be a full-on cock-hardening fantasy. Not now.

Right now, I was mortified.

"Get me my goddamned pants!" I barked, swaying with the effort to hold myself upright. And yes, I felt like shit for yelling at Aubrey like that. I didn't miss the way she flinched. It was like a knife to the heart. This girl did something to me that made me feel things I wished I didn't.

Guilt, shame, the desperate fucking need to be with her all the time.

But I realized there was good stuff too. She made me feel like a little kid on Christmas morning every time I knew I was going to see her. She filled me with anticipation and something else entirely—a desire to be something better.

And that made me both want to run as fast as I could in the other direction and to hold on to her with everything I had.

Aubrey slowly walked across my destroyed bedroom, leaned down, and picked up my jeans. Deliberately she closed the space between us. My chest felt tight. I was twitchy and weak. Watching her out of one eye was throwing me off-balance. I wanted to back away. I wanted to crouch in the corner and cower in shame. I hated her seeing me at my worst. I never wanted to be anything but my best around her.

But here we were. And there was no escaping the reality of what I knew she saw.

She gripped my pants in her hand and held them out for me to take, her eyes never leaving my face. Normally I would have met her bold stare head-on. I would have taken her challenge and enjoyed it.

This time I looked away, my gaze dropping to the floor to escape her.

I grabbed my jeans and put them on as quickly as my quivering body would allow.

"You'll probably need some help," Aubrey said matter-of-factly, holding up a button-down shirt. Why in the hell would I need help getting dressed?

I yanked the shirt out of her hand, not bothering to respond. But when I lifted my arm to push it through the sleeve, I was bowled over by a sharp pain in my ribs. It wasn't that sort-of-hurts kind of pain. This was a cry-like-a-little-pussy-and-curl-into-a-ball agony.

My hand went up to the right side of my ribs, and the barest touch made me wince and gag. I looked down to see my rib cage covered in a pattern of yellow and green bruising.

"I think you've got some cracked ribs. Now that you're awake, you should probably go to the hospital. Get yourself checked out," Aubrey said. I glanced at her and noticed she hadn't moved any closer to me. She hadn't left, but she was giving me space.

I was both thankful and masochistically hating it.

I gingerly ran my fingers down the length of my battered flesh, and vague memories of Gash and Vin tickled my subconscious. I had the feeling I had gotten myself into some serious trouble.

As much as I wanted Aubrey to leave to spare myself the awkward embarrassment of admitting I needed her to help me, I was stuck. Right now I couldn't do this on my own.

I needed her.

My god, I *really* fucking needed her.

The weight of that thought hit me with a bone-crushing force.

"Can you help me?" I asked begrudgingly. I wouldn't meet her eyes when I conceded defeat. It was too much.

Aubrey didn't say a word, but I felt her, I smelled her, I could practically taste her on my tongue as she stood in front of me, her fingers carefully buttoning up my shirt. Her hair brushed my face as she bent her head down. I couldn't help but lean in, my nose brushing the crown of her head as I breathed her in.

She made sure not to touch my bare skin as she hastily did up the buttons. When she was finished, she gripped me by the arms and pushed me back down on the bed.

"Let me get you something to eat," she said firmly, propping me up against my pillows. I couldn't remember the last time I had been taken care of. Definitely not since my parents had died.

I had still been young when my mother passed away and my dad stopped caring about himself, let alone his two small sons, after she was gone. And then he had died too, and with him the last person responsible for taking care of me at all.

I had forgotten how it felt to be tended to. To be treated gently.

It had been a long time since anyone had done anything for me. I didn't know what to do with the unexpected feelings Aubrey's innocent offer to make me food created inside me. She made me feel cared for. Wanted. The blossoming of emotion in my chest suffocated me with a violent awareness. This woman could change everything.

"I'm not hungry," I lied, trying to swallow the thick lump in my throat.

Aubrey ignored me and left me alone with my out-of-control emotions and aching body, lost in a minefield of feeling that was ready to detonate in the worst way possible.

I had too many questions and zero answers. If the state of my room was any indication, things had gotten ugly. I only hoped it had happened *before* Aubrey had arrived on the scene.

And what the hell was she doing here at all? That was the question I was having the hardest time wrapping my head around.

I reached over to my bedside table, searching for my tried-and-true fix to any problem. I pulled out the drawer and realized that it was empty.

"Shit," I groaned, pulling myself off the bed, ignoring my protesting muscles as I fell to my knees to search for the bottle that was always there.

"Looking for something?"

I sat up so quickly that I felt light-headed. Aubrey put a bowl of soup down on the same bedside table I had been ransacking before squatting down beside me. I sat back on my haunches and put my hands through my hair.

"No, I was just . . ." I didn't have an explanation and fuck it, she didn't need one. This was *my* home. *My* room. *My* business.

Aubrey pulled something out of her pocket and held it up.

"What the hell?" I growled, reaching out with a trembling hand for the bottle she held.

Aubrey got to her feet, still holding my salvation between her fingers without a care for what that small brown bottle meant to me. Right now, it was everything, more than the girl who dangled it in front of me like a fucking carrot.

Was she taunting me? I saw red.

"Give it to me, now!" I demanded, advancing on her. I forgot about how shitty I felt. Adrenaline coursed through my system as I focused on getting the bottle away from her.

Aubrey looked unsure. In fact, she looked scared. I didn't blame her. I could imagine what I looked like stalking toward her, ready to wrench the bottle from her fingers, viciously if necessary. I didn't give a shit if I had to snap each one of those pretty little digits, I'd get what my body needed.

"Now, Aubrey," I whispered, my voice shaking with anger. Aubrey's lips trembled, and I could see she was trying not to cry. I didn't care. There was only one thing I cared about right now.

She held the bottle out to me and hurriedly crossed the room to the door. I snatched it up and shook it. It was deafeningly silent. I ripped the top off and turned it upside down.

Empty.

"Where are they?" I roared. My rage was white-hot. Aubrey was shaking. But she didn't leave the room. She didn't run from me. She faced me on unsteady feet.

"They're all gone, Maxx," she said quietly.

No, I couldn't have heard her right.

"That's not possible," I bit out, throwing the bottle across the room.

Aubrey shook her head, her hair flying around her face. "I swear, they're gone. There's nothing left," she said.

I clenched my fists. I was going to fucking lose it.

And then Aubrey did the strangest thing. She walked back toward me and grabbed my face between her hands.

I tried to wrench myself away from her confining grip. I took hold of her wrists and squeezed them hard enough to crunch bone. Just then, I hated her. I wanted her to hurt the way I hurt.

Yet . . . I wanted *her* . . .

"Maxx, you don't need that stuff," she told me, with such confidence that if I were in my right mind, I would have believed her.

I yanked her hands off my face, still squeezing her wrists. "Don't tell me what the fuck I need!" I yelled.

Then she kissed me. That crazy, delusional girl kissed me.

As if that would make me forget what it was I wanted.

As if she could ever replace what my body craved.

I pulled my mouth back from hers, infuriated. Enraged. She was breathing heavily, her eyes glassy with tears.

"Please, Maxx. Don't do it. Be here. With me," she begged. And then she was kissing me again, and she was telling me "I won't leave you. I won't ever leave you."

And there was something about those words and the feel of her lips on mine that broke through the red haze of my anger, the inconsolable need that plagued me.

She wouldn't leave me.

How could she know how desperate I was to hear that from her? From *anybody*?

And then I was kissing her back. Devouring her as though she were the drugs I hungered for. And for that brief moment she was something even better.

"Don't leave me," I sobbed against her mouth, my teeth bruising her lips as I punished her with my tongue. I meant it with every fiber of my being. I couldn't survive without her. What a terrifying thought that was. But it was the honest-to-god truth. In that split second she had become the most vital thing in my world. She was the thing that could keep me sane. Keep me here. Keep me from diving off the cliff after the drugs my body wanted so badly.

She was the string holding me together. She was the only person to stay by my side even when I hadn't asked her to. I hadn't demanded a thing of her, yet she had given me everything. How could I not latch on to that like a parasite? How could I not try to suck every last drop out of her to keep myself alive?

How could I not begin to live in a fanciful delusion where she would be all that I needed and everything would be okay?

But she wouldn't leave me. Those words held a promise I'd cling to.

The kiss began as the pinnacle of every hateful emotion, every negative, self-loathing thought. It wasn't hearts and flowers and skipping through the sunshine. This was soul-filled angst shit that no one should ever want but delusional people chase after anyway.

But somewhere, somehow, it morphed into something else entirely. Aubrey took control and gentled the kiss. Her lips softened, her tongue an inviting caress. Her fingers curled into my greasy, filthy hair as though she never wanted to touch anything else ever again.

And then I wasn't assaulting her mouth but worshipping it. Loving it. Tasting and enjoying it.

I knew I needed Aubrey. I needed her in the worst way possible. I was selfish and frantic, and I honestly didn't care if I took her to hell with me because she would make the trip the sweetest thing I had ever experienced.

She was mine.

And I'd never let her go.

chapter
nineteen

aubrey

$t$wo days.

That's how long I had spent with Maxx at his apartment.

It was two days since I had driven him home after he had been beaten nearly to death at Compulsion.

It was two days since he had lost his mind as he went through the most intense and agonizing withdrawal I could ever imagine.

Two days, and my life had changed completely.

The shower was running. It was thirty minutes since Maxx had gone into the bathroom to clean up after I had forced him to eat some soup and bread. He had looked a sickly green after swallowing my less-than-palatable attempt at cooking, but he had kept it down.

We had done very little talking after I had kissed him. I don't know why I had done that. It was such a stupid thing to do. My only excuse was that I had been at my wits' end and terrified of the crazed glint in his eyes, as he demanded that I give him his drugs.

His withdrawal was bad. I knew that without ever having seen one firsthand before. I had read enough case studies to know that he was feeling the worst kind of physical and mental pain imaginable. His cravings had to be unreal.

And there were definitely moments when I didn't doubt he'd hurt me to get what his body wanted so desperately.

But I stayed. Because I cared too much for the messed-up boy and his fucked-up life to ever walk away.

So while he had been railing against me, hurling threats that I was all too sure he'd keep, I had used the only weapon in my arsenal. My mouth and my hands.

And it had worked.

Well, sort of.

I'm by no means proclaiming a miracle. This wasn't some sort of cheesy romance where the love of a good woman saved the boy from his demons.

If only it were that easy.

But my actions had shocked him. They had stayed the nastiness spewing from his lips. He hadn't expected me to do that.

And afterward, it wasn't as though we had fallen into each other's arms and hugged while I told him everything would be all right.

Nope. Maxx had taken the bowl of soup and started eating. He hadn't looked at me. No eye contact was made. No mention of feelings or futures. But damn it, he was eating.

And that small success was enough.

"Christ!" I heard Maxx yell from the bathroom. I jumped off the couch, where I had stationed myself like a sentry, waiting for him to emerge. I knocked on the door.

"Everything okay?" I asked.

The door swung open as steam rolled out into the living room. I tried not to fixate on the fact that Maxx wore only a towel draped around his narrow hips. His chest, while not overly muscular, was defined. He was tall. Much taller than me. So my eyes were at just the right height to get a good, long look at the lean body in front of me.

My gaze traveled up to Maxx's battered face. His blond curls were slicked back, and his one good eye was glinting in anger.

"What the fuck happened to my face?" he demanded.

Maxx's fingers touched the red, raw skin on his face. He winced, a hissing breath sucked through teeth.

"I followed you to the back of the club and found you getting your butt kicked by two guys," I told him.

Maxx's shoulders tensed. "What did they look like?" he asked. I couldn't tell if he was angry or scared. Maybe it was a combination of the two.

I tried to remember his assailants, but the memory was fuzzy after forty-eight hours of very minimal sleep. My instinct had been to help Maxx, not to identify the guys who had hurt him.

"I don't remember much about them. It was dark. I was focused on you bleeding all over the place. Sorry," I muttered.

"How in the hell did you get me home? There's no way you were able to drag me to your car by yourself," he continued. Why did I feel like I was being interrogated? Where was the thank-you?

"Some guy helped me. I recognized him from working the front door," I offered shortly, annoyed with his curtness.

"Marco," he prompted. Yeah, Marco. That sounded right, so I nodded.

Maxx pushed past me and walked to his bedroom. He was still weak, his steps slow and clumsy. I followed him and froze.

Maxx stood stark naked in the middle of his room, the towel fallen at his feet while he rooted around in his drawer for clothes.

I swallowed thickly and averted my eyes while he dressed. The urge to chance a peek was overwhelming, but I refused to give in. It wasn't right to ogle the guy after everything he had been through. Sure, I had crossed every boundary in our relationship, but I had some lingering morality left.

"Have you seen my phone?" he asked a few minutes later. I turned to look at him and squelched my disappointment at finding him fully clothed. I pointed to his desk.

"I put it over there. It was in your jeans pocket," I told him.

Maxx grabbed it and put it to his ear. He looked up at me, and I knew that currently I wasn't welcome. It was time for me to go.

He turned his back, shutting me out as surely as if he had slammed a door in my face.

I bristled at his rejection, infuriated by his dismissal.

Even more humiliating was the burn of tears I felt in the back of my eyes. I *never* cried anymore. I hated tears.

I stood there for another moment listening to Maxx leave a frantic message on Marco's voice mail. He was talking in quiet, quick sentences that I couldn't quite hear. One thing was obvious: Maxx was agitated.

I quietly closed the bedroom door and made my way back to the shabby living room. I had made an effort to clean up while Maxx had been in the shower, but not much could be done to make the space comfortable.

I thought about leaving a note, but then decided against it. What was the point?

I grabbed my purse and dug out my car keys, ready to make my escape.

"Where are you going?"

I looked over my shoulder to find Maxx walking toward me. He looked drawn and tired, but some of the spark had come back to his eyes.

"I just thought I should head home. You know, get out of your way," I said, lifting my chin defiantly.

Maxx put his hand flat against the front door, barring my exit. His face, which had been hard and anxious a few moments earlier, was now troubled and vulnerable.

He leaned down until his face was a mere few inches from my own. I could smell the mint from his toothpaste on his breath. His eyes drilled into mine, piercing me.

"What you did, how you helped me, stayed with me . . . I don't know why you did it. But thank you," he said quietly.

And there it was, the acknowledgment I had wanted. But now that he had given it, I wasn't sure what he wanted from me. Or what I wanted from him.

I leaned back against the door, his proximity overwhelming me. "It was nothing," I replied, shaking my head.

Maxx brought his other hand up to rest on the wood beside my head. I was captured between his arms, no room for escape.

"It wasn't *nothing*," he argued. "Why were you at the club?" he grilled.

"I don't know . . . ," I started, but he interrupted me.

"You do know, Aubrey. Why were you there?"

"For you, Maxx. I was looking for you," I admitted breathlessly, my heart pounding in my chest. "I was worried about you."

"You don't even know me, Aubrey. Why would you concern yourself about me at all?" he pressed.

I closed my eyes, needing some distance from the intensity of his gaze. "I just . . . I wanted to help you." I opened my eyes and looked unflinchingly up at him. "I care about what happens to you. You seem to need someone to give a damn. And I do, Maxx. So much," I said, my voice barely above a whisper.

Maxx swallowed, his lips trembling at my admission. His bruised face twisted with an emotion I couldn't quite read. He dropped his face and pressed his forehead against mine, our noses brushing.

"You shouldn't. I'm not worth it, Aubrey," he pleaded in a strangled groan.

I slowly moved my hands up to gingerly touch his face, my fingers sliding down the length of his cheek. He leaned into my hand and seemed to be at war with himself.

"You *are* worth it, Maxx. You need to learn that and believe it," I said. Maxx captured my hand, his eyes opening and blazing into mine.

"You need to know that if you decide to do this with me, I'll never be able to let you go. Not ever." His words quivered. A small part of me was terrified by his promise.

But a larger part of me hoped he would hold me tight . . . forever.

I pulled my hand from his and touched his face again. I brushed my thumb along the curve of Maxx's mouth. He parted his lips, kissing the soft pad of flesh, his tongue tentatively tasting.

I shook at the tidal wave of emotion that simple touch unleashed in me.

"Maxx, let me help you," I begged, knowing I was slowly climbing over his wall.

His hands were around me in an instant, pulling me to his chest. I could hear the thudding of his heart beneath my ear. "You already are," he said, his voice vibrating in my head.

I pulled back slightly to look up at him. He looked grieved, as though he hated himself for what he was doing but couldn't help it.

"What are you doing to yourself?" I asked, cupping his face with my hand, gently touching the bruised skin.

Maxx didn't answer me. He grabbed my hand and pressed a kiss to my palm before resting it over his heart. And then we held each other tightly, neither of us willing to let go, neither wanting to upset the tenuous beauty of the moment with the ugly reality he lived in.

Because for now, we had *this*.

◆

"My mother died when I was ten and Landon was five. It was cancer. I don't remember much about her being sick. I have vague memories of her being in bed for long periods of time and going to the hospital to visit her. But other than that, my mind seemed to have blocked it out. I guess I carried on my life like nothing earth-shattering was going on." Maxx snorted in disgust, his arms tightening around me.

We were sitting on the couch. It's where we had been for the past two hours. We hadn't talked much; Maxx had been mostly quiet. I was hesitant to break the silence, not knowing what would come next.

He seemed to need to hold me. He ran his fingers through my hair and softly kissed my temple. That was all. For him, right now, that appeared to be all he needed.

I couldn't help but continue to notice the fine tremors in his body, his erratic heartbeat under my palm, the fine sheen of sweat on his face. He was still trying to climb out of his horrible withdrawal. He was unhealthily pale, dark circles ringing his eyes, their normally vibrant blue dull and listless.

I had grown accustomed to the silence, so when he spoke I started in surprise. The noise was almost obscene in the hush.

"What sort of person doesn't remember his own mother dying?" he asked. I wasn't sure he was looking for an answer, but I gave him one anyway.

"You were a child, Maxx. You couldn't possibly understand what was going on."

Maxx was quiet again. I wasn't convinced he even heard what I said. His hold on me was as tight as ever, his fingers digging into my skin as though he was trying to fuse us together.

"My dad sort of disappeared from our lives after that. He was there, but he wasn't. He worked a lot, and I took over taking care of Landon. I would get him breakfast and dinner, help him with his homework. I made sure he had clean clothes to wear and went to bed when he was supposed to. He became *my* responsibility. I became a mom and a dad at ten fucking years old."

I wasn't sure what I had been expecting him to tell me. I had conjured up a thousand explanations about how he may have come to be the way he was, what had pushed him into the dark world he lived in. But hearing about a boy who had lost both his parents and was forced to become an adult before he was ready wasn't what I had expected.

I had guessed at a less-than-rosy past. Maxx hid too much away for his childhood to have been idyllic.

I had seen his protectiveness toward Landon. It had been more than obvious that he felt responsible for the younger boy. But the story Maxx began to share showed a side of him that was sad, yet it strangely gave me hope for the person he could be.

"And then my dad died of a heart attack two weeks after I started high school. I don't think I ever really knew him. I don't even remember the person he had been before my mom died, when he wasn't depressed and grieving. Christ, I don't know what the fuck I'm talking about," he muttered, running his hand through his hair while his other arm still clung to me tightly.

I could tell he was trying to sort through everything going on in his head, trying to find the words he wanted to share with me.

"After that, I realized there were varying degrees of shit. And the shit before my dad died was nothing compared to the shit *after* he died," Maxx said, his voice cracking a bit.

"My uncle David had never been in the picture. I barely even knew that he existed. He's my mom's younger brother. It was pretty obvious after we went to live with him why we never knew him. He's an asshole. Worse than that, he's a self-serving, sadistic asshole, a guy who gets off on treating others like shit if it makes his life easier. He got custody of Landon and me because there was no one else. Both sets of our grandparents were dead, and my dad was an only child. So that left just David. At first he refused to take us on. But when he realized we came with a hefty Social Security check every month until we turned eighteen, that changed his tune pretty damn quickly. The fucking douche bag took our money and made sure we never saw a dime. He said it's what we *owed* him," Maxx growled.

I took his hand in mine and laced our fingers together. "I'm so sorry, Maxx," I said earnestly, hoping I didn't sound condescend-ing. There was something so ridiculous about the words *I'm sorry*. As if I could in any way empathize with what he had experienced.

For all the crap I had gone through with my parents after Jayme had died, I didn't understand what it was like to feel unloved and unwanted.

My childhood before Jayme's death had been pretty close to perfect. I had parents who gave me everything. I couldn't fathom the feelings of abandonment and isolation Maxx must have experienced. And to have had to take on the role of parent when he was only a child himself was unimaginable.

I had lost the relationship I once had with my parents in the last few years. But for the first time I wondered whose fault it was. Did the blame completely rest on my parents' shoulders, as I had convinced myself? Or had I been too lost in my selfish grief to realize I was pushing away the two people who had loved me the most in my life?

Self-realization was a scary business. It shook your foundation to the core. How strange that it was this fucked-up boy, with a life full of pain, who made me question what I thought I knew about myself.

And how strange that he could make me doubt absolutely everything.

"I just want to take care of my brother. It's all I've ever wanted. But David is his legal guardian, and he holds that over my head every chance he gets. I try to make sure Landon has money to live on, but David just ends up taking it all. I'd kill the bastard if I could. I've thought of so many ways to get that fucker out of our lives. Sometimes this anger"—Maxx gripped the fabric of his shirt over his chest and pulled it—"it hurts. It hurts so fucking badly. I can't think, I can't see anything beyond it. The hatred eats me alive. I hate David for using my brother and me. I hate my parents for leaving me. Sometimes I even hate Landon for depending on me so much. And most of all, I hate myself. Because I'm weak and selfish. Because I don't want the responsibility of taking care of anyone but me. I just want to live my life for me and not for anyone else. I hate knowing that in my heart I feel that way. I hate that I resent Landon and my parents for the shit they've put on my shoulders, whether they meant to or not. I feel like I'm drowning with no way out."

Maxx's face contorted in grief and self-loathing. It ripped a hole in my heart. God, I just wanted to take all of his pain away.

"How did you end up at Compulsion . . . doing . . . what you do there?" I asked tentatively, not sure how to pose the questions I wanted to ask. I wanted to know how he ended up immersed in that dark and scary scene, how he had grown so comfortable in a place that seemed to suck you dry and leave you with nothing but regret.

"I've known Marco most of my life. He's a few years older, but I knew him from high school. After my dad died and Landon and I went to live with David, I was in a pretty fucked-up place. I didn't know if I was coming or going. I was depressed. And then Marco handed me a flyer for Compulsion. He got me in, introduced me to Gash, who runs the place. I wanted somewhere to belong, to do something that made me feel good. It started simply enough. I'd help Vin scout locations for the club every week. I was getting paid decent money, but it wasn't enough for me to take care of Landon. And then I got accepted by Longwood University. I had applied on a whim, convinced there was no way in hell I would ever go, even if I got in. But then the letter came, and I thought, *Hey, this could be my chance to get out of here, to build that life for Landon.*

"But that took money—a lot of it. Between school tuition, finding a place to live, and making sure Landon was okay, I couldn't survive on the little bit of money location scouting was bringing in. Then I realized I could make so much more selling club drugs. You know, some ecstasy, a little oxy. A bit of cocaine here and there. Maybe some crank. Before I knew it, I was flush with cash. Gash gave me the drugs, and I sold them, taking my cut. And because of it, I was living the life I had always wanted. I lived on my own terms, no one else's. I was on top of the world."

Maxx's eyes had gone unfocused as he talked. He was showing

me the bigger picture, and I felt like I was finally being given a glimpse of who he really was. No pretenses. No illusions. This was Maxx. The real Maxx.

"For the first time, people were seeking *me* out. They *wanted* to be around me. They liked what I offered. And I was the only one who could give it to them. For the first time in years, I was somebody people *knew.* Someone people *needed.* Someone people *wanted.*"

Maxx's face brightened with a fanatical light, and I knew that this power, however wrong it was, fed something inside him. It gave him a purpose, no matter how shady it was.

"I like how it makes me feel, Aubrey. I won't apologize or feel bad about that. It helps me take care of my brother. It keeps a roof over my head. It lets me stay in school and try to make something out of this shitty life I've been given," he stated defensively.

"Do you honestly like the way you've felt the past two days? You're hurting yourself, Maxx," I tried to reason. I brought his hand up to my lips and kissed his knuckles, positioning my body so that it pressed against him.

"You don't need that stuff to feel good about yourself. You have so much more going for you than that," I appealed to him.

Maxx laughed humorlessly, pulling away from me slightly. Even though it was only the barest of inches, it felt like miles now separated us.

"I know what you think. I see the way you're looking at me. How you always look at me. I know you think I'm just like every other fucked-up junkie out there. That I can't function without drugs. That I'd suck dick for a fix if I had to." I tried not to cringe at his anger. He was pissed.

"But I'm not like that, Aubrey. I'm not some cracked-out fiend who wakes up in the morning thinking of where and when he can get high. I can function without it. I was able to live most of my life without it. I can quit any time I want to. But why would I want to when it can give me something nothing else can?"

I frowned in confusion. What was he talking about? I didn't understand. I couldn't even pretend to. I didn't get his logic at all. But I could tell that in his mind, he was making perfect sense.

"It stops me from thinking, Aubrey! And for a guy like me, thinking sucks! I need the peace," he explained, as though it were the most obvious thing in the world.

I wanted to shake him. I wanted to smack him upside the head and tell him to wake up and see the state of the world he was living in. I wanted to tell him that his few moments of peace came at a hefty price. He might not remember the violently ill, barely conscious person he had been two nights ago, but *I* did! And from what I could see, those pills weren't giving him peace; they were pushing him that much closer to total obliteration.

He honestly thought he didn't have a problem. He had a clear idea of what it meant to be an addict, and in his mind, he wasn't ticking any of those boxes. His delusions would destroy him.

I remembered clearly the person who had lain curled up in a ball on his bed, throwing up on the floor, shaking and sweating as the drugs left his system, and the way he had cursed and threatened me when he couldn't get the fix he thought he needed. This was not a person who could quit when he felt like it.

His mind wouldn't let him quit, and his body sure as hell wouldn't either. He was trapped in the prison of his addiction, whether he realized it or not. And his denial was what was keeping him there.

But I wouldn't argue with him about it. It was a waste of time. You couldn't help someone who wasn't willing to help themselves. All I could do was be there and hopefully stop him from losing everything. I'd be there if he fell, and I would pick him up when he hit bottom.

I needed to do this for him. I needed to do this for *me*.

As I listened to Maxx talk, I could see my sister, crying out for the help I never gave her. Not this time. I'd hold on tight to Maxx and weather this storm with him.

"I want to be the guy who can take care of his brother. The guy who can go on and save the fucking world like my mother thought I could. But I also like being the other guy, the one who doesn't let anything touch him, who can't be dragged down—the guy who can be *everything*. And I want to be that guy for you," Maxx said, with so much conviction it was easy to believe he could be all those things. But the cost of that was too much.

"Why can't you just be Maxx Demelo? I kind of like that guy," I said, cupping my hand behind his neck.

Maxx smirked, a ghost of the smile I was familiar with. "I can be so much more for you. I want to be everything you could ever want."

I shook my head, not understanding where this was coming from. Why did he feel like he had to be superhuman? Why couldn't he just be happy with the person he was?

"I just want *you*," I told him, hoping he heard me.

"And I want *you*, Aubrey. All of you. Every tiny, perfect part. I want you to belong to me, only to me, so that you'll never leave. Please don't leave," he whispered, a choking plea.

God, how could I deny him anything? He was practically shoving his heart into my hands, insisting that I take it. He wasn't giving me a choice. And even if I had been given one, I knew the decision I would make. I would hold on to him—his heart, his soul—with everything I had.

Here was a man who tried desperately to mute the insecure little boy inside him, who was terrified of being abandoned or not ever being enough.

I wished I could get him to see the wonderful person he was without all the other stuff messing it up.

I leaned up and kissed his swollen eye, letting my lips linger as they traveled down the side of his face. Maxx had sucked me in, and there was no escaping it.

I just hoped I wouldn't regret my decision to stay.

chapter
twenty

My heart had betrayed me.

It held me prisoner to a fierce whirlwind of emotions that were unfamiliar and overpowering.

Taking care of Maxx, seeing his brutal struggle, had altered something inside me. I had stopped looking at him as the man he wanted me to see, and I began to view him as the person he *was*. The sad, lonely, scared boy who had lost so much and was trying to hold on to the last little bit of control he had.

Seeing him at his worst had inexplicably softened me toward him. The last bricks in my formerly impenetrable wall had come crashing down. A shift had taken place. I no longer just thought about fixing him. My feelings had become more complicated than that. More confusing.

And a hell of a lot deeper.

And while I was still petrified as the parameters of our relationship stretched and strained to make room for this new reality, I was also eager for it. I wanted it. I wanted *him*.

I should have been wary and hesitant. Here I was, jumping

into a heady, soul-consuming relationship with a guy I had met under the most unconscionable of circumstances.

Where was the girl who worried about screwing up? She had apparently taken a backseat to the girl who was discovering true emotional connection for the first time.

I knew it was wrong. I was already paranoid that people would catch on, that when my classmates looked at me, they'd see a girl doing something she definitely wasn't supposed to be doing.

But I couldn't stop myself.

Leaving Maxx's apartment was jarring. I had lived in this self-contained bubble for two days, forgetting that anything or anyone existed outside of it. It was easy to forget about trivial things like schoolwork and friends when I was in Maxx's world. That was how quickly he absorbed me.

But reality was a cold, hard slap in the face when I realized as I left that tonight I'd have to face Maxx in an entirely different setting, one that would most likely be trying and difficult and definitely more than a little bit awkward.

Support group.

Renee was home when I returned from Maxx's apartment. I had texted her over the last two days, explaining my absence as school-related. She hadn't questioned me. I hadn't really expected her to. She was too busy trying to get her own floundering life back on track now that Devon was out of the picture.

She had been happy to see me, and I was tempted to tell her everything about Maxx—about what had happened to him at the club, about why I had been gone for the last two days.

Once upon a time there was a good chance I would have done just that. But given the tenuous footing our friendship was on, I wasn't comfortable with the thought of sharing Maxx with her yet.

It felt crappy to lie to her, to look her in the eyes and tell a story that was one hundred percent not true. But I was faced with little other option.

Renee mentioned that Brooks had been by several times and that he seemed less than happy. She looked as though she wanted to question me about it all, and I was thankful when she didn't.

That was yet another part of my story that I didn't want to share with Renee. And I'd have to deal with Brooks and his hurt disapproval soon enough.

My phone rang just as I was walking across campus toward the psychology building for group that evening. I was surprised to see Kristie Hinkle's number on my screen.

"Hello?" I said after answering.

"Aubrey, I'm glad I got hold of you. I'm sorry to call so close to the start of group, but I'm going to need you to be the head facilitator tonight."

Shit!

"Why?" I asked bluntly, cringing at my rudeness, but her news had thrown me.

Kristie let out a wet cough. "I'm sick," she answered shortly, but the fact that she was hacking up phlegm was all the answer I needed.

"Can't we cancel?" I asked, hoping she was feverish enough to go along with that suggestion. Facing Maxx so soon after everything that had transpired, and in such a challenging setting, felt like a recipe for disaster.

One would hope that I could trust my abilities to remain professional and dispassionate. But the second I had acted on my feelings, and had allowed Maxx into my life, those nicely constructed boundaries flew, suicide-style, straight out the window.

I didn't trust myself . . . at all.

I wasn't sure if I could look at Maxx during group and not see the boy who had just bulldozed his way into my life and my heart. I was still raw and reeling from the realization of how much my feelings toward him had changed.

How would I ever be able to treat him like everyone else? Because he most certainly was *not* like everyone else.

I was a mess. A giant pile of my-life-is-out-of-control mess.

"No, that's not an option. We can't disrupt the flow of the group, particularly at this point. I need you to step up tonight, Aubrey. I trust that you've read over the lesson plan," Kristie said in between mucus-filled hacks. Yuck.

"Uh, yeah. I reviewed it last week," I answered, clearing my throat. There was no way to get out of this. *Suck it up, Aubrey, and pull up your big-girl panties.*

"I really think this could be a great opportunity for you to gain some valuable facilitating time. Starting tonight there will be another counseling student on hand as an observer. He will be able to step in should you need it," Kristie said. Blah, blah, blah, yadda, yadda, yadda.

And then I realized what she'd just said.

"Another student?" I asked. Just great, someone else to witness my abject humiliation.

"Dr. Lowell called me earlier to say that one of her senior symposium students needed a few more observation hours before graduation and asked to sit in on the group for the remainder of the semester. I haven't had the chance to meet him yet, and I wrote his name down but it's at the office."

Apparently the universe liked to fuck with me. I had somehow become the brunt of a huge cosmic joke. I should have known who that student would be.

And when I walked into the classroom a few minutes later to find Brooks setting up the chairs, I could only laugh at the ridiculousness that was my life.

"What are you doing here?" I asked, trying to get my almost hysterical laughter under control.

Brooks looked up, giving me that "you're bat-shit crazy" look he was so fond of.

"Didn't Kristie call you?" he asked coldly. His iciness put the kibosh on my amusement.

"You're the senior sitting in?" I asked stupidly.

"Obviously," he muttered, his face purposefully turned away from me. The distance between us was becoming uncomfortably familiar. I hated that I was getting used to his cold shoulder, that his disdainful disappointment was a frequent visitor.

"Well, um, that's great," I lied.

Brooks slammed the last chair onto the ground with a loud bang before he turned to face me. "Where have you been for the last two days, Aubrey? I've tried to call you. I went by your apartment, but Renee said you had schoolwork to do." He made quotes with his fingers. He was really, really mad.

"Yeah, if 'schoolwork' is Aubrey-ese for that druggie I saw you with on Saturday night. So why don't you explain what the hell that was about?" Brooks walked across the room until he stood directly in front of me. I had never felt intimidated by Brooks. It wasn't in his nature to be aggressive. But right now I felt like kneeing him in the nuts and running out of the room. I didn't appreciate the way he was looking at me as though I had just beamed down from the planet I Make Stupid Decisions.

"Um . . . ," I stumbled. Lie, lie, lie. That's all I was doing anymore.

Brooks took my hand, his face softening. "Aubrey, you can talk to me," he promised, his thumb rubbing the back of my hand. I opened my mouth, not sure what would come out.

Maybe I'd tell him the whole sordid truth. Maybe I'd stick to the schoolwork story.

Maybe I'd start speaking in tongues while my head rotated a full 360 degrees.

Someone cleared his throat before I could find out.

I looked over my shoulder to find Maxx, his arms crossed over his chest, leaning against the doorframe. Our eyes met, and a flash of heated awareness blazed between us. He looked better. The dark circles weren't as pronounced, and his skin was less sallow.

Maxx's gaze darted down to my hand, where it was still held by Brooks, and I instantly pulled away. I shot a look at Brooks, who narrowed his eyes.

Maxx entered the room and took his usual chair, never looking away from me. I licked my lips nervously, my mouth suddenly dry. My cheeks and neck flushed, and I knew without a doubt that tonight would be a lesson in avoidance.

Brooks walked over to Maxx and held out his hand. "I'm Brooks. I'm going to be sitting in tonight. What's your name?"

Maxx looked at Brooks's outstretched hand and then returned his eyes to me, ignoring him completely.

The silence was deafening as it became apparent that Maxx wasn't planning to answer.

"This is Maxx Demelo," I hurriedly answered for him. Brooks's lip curled up in a sneer before he turned his back to Maxx. His expression said it all. He was going to make this as awkward and difficult as possible.

Just flipping fabulous.

Thankfully, the rest of the group members arrived after that. Brooks went around introducing himself to the others, and I couldn't help but be impressed with how easily he interacted with them, even Evan and April. He spoke with them, and they responded with a lot less venom than I was used to seeing. Of course, Brooks was a natural.

A natural pain in *my ass*.

After everyone had taken their seats, I let them know that Kristie was sick and I would be leading group that evening. Twyla snorted and rolled her eyes, but that was the only reaction I received. I was relieved. I hadn't been expecting rioting in the streets, but I had been anticipating some substitute-teacher shenanigans.

I started my discussion on the stages of the recovery process. I knew this material backward and forward.

And while my mouth moved, the words flowing easily, my brain was engaged in a desperate battle. My willpower was flagging and threatening to give way under the force of Maxx's eyes.

Do not look at Maxx! I admonished myself over and over again.

I tried to ignore the tingling sensation as I passed out the evening's worksheet and just happened to brush my fingers against his.

I was failing miserably.

"Tonight you're going to be writing a letter to yourself. I want you to think about where you want to be in six weeks, six months, six years. Write about the challenges you see for yourself, but also the successes you've had. You're also to include some positive self-messages that your future self would want to hear. Be honest. Be realistic," I said.

"Can I get some extra paper?" Maxx asked.

I cleared my throat and responded with a barely audible, "Sure."

I handed him the paper, and when he took it from my hand, his fingers purposefully caressed the skin of my palm. His touch lingered, his eyes burning into mine. The room around us receded, and there was only us.

"Aubrey," Brooks called out, returning me to reality. I instantly pulled my hand back as if the touch had singed me.

Maxx's face darkened. He looked at Brooks, who watched us like a hawk. Maxx's expression was murderous.

"Can I get a pencil and paper?" Brooks asked stiffly, arching his eyebrow. Maxx opened his mouth as if to say something, but I hurried over before he was able to speak.

"Here," I said, thrusting the paper into my friend's hand. Brooks's eyes flashed as he looked at me.

"Thanks," he muttered.

I returned to my chair and made nonsensical notes on my pad of paper, trying to calm the pounding of my heart. Everyone was silent; the only sound was that of the scratching of pencils on paper.

I watched Maxx as slyly as possible, but he seemed to be en-grossed in writing his letter.

When the time was up, I handed out envelopes and instructed everyone to put the letters inside, writing their addresses on the outside. Kristie had explained to me that she would mail the let-ters at the end of the group for them to read.

"This is so fucking stupid," Evan stated as I went around, col-lecting the letters. Here we go. I should have known I wouldn't be able to get through the group without Mr. Pleasant telling every-one his opinion about *something*.

I tried not to roll my eyes. Honestly, I did. But I was having a hard time with self-control. "Why is that?" I asked him blandly and knew I had pissed him off.

"Like a fucking letter will change what we do with our life. This psychobabble bullshit won't do anything. You prissy bitches on your soapboxes lecturing about what we should and shouldn't be doing need to fuck off and worry about yourselves," he spat out. I felt my face get hot as a few others made noises of agreement.

I held my hand out to take his letter, refusing to engage with him. *Deep breaths, Aubrey. Rein it in. Ignore him.* I chanted sooth-ing phrases over and over in my head.

I knew that Evan was looking for a reaction. He wanted an ar-gument. And I wouldn't be giving him one even if I had some choice, colorful comments that I'd like to make.

Evan glared up at me, clicking the ring in his tongue across his bottom teeth. "I'm not giving this to you," he said angrily. April looked between her boyfriend and me nervously.

I retracted my hand. "That's your choice," I said mildly, moving to take the next person's letter.

"You're not taking any of our letters," he announced, getting to his feet. Evan drew his body upright, apparently trying to make himself more intimidating.

Okay, and maybe he was a little intimidating, particularly since it seemed no one was in a hurry to intervene. *Thanks a lot, guys.*

"That's not your call to make, Evan," I replied carefully, making eye contact with him. It was important to not show weakness, to not let him know he was getting to me—even though he was. He worried me. His behavior was decidedly unhinged.

Evan smacked the pile of letters out of my hand and kicked them out of my reach with his feet. "Fuck this shit!" he growled.

Brooks was on his feet and by my side in an instant. He held his hands up in a placating gesture. "Let's just take a moment, Evan, and calm down," he said soothingly, employing all of those superb counseling skills he had been developing over the last four years.

Well, apparently, the words *calm down* had the exact opposite of the intended effect on Evan. He kicked his chair, sending it clattering to the floor. He started to escalate quickly, his eyes bulging out of his head. Now that I was looking directly at them, it was obvious that both he and April had been using before group.

So employing reason and logic wasn't going to be an option.

"Evan, I think it's time you left," Brooks said firmly, making small, inconspicuous steps toward Mr. I'm-ready-to-go-psycho-on-your-ass.

April tried to put a hand on her boyfriend's arm, but he threw it off with enough force to knock her backward. The rest of the group members were slowly moving away. *Cowards.*

"I'll leave when I'm fucking ready to leave!" Evan yelled, spit flying from his mouth. He looked crazed. He looked ready to inflict some serious damage . . . to Brooks's face and mine.

He took one menacing step toward me, and I couldn't help but back up. I didn't care if it showed weakness, if I was practically announcing to the entire room that this guy scared the crap out of me. My survival instincts kicked in, and my need to get away from him outweighed everything else.

Before Evan could move toward me again, Maxx had him by

the front of his shirt and shoved against the wall. He pressed his forearm against his throat and leaned in, his face so terrifying it made Evan instantly stop struggling.

"Don't you *ever* fucking talk to her like that!" Maxx pressed into his throat again, making Evan gasp for breath.

"Do you hear me, shit stain? If you ever put a hand on her, I'll kill you!" he roared. Evan flinched, and the fight had left him completely. April was sobbing in her chair, and the rest of the group members were gaping in shock at the turn of events.

Brooks grabbed Maxx's arm and pulled on him. "Get off him, Maxx! Now!" he hollered, but Maxx was like a wall of stone as he continued to glare at Evan, not bothering to acknowledge Brooks at all.

"You need to apologize to Aubrey. Right now. If you don't, you'll be pissing out your teeth for a week!" Maxx said, his voice low and cold. He pressed his arm harder into Evan's throat, and the other man started to turn an unnatural shade of blue.

Brooks yanked on Maxx's arm again, and finally he let himself be pulled back. Evan gulped in a breath, his eyes darting to me. "I'm sorry," he rasped, rubbing his throat.

I could only nod, just as shocked as the rest of the room with Maxx's He-Man transformation. Evan grabbed April's hand, and they practically ran from the room.

Brooks was saying something to Maxx, but Maxx moved past him and headed straight to me. He took my hands and brought them up to his mouth. He didn't kiss my skin, only held them against his lips as he closed his eyes and tried to get himself together.

The room was deathly still, everyone watching us. This was bad. I really should put a stop to it. But I couldn't move. I was trapped by the mass of quivering need that unleashed in my belly the moment Maxx touched me.

He finally opened his eyes and brought my hands down. "Are you all right?" he asked me quietly.

I could only nod, as I was finding even breathing difficult. The intensity of his gaze was unsettling, but God help me if I didn't want to throw my arms around his neck and hold him.

His fingers slowly uncurled and released me. My hands fell to my sides, where they hung limply. We stood so close, our chests were touching. He lifted his hand to brush my cheek but stopped himself before making contact.

Then without another word, he backed away, leaving the room.

No one moved for an endless moment, and then it was as though everyone started heading for the door at once. I tried to make a general sort of announcement about next week's session, but my voice was gone. Brooks had to take over.

I continued to stand there, reeling from what had happened, from the fact that Maxx had made crystal clear to everyone in the room that there was something going on between us, something that could get us both into a lot of trouble.

Once the room was empty, Brooks slammed the door closed and whipped around to face me.

"I can't believe you, Aubrey! Are you stupid?" he bit out hatefully.

I flinched but didn't say anything. I couldn't deny what he was saying, yet I couldn't put an admission into words. I was mute in my guilt.

Brooks angrily closed up the metal chairs and shoved them against the wall. I pulled myself together as best I could and cleaned up the papers that Evan had scattered across the floor.

"You're going to ruin any chances you have at becoming a counselor. This is 101 shit, Aubrey! You don't get involved with clients! I can't believe you're being so reckless. And for that guy? Seriously?" Brooks yelled.

But then my own anger rose up to meet his. I couldn't take his sanctimonious condemnation a moment longer.

"Don't you think I know all of this?" I was breathing fast and heavy. Brooks stood with his hands jammed in his pockets as if to stop himself from wringing my neck.

"I can't explain why it happened. I didn't want it to!" I implored.

"So you admit that something *has* happened, then?" Brooks asked, looking pained, and I knew that I had no right to be angry. Brooks was only looking out for me as a friend would.

"Not really. Not yet," I said quietly.

"Then you still have time to put a stop to it, before you can't undo it. You'll get thrown out of the counseling program, Aubrey. This is a major violation of ethics," Brooks argued, his anger fading, his shoulders drooping.

"I can't, Brooks," I let out on a choked whisper.

Brooks's mouth tightened in frustration.

"Why not? Why him?" he asked me.

I shook my head, pressing my fingers into my temples, trying to stave off the headache that had started to throb behind my eyes.

How could I possibly explain to Brooks why I couldn't walk away from Maxx? That I saw something in that desperate man that made me want to help him. That I just knew there was something great, something beautiful, under the surface that only I would be able to see. That my heart, my soul, hungered for him in a way that I had never experienced before.

It sounded ridiculous. Illogical. Hormonal. Those thoughts made me look like a fool, and maybe on some level that's exactly what I was.

But all I knew was that he needed me. And that *I* needed *him*. That we could heal each other.

How could I turn my back on that?

So I didn't say a word. I let Brooks make his own deductions. As the silence between us lengthened, my friend sighed sadly.

"I can't stand by and watch you throw everything away like this," he said, appealing to me in a last-ditch effort to get me to see reason.

But I had come to learn that my feelings for Maxx weren't reasonable.

"Then don't watch," I murmured as I gathered my things, leaving Brooks alone with his disappointment in the crumbling remnants of our friendship.

I hurried out to my car, keeping my head down, wiping the tears that fell down my cheeks.

"Aubrey."

I looked up, the wind whipping my hair and obscuring my vision. Maxx stood in the shadows. He was recognizable only by the slope of his shoulders and his head full of blond curls, which was uncovered in the cold air.

But now I would know him anywhere.

I started to walk toward him as though pulled by an invisible cord. He met me halfway, his arms reaching out. I froze, looking around, worrying about being seen.

Maxx picked up on my hesitation. "What is it?" he asked.

I put my hand on his arm, resisting the need to fall into him. "We just have to be careful, Maxx. You can't be touching me in public. What happened tonight in group, while I appreciate it, was too much. People will think there's something going on between us," I rebuked gently.

Maxx frowned, his mouth thinning into a line. "Well, there *is* something going on between us. Right?" he asked, taking a step back, his voice gruff, a shutter going down over his eyes.

I could sense the impact of my rejection. He was pulling away from me, preparing to be hurt. With little thought to common sense, I grabbed him and yanked him toward me, my hands coming up to frame his face.

"There is so much going on between us that it scares me, Maxx. This"—I indicated the space between us—"could get the both of us into a lot of trouble. You're in a group that I'm helping to facilitate. I could get kicked out of the counseling program. This would most definitely be in violation of your probation. We have to think about all of the implications here," I reasoned.

As if angered by my appeal, Maxx grabbed my face and roughly pressed his lips to mine, his tongue parting my lips and invading the deepest recesses of my mouth. He plundered and took without waiting for my compliance. This wasn't about me. This kiss was all about *him*. He pulled away before I could react.

"I don't give a shit about the *implications*, Aubrey," he warned, his eyes flashing in the shadows.

My heart beat furiously in my chest. Maxx was a loose cannon. There was no way to control or dictate how he would handle the situation we found ourselves in.

He felt it, he reacted.

He thought it, he acted.

How could I *not* expect this to blow up in my face?

And even more perplexing was why a part of me did not care at all. Why was I thrilled at the intensity I saw when he looked at me, no matter the consequences? Why did I find myself arching my body to get closer to him as we stood in a darkened corner of campus where we could be discovered by anyone?

"Come home with me," Maxx murmured as he bent his head low, nuzzling my ear. I shivered, and it had nothing to do with the cold.

"Please," he whispered against my neck.

"We have to be careful," I cautioned before my wits left me. Maxx didn't acknowledge my words. He didn't alleviate my worries. He didn't comfort or placate. Instead, he pulled me into the black and devoured me there. And I was happy to go with him.

And later at his apartment, as he undressed me, slowly, reverently, I convinced myself that this choice to be with him was the only one worth making.

Maxx kissed every inch of my body, spreading my thighs with his strong hands and using his tongue and lips on the most intimate part of me.

I had given myself to him completely, bared my heart and soul.

I watched him as he removed his clothing and then covered me with his body, positioning himself between my legs.

One last twinge of reluctance buzzed around in my head. The fear that this step wasn't one I should be taking. That sex with Maxx was binding and final. He would own me.

And I wasn't confident his possession was something I could survive intact.

But then Maxx kissed me deeply and thoroughly, and all thoughts of denying this moment were gone.

I wrapped my arms around him, my legs securely at his hips. The tip of him pushed slowly inside me, joining us together.

I gasped, he cried out. I moved, he held on. He pressed himself as deeply as my body would allow. Every inch of us fitted together, uniting perfectly.

Maxx growled romantic nonsense in my ear as he slid in and out of me. "I've been waiting my entire life for you." He kissed the sensitive skin beneath my ear.

I couldn't say anything. I didn't want to make promises and declarations I was scared neither of us could keep.

Maxx dug his fingers into my thigh as he lifted it up and over his hip. He cupped my cheek and looked down at me, his eyes dark and full of a tenderness that took my breath away.

"I want this, forever," he whispered, his voice hitching as he angled his hips and pushed deeper. I matched his rhythm, his desperate words ringing in my ears as we climaxed.

These were sentiments I didn't think it possible he should be feeling. Not yet. I wasn't sure I was ready for his pleas of forever.

Yet I longed for it.

And in the heated darkness, I couldn't deny I felt these passionate truths as well.

chapter
twenty-one

aubrey

Waking up the following morning, I was on the edge of a full-on freak-out. I blinked my eyes in the dimness, trying to make out where I was. My brain couldn't compute why I wasn't at home, in bed, surrounded by my stuff.

Then arms tightened around me, lips brushing the back of my neck, and I froze. Well, shit, now I remembered.

I had slept with Maxx Demelo.

His words from the night before drifted back through my sleepy brain. Did he really want me forever? Or was it the sex talking?

My chest felt tight as I remembered the look on his face as he stared down at me, his eyes soft and aching with a need I felt just as intensely.

But right now, I really needed to use the bathroom.

I squirmed in Maxx's embrace. My bladder felt ready to burst, but Maxx didn't seem to want to let me go anytime soon.

I turned on my side, thinking I could slide out from beneath his arms. But now that I was facing Maxx—his eyes closed, his sleeping face looking surprisingly young—I didn't want to move.

I loved looking at him like this, without the cocky confidence or the pained vulnerability. Both ripped at my chest. But here like this, quiet in his sleep, he seemed content.

His lips curved up in a smile. "I know you're looking at me," he mumbled. I rolled my eyes.

"I really need to use your bathroom, but I'm sort of pinned to the mattress right now," I remarked dryly, wriggling again.

In one fluid movement, Maxx opened his eyes and rolled me on my back, his hips fitting between my legs and lining up with me perfectly. We were naked, having not bothered to get dressed the night before. My body instantly responded to his proximity.

"I like waking up with you here," Maxx said with a smile, slipping inside my wet entrance just a fraction of an inch.

My breathing became shallow, and the coil of burning lust knotted itself in my belly. "Oh, god," I moaned as Maxx pressed farther inside me.

I arched my back, my breasts pushed forward, and Maxx took one of my nipples into his mouth, his tongue swirling around the tight, hot bud.

He still hadn't pushed in the rest of the way, and I was a squirming, writhing mess beneath him. I dug the heels of my feet into his ass, trying to push him forward, but he resisted me, chuckling against my breast.

Then, just as I thought he'd slam himself home, he pulled out and rolled off me. I sat up, bewildered, my heart beating wildly and my head fuzzy with my unfulfilled orgasm.

"What the hell?" I glowered at him. Maxx leaned back, his arms crossed behind his head, and grinned like mad.

"Go to the bathroom, do all of your girlie stuff. I'll be here when you get back," Maxx teased, giving me a mischievous wink.

I got up in a huff and walked down to the bathroom. The distance from Maxx's body cleared my head, and I was able to think about the situation I found myself in more rationally.

I thought about what had happened in support group last night, and my blood froze. We had been careless and more than a little reckless. It was only a matter of time until Kristie found out, and then Dr. Lowell and then the rest of the faculty in the Psychology Department.

There was no way to explain away Maxx's behavior or my inability to respond appropriately in his presence. It was more than obvious how we felt about each other. It was my worst nightmare come true.

But I was quickly becoming addicted to him.

He was all I wanted.

I took several deep breaths before returning to the bedroom. It was still dark out. I had no idea what time it was. It was too early to be awake, but I wasn't tired anymore.

Seeing Maxx laid out in the bed, waiting for me, filled me with a glowing warmth that could no longer be confused with simple lust. It burned so much brighter than that.

I crawled in beside him, cuddling down beneath the covers, my leg wrapping around his hip, my arm resting on his chest. I tucked my head underneath his chin, and he squeezed me to his side.

It was nuts how Maxx could make me lose my head with desire but then lull me into a contented relaxation in his arms. The emotions were waging a battle against each other, but I felt each so deeply. The battle made me feel weak in the knees and on the cusp of losing control.

The appeal of that was the same as when I had been at Compulsion. The opportunity to surrender and embrace a side of myself that had lain dormant for most of my life.

Maxx's fingers swept up and down my arm, a soothing gesture that made my eyelids start to droop. But then he spoke, and all thoughts of falling asleep were gone.

"Thank you," he whispered, kissing the top of my head.

"For what?" I asked, turning to rest my chin on his chest. His face was shadowed in the dark, a grim reminder of the person he was for part of the time—my mystery man, the person I wasn't sure how to reconcile with.

"For being here with me. For not leaving that night after the club. For staying by my side even when it got ugly." His voice broke, and he cleared his throat, smiling sheepishly. He quickly leaned down to kiss the tip of my nose.

"For being who you are," he finished, his hand cupping the back of my head as he pulled my face to his. He captured my mouth in a searing kiss, and I couldn't help but melt into him. That was the power he had over me. It was total and absolute. I was helpless to resist him.

I could feel his heartbeat beneath my palm, and it was steady and strong. So far there were no signs of withdrawal. I just hoped that didn't mean he had already used that morning before I had woken up. I wanted to know, but I was scared to ruin our moment with questions that would only infuriate him.

I let him kiss me until we were both breathless. He pulled me on top of his body so that I straddled him. My desire was awake and ready. I couldn't help but rub against him, grinning at his low, throaty groan.

"Spend the day with me," Maxx demanded with a smile that quickly turned to a moan as I rubbed against him again.

I lifted up and positioned myself over him. Slowly, purposefully, I lowered myself down until he filled me completely. The action caused us both to moan loud and low.

"I have class. I have a paper to write. Don't you have schoolwork to do?" I asked between gasps. Maxx gripped my hips and rocked me over him, guiding me as he thrust upward.

Maxx flipped me so that I was beneath him, his hand coming up to caress my face, slowing his rhythm. "Just for today," he pleaded. I started to shake my head, but then he kissed me deep and long.

"No classes, no work. Just you. Just me. Just us together," Maxx begged in time with our heart-pounding rhythm.

"Yes," was all I could say, my nails digging into the skin of his shoulder blades, my back arching up.

I came with a violence that shocked me. Then he came on the tail end of my orgasm. We lay in the aftermath, trying to control our breathing, waiting for our hearts to slow.

Our bodies were slick with sweat, and normally I would have been grossed out at the way our skin stuck together, but strangely it didn't bother me. My hand was definitely lying in a wet spot, but all I could think about was how good it felt to lie sprawled across him, the two of us still attached intimately.

Maxx ran his hand down my spine and smacked my ass. "Let me make breakfast. I'm starving!" I wished his energy was contagious, but I was feeling languid and lazy and not in the least bit hungry.

But I let him pull me out of bed and down the hallway while he flipped on all the lights in his tiny apartment.

"Sit. I'll get everything together," Maxx urged, buzzing around animatedly. He was so happy. And it was more than a little flattering to think I may have had something to do with the smile on his face.

We were both still naked, and I was starting to feel self-conscious. I wasn't one to make a habit of hanging out in the buff. For me, nakedness was confined to showers and changing clothes. I started to pull one of the couch pillows over my chest when Maxx grabbed it and tossed it on the floor.

He dropped to his knees, his arms curling around my waist, his face tilted up as he looked at me. "Don't ever cover yourself in front of me. I need to see you," he murmured, pulling my legs apart. I was completely exposed. It made me uncomfortable, but it was also extremely erotic.

"All of you," he finished, running his nose along the inside of my thigh, his breath warm on my center. I shuddered, too turned on to be embarrassed by my body's blatant reaction to him.

He rocked back on his heels, his fingers still gripping the flesh above my knees, and he looked at me, all of me, as though I were the most beautiful thing in his universe. He was really good for the ego.

"Stay here, like this," he commanded, getting to his feet.

I sat there on his couch awkwardly for a moment before going against his wishes and curling my legs up underneath me, though I didn't cover up, against my every instinct to do so. I wasn't sure I could make this a habit. It was too weird.

Maxx came back only a few minutes later with two plates. He handed me mine and sat down beside me, as close as he could get.

I looked down at the plate and laughed. Maxx grinned shyly. "I don't have much in the way of groceries, sorry," he muttered.

I picked up a string of licorice and popped it into my mouth before grabbing a handful of Doritos. Not the most nutritious breakfast but definitely one of the most interesting.

I worked through my selection of junk food, thinking to myself that this was perhaps the best meal I had ever eaten.

When I finished, I was full, mildly nauseous at the excessive amount of sugar and carbs first thing in the morning, but completely content.

Maxx picked up the remote control. "What do you like to watch?" he asked, flicking on the television. I looked at him blankly.

"We can watch Bob Ross paint some trees or . . ." He flicked through a few more channels before settling on a fashion design show I had seen a few times before. "What the hell is this shit?" he asked, frowning.

I snatched the remote and turned it up. "It's obvious you need to get in touch with your inner diva, Maxx," I teased, settling back into the couch.

We watched for a few minutes before Maxx couldn't take any more. He turned to me and grabbed the remote, muting the show.

He hauled me onto his lap. "Fuck TV, tell me about you," he said, smoothing my long hair behind my shoulders.

"I love your hair. It's so soft," he said quietly, threading the strands through his fingers.

"*She is beautiful without knowing it, and possesses charms that she's not even aware of,*" he murmured, his fingers pacifying me into a quiet comfort.

I looked at him under heavy lids. "Why the quotes?" I asked, leaning into his touch. "You do that a lot."

Maxx smiled, a soft expression on his face. "Sometimes the words in my heart have already been written down by someone who can say it a hell of a lot better than I ever could."

I ran my finger along his bottom lip; he opened his mouth and bit down lightly on the tip. "Well, the whole sensitive guy thing *is* pretty hot." I grinned.

Maxx rolled his eyes and squeezed my hips, making me squirm.

"Stop changing the subject, I'm on a discovery mission here." Maxx winked and went back to running his hands through my hair.

"Favorite food?" he asked.

"Fettuccine Alfredo and garlic bread," I answered. Maxx nodded.

"Noted. What about favorite color?"

"Orange," I replied.

Maxx raised an eyebrow. "Orange? Not something girlie like sparkly pink?"

I stuck out my tongue, making him laugh. "Nope. It's impossible to be in a bad mood when you're wearing orange," I volleyed back.

Maxx tapped the side of his head. "Got it. Okay, favorite flower."

"Why all the questions?" I asked, curious as to where he was going with all this.

"I want to know everything. Plus it's good to know how I can butter you up later," he joked, pulling on my hips so I was pressed hard against him.

I rolled my eyes but couldn't help smiling.

"Well, I'm not really a flower kind of girl." I leaned forward and touched my lips to his ear before saying, "But if you really want to get me hot and bothered, buy me some chocolate. I'll do just about *anything* for chocolate."

Maxx chuckled, but I could feel him getting harder against me. "Chocolate is the way to get in your pants. Good to know."

I rubbed against him and kissed the skin below his earlobe. "If you couldn't tell, I'm already out of my pants."

Maxx cupped my ass and started rubbing me rhythmically against him. "Oh, I could tell," he said, his voice cracking as he moved me faster.

And then we were done talking for a while.

◆

Hours later, when we finally came up for air, Maxx urged me to take a shower and get dressed. "Take your time," he said, giving me a kiss as I went into the bathroom.

I frowned. "Okay, I will," I told him, confused.

Thirty minutes later, I emerged from the bathroom, dressed and feeling a bit more human. Maxx had gotten dressed as well and was standing in the living room, grinning from ear to ear.

I walked out to meet him and stopped. On the coffee table were several boxes of chocolates. He had gotten assortments of every type imaginable. Beside them in a vase was a bunch of orange lilies. He held a grocery bag in his hand.

"What's all this?" I asked, ridiculously touched by his thoughtfulness. Who knew Maxx Demelo could be so romantic?

Maxx was downright giddy. "I've never done the whole boyfriend thing before, but I want to do this right, Aubrey." He held out the grocery bag. I took it and looked inside.

"I'm going to make you fettuccine Alfredo for dinner. I'm not a cook, but I figure even I can follow a recipe." He kissed me hard on the mouth, his eyes twinkling.

We spent the remainder of the morning wrapped up in each other while Maxx continued his version of Twenty Questions. When he'd get tired of quizzing me, he'd devour me. We couldn't get enough of touching and tasting each other.

I had never been so physically and emotionally drawn to someone before. I had tried the monogamous dating thing in the past, and it had never ended well for me. Whenever I had gotten to a certain point in the relationship, I had instinctively retreated, unable to move forward.

But with Maxx it was different somehow. Maybe it was knowing that this was someone who needed a connection almost as badly as I did. Looking at Maxx was like seeing a darker, more troubled version of myself. He was closed off and isolated, just as I had been for the past three years. And by giving him tiny pieces of myself, I was hoping to make both of us less lonely.

I had moments when my better sense tried to take over, moments of wondering what it would really mean to open myself up to him. And then I thought about what waited for me when I left the safety of Maxx's apartment. I felt paralyzed with uncertainty.

"What are you thinking about?" Maxx asked. In fact, I was thinking perhaps a little too hard about possible suspension, a ruined career, a derailed academic future, friends pissed at me for life.

I plastered a smile on my face. "Nothing," I lied. Maxx frowned, obviously not sure whether to believe me or not. I leaned up on my knees and pressed a kiss on his mouth. He instantly molded his lips to mine.

Pulling away, I laced my fingers with his. "You've been hearing all about me. I'd like to know about you." Maxx stiffened slightly but then gave me a blinding grin.

"What you see is what you get, Aubrey," he said, yanking me forward. He grabbed the back of my neck rather aggressively and tilted my head to the side, his lips sucking and nipping along the column of my throat.

"I don't believe that," I argued, pulling back. I knew there had to be a whole mess of stuff going on with Maxx. A lot more than he had revealed so far.

"I promise you, there's nothing to know that you don't know already. I told you about my parents, about Landon and my uncle. That's more than I've ever shared with anyone. Honestly, there's nothing more to tell," he said, kissing the tip of my nose.

I opened my mouth to press the point when his phone started ringing.

He checked the screen and scowled but answered it instantly. "Is everything okay, Landon?" he asked.

Maxx's transformation as he spoke to his brother was fascinating. He literally became someone else. He was soft-spoken and calm, his voice warm.

His eyes flicked toward me. "I don't think so, buddy. Not today.

"I've got plans.

"Yes, Landon, it's a girl.

"Shut up, will you?"

I snickered. Even though I could hear only Maxx's end of the conversation, it was obvious he was getting a ball busting from his younger brother. I didn't know Landon, but already I liked him.

Maxx grimaced. "That's probably not a good idea. I can come by during the week."

I put my hand on his arm, interrupting him. He looked down at my fingers curling around his wrist and then up at me.

"I'll come with you," I offered, hoping he'd take me up on it.

Maxx pulled the phone away from his mouth. "I'm not sure that's cool." He frowned, clearly not happy with my suggestion.

I squeezed his arm. "Please. I'd like to see Landon again."

Maxx closed his eyes, as though he was having some sort of internal battle. He opened them and looked at me for a long moment before putting the phone back to his mouth.

"Yeah, we'll come by. We'll be there in an hour. And David's not there, right? Okay, see you then."

Maxx hung up and got to his feet, holding his hand out. "Come on, let's go see my baby brother," he said, and I knew he was glad we were going to see him. And I couldn't be more excited about having the chance to see the two of them together again, to see once more the side of Maxx that had drawn me in.

The Maxx that I hoped to see more of.

chapter
twenty-two

We pulled up in front of Maxx's uncle's house a little after one in the afternoon. I wondered why Landon wasn't in school and asked Maxx about it.

"It's a teacher workshop day. He's been on me to come by and help him with his car, but I've been busy," Maxx answered, sounding defensive. Something told me being busy wasn't why he hadn't been by to see his brother, but I didn't push it.

Maxx went around to my side of the car and opened the door for me. My heart fluttered at the gesture. I had never pictured Maxx as being the sort of man to open doors for women. I was happy to be wrong.

I went up on my tiptoes and pressed my mouth to his. The kiss was warm and comforting and over far too quickly.

Maxx pulled back slightly and gave me a tender smile. "What was that for?" he asked.

I kissed his chin, then loosened my hands from around his neck. "For surprising me," I answered. Maxx's smile became questioning, and he chuckled under his breath. He pulled me tighter into his embrace.

"Remind me to surprise you more often," he murmured, and it was my turn to laugh.

"Get a room!" a voice called out. Maxx and I broke apart, and he grinned over his shoulder at the young boy who stood on the porch.

"Shut up, Landon," he called back, rolling his eyes at his brother.

Maxx grabbed my hand and pulled me toward the modest ranch-style house. It was a bit on the shabby side and needed a new coat of paint, but other than that it was being maintained.

Maxx ruffled his brother's fine, blond hair as he walked up the porch steps. "How's it going, buddy?" he asked Landon, who ducked out from beneath Maxx's hand.

Landon smiled when he saw me. "I remember you! You're that chick from Maxx's school!"

Maxx smacked the back of his head, then put his arm back around my waist. "This is most definitely not a *chick*, Landon. Show some respect," he reprimanded, and I could only laugh.

"Well, she's a hot chick. Is that better?" Landon asked, wearing a smirk almost identical to his brother's.

"That's it. You're overdue for an ass kicking," Maxx teased, feigning a lunge in the younger boy's direction.

Landon jumped off the porch and sprinted around the yard, Maxx not far behind him. The two ended up on the ground, wrestling good-naturedly. I couldn't stop laughing as I watched them roughhouse.

When Landon finally freed himself, he punched Maxx in the back, and the two carried on with their antics until we were inside the house.

Maxx put an arm around my shoulders and grinned. He was relaxed and comfortable. It was obvious he was happy being with his brother. He kissed the top of my head, and I placed my hand on his chest as he pressed me to his side.

Maxx turned to his brother, who was pulling grass out of his hair. "Landon, I want to introduce you to my girlfriend, Aubrey Duncan. Aubrey, this is my little brother, Landon," Maxx said, beaming at the two of us.

Landon's eyes widened. "Girlfriend? Really? I don't think you've ever had one of those before," he joked. I felt my face get hot. Had he really called me his girlfriend?

Shit, I was Maxx Demelo's girlfriend!

I couldn't stop myself from grinning like an idiot.

Maxx reached around me to smack Landon on the back of the head. "You really need to disengage your mouth from your brain before I kick your ass again," he warned, though there was no threat in his tone. I had never seen Maxx like this before. He was laughing and smiling. His entire demeanor had changed drastically. Gone was the tortured man I had grown accustomed to. This person was someone who was content with his life.

Landon kicked off his shoes and led Maxx and me into the house. It was very apparent that guys lived here. It wasn't filthy or dirty, but any former tidiness had been replaced with clutter and mismatched furniture. I was in eye-twitching hell.

"Thanks for coming over. David shouldn't be home until later, so I thought we could work on the car." Landon darted a look at me. "But we don't have to. We can just hang out or something."

I held up my hands. "No way, I want to watch your super-mechanic skills in action. Don't let me stop you."

Maxx, who hadn't let go of me, rubbed my arm. "You just want to see me all sweaty and dirty, don't you?" he murmured in my ear. I flushed and cleared my throat, shooting a look at Landon, who thankfully wasn't paying us any attention.

I smacked Maxx's chest weakly, and he chuckled into the side of my neck before placing a soft kiss on my skin. I tried not to shiver at the innocent touch.

We headed into the kitchen. It was small and cramped, with a table and chairs pushed against the wall and dishes piled up in the sink. I had to suppress the urge to start washing them.

Maxx headed over to the refrigerator. "You got anything to drink?" he asked, pulling it open.

"No, uh, why don't you have some water," Landon replied hurriedly, trying to shove the fridge door closed.

Maxx frowned and gently pushed his brother aside. He opened the door and let out a growl.

"When was the last time you went to the store?" Maxx asked, clearly unhappy, his mood changing instantly.

Landon hung his head, his shoulders slouched. "I don't know," he mumbled.

I peered around Maxx into the open refrigerator and saw that it was empty save for a few cartons of beer.

Maxx slammed it shut and hit it hard with his fist. I jumped, his violence catching me by surprise. He had been happy only moments earlier, but now he was fuming. Landon, however, didn't so much as blink an eye. Clearly, Maxx's fits weren't unusual.

Maxx pulled his keys out of his pocket and marched to the front door. "Get your jacket; we're going to the store," he announced.

Landon and I followed behind him. "You don't have to do that, Maxx. I can go during the week," Landon protested.

Maxx whirled around to face his little brother. "This is bullshit, Landon! The money you get every month is for *you*! Not so David can fuck off and piss it away on hookers and poker!" Maxx's hands clenched into fists. "I'll start coming by once a week and taking you to the store. That way I'll *know* you have something to eat." He took a deep breath and leveled his brother with a look that brooked no argument.

Landon glanced at me, and I could tell he was embarrassed. "Sure," he muttered, walking past his big brother and back out onto the porch.

Maxx rubbed his temples, closing his eyes and letting out a

frustrated breath. When he had collected himself, he looked at me and gave me a sheepish smile. "Sorry about all this," he apologized.

I shook my head. "Don't. He's your brother. I understand wanting to take care of him. Let's go to the store," I said, tucking my hand in his.

He wrapped his fingers around mine, pulled me in, and gently kissed my lips.

The three of us went to the store and loaded Landon up with enough food to feed an army. Landon argued every time we put something in the cart, but Maxx wouldn't hear any objections.

It took us half an hour once we got back to the house to bring in the bags and unload everything. Maxx had Landon put several boxes of Pop-Tarts, crackers, and cereal bars in his room.

"So *he* can't take it all," Maxx told him as he stuffed the boxes in the younger boy's closet.

Slowly, Maxx's anger disappeared, replaced by the easy companionship I had witnessed earlier. Watching the brothers together, my heart felt heavy, and I couldn't help but miss Jayme.

My story had ended badly. I just hoped this one had a better ending.

"Come out to the garage! I want to show you what I worked on this week," Landon enthused once we were finished putting everything away. Maxx grinned at his brother, slinging an arm around his narrow shoulders.

Seeing Maxx with Landon made it impossible to ignore the feelings I was developing for him. The caring nurturer that Maxx became around his brother made it easy to forget the parts of him that scared me.

I went with the boys out to the garage. The air was thick with paint fumes, and Maxx immediately hit the button to roll back the bay. "I hope you're leaving the place open if you're painting in here. You'll catch stupid if you're not careful. And you don't have a whole lot of brain cells to lose," Maxx joked, giving Landon a playful nudge.

Landon grinned at his big brother. He clearly loved being the focus of Maxx's attention. He soaked up everything Maxx said, hanging on his every word. Landon had a major case of hero worship.

"I only did some touching up in here. Don't worry," Landon explained as he pulled the drop cloth off the large object in the middle of the room. The old Mustang had been painted recently, a bright, cherry red, with long flames down the back end.

Maxx was grinning as he walked around the body of the car. "Who did the paint job?" he asked, running a finger along the glossy exterior.

Landon's grin was huge as he watched Maxx appreciate the car. "My buddy Tate has a cousin who owns his own body shop. He came and towed it over there earlier in the week. He did the paint job in exchange for me doing a bunch of odd jobs for him. Looks pretty sweet, right?" he asked, bouncing on his feet in excitement.

Maxx nodded, coming over to clasp Landon's shoulder. "It looks awesome. Did you paint the flames?" he asked.

"Yep! I'd never used an airbrush before, and I thought I'd screw it up. But I think it turned out pretty cool! I designed the flames and did everything," Landon said modestly.

Landon's talent blew me away. The flames were done in varying shades of red, orange, and yellow, with shadings of black and gray. They had texture and depth, and it looked as though fire was literally licking up the side of the car.

"It's amazing, Landon. This looks professional," I piped up, walking closer to the car to have a look. I knelt down and ran my fingers along the paint job.

"You really think so?" Landon asked, coming to stand next to me. I straightened up and gave him a wide, genuine smile.

"Definitely! Maxx said you were an artist, I just had no idea you were so good," I commented. Landon flushed with pride, puffing his chest out.

"Thanks, Aubrey! I'm hoping to go to art school when I graduate. Get into graphic design or something." Landon glanced at Maxx, who still wore a smile, though it was now decidedly strained.

Landon turned back to me and shrugged. "We'll see what happens, I guess," he said, picking up on Maxx's pointed silence.

I gave Maxx a tiny frown, but he wasn't looking at me. His eyes were on his brother, his expression sad.

I cleared my throat, feeling the sudden tension. "So what's left to get this thing road ready?" I asked, slapping my hand on the hood.

Landon's face brightened. "We just need to swap out the alternator, put in new brake pads, and replace the fuel line."

I turned to Maxx, who was digging around in the toolbox. "You do the work yourselves?" I asked. Maxx nodded.

"Where did you learn how to do this stuff?" I asked. Landon chewed on his bottom lip before answering.

"Actually from Uncle David. He's really into cars, and when we first came to live with him, he'd work out here for days. If we wanted to spend any time with him then, we had to learn how to help. It's a pretty good skill to have in the long run, though. It saves us a fortune in mechanic's bills," Landon said, popping the hood of the car and peering down.

"I'll say. I always wanted to know more about cars. It's tough being a girl and dealing with mechanics. They see a female and think they can charge double," I said, staring down into the car. It looked like a mess of metal and dirt to me.

Maxx came up beside me and pointed. "Well, that's the engine," he teased. I elbowed him in the gut and he grunted.

"Smart-ass," I muttered.

"Pull up a chair, Aubrey, and watch. We'll turn you into a gearhead in no time," Landon promised, smiling in that way of his that was so much like his brother's. The two of them together wreaked havoc on my heart.

Landon turned on a small radio, and the boys started working together under the hood of the Mustang. I watched them, amazed at how deftly they maneuvered around the insides of the car.

They laughed and joked, and the atmosphere in the garage was cheerful.

Until a diesel truck pulled into the driveway, the engine gunning in warning.

Landon looked up at the sound and started hastily putting tools away. Maxx's shoulders tensed, and his jaw stiffened. He started to help Landon clean up, purposefully not looking toward the figure coming our way.

"It's about damned time you came by," the voice called out. I looked from Maxx to the man who was approaching. As he got closer I was surprised to see an older version of Maxx and Landon.

Their uncle David was a good-looking man, if a bit on the paunchy side. He looked to be in his midthirties and walked with a confident swagger that reminded me a lot of Maxx.

But it was clear there was no love lost between David and his older nephew. Maxx gave his uncle a look of disgust as he entered the garage. David sneered down at the Mustang, kicking a tire with the toe of his boot.

"I don't know why you bother with this piece of shit. You'll never get it running," he mocked nastily. Landon deflated a bit, and I wanted to smack the hateful smile off David's face.

Landon continued to clean up, but he seemed to shrink in on himself. "I told you to keep this place neat and tidy; otherwise I'll have this fucking car towed out of here," David warned, knocking over a pile of boxes.

"Sorry, Uncle David. I'll clean it up," Landon replied hastily.

Maxx held his arm out to stop his brother from rushing over

to pick up the boxes. "Landon didn't make the mess, David. Why don't you move your fat ass and do it yourself?" he growled.

David's face turned red, and then his attention shifted in my direction. His dull blue eyes swept up and down my body, his lip curled in a lascivious grin. "Is this pretty piece of pussy an early birthday gift?" David asked. His blatant interest made me want to take a shower.

"Don't talk about my girl like that," Maxx snarled, grabbing my arm and pulling me behind him.

David laughed. "There's no way you can hang on to a piece of ass like that, Maxxy." David inclined his head in my direction. "A word of advice, baby, ditch the limp dick and find yourself a real man." David licked his lips, and I shuddered in revulsion.

Maxx made a choking noise in the back of his throat, and for a brief moment I thought things were going to turn gladiator. David and Maxx stared each other down, neither giving an inch.

I gripped Maxx's arm, digging my nails into his flesh, trying to stop him from what he seemed about to do. Finally, he looked at me. "We need to leave now before I take a crowbar to his thick skull," Maxx snarled through clenched teeth.

He turned to his brother, who was picking up the boxes David had knocked over. "We've got to go, Landon. I'll call you in a few days," Maxx promised, his face regretful.

Landon nodded but didn't lift his head as we left. Maxx pushed past his uncle, who reached out to grab his arm.

Maxx wrenched out of his grasp. "Keep your fucking hands off me," Maxx snarled. David lifted his hands in surrender and chuckled a little nervously.

"I hope you left me some cash. Things have been a little tight around here." David's words were mild but clearly threatening as his eyes darted back to Landon, who was still cleaning up the mess his uncle had made.

The position Maxx found himself in as a result of his uncle was all too clear. David used Landon to get what he wanted from Maxx. And Maxx loved his brother too much to say no. How easy it had been for me to condemn his life at Compulsion; I hadn't understood his motivations.

This was his motivation.

Maxx pulled out his wallet and threw two hundred-dollar bills onto the sidewalk before grabbing me by the arm again and pulling me after him.

"Thanks, Maxxy!" David called out, and I looked over my shoulder one last time to see the older man crouched down, picking the money up off the ground and Landon standing just inside the garage, watching us leave.

I lifted my hand to say good-bye, and Landon waved back. My stomach twisted in knots at leaving the younger boy by himself with his uncle. I could only imagine how Maxx felt each and every time he had to go home.

"Get in!" Maxx said gruffly, holding the door open for me. His entire body was trembling, and his eyes were manic.

I scrambled inside. Maxx slammed the door shut behind me before getting in the car. He pounded his fists on the steering wheel and yelled. It was a deep, painful sound that made me want to touch him, to comfort him. But something told me my actions wouldn't be well received right now.

In quick, jerky movements, he started the engine and pulled away from the curb, not bothering to look for oncoming traffic.

"I hate that fucker!" Maxx howled, jerking the car right, then left, as he began the drive back to his apartment.

"I'm going to fuck that bastard up one day! When Landon doesn't have to live there anymore, he's going to find himself at the bottom of a seven-foot hole," Maxx raged, swerving in and out of traffic.

My heart was beating wildly in my chest. I was worried about us getting back to the apartment in one piece. But I didn't say anything. I didn't want to be on the receiving end of his anger.

And something told me he wouldn't hear anything I had to say anyway.

Once we got back to the apartment, I hurried to follow Maxx up the stairs. He didn't wait for me.

He headed straight for his bedroom, not stopping to turn on lights or even to take off his jacket. The Maxx he had been earlier that morning was gone.

Maxx pulled out the drawer of his bedside table, sending it crashing to the floor. He fell to his knees and picked up the brown bottle that he always kept there but that I had hoped he'd never need again.

All the warm, fuzzy feelings I had been enveloped by earlier disappeared into a mixture of distress and revulsion as I watched Maxx shake several pills into his palm, then put them in his mouth. They made a sickening crunch as he smashed them between his teeth.

Then he shook out a few more, and they followed the first lot down his throat.

It was then that he looked up and realized I was still there.

"Go home, Aubrey," he said tiredly, getting to his feet so he could fall onto his bed.

"Why?" I couldn't help asking. I wasn't sure what my question meant. Why did he let his uncle get to him like that? Why had his first instinct been to come home and get loaded? Why couldn't he turn to me when he was upset? Why was I always competing with the bitch at the bottom of that bottle? He said he needed me, that he wanted *me*! But what did he turn to when things got rough?

Why couldn't I be enough?

Maxx shook his head, putting an arm over his eyes. "Just go home," he repeated dully.

And with a sad resignation, I left him, unable to watch as he fell down the dark pit he seemed determined to throw himself into.

chapter
twenty-three

maxx

I wished Aubrey could be enough.

And even though I couldn't stay away from her and even though I wanted to be with her all the time, I couldn't let myself depend on her completely.

Why *couldn't* I allow myself to turn to her when I was at my lowest, when I fell down and smashed into pieces?

I was a man split in two. And the part of me that craved Aubrey was fighting the part of me that craved something else entirely.

When Aubrey and I were together, I didn't hear the noise in my head. My body didn't ache with the cravings I had become so familiar with. I couldn't think about anything but losing myself in her.

She was my balm. And while she was with me, her hands, her lips, her smile, her laugh were the only drugs I wanted.

Until the anger took over. Then I needed something more than Aubrey's calm to erase the raging inside me.

And when Aubrey would leave, *she* took her place.

She didn't like to be ignored. *She* howled in my brain and twisted my body in her rage. *She* needed to be appeased before she ate me alive.

In those desperate moments, I was only too happy to give in. It was as though the hours with Aubrey were a dam, and when she was gone, the waters were released, sweeping me away without mercy. It hurt to resist. So I didn't.

I used to need only one pill to get high. Then it was two. Then three.

Now it was four pills until I was experiencing the kind of bliss that easily replaced everyone and everything.

And for a time, even Aubrey.

They were at war against each other, Aubrey and the drugs. Both had a claim on me. I needed both. But they couldn't coexist.

I had to hide the drugs from Aubrey. I had to be careful. I understood that, given what had happened to her sister, she hated them. She was as straight-edged as they came.

She didn't understand that it was my choice to use. That *I* dictated when and how much I took. That being high was the greatest form of control I had in my life.

I wished things could have been as easy as holding Aubrey's hand and skipping off into the sunset of our happily ever after. I really wanted that.

But I had responsibilities. Landon relied on me. My uncle used me. Gash and the club had me by the nuts if I didn't do my job. And the drugs . . . they owned me. They were my key out of the prison. And even the promise of Aubrey wasn't enough for me to throw that key away. My heart wanted to, but my mind wouldn't let me.

So I kept *her*.

We all had our secrets, and the pills were mine.

And I was Aubrey's.

She was terrified we'd be found out. She agonized over the consequences of being with me. Without realizing it, she had turned me into something ugly and shameful. And I couldn't even blame her for that, because I already felt those things about myself.

But when Aubrey kissed me, when I was inside her, I could pretend I was enough.

She told me I was perfect, that I was smart and worthy. She tirelessly worked on building me up so that I would never have the temptation to fall.

When we were together, I believed it all. But when she left, I doubted, at least until I was with *her* again.

I'd put the pills between my teeth and smile while I swallowed my self-destruction.

Is there any better feeling than knowing that every pain, every hurt, every disgusting, guilt-ridden thought could be erased . . . just . . . like . . . that?

I wasn't expecting Aubrey until after her evening class. I had roughly five hours to kill before I had to be sober. So I decided to use the time wisely. I found the bag of oxy in my dresser drawer and shook four pills out onto my palm.

I took a quick inventory of my supply. I'd have to double my price for the remaining pills to make up the difference. I should have been more worried about using the drugs that I was meant to sell.

The beating I'd received from Gash and Vin had been the warning. I wouldn't be lucky enough to walk away next time. Marco had ripped me a new asshole a few days after I had recovered. He was pissed as hell and feeling paranoid that our other side venture would be discovered because I was being sloppy.

My drugs wouldn't take only me down, but Marco as well. We had been skimming a cut of the door profits for over three months now. It was not enough to be noticeable, but over time it was a good bit of cash.

I wasn't alone in my stupidity. Marco was right there with me. Greed was as much a high as the drugs. The adrenaline rush from slipping the money in our pockets was almost as addictive as the pills.

Gash was already onto me since the money from my sales didn't equal the supply I was given. I should have been smart enough to cover my tracks. It was a moronic move, one that I would eventually pay for.

But now I'd have to toe the line and not give Gash or his trained monkeys any reason to doubt I was doing my job. And that would keep Marco's nose clean and far away from Gash's fist.

My head lolled on the back of the couch, my arms heavy and my head thick. I'd worry about selling the rest of the bag over the weekend.

I wondered whether Aubrey would expect some sort of boyfriend crap. I'd been inside her, laid my heart on the ground at her feet, yet I never knew what to do around her. She had me second-guessing everything.

God, when had I become such a chick about this shit?

I still had things I had to do, and as much as I wanted to spend all of my time with Aubrey, that couldn't happen.

Now that I was thinking about her, I couldn't stop. Even as fucked-up as I was—unable to move my limbs, my body weighted down, and stoned out of my mind—my heart slammed madly in my chest at the memory of her face. A goofy smile stretched my lips as I thought about how easy it was to be myself around her, the person I had almost forgotten how to be.

"Yo, Maxx, let me in!" a voice yelled from the other side of the door, followed by a pounding that rattled my skull.

There was no way I was getting my ass up off the couch. Fuck whoever wanted in. They needed to take a number.

I closed my eyes, trying to ignore the persistent knocking.

"I will kick this door down if you don't open up!" the voice threatened.

Fuck me, chill out already.

I slowly got to my feet and sluggishly made my way to the door.

Marco shoved past me the moment I opened the door. "What the hell, man? I've been trying to get hold of you for days!" Marco scowled as he made his way into my apartment. He headed straight for my bedroom.

The fucker had serious issues with personal boundaries.

I was having a major problem seeing straight. I knew I should be worried by Marco's aggressive entrance, but like every time I was doped up, I couldn't summon the energy to care.

I leaned against the doorframe and watched Marco pull out my bedside drawer, rooting around until he found the baggie of pills I had put there. He held them up to the light and started counting.

"Make yourself at home," I slurred, swinging my hand out in front of me in a sweeping gesture.

Marco tossed the bag onto the bed and advanced toward me. My mouth was frozen in a lazy smile, which I could tell pissed Marco off.

He grabbed me by the front of my shirt and shook me. I tried to shove him off but with no success.

"What the fuck?" I mumbled, trying to get away from him.

"You've been taking them, haven't you? You're supposed to be selling them, not eating the shit for breakfast!" he yelled into my face.

Marco was a scary dude to most people. But I remembered him when he wore his pants around his knees, was covered in acne, and had no game whatsoever. He'd been a joke. Now he liked to think of himself as a badass. But a few years of weightlifting and covering his face in metal didn't erase the fact that he used to be the biggest douche on the planet.

"Don't start with your goddamned lectures. If I wanted advice, I wouldn't be asking for it from the guy who let some cracked-out chick pierce his junk with a needle," I said with a smirk, shoving Marco hard in the chest and sending him stumbling backward.

Even fucked-up out of my mind, I could still take him. I grabbed my dick crudely and flipped him off. I went to the bed and picked up the baggie, shoving it back in the drawer.

"Stay the fuck out of my stuff," I warned, pointing at him with a wobbly finger.

Marco sneered, stretching his lips in an ugly grin.

"So what's your great plan, Maxx? How the fuck are you going to make the money back so Gash won't shove your nose up your own asshole? Come on, tell me your latest stroke of genius! I'm dying here." Marco flopped down on the bed and put his muddy combat boots up on my sheets. Not that they were clean or anything, but I didn't appreciate him messing up my shit.

"Get your boots off my bed, man," I told him, though my voice sounded weak in my ears. Messed up and wanting a nap was not the way to have a confrontation. I could barely keep my eyes open. Marco was seriously screwing with my high. I'd have to kick his ass for that later.

Marco ignored my comment as he continued to regard me. "Look at you, Maxx. You are *fucked-up*. If Gash saw you like this, you'd be wearing your rib cage as a hat. What the hell is up with you?" he asked, sounding a mixture of angry and concerned.

When it came down to it, for all his shank-you-in-the-gut skinhead act, he was just looking out for me. Marco and I had been friends for years. We went back a long way. And we'd always had each other's backs. It was because of Marco that I landed the extremely well-paying job I had to begin with, a job that allowed me to take care of my brother, keep a roof over my head, and pay for school.

"I'll charge double," I offered with a shrug, as if that were the most obvious answer in the world.

Marco barked out a laugh. "Are you fucking with me?" he asked incredulously.

I frowned. I had thought it was a good idea.

"Why is that so funny?"

Marco snorted. "Dude, there are enough people slinging around this city, you charging double for midgrade pills won't make you a cent. It won't make Gash the money he expects. You, my friend, are a fucking moron."

"You don't know shit, Marco. You just sit at the door and tell the chicks if they look pretty and leave the hard stuff to me," I derided.

Marco's face darkened. He dropped his feet down to the floor with a loud thud. "Don't fuck around. You're not just messing up stuff for you, but for me too. What do you think will happen if Gash figures out you're taking more than you're selling, that you don't have the money to give him?" Marco got to his feet and started pacing, something he did when he was ready to lose it.

Why the hell was he freaking out so badly? I should be the one worrying. My head started to pound, and the pills across the room were screaming for my attention.

"He'll start looking at all of us, man. I've been smart about the door money, but Gash could figure it out, you know! He'd have us both taken out!" Marco smashed his hand into the wall beside my desk.

"Stop being such a pussy about it. No one put a gun to your head and made you steal from the door. So don't start bitching about it now," I stated matter-of-factly. Marco's jaw started to tick.

"Have you found a location yet?" Marco asked, changing the subject.

I shrugged. "Not yet," I said unemotionally. I really should have more of a sense of self-preservation than this. I was walking on some pretty thin ice.

Marco gripped his skull, which was covered in a badly done tribal tattoo. Dude really had bad taste when it came to body art.

"Are you trying to kill me? Seriously. Well, get your shit, we're finding something now. Gash expects the information tonight." Marco marched past me and into the hallway.

"I can't make it tonight. I've got plans," I called after him, trying not to laugh as he became even more enraged.

"The hell you can't. Get. Your. Shit. We're leaving," Marco announced, slamming my front door behind him as he left.

I should have called Aubrey. I should have explained that I wouldn't be home this evening.

But I didn't.

The drugs made everything but the here and now a vague, hazy memory.

They made it easier to think I could just deal with it all later.

✦

Marco pulled up outside an unassuming office building a few hours later. It was a little after eight, and Marco and I had just returned from finding a run-down middle school. We had gone through the building, and even though it looked one step away from being condemned, it would work for the club.

Marco had stopped at a diner on the way to Gash's office and plied me with food and coffee in an attempt to sober me up. I was already coming down, which of course left me shaky and sick to my stomach.

The burger I had eaten earlier threatened to come back up. I grabbed Marco's arm before we headed into the office. "Dude, do you have anything?" I asked, trying not to beg. "Seriously, I just need one."

Marco grunted, giving me a look of disgust. "You've really got to get your shit together, man," he muttered, fishing in his pocket for a small bag. He shook out one tiny white pill and held it up between his thumb and forefinger.

I went to snatch it from his hands, but he held it back. "Aren't you supposed to be going to some support group or something? Because if this is how the whole twelve-step thing works, it sucks," he commented.

I glared at him, not bothering to correct the twelve-step comment. I was too busy swallowing down the bile that filled my mouth. "Just give it to me and save the sermon for someone who gives a damn," I said as I tried not to throw up on my buddy's shoes. My head had started hammering, and I knew there was no way I could face Gash without something to take the edge off.

Marco shoved the pill in my hand. I hurriedly put it in my mouth, crunching it between my teeth. "Just give me a second," I said, leaning against the side of Marco's beat-up Volvo.

Ten minutes later, the shakes had stopped, and the nausea was almost gone. I still felt spaced, but I was good enough to go inside.

Gash's office was not what you'd expect from the guy who ran the most successful underground club on the East Coast. The first time I had come here, I had anticipated black lights and mood lighting, and at least a muscled henchman or two.

It was completely empty, which wasn't surprising given that it was after eight in the evening. Gash kept . . . *unusual* hours.

The place was sterile and nondescript. The office was in the kind of building where you'd expect to run into a herd of accountants. Marco and I stuck out like sore thumbs in this environment of cream walls and bad art reproductions.

In Gash's other life, he was known as Trevor McMillan, and he worked as an IT analyst for a small security firm.

So how did Trevor become Gash? That was the question of the decade. There were plenty of rumors as to how he'd started Compulsion, just as there were a million stories of how he had earned the nickname he was known by—and I seriously doubted any of them were true.

Who the fuck knew? Did it really matter? The answer didn't change the fact that he was one scary motherfucker for a scrawny IT guy who played club manager goon on the side.

Marco knocked on the door and went inside without waiting for an answer. Gash sat behind a plain wooden desk, his head bowed over a keyboard. He could have passed for someone's pedophile uncle or a used-car salesman. He wasn't particularly intimidating, just sort of smarmy . . . until he looked at you.

His cold, dead stare could make a lesser man squirm. I wasn't too macho to admit I'd been close to pissing myself a time or two in his presence.

Marco closed the door and had a seat at one of the two upholstered chairs against the wall. I followed, hands shoved in my pockets, shoulders hunched defensively. You never knew what you were going to get when you had a meeting with Gash.

Some days he was fine, civil even, though he very rarely cracked a smile.

Then there were the days when you were waiting for him to pull a knife from his coat and slit your throat. He was unpredictable, which should have made Marco and me think twice before stealing from him. We should have been smarter than to mess with a guy like Gash. But as I said, money and drugs were a temptation neither of us could turn away from, sad, sick bastards that we were.

Marco handed Gash the slip of paper where he had written the address for the old school. Without looking at either of us, Gash turned back to his computer and started clicking away, looking at a map on the screen.

"Is this in a residential area?" he asked, finally looking at us. He turned his unemotional stare on me.

I shook my head. "It used to be, but the area is run-down now. Most of the houses have either been foreclosed or abandoned. Not many people still live there, and the few that do are old. No families. No kids," I reported.

I curled my hands around the arms of the chair. I was sweating bullets. Damn, I needed another pill.

"Police?" Gash asked.

"The police station is on the other side of town. The force just laid off three officers, so they're bare-bones right now. I don't see much of a problem," Marco piped up, filling in what I should have already known.

This is the sort of research I normally would have done. Marco was picking up the slack, and I definitely owed him one.

"I'll get one of the guys to poke around a bit, see if there's some-one we can talk to about making sure we don't have any problems on Saturday," Marco said, glancing at me out of his peripheral vision. Could it be any more obvious I hadn't done a thing?

And it wasn't lost on Gash. He regarded me as though I were shit on his shoe.

"And what the fuck have you been doing while Marco has been doing your job? What the hell am I paying you for? A little painting here and there doesn't cut it. Sit up and stop fucking slouching!" Gash demanded. I felt like a kid in the principal's office. Would my punishment be detention or an ass beating?

I sat up in my chair slowly. I couldn't help but be oppositional about it. I was a tit like that.

"I've had a lot of shit going on," I offered by way of an excuse, though I knew it was lame at best. My pathetic justification obviously made Gash really, really angry.

He leaned over his desk, his lips peeled back to bare his yellowed teeth, lines forming between his eyebrows. "I don't care what is going on, you have a job to do, so do it! Marco shouldn't be doing the shit I pay *you* for." Gash jerked his thumb at Marco, who had all but disappeared into the upholstery of the chair. Not drawing attention to yourself when Gash was pissed was a matter of survival, plain and simple.

I nodded curtly. "I get it; it won't happen again," I said.

"Vin said he dropped off the week's product to you a couple of days ago. I want the money on Sunday. Not Monday. Not Tuesday. But fucking Sunday! I've got my eye on you and I'm not happy with what I'm seeing," Gash warned, running his finger along the scar under his eye.

He had been stabbed in the face by a junked-out crackhead a few years ago. The crackhead was dead. Gash was still here. Point made.

I nodded again. "You'll get it, not a problem." Too bad it was actually a very big problem.

"You're looking a little shaky. You all right?" Gash asked, eyeing me shrewdly. He was no dumb shit. I knew that *he knew* I was coming down . . . hard.

"It's those downers. You need something to bring you up. Try this. Just get yourself together. I don't need a damned junkie selling my shit. That's a liability I do *not* want," he growled, tossing a baggie of dried leaves in my lap.

I opened it and gave it a sniff. What was this? It didn't smell like weed. Maybe it was some crazy hallucinogenic.

"It's an herbal tea, dipshit. Ginkgo biloba, a little bit of ginseng. It's good for the blood flow to the brain. Go home and make yourself a cup."

I wanted to laugh my ass off at the irony. Gash, the biggest drug pusher this side of New York, was offering me a bag of herbal fucking tea.

I chanced a look at Marco, who was chewing the inside of his cheek as he also tried not to laugh at our boss peddling his hardcore herbal remedies.

"Sure, sounds great," I said, tucking the bag in my pocket.

Gash pointed at me. "I'm serious, you have this weekend to show me you can still handle all of this. Because next week I'm getting a shipment of stuff up from Mexico that can make *everyone* a hell of a lot of money. I need to know you'll do what I need you to do."

Marco and I got to our feet. "You got it, Gash," I promised.

"And drink some of that tea," our boss instructed as we left. I patted my pocket in agreement.

Out in the parking lot, I wiped sweat off my forehead. I needed to get home. I needed to even myself out. Fuck the tea.

"You got off pretty easy in there, Maxx. You need to listen to what Gash was telling you," Marco lectured.

I rolled my eyes, sick of hearing the same ol' shit.

It's only when I'd gotten home and had taken another couple of pills that I remembered Aubrey. Before passing out, I wondered if she had come by. Maybe I should call her. Explain what had happened.

But then the high took over, and I forgot all about Aubrey.

I forgot about everything.

chapter
twenty-four

aubrey

I was pissed.

No, I was *livid*.

I had gone by Maxx's apartment last night and pounded on the door. He hadn't answered. So I had waited outside. In the freezing cold. For hours!

And he had never showed.

I had tried phoning him, but the call went straight to voice mail. I had been tempted to call back over and over again, but I had controlled the urge.

So now I was not only angry and hurt but also ready to inflict bodily harm the next time I saw him.

Our relationship was only weeks old, but already we were failing at it miserably. What chance did we have when I was mired in distrust and wariness? I knew that if he wasn't with me, he was most likely doing something that would break my heart.

I knew he was being unfaithful.

But he wasn't with another woman. He was spending all of his time with the tiny white pills he was so fond of.

I came out of the psychology building and pulled my hood up

over my hair. It had started to snow while I was in class, and I wished I could appreciate the white silence that had descended. But I couldn't. I was too wound up.

"Aubrey!"

My head snapped up to see Maxx hurrying across the quad, his book bag slung over his shoulder. His hair was wet from the falling snow, his curls plastered to his forehead. He was smiling a megawatt grin as he hurried toward me. I had been hoping to get off campus before seeing him. I should have known better. His knowledge of my schedule was disconcerting.

And to see him now, he looked like any other college student. But I knew what dwelled beneath the surface—an ugly darkness dressed up with his beautiful face.

I thought about ignoring him and walking away, but I knew he would only follow me. And I wasn't going to try to outrun him across campus.

So I waited until he caught up with me.

He reached out to grab my hand, but I pulled back before he could touch me.

Maxx grimaced. "Right, I forgot where we were. Sorry," he said, but his smile returned, brighter than ever.

"Are you done with classes for the day?" he asked, falling into step beside me.

I didn't answer him, my irritation and frustration making communication impossible.

As the silence between us grew, Maxx's smile slipped, and he frowned. He grabbed hold of my arm to stop me. "What's wrong?" he asked, puzzled.

"I waited for you last night," I told him coldly, narrowing my eyes.

Maxx hung his head. "Right. I knew you were coming by. I'm sorry," he said. He lifted his eyes to look at me, his face a plea for me to forgive him.

"Where were you?" I asked, letting my annoyance bleed through.

"Marco came by. We had to go out for a bit," he told me, giving a minimal explanation.

I could ask what they were doing, but I probably didn't want to know. And I doubt he would have told me anyway. His life at Compulsion was something we never talked about. It was the wall between us.

"Why didn't you call me then? To at least tell me you wouldn't be at home?" I asked, trying really hard to hold on to my irritation. It was hard when Maxx looked so contrite.

He began to gnaw on his bottom lip as drops of melting snow slid down his face. "I should have called you. I didn't. I don't have an excuse, at least none that would make you feel better. Just know that I'm sorry and that I'd rather be with you than anywhere else in the world," he said, and for some reason, his lack of justification went a long way toward soothing my anger.

He wasn't making excuses. He wasn't trying to get himself out of trouble. He accepted that he had messed up, and he apologized. And, strangely, I appreciated that.

I let out a deep sigh, my shoulders dropping. "Just try to remember next time, all right?" I said. Maybe I was letting him off too easy. Perhaps I should make him feel even guiltier for standing me up. But what would be the point? Why prolong the unhappiness of us both?

"I will, I promise," he swore, and I almost cringed. *I promise.* Why did it feel as though he was setting himself up to fail by uttering those words?

Maxx hoisted his book bag up higher on his shoulder, and his smile returned. "Can I take you somewhere?" he asked, his eyes sparkling with excitement.

I rubbed my hands together, trying to keep them warm. "You want to take me somewhere?" I asked him, raising my eyebrows.

Maxx chuckled. He chanced a look around before he reached

out to cup the side of my face. "Somewhere special. Is that okay?"
he asked, his thumb stroking my cheek.

I closed my eyes briefly, knowing I'd cave. "Fine," I said.

Maxx's grin was contagious, and I couldn't stop my own smile
from making an appearance. "Let's go then," he said, dropping his
hand from my face and grabbing my hand, not caring who saw us.

He headed me toward the parking lot. He opened the passenger door of his car, letting me inside. My stomach fluttered every
time he did that.

Once Maxx was inside, he started the car and cranked the heat.
He took my hands between his and blew his warm breath over
them. He kissed my fingers one at a time, smiling into my skin.

The snow was falling more heavily now; it was settling in a
thick coating on the grass. So far the roads seemed to be okay, but
I worried about how safe his car would be on the road.

"It looks like it's getting pretty nasty out. Maybe we should do
this another day," I suggested, peering out my window.

Maxx shook his head. "No way. This is perfect weather for
what I have in mind," he enthused, wrapping a hand around mine
as he maneuvered his car out of the parking lot.

"Why does that make me nervous?" I teased as Maxx pulled
into traffic.

"Don't be nervous. I'll take care of you," he stated with total
sincerity. I really wanted to believe him. When he was like this, relaxed and carefree, it was easy to let myself trust him.

Maxx drove with little concern for the rapidly deteriorating
weather conditions. The snow was coming down in heavy bands.
"Maybe you should slow down," I suggested, gasping as Maxx took
a turn a little faster than I liked.

Maxx snorted. "I can tell you're from the South. Aubrey, this is
nothing. I've driven in worse weather than this," he placated.

"Not with me, you haven't," I muttered, and Maxx laughed,
though he did slow down considerably, much to my relief.

A few minutes later, he parked along a nondescript residential street.

"Where are we?" I asked, surprised when Maxx got out of the car. He came around to my side and held the door open for me to get out. He tilted my chin up and softly kissed my mouth, cold, wet snow mixing with the heat of his lips.

"You'll see," he said, his eyes dancing. He went around to the trunk and popped it open.

"Put these on," he said, handing me a clunky pair of black snow boots.

"No way will these fit me," I scoffed, holding them up by their laces.

"Just tighten up the straps on the sides. They'll be fine," Maxx assured me, leaning down to put on his own pair of boots.

I did as he asked and took off my sneakers and handed them to Maxx, who tossed them into the trunk. I slid my feet into the boots, which were easily five sizes too big. I tightened the laces and buckled the straps on the sides as much as I was able to, though I knew I still looked ridiculous.

I put my hands on my hips and gave him an irritated scowl. "Are you going to explain why you're having me dress like Bozo the Clown?" I asked.

Maxx handed me a thermos while he grabbed two final items from his car. He had obviously come prepared.

"Sleds?" I asked incredulously.

Maxx tucked the two red plastic sleds under his arm and smiled sweetly.

"Yep, these are sleds," he teased.

He slammed the trunk closed and cocked his head in the direction of a wooded path between two houses. "Come on."

I clomped after Maxx in the snow, which had already accumulated up to my ankles. Walking in Maxx's boots slowed me down considerably, and he had to stop periodically to allow me to catch up. He led me down a small lane that cut through a shaded group of trees.

I could hear laughing and yelling off in the distance. We broke through the trees to find ourselves at the back end of a subdivision. Behind the row of houses was a steep incline that ended at a soccer pitch at the bottom.

The place was teeming with kids. Obviously, the schools had been dismissed early because of the snow, and most of the local children had congregated at the most epic sledding hill I had ever seen.

"This is where you wanted to take me?" I asked Maxx, looking up at him in astonishment. By this point, I should have given up on being surprised by anything Maxx did. But I couldn't reconcile the man I had come to know with the person standing beside me now, holding two children's sleds and looking as ecstatic as the kids around him.

He shoved his hands in his pockets and took in the scene in front of him, a distant look in his eyes and a soft smile on his lips. "My mom used to bring me here on every snow day. It was something special that was just between us. She would let me sled down that hill until I couldn't stand, and then she'd give me some hot chocolate and carry me back to the car."

I didn't say anything, not wanting to ruin this rare moment of transparency. Maxx pointed to an outcrop of stone at the bottom of the hill. "I broke my arm after I hit a rock down there."

He laughed, and it was a sad and lonesome sound. "My mom freaked out. I got to ride in an ambulance, which for a nine-year-old was the coolest thing ever. So I didn't think a lot about the fact that my bone was sticking out through my skin."

His smile faded and twisted into a grimace. "I haven't been here since I was ten," he murmured, staring ahead, lost in his memories.

I felt my throat tighten and my eyes burn. I knew what he was doing, even if he didn't realize it. He was giving me a piece of himself, a part of him that belonged to a time before the drugs. Before the club. Before his life had derailed.

I took a deep, shuddering breath and tried to calm the erratic thump of my heart. How could I not lose my heart to the man who stood in front of me, giving me the most precious thing he had? His memories. His happiness. The parts of his life that were untainted.

Maxx blinked a few times as if reminding himself of where he was. He turned back to me, his lip quirking upward slightly. He took the thermos from my hands, set it down beneath a tree, and handed me one of the sleds. "It'll be fun. I promise," he said, pulling his beanie out of his back pocket and putting it on.

There were those words again. *I promise.*

But this time, with his eyes sparkling and giddy, I actually believed him.

I rolled my eyes. "Sure, if I don't break my neck first," I deadpanned, and Maxx kissed the tip of my nose.

"Stop being so pessimistic," he chastised, grabbing my hand and heading toward the crest of the hill.

I chewed on my bottom lip as I watched little kids zip down the hill, screaming the entire way. I could admit I was a bit of a wimp. Plus the incline was really steep, and I had already witnessed a few wipeouts.

"Yeah, I'm not so sure." I hesitated as Maxx settled down on his sled. We were getting some strange looks from the children around us. I'm sure it was more than a little odd seeing a couple of adults playing in the snow alongside them.

Maxx looked up at me. "You've never been sledding before, have you?" he deduced.

I shook my head. I felt like an idiot. But we didn't get a whole lot of snow in North Carolina. A few flakes and the world shut down. Half an inch closed school, but it had never been enough to sled in.

Maxx scooted back in his sled and patted the spot in front of him. "We'll go down together," he said.

"We'll be too heavy. There's no way that will work," I reasoned.

"Actually, you go faster with more weight," a little boy standing beside me piped up. I looked down at him and frowned.

"That's not helping right now," I told him.

The boy, who didn't look a day over seven and was decked out in head-to-toe snow gear, rolled his eyes.

"Don't be such a wimp," he said.

Maxx snorted, and my mouth dropped open. Was this kid making fun of me?

"You heard the little dude. Don't be such a wimp," Maxx goaded. Not wanting to look like an ass in front of a grade-schooler, I sat down on the sled in front of Maxx and squished my legs inside the frame.

Maxx's legs pressed into mine, and he wrapped his arms around my middle, pulling me back tightly against his front. Even through the layers of our clothing, I felt the heat of his body.

He rested his chin on my shoulder and kissed my neck. "Here we go. Hold on tight," he whispered softly, stirring the hairs by my ear. The boy was smirking at me, and I stuck my tongue out at him. He widened his eyes and ran off.

"Wow, that was mature, Aubrey." Maxx laughed. I shrugged.

"He deserved it," I quipped, feeling warm and tingly as Maxx's chuckle vibrated against my back.

And then, without giving me a chance to prepare myself, Maxx pushed us off and we sailed down the hill. My hair blew back, and the wind was cold on my face. I screamed like a wuss the whole way down.

When we got to the bottom, we hit a snowdrift and popped up into the air. Maxx and I both went flying off the sled. I landed with a thud on my back, wet sludge sliding down my face. I stayed that way, staring at the sky, trying to get my breath back.

Suddenly Maxx was leaning over me, grinning like a fool. "Wasn't that awesome?"

He helped me to my feet and brushed snow from my jeans. I patted my arms and legs, searching for broken bones.

Maxx grabbed my hand and started marching back up the hill. "Let's do it again," he called out, pulling me after him.

I tripped and fell, bringing Maxx down with me. I laughed and grabbed a handful of snow and shoved it down the back of his shirt. He yelped and tried to remove it.

I was doubled over in fits of near hysterics as I watched my boyfriend hop around trying to get the snow out of his shirt.

And then he stopped, and I knew that mischievous glint in his blue eyes was bad news. He slowly and purposefully bent down and scooped up a handful of snow. "You wanna play like that, huh?" he asked me, patting the cold stuff into a tight, compact ball.

I held my hands up and started to back away. "Don't you dare, Maxx! I swear to God . . ." I let my threat trail off because then I was running and Maxx was chasing me. I felt the snowball hit the center of my back.

"Get her!" I heard the same little boy from earlier yell, and then I was running not only from Maxx but from four kids who were all hurling snow.

Maxx tackled me in the snow and shielded me as the kids pelted us. "I say we join forces," he said into my ear.

I nodded, and then we were on our feet and running after our would-be attackers. They screeched as we began our epic snow battle.

By the time we called a cease-fire, I had laughed so hard my cheeks hurt and my sides ached. The kids loved Maxx. I snickered as he walked up the hill with three boys hanging off him like monkeys. He was a natural with them, and watching him interact so easily with the children made my heart constrict tightly in my chest.

I never thought I could have so much fun freezing my ass off. By the time we left the field, I was exhausted and happier than I could remember being in a long time.

Maxx handed me the thermos as we trekked back to the car. I

unscrewed the top and took a drink of the still-warm hot chocolate. I gave him a sideways grin. "Chocolate?" I asked.

Maxx smirked. "I remember what it takes to butter you up," he
replied.

I stopped in the middle of the darkened path and turned to
him. I twined my arms around his neck and pulled his head down
so that my lips could touch his.

I opened my mouth and slid my tongue along his. He groaned
in the back of his throat and gathered me tighter against him. The
snow was still coming down, and my clothes were drenched, but I
didn't care.

The only thing I cared about, the only thing that mattered, was
this man in my arms.

I pulled away, and Maxx rested his forehead against mine.
"What was that for?" he asked softly.

I ran my fingers through his wet hair, ignoring the numbness
of my fingers. "For surprising me," I answered just as softly, grinning up at him.

Maxx's fingers dug into my back. "Remind me to surprise you
more often," he growled, nipping at my bottom lip.

I giggled and reached up to kiss him again, but Maxx stopped me.

I cocked my head questioningly as I looked up into his suddenly serious face.

"What is it, Maxx?" I asked him.

He closed his eyes and swallowed.

"I love you, Aubrey," he said in an almost agonized whisper, as
though his confession was ripped out of him by force, as though
saying the words pained him.

I frowned and touched his face with the back of my cold hand.
He opened his eyes, and they shone in the growing darkness. My
lips parted and I wanted to say something back.

I wanted to tell him that I loved him too.

Because I did.

It had been a gradual building of emotion that I recognized even without ever having experienced it before.

It was love. Pure and total love.

But for some reason, the words stuck in my throat. I stood there gaping like a fish as Maxx stared down at me, his eyes beseeching, pleading with me to reciprocate.

And I *did*.

So why couldn't I say the words he needed to hear? The words I wanted to say?

The silence stretched and lengthened, and still I said nothing.

Finally Maxx let out an awkward laugh and looked away. I felt horrible. I had held back from him when he needed something from me so desperately. I hadn't been able to give it to him.

And why?

I couldn't explain why I was so hesitant to verbalize the feelings inside me. Perhaps it was the lingering mistrust or the mounting fear of failure.

I was furious with myself for ruining a perfect day with my insecurities.

Maxx lifted my hand to his mouth and kissed my knuckles. He smiled, but his eyes, which had been happy and content minutes before, were now tinged with sadness.

"Let's get back to my place. I think I still owe you a fettuccine Alfredo," he said, threading his fingers through mine as we made our way back to his car.

"Maxx," I began, but he shook his head before I could continue.

"Don't say anything, Aubrey. Let's go home, and I'll make you the best damned Alfredo you've ever eaten," he stated, his voice hard even as he tried to act unaffected.

I blinked away the tears that were building, and I gave him a shaky smile.

"Sounds great."

chapter
twenty-five

aubrey

After our day in the snow, I thought we had hit a turning point in our relationship. Even after my inability to verbalize my feelings, we had a wonderful evening together.

We had gone back to Maxx's apartment, and he had made me dinner. He had obviously taken the time to straighten up his small apartment and had even vacuumed the carpet.

He had put a lot of effort into making the night special. I had helped him mix the sauce and make the salad. Then we had eaten his overcooked pasta and slightly burned garlic bread by the light of a dozen candles.

After cleaning up, Maxx had suggested we watch a movie. He had been careful in his selection, choosing *The Doom Generation* as an homage to our first date. I had misted up at his romantic sentiment.

Without bothering to watch the movie, I had dragged him back to his room and made quick work of removing our clothing. We made love until the early hours of the morning.

Everything had been so beautiful in its ease and simplicity.

And I clutched at those moments greedily, scared that they would slip through my fingers.

Because the nature of our relationship wasn't one of quiet happiness. And the weeks following our one amazing day together had shown me that we were destined for something much darker.

Because Maxx kept disappearing. He would slip away without my realizing it, and I would be left in a dark torment, worrying about what he was doing, what drugs he was taking, what ways he was destroying himself.

When we were together and he was touching me, I tried to ignore the anxious awareness that this was *temporary*, that when our breathing had slowed and the sweat had dried he'd leave me again. But I kept coming back for more.

Maxx overtook me.

He overwhelmed me.

I was drowning.

The moments of happiness when we were together felt bittersweet because they never lasted long enough.

I knew where he was going, I wasn't stupid. But Maxx deftly evaded my questions when I asked them. But I never pushed too hard. I never grilled too much.

If I was being honest with myself, I simply didn't want the confirmation that he was still selling, still using, still screwing up his life in the worst way imaginable. I was terrified that if my suspicions were confirmed beyond a doubt, I'd be forced to make a decision about our relationship. And I was worried that my choice would make me hate myself.

I was worried that I'd follow him wherever he wanted to lead me.

A strong part of me still wanted to go back to Compulsion. Even though I now knew the reality of what that place was and its role in Maxx's world, I could still remember the thrill I felt when I was inside. The temptation was tantalizing.

So I stuck my head in the sand and tried to carry on as though this dark hole in his life didn't exist.

Some days Maxx was the perfect boyfriend. He was romantic. He was doting. He loved me with all that he had. We laughed and talked together and lived in stolen moments of pure joy. He tried so hard to give me everything I needed.

But not the only thing that I would ever really want: for him to stop—the drugs, the club, all of it.

I knew he wouldn't. So I never asked him to, knowing his answer would break my heart. There were times when he was lucid, his blue eyes clear. He didn't shake or sweat or double over from the nausea of withdrawal. I could almost convince myself that the beast had been slain, that the worries in the back of my mind were unfounded.

But the worries were there nonetheless, rooted in a painful reality that was never far from the bubble we were trying to survive in.

Maxx wouldn't talk to me about the club or anything that had to do with that part of his life. I hated it. I didn't want Maxx to hide things from me, even the ugly parts that I wished weren't real.

And while he kept so much of himself shrouded in secrecy, I knew that he loved me. And even though I had yet to verbally return the sentiment, Maxx never wasted a moment to tell me how he felt.

I love you sat on the tip of my tongue. And when I'd be ready to give it voice, Maxx would leave again, and I would be left with the black, twisted worries that were becoming all too familiar.

◆

"Well, if it isn't my roommate! I was beginning to think I'd have to fill out a missing-person report," Renee teased as I came into the apartment after class on Thursday. I hadn't seen much of Renee over the past few weeks. And I had missed her. While I lived my roller coaster, I wanted so much to confide in her the way I used to be able to. Even though we were crawling slowly back to a more comfortable form of our earlier friendship, I wasn't sure I was ready to share my painful situation.

She looked happier. The bruises from Devon's fists were long gone, and I could tell she had started to put on some much-needed weight. Her skin had a healthy glow, and she was starting to dress in some of her old clothes.

This alone was proof that Devon was no longer in the picture.

"Ha, ha." I rolled my eyes, dropping my book bag on the floor. I had just gone by Maxx's apartment, hoping to see him before class. Of course he hadn't been there. I had waited for twenty minutes, but he hadn't shown up. I had left only when it started raining.

"When was the last time you spent the night here? I was beginning to think I lived by myself," Renee said, closing the book she had been reading and putting it on the couch beside her.

When I didn't say anything, she gave me a small smile.

"So who's the guy, and why haven't I met him yet?" she asked, following me into the kitchen. I opened the refrigerator and pulled out a soda. Popping the top, I took a long drink, thinking about how I was going to answer her.

I continued to live in a constant state of paranoia about being found out. I agonized over what would happen should the wrong person see Maxx and me together. I invented horrific scenarios in my head about the moment when my entire world would implode and my dreams would be dashed to the floor.

I put my soda can down on the counter and let out a sigh. Renee crossed her arms over her chest and regarded me steadily. Despite how much our friendship had changed over the past year, she still knew me better than most anyone.

"What's wrong? Is it this guy?" she asked, sounding concerned. I sighed again. Renee frowned.

"Take it from me, no guy is worth making you feel like shit," she stated firmly.

I leaned against the cabinets, bracing myself against the counter. "I think I love him," I said quickly, shocking myself. The words had slipped out without my usual resistance restraining them. I covered my mouth with my hand as though I could shove the words back inside where they were safe. But now that they were out, there was no putting them back.

Renee blinked in surprise. "Huh? You love a guy I've never even met? Someone you never mention at all? Sorry, but I find that hard to believe," she scoffed, cocking her eyebrow at me in disbelief.

"I can't talk about him, Renee," I begged, hoping she'd let it go. But there was no walking away from it now.

"Uh-uh, you and I are long overdue for a good, long girl talk. Grab the ice cream, I'll get the chips, and we're parking our asses on the couch," Renee instructed, and I couldn't help but smile. After keeping secrets for so long, I found myself looking forward to letting some of them go.

I pulled two pints of Ben & Jerry's out of the freezer and met her in the living room.

"You need to start at the beginning and go from there. Why is this relationship so secret? It's not like you," Renee said as we settled on the couch.

I put a spoonful of ice cream in my mouth, hoping the resulting brain freeze would knock some sense into my otherwise thick skull.

"He's in the support group I help to facilitate," I admitted, confessing my sins quickly. It was like ripping off a Band-Aid—better to do it all at once.

Renee's eyes widened. "Well, that can't be good," she observed.

"Uh, no, it's really bad actually," I mumbled, scooping more ice cream into my mouth.

"Well, the secretiveness makes sense now," Renee mused, putting the Ben & Jerry's aside to start on a bag of sour-cream-and-onion potato chips.

"It started before I realized anything was going on. He sort of snuck up on me, and then it was like a full-blown meltdown. Does that make any sense?" I asked. Actually talking about my relationship with Maxx made me realize how reckless the entire situation was.

"Completely," Renee answered, grimacing. I knew she was thinking about Devon, and not for the first time, I felt guilty for how judgmental and unsympathetic I had been about her feelings for her ex. I now understood how difficult it could be to let go of someone you cared about, even if you knew he was bad for you.

"Brooks knows," I said.

Renee surprised me by rolling her eyes. "Good. He needs a reality check."

"Huh?" I asked.

Renee handed me the chips. "That guy has been panting after you for entirely too long. It's embarrassing to watch."

I shook my head. "No way. We're just friends. We've been there, done that, got the crappy T-shirt," I argued.

Renee rolled her eyes again, making me feel as though I had missed something glaringly obvious. "Well, you're blind then. Because that boy wants a return ticket on the Aubrey Duncan express train straight into your panties. You guys have known each other . . . biblically. There is no way you can go from *that* to friendship without having all sorts of complicated shit under the surface. And Brooks Hamlin wants you . . . bad. So I say, good! He needed something major to make him move the hell on," Renee remarked, not unkindly.

Her crass observation brought a whole new level of complication to an already convoluted equation. Was Renee right? Of course she was right. Deep down I had suspected the same thing for a while now.

"But he knows. And if you're right and he's got these unrequited feelings, what's to stop him from telling someone?" I moaned.

Renee didn't say anything. There was no need to point out the obvious: If I was so worried about repercussions, I shouldn't be doing it in the first place. If I really cared about my future, I should end things with Maxx and forget about him.

But that would make things entirely too simple. And clearly my heart didn't like simple.

Renee reached out and stroked the back of my head. "I honestly don't think Brooks would do that to you. He's your friend, Aubrey. You would never have gotten close to him if you thought him capable of such bitchy behavior." Again, my suddenly wise roommate was right. I couldn't imagine Brooks being so hateful.

Then again, it was hard to forget the anger and hurt on his face when he realized what was going on between Maxx and me. The truth was, I just didn't know who and what to trust anymore.

"I wish I could tell you what to do, but if you hadn't noticed, I'm not the best one to give relationship advice. I can only tell you to be careful. I don't want to see you getting hurt," Renee continued, giving me a look full of sympathy.

Oh, how times had changed. Not too long ago I was bestowing those particular looks on her. I had sunk so low.

Before I could drop to the floor in a flood of self-pity, Renee's phone dinged, letting her know she had a text message. She picked it up off the coffee table and read it, her face contorting in a mixture of anger and fear.

"What is it?" I asked, watching as she hastily deleted the message.

Renee forced a smile and tucked the phone into her pocket. "It's nothing," she lied.

I narrowed my eyes at her, and she lifted her shoulders in a shrug. "It's just Devon," she replied.

"Devon? I thought you guys were done?" I asked, hoping I

hadn't missed a major shift in my roommate's circumstances while I had been wrapped up in Maxx.

"Oh, we're done. He's just having a hard time accepting it," she muttered.

"What did his text say?" I asked. Given Devon Keeton's stellar personality, I could hazard a guess at the contents.

"Nothing, really. He just has a fondness for some not-so-nice words." She shrugged again.

It was on the tip of my tongue to say something nasty about her ex. But I stopped myself. Renee was holding strong, though I worried about how long that would last. And I knew my hateful remarks wouldn't help anything, even if they made *me* feel better. Looking at Renee, I could see how much Devon and their relationship had taken their toll. But she still loved him. I could see that plain as day. And that love was hurting her.

I couldn't help but wonder if I was in a similar situation. My feelings for Maxx were causing me to make decisions I never would have made in the past. I was forgetting about everything that had mattered to me, potentially throwing it all away to save a boy I was pretty sure didn't want to be saved.

Love made us stupid.

Love made us blind.

Love could incapacitate us and leave us powerless.

And love could also make everything better.

I couldn't let myself think anything else.

But Renee's love had come close to destroying her. It hadn't fixed anything. There was a new realization in my friend's eyes that had never been there before.

I reached out and squeezed her hand, offering support, which ultimately is all that any of us wants. She tried to smile, but her mouth twisted into more of a grimace.

"I've got to head to the library. Will you be here tonight?" Renee asked.

"I'm not sure," I answered honestly. Because I knew if I could find Maxx, I wouldn't be coming home. Already, I was twitchy and anxious to be with him again. We had been together just that morning, yet here I was fidgeting and restless like a junkie needing my fix.

Maxx was my drug.

Renee's lips turned upward in a sad smile. "Just don't get dragged down by him, Aubrey. Learn from my mistakes," she cautioned. I wanted to blow off her statement, but I couldn't. She was right.

After Renee left, I gave in and tried to call Maxx again. And again he didn't answer. I thought about leaving a message but decided against it. He'd see that I had called. I only hoped he'd call me back.

I couldn't sit around my apartment waiting for my phone to ring. It was sad and pathetic. I had things I should be doing. I had work that needed to be done. I had been neglecting school in the past few weeks, and I would have to work my ass off to get back on track.

I gathered my book bag, trying not to focus on the state of my bedroom, which also had been neglected due to my obsession with Maxx. The amount of dust had me fleeing quickly.

Once on campus, I headed for the back entrance of the psychology building. I had forgotten to check Dr. Lowell's symposium schedule for the week, and I didn't want to make things worse for myself by not showing up to the class.

I hoped I wouldn't run into my adviser, but I should have known I wouldn't be that lucky. The universe seemed to be turning up its middle finger in my direction lately.

"Aubrey! Come in and talk to me for a minute," Dr. Lowell called out as I tried to slip into the reception area outside her office without being noticed. Clearly I needed to work on my stealth skills.

Facing my professor, whom I had a lot of respect for, knowing I was betraying the confidence she had in me, was a new kind of torture. I was fearful she'd look at me and know all my secrets.

I hated that this shiny new love I felt for Maxx also brought with it immeasurable amounts of guilt and shame. Why couldn't Maxx and I have met under different circumstances?

But a part of me knew that a lot of what drew me to Maxx was the messy chaos inside him that had landed him in the group in the first place.

God, what did that say about me? Maybe it wasn't Maxx who was the truly messed-up one? It was apparent my issues were just as damaging.

I walked into Dr. Lowell's office and stood awkwardly inside the door. My professor looked up and gestured for me to have a seat. I scrutinized her face, looking for displeasure or anger. I was festering in my own distrust.

"Just give me a moment to finish this," Dr. Lowell said, sorting through a pile of papers.

While I waited, I looked around the office I had spent so much time in. I could remember taking my first class with Dr. Lowell my freshman year. Psychology 101 hadn't been the most riveting class, but I had loved Dr. Lowell's teaching style. She had a way of inciting passion in her students that was awe-inspiring.

I had been lost and miserable that first year, after losing Jayme. My relationship with my parents was strained. I was hundreds of miles from home, and I was alone. I had cut ties with all my friends from high school and hadn't been looking to make any new connections with anyone.

But somehow, Dr. Lowell had seen something in me and had quickly taken me under her wing. I respected her refusal to make or accept excuses for anything. I had been drawn to her gruff yet kind personality and the way she expected me to hold myself accountable but be ever mindful of my grief.

She nurtured my desire to be a counselor. She guided me down the path I had chosen. She was my mentor. My adviser. My favorite professor. And the thought of letting her down made me sick to my stomach. I was terrified of looking in her eyes one day and seeing disappointment.

Finally, Dr. Lowell gave me her attention, and I almost sagged in relief when I saw her smile. This wasn't someone who was unhappy to see me. On the contrary, she seemed pleased.

"I don't want to keep you, Aubrey. I know you must be busy. I just wanted to take a moment to tell you I've heard such great things from Kristie about group," Dr. Lowell said, shocking me.

"Really? I was pretty sure that after my screw-up I had been written off," I said, making Dr. Lowell laugh.

"I think she's gotten over it. Kristie can be a tough sell. She comes across nice enough, but she's pretty inflexible about things. So the fact that she's come around is a huge compliment."

The praise didn't bring with it the warm glow of pride it normally would have. No. In fact, it made me feel worse. What would Dr. Lowell and Kristie say when they realized how inappropriate I was actually being? I shuddered at the thought of their faces if the truth ever came out.

So why wasn't that enough to make me walk away?

Because I suffered from my own addiction, which sucked away all logic.

"Thank you," was all I could squeak out. Dr. Lowell beamed at me, and I wanted to flee. Run away. Now.

"Check my schedule on the door, and put yourself down for a one-on-one after group is over. We can talk about how things went and look at options for your next volunteer placement," my professor instructed, dismissing me.

I didn't say a word as I got to my feet. I hurried out of the office and did as Dr. Lowell requested. I already dreaded the meeting.

I should go to the library. I had a mountain of work to catch up on, but right then I just wanted to get off campus. I wanted to go to Maxx's apartment and submerge myself in the feelings I experienced only when he touched me.

I pushed through the doors that led out onto the academic quad. I rushed down the sidewalk and came up short. The sight of color at my feet caught my attention. I looked up and saw that the entire length of the pavement was covered in a drawing.

I backed up so I could get a better look at what was an elaborate kaleidoscope of images. At the center were two figures that looked like marionettes on strings. Their joints were depicted as jagged, bloody seams held together by nuts and bolts. The strings holding them up disappeared into a thick, raging fire above them.

The marionettes were clutched together, their awkward limbs trying to hold on to one another. The ground below them was giving way, crumbling and disappearing. The long blond hair of the female puppet was wrapped up in flowers that obscured her face, the fair strands an intricate weaving of the letter X.

While I stood there, transfixed by the strange yet unbelievably beautiful image, water hit the tip of my nose, followed by more drops on my cheek. Looking up, I saw clouds moving in and watched with sadness as rain flooded the drawing on the sidewalk, erasing it.

It seemed such a shame for something so amazing, something someone clearly spent a long time creating, to be ruined by a rain shower.

I hadn't prepared for the turn in weather, so I stood there in the downpour, getting soaked. I watched with morbid fascination as the vibrant colors mixed together, washing down the pathway. The two puppets, locked in their passionate yet uncomfortable embrace, faded away until there was nothing left.

"Why can't he just draw on paper like a normal person?" a hateful voice asked from behind me.

Brooks stood beside me, moving his umbrella so that it

shielded me from the rain. I hadn't spoken to him in weeks, not since our confrontation after support group. He continued to sit there week after week, but he hadn't initiated any sort of interaction since. Nevertheless, I felt him watching me closely. And he wasn't the only one. I knew that others were watching me as well, which didn't help my paranoia, which was already near the breaking point.

The marionettes were completely gone. "I thought you liked X's paintings," I remarked, still not taking my eyes away from the rain-soaked pavement.

Brooks snorted. "It's like that club, just a delusional waste of time. Sure, it looks pretty, but it only hides a heart that's rotten to the core," he spat out. I knew he wasn't talking about the painting.

"Why so bitter, Brooks? It takes a lot of talent to create something like this," I argued, shivering from the cold and the wet clothes clinging to my skin.

The rain beat down on the umbrella, pouring in rivulets around us, splashing my shoes and jeans as it hit the ground.

Brooks shook his head. "I get it, Aubrey. It's easy to be distracted by something like *this.* But don't forget the ugliness underneath. It may be nice to look at, but it's only paint, and it washes away eventually."

Brooks's metaphors were making my head hurt. But his meaning was crystal freaking clear. If I had wondered about the state of our friendship before, I didn't now. I could practically taste his disapproval.

I stepped out from underneath the protection of his umbrella. I looked up into my former friend's eyes and saw nothing of the kind, compassionate man I used to see.

"I feel bad for you, Brooks. It's so easy to criticize what you don't even try to understand. To pass judgment without looking at what's really there. I'm sorry if I haven't lived up to the expectations you had for me. That I disappointed you. But I had to come down off that pedestal eventually." Brooks opened his mouth, looking like he wanted to say something, but then shook his head.

"I'm sorry too, Aubrey," he said sadly.

I looked down at the ruined painting again. All that was left was a puddle of color in the grass.

"You'll miss out on some amazing things in life if you can't look past your nose to see the beauty that's out there in the most unconventional places. And complexity isn't ugliness. It's the complication that makes it worth it," I said softly, turning and walking away.

I pulled out my phone and tried calling Maxx again. No answer. I was freezing, the tips of my fingers going numb. But I couldn't go back to my apartment. I couldn't be on campus.

There was only one place I belonged. Only one person I needed.

So I walked the four and a half blocks to find him.

And when he wasn't there, I waited.

I'd always wait for Maxx.

chapter
twenty-six

"Why can't I come with you?" I asked Maxx as I lay naked and tangled up with him in his bed. His fingers stroked up and down my back, making me squirm.

We had been wrapped up in each other for most of the day. It had been almost a week since we were last together, and when I finally saw him again, there was no explanation for his disappearance. There never was.

I wanted to be angry with him. I wanted to be upset and sad. But I couldn't be. Not when he touched me and held me like his life depended on it. Not when my own feelings were jangled and raw from my burst of self-realization.

I loved Maxx Demelo. I felt it deep in my bones.

I was bursting with wanting to tell him. To lay my heart at his feet as easily as he had done. I imagined the way his eyes would light up when I told him. I fantasized about his reaction. He would kiss me, make love to me, worship me with his beautiful words.

But *I love you* was quickly being swallowed by other things.

Primarily it was the life he led when we were apart, the life I hated as surely as I loved the man who lived it.

The need to protect what little hold I had left on my heart rendered me mute. So the words remained unspoken, even as they tattooed their presence on my heart.

"I won't be there long. Just a few hours. Why don't you stay here, just like this? So that when I get home, I can do *this*," Maxx replied huskily, rolling me onto my back and fitting himself between my thighs.

I had learned that Maxx used sex as a way of shutting me up. When I questioned him or expressed concern, he'd flop me on my back and fuck me into silence.

And while I couldn't help but enjoy the methods he used to control the direction of our conversations, it was also frustrating.

So when he pressed the tip of himself between my wet, warm folds, kissing me so that our talk was finished, I resisted.

I pulled my hips back even as my body begged to join with his. I tore my mouth away and turned my head to the side. I pushed against his chest. "I want to go to Compulsion, Maxx. Please, take me with you," I pleaded.

I'm not sure why I was making a big deal about going to the club with him on Saturday. Except that I was tired of spending my weekends wondering what he was doing while he was there, though I didn't have to imagine too hard to figure it out.

While he tried really hard to keep the drugs away from me, I knew they were still there. The bitch demanded so much of his time. While he denied his addiction was there at all, it was a constant presence in our relationship. And he gave *her*, his need for pills, more attention than he gave me.

I was jealous.

I was scared.

Maxx was turning me into a mess of emotions both good and

bad. I didn't know what to do. I didn't know how to help him. Here I was, studying to become an addictions counselor, and I couldn't do anything for the man I had fallen in love with.

Every time I had tried to bring up his drug use, he claimed that there wasn't a problem, that I needed to stop worrying about him. He didn't see himself the way I did, as a sad, desperate man who had no idea of the destruction he was unleashing on himself. He thought he had it under control. He thought *he* was in charge. He thought that he could hide the worst of it from me, that I'd never know.

He was so, so wrong.

I could tell the difference between the Maxx who was high as a kite and the Maxx in the grips of withdrawal, both of which were starting to occur with more frequency and severity, and the Maxx who fell somewhere in between.

The two extremes were quickly becoming the only state he lived in. The in-between Maxx was slipping away. I knew he struggled, he hurt, he craved. And though he didn't use in front of me, not since that time after we went to see his brother, I knew he still spent the majority of his time high.

I wanted to press him, demand to know the truth, but I was scared to. I knew that if I did, he'd freeze me out, and then I'd never have a chance to help him. So I let myself be quieted, hating that I was allowing it, yet frantic for him all the same. I was letting him use our bodies to make us both forget the truth.

But I was growing weary of my willful ignorance. I was frustrated with the levels of my own denial. I was sick and tired of turning a blind eye even as Maxx shredded us both.

I wanted to go to the club with Maxx.

I had decided that being with him was a hell of a lot better than obsessing about it all alone. All I could think about in those dark hours until I saw him again was whether this would be the time he wouldn't come home at all. I was afraid that eventually the limits wouldn't matter and he'd go over the edge.

Maxx let out an irritated breath and sagged his body, resting his forehead on my collarbone. "Why is it such a big deal to you?" he asked, sounding annoyed. "You've been there, and I can tell it's not your scene."

I pushed out from under him and rolled onto my side. I folded my hands beneath my cheek and regarded him steadily. "Because I want to be with you. I hate waiting around for you to come home, wondering what you're doing," I explained.

Maxx folded his arm under his head and looked up at me, lines forming between his eyebrows. "You know what I do there, Aubrey," he said softly. Yes. I knew what he *did* at Compulsion. He made money selling drugs to the miserable and hopeless. How could I ever accept this part of him?

"You don't want to see that," he finished, running the pad of his thumb along my bottom lip.

I kissed his finger before saying, "But I want to be with you."

"How can I ever say no to you?" he asked me, smiling. My stomach knotted up at his statement.

Because it was a lie.

I didn't have the power to make him stop using drugs. He'd deny me if I asked him to never sell drugs again. I knew what his response would be if I insisted he stay away from Compulsion and all the temptations it held for him.

As much as Maxx wanted me, as much as he loved me, my influence went only so far. And he was still saying no to me each and every day.

"I'll pick you up tomorrow night at nine. I have some stuff to do before then," Maxx said, wrapping an arm around my waist and dragging me across the bed. "Now can we get back to this?" he asked, picking up my leg and hooking it up and over his hip. He dipped his hand between our bodies.

"Yes," I breathed out, followed by a guttural groan as Maxx pushed two fingers inside me. He moved his hand, his mouth conquering mine, and once again I let myself forget.

◆

"So I'm finally going to meet the mystery man?" Renee asked on Saturday evening. I was getting dressed to go to the club with Maxx. I was a bundle of nerves. This was a big step for us. He was taking me into his world, by his side, where it would be obvious who we were to each other.

We had gone through the early days of our relationship within the walls of his apartment. We had a connection built in secret. Aside from the day we went sledding, we had spent very little time in public. We had been out to dinner a few times, a movie twice. But the majority of our time was spent in the safety of his home.

This was taking our relationship out into the open. This was announcing to everyone that he was mine. It was exciting and terrifying at the same time.

Because I knew who I'd be walking into the club with. It wasn't *my* Maxx. It was the Maxx who belonged to everybody else.

I was forcing two worlds to smash into each other.

I was nervous and fitful about the possibilities this night would bring. While Renee was happy to finally meet the guy who had twisted me up inside, I wished my feelings could be that simple.

"I suppose," I answered, pulling a short red dress over my head. I was borrowing my outfit from Renee, who had insisted. And it was short, as in barely-covering-my-ass short. I felt way too much air where I shouldn't be feeling it.

"Well, you look amazing. What are you guys doing tonight?" she asked, but before I could answer, her phone vibrated in her hand. Without bothering to look at the screen she turned it off.

"Was that Devon again?" I asked.

"Yeah," Renee said, giving me one of her all-too-common forced smiles.

"Still being his charming self?" I couldn't help asking. Renee gave me a look but then snorted.

"Of course," she replied, walking over to my jewelry box and digging through it. I wisely let the subject drop. I knew she didn't want to talk about it, and I was freaking out too badly to dig for more than she was willing to give.

"I knew you still had these!" she accused good-naturedly as she held up a pair of dangly earrings with huge sparkly stones at the bottom.

"I am not wearing those," I told her. I remembered all too well how Renee got when she wanted to play makeover. When we first became friends she had made it her mission to revamp my wardrobe, getting a lot of joy out of introducing me to stilettos and earrings the size of melons.

I hadn't been subjected to her ministrations in quite some time, but it was easy to recall how much I hated them.

"Oh yes you are. And . . ." She trailed off, going through my shoes and coming up with a matching pair of black strappy things with heels as tall as skyscrapers.

"I'll break my neck!" I complained, but Renee put them down in front of me, and I oh so carefully slipped them on.

I tried standing up in the four-inch heels Renee was insisting I wear. I stuck one foot out and examined the modern torture device attached to my foot.

"Really, Renee? Why not put spikes on the bottom of my feet? These bitches are gonna kill my toes! I'm going to need to amputate a few by the end of the night," I groaned, hating the way the shoes pinched my skin.

Renee rolled her eyes and laughed at my pained expression. "You always did make dressing up a chore. Just trust me. Your man will be drooling at your feet," she said, smiling at my reflection in the mirror. I met her eyes, and there was a moment when I thought things would be okay.

And then I heard a knock at the door. "Mystery man arrives!" Renee announced, arching her eyebrow.

I ran the brush through my long hair one more time and gave myself a perfunctory once-over. I looked good. Really good. It had been a long time since I allowed myself to dress up and enjoy it. I just hoped Maxx liked it.

"Can I get it?" Renee asked.

I nodded, hanging back so she could answer the door. When she did, it revealed a Maxx I had only ever seen in one place . . . Compulsion. This was the man who had first captivated me.

He oozed sexuality and confidence. He wore distressed jeans that hung low on his narrow hips, a tight-fitting blue Henley the color of his eyes, and worn brown Doc Martens. His blond curls were in haphazard disarray and hung down into his hooded eyes. His full lips curved upward in a lazy, sure smile, and his thumbs were tucked into his belt loops.

Maxx was the man your mother warned you about. He was sex and danger and secrets. He was the very worst kind of temptation and the very best kind of distraction.

And even though the sight of him set my hormones on fire, there was something in his eyes that concerned me, something slightly predatory and violent. He scared me. He pulled me in. I felt like running. I felt like giving him everything.

I had come undone.

"I'm Renee," my roommate said, holding out her hand as she watched him closely. Maxx pushed off from the wall and took her offered hand.

"Nice to finally meet you, Renee. I'm Maxx Demelo." He covered their joined hands with his other palm, a touch that was meant to alleviate all worry. He looked over at me, and his eyes widened a fraction, the first genuine expression I had seen on his face since Renee had opened the door.

I had surprised him, and maybe unnerved him a bit. It was a heady and powerful feeling.

"I'm Aubrey's boyfriend," he finished his introduction, his lips lingering over the word *boyfriend*. As if that word could ever adequately describe who he was to me.

Obsession. Fixation. Owner of my heart and soul. Those were more appropriate descriptions.

Renee looked over her shoulder as I came closer. Her mouth was smiling, but her eyes were concerned.

Maxx released Renee's hand and turned to me. "God, you're beautiful," he said softly, his eyes twinkling. And just like that, he was *my* Maxx again. He leaned forward and placed a soft kiss on my lips. He tasted like cigarettes and peppermint.

"Thanks," I said, smoothing down the tight skirt of my dress. I wasn't entirely comfortable in my clothing, but the heated look in Maxx's eyes made me glad I was wearing it.

Maxx, obviously not bothered by our audience, grabbed the back of my neck and smashed his mouth down over mine. His tongue plunged between my lips as he kissed me senseless. He emitted a growl deep in his throat, and all I could taste, all I could feel, was *Maxx*.

"Ahem." Renee cleared her throat from behind us, and I yanked myself away from Maxx's restrictive hands.

"I guess we should get going," I said, my voice sounding shaky. Renee looked from me to Maxx, and I knew she was seeing something she wasn't happy with, but she plastered a smile on her face all the same.

How many times had I done the same thing when she had left with Devon? How the tables had turned.

Maxx is nothing like Devon. He would never hurt me, I told myself, hoping I'd believe it. And it was true. Devon was a bully. He took satisfaction in hurting others. Maxx was nothing like that.

The pain he caused was unintentional and most often self-inflicted.

But did that make it any better?

"I'll be home sometime tomorrow," I told Renee, who only nodded.

Maxx kissed my temple, nuzzling my hair. "Don't count on being anywhere but in my bed tomorrow," he whispered, goose bumps breaking out across my skin.

I let my boyfriend lead me out to his car. He held open the passenger-side door for me to get in. It was funny how something as simple as holding the door open for me melted my heart. It made it easier to overlook the things that left me cold inside.

"So I guess we don't have to go find the painting, huh?" I asked as Maxx pulled out into traffic.

Maxx smirked, as if laughing at his own private joke. "I know where I'm going."

"Do you know who X is, then?" I asked. It was a mystery I could admit I'd like to figure out. I had definitely become a fan.

"Yeah," Maxx answered shortly, not giving me any more information.

"Well, who is it?" I prodded.

"What do you think of his stuff?" he asked me, changing the subject.

"It's . . . strange and beautiful and dark and crazy. I've heard that a bunch of galleries are interested in his art. Is that true?"

Maxx smiled. "Yeah, it's true."

"So why doesn't he sell some of it? He'd make a killing!"

Maxx stared straight ahead at the road. "Because his art isn't about money! It's about more than that. He doesn't want to taint it with a desire to earn some quick cash. It's probably one of the few pure things he has left in his life."

Maxx was talking knowledgeably about the artist, speaking as though he understood, on an intimate level, what motivated the unidentified painter. Suspicion started to blossom inside me.

"And how do you know all that? You seem to know this X really well," I said carefully.

Maxx's jaw tensed, and his hands gripped the steering wheel so tightly, his knuckles turned white. "I don't know him at all," he barked.

Okay then. Clearly X was a sensitive subject. But his gruff dismissal had sparked a hunch I couldn't ignore.

"So where are we headed?" I asked when the silence became uncomfortable.

"A warehouse down in the city. Pretty close to one we've used before. It's a good location," Maxx said after a beat.

"How do you find the spots for the club?" I asked, posing the question I had wondered about since first going to Compulsion. The spots were picked with care and consideration.

Maxx's smile returned. "I look for places out of the way that can hold a lot of people, where we can run a few transformers off the local grid. Most important is that it be as far away from the police as possible."

"That makes sense," I replied.

I tried to think of other things to ask him, since he appeared to be in a full-disclosure kind of mood, but my mind went blank. Maxx wasn't in a hurry to fill the silence, so I let it go and tried not to feel tense in the quiet.

Once we got to the club, it was already heaving. The line to the front door wrapped around the block. But this time I didn't have to wait my turn like the rest of them.

Maxx took my hand and led me to a door around the back of the building. Before going inside, Maxx turned to me and became serious. He grabbed my face and kissed me hard. "Don't talk to anyone. Not unless I'm with you," he warned.

I smirked. "I *have* been here before, you know," I said, trying to lighten the mood. Maxx's transformation had already occurred, and I felt immediately apprehensive.

Maxx narrowed his eyes at me as he pulled a baseball cap out of his back pocket and fitted it on his head. "Yeah, and you were almost trampled to death and had your drink spiked. And let's not forget you ended up with a guy like me. I think that says a lot about your judgment." His words came out like an accusation.

He grabbed my hand and pulled me through the back door. It was pitch-black. I couldn't see two feet in front of me. The thumping bass filled the space, vibrating my bones and buzzing in my head. Maxx gave my hand a small yank, and I stumbled forward, catching myself on the wall as I collided with his back.

"You okay?" he yelled into my ear. I nodded, though I knew he couldn't see me. And then I was being pulled farther into the building. We headed down a dark hallway, and I could see the familiar throbbing red lights ahead. The hallway led into a cavernous space, very similar to what I remembered from that first night when I had come to find Renee.

It was sweltering. Sweat was already beading along the back of my neck, and I had to lift my hair to get some relief. Maxx's hold on my hand was bone-crushingly tight as he navigated us through the crowd.

His shoulders were rigid and his chin thrust forward. His narrowed eyes flicked through the mass of people. He was assessing, taking note. If it weren't for his fingers gripping me, I would have thought he'd forgotten I was there.

People reached out to grab him as we passed. "X! You're here!" a man said, walking into our path. He had called Maxx X. My hunch had just been confirmed. The artist and my boyfriend were one and the same. I thought back to the paintings—the woman who had appeared in every single one since I had met him, the girl with the long blond hair who always seemed to be walking toward her doom.

I shivered in spite of the heat.

Maxx's shoulders stiffened, and he shoved the guy out of his way and kept walking. I was shocked by his sudden display of aggression but allowed him to pull me along.

Girls tried to get his attention with their skin. Guys tried to talk to him, pleading for a moment of his time. They all wanted him. And I could tell he loved it.

He had changed, and he was most certainly no longer *my* Maxx. He was that *other* Maxx.

He was X.

No one spared me a look. Their focus, their *desire*, was entirely for him.

As we made our way through the crowd, Maxx's hand wrapped tightly around mine, my front pressed into his back, I thought I saw a familiar pair of faces. I peered into the shadows, the red light obscuring my vision.

I thought I had seen Evan and April. God, I hoped I was wrong. I pulled back from Maxx a bit, trying to get a better look.

Maxx stopped walking, turning back to see why I had stopped. I pointed toward the far wall.

"I think I saw Evan and April," I yelled over the din. Maxx shook his head, grabbed my chin, and tilted my head back.

"Stop worrying, baby," he said against my lips just before he kissed me hard enough to leave me rattled. Pulling away, he gave me his characteristic cocky grin and started to push through the people again.

He headed straight for the bar, not responding to anyone who attempted to speak to him. He motioned for the bartender to attend to us. The man came over, acknowledging Maxx with a nod of his head. He had a multicolored Mohawk and the customary piercings in his nose and lip.

"Eric, this is Aubrey. She's my girl. Make sure she gets whatever she wants," he commanded.

"Sure thing, dude," Eric said, smiling in a way that was almost attractive. He turned his attention to me.

"What can I get you?"

"Uh, just a beer, thanks," I said, yelling to be heard over the music. After getting my drink, I cradled it close to my chest, causing Maxx to smirk.

"I see you've learned your lesson," he said, motioning to the drink I had tucked close to me.

"Fool me once," I replied, raising my drink and saluting him with it.

He leaned in close so that his lips touched my ear. "No one will mess with you as long as you're with me. They know better. And if they don't, I'll make sure they do."

His words were hard and cold, and I had no doubt he meant them. I pulled away from him slightly, putting the bottle to my mouth and taking a drink. His mood was edgy, and it was contagious. I felt restless and disquieted.

Maxx had one arm wrapped tightly around my middle, his other hand jammed in his pocket. He watched the crowd closely. He rocked a bit to the beat, but I held myself rigid beside him.

"Why did that guy call you X?" I asked him, practically yelling in his ear. Maxx's lazy smirk slipped a bit at my question. Even though he continued to hold me close, I felt him distancing himself.

"It's my name," he replied shortly.

"No, X is the person who paints those pictures. The person I was asking you about earlier," I remarked, my accusation clear. He had been dishonest . . . *again*.

Maxx shrugged, still not looking at me, still moving in time with the beat. "So what? I paint some pictures on fucking buildings. What's the big deal?" he asked, his words clipped and angry.

What was the big deal? Was he serious?

Those pictures had been my first link to him. They had drawn me in with their raw beauty. And now that I was connecting the man I loved to the mysterious figure who had painted them, I was both furious and exhilarated.

Because I had seen something in those paintings that gave me hope that deep down Maxx believed he could be something *more*.

But he hadn't been truthful. When I had given him the opportunity to come clean, he had evaded and withdrawn.

We were running around in a circle, constantly repeating the same tragic mistakes over and over again.

"You lied to me!" I shouted, feeling my anger flare up at his casual dismissal.

Maxx's arm dropped from around my waist. He twisted me so that I was pressed against his chest. He grabbed my chin and held it firmly between his fingers.

"I did *not* lie to you! I omitted a truth. That is *not* the same thing," he reasoned, his eyes hidden beneath the bill of his cap.

I wanted to laugh at the absurdity of his statement. But I didn't. Because I could tell he believed his words wholeheartedly. In his mind, eliminating a few key facts was not the same thing as being deceitful. I knew instantly that this was the only way he was able to justify his actions and his continued dishonesty, his *omission of truths* from Landon and from me.

It was how he was able to look in the mirror and not hate himself. It was how he was able to so readily put on the mask and play the part of X.

For the first time, I saw just how totally he separated himself, why he purposefully kept his lives apart.

It made me sad. It made me heartsick for him.

And God help me, it made me love him more.

I opened my mouth to say the words I had been denying him. Here in this crazy, messed-up world, I wanted to tell him that I loved him and that I accepted *all* of his truths, whatever they were.

Before I could utter a syllable, a girl came up and leaned into Maxx on his other side. She either didn't realize or didn't care that his arm was around *me.* She lifted her hand and ran a finger down the side of his neck. He jerked away from her touch.

"Don't," he warned. She was either stupid or irrationally horny, because she didn't listen. Before I knew what was happening, she had pushed her pelvis up against Maxx's hip and started to rock against him, pressing her breasts into his arm. I could only stand there, gaping in shock at her forwardness.

"I know you've got it. I'll give you whatever you want," she shouted over the music. Was this chick for real? And was this how my boyfriend, the man I had been about to confess my feelings to, conducted his "business"?

Maxx shrugged her off, and she stumbled a bit before looking at me. She grimaced and had the decency to look embarrassed by her behavior.

"I'm sorry. I didn't know you were here with someone. I just thought . . . ," she began, and Maxx glared at her, shutting her up.

"You thought wrong. Now get out of here!" he told her firmly. The girl suddenly looked meek, and I sort of felt sorry for her. She was pretty, wearing clothes that weren't cheap, and I found myself wondering what brought her here, and why she wanted what she thought only Maxx could give her. All of these people were the same. They were running from something. Including Maxx.

Including me.

The girl scampered off, and I looked up at Maxx, whose eyes were now trained on the people around him. Had my boyfriend traded drugs for sexual favors? I thought I was going to be sick. What would have happened if I hadn't been there? Would he have gone off with her? Would he have given her drugs if she spread her legs for him?

I tried to pull away from Maxx, revolted by the thought. How quickly my feelings had changed. Only moments before I had been full of an all-consuming love for this man. Now I wanted to get away from him as fast as I could.

He squeezed me tightly against him, not letting me move. "It's not what it looked like, Aubrey," he said, tucking his head down into the crook of my neck.

I struggled against him, knowing he'd use his hands to subdue me, to make me compliant. Damn him, not this time!

Maxx took my shoulders in his hands and pulled me to face him again.

"I don't do that shit. Not anymore. And definitely not since you," he swore, his eyes pleading.

"But you used to. You gave girls drugs if they what? Sucked you off? Had sex with you?" I accused, curling my lip up in disgust.

Maxx shook his head. "Don't judge me for the person I was before you came into my life! I did ugly things that I hate myself for! I would never do that again. I would never do that to *you*." His thumbs brushed the length of my jaw, his fingers curling into my hair as he held me firm.

"I love you, Aubrey! I will *never* touch another woman. I will never *look* at another woman. There will never be anyone in my life but *you*. I won't cheat. I won't play you false. You are it for me. Forever," he swore, looking down into my face.

I gulped, my mouth dry.

"But you're still selling and doing drugs, Maxx. How can you say you love me when you try to hide it from me? I'm not stupid. I know how often you take those pills. I know why you disappear and won't answer your phone. I've seen it. I've seen what you do. How can you say you love me when you won't give that up? You won't give *this* up?" I demanded, trying not to wince as Maxx's fingers dug into my skin.

His eyes flashed at my accusations. He didn't deny anything.

He stood there, the press of bodies all around us, not moving as he stared into my eyes. I saw a conflict on his face. I saw the two sides of him fighting for dominance. And I knew without a doubt that this lost and deeply troubled man loved me. But did he love me *enough*?

He dropped his hands and looked away from me. My heart broke. It shattered. It fell into a million tiny pieces at my feet. I had my answer.

"I'm not doing this here, Aubrey!" he hissed.

"Well, it's not like we'll do it any other time," I bit back.

"You wonder why I don't talk to you about everything going on in my life? You ask me why I keep things from you?" He whirled around to face me again, and I saw that he was angry. This was a man so deep in his denial that he couldn't see the destruction all around him. He couldn't see that this world was stealing his soul.

"Because you stand there on your fucking soapbox without a goddamned clue as to what it's like to be me. It's so easy to judge, isn't it, *Aubrey*," he spit out hatefully.

"I'm not judging you!" I argued, but he didn't hear me.

Maxx grabbed me by the shoulders and pushed me back up against the bar. "I've got shit to do. You need to stay here. Don't move!" he commanded, his eyes making it clear that he expected me to listen.

I had never seen him so angry, not toward me, anyway. I didn't know what to do, so I didn't do anything.

Without another look in my direction, Maxx disappeared into the crowd. Eric the bartender was at my elbow the moment I was alone.

"Can I get you another drink?" he asked me. I looked down at my empty bottle and nodded.

So I drank another beer. Then another. Then another. And then I thought, to hell with Maxx and his demands. I pushed myself off the bar and headed straight for the dance floor.

I was mildly drunk and feeling a nice numbness. The dull pain in my chest from Maxx's earlier behavior had faded a bit, and all I wanted to do was dance and forget.

I found myself a pocket between dancers to station myself. The music was fast, and I started to bob around on my feet. I rocked my head back and forth, my short skirt riding up my thighs. I was probably in danger of showing the world my ass, but I didn't particularly care.

My feet were starting to ache from the heels, so I kicked them off, my bare feet making contact with the filthy floor. I didn't think about what I could be standing in. Here, I didn't care. I felt myself let go, just like the last time I was here. And it was liberating.

The pleasurable release lasted for a few more songs. I danced with complete strangers, not pulling away when they touched me. I belonged in this amazing communal experience. Someone handed me a flickering glow stick, and I stuck it into the bodice of my dress as I continued to dance.

I was slick with sweat, my bare feet dirty and aching, my head fuzzy from the alcohol, and I was feeling pretty damned great.

Until I opened my eyes while I danced and saw Maxx, my *boyfriend*, up against the far wall, two girls standing in front of him with their boobs out on full display.

I didn't know what they were saying. I could tell by Maxx's body language that he wasn't looking in the direction they hoped he would. Their blatant efforts at trashy seduction would have been bad enough. But it was the sight of the money leaving their hands and tucking into Maxx's outstretched palm that gave me pause.

He pulled a baggie out of his pocket and tossed it toward one of the girls. She opened it up and poked her finger inside, pulling out what I only imagined was a pill of some sort. She handed one to her friend before slipping another under her tongue. Then she gave one to Maxx. He held it in his palm, not moving. Slowly, his

head came up, and I saw him scouring the crowd. He was searching. Looking.

For me.

I ducked behind the people dancing closest to me, not wanting
to be spotted.

After a heartbeat, Maxx lifted his hand and dropped the drug
into his mouth.

I couldn't help but stare as he pulled out another baggie and
shook several more pills into his waiting hand. They followed the
first onto his tongue. Without another look at the boob twins, he
turned away and walked back through the club.

X was in his domain.

This wasn't the first time I had seen him do this. So why was it
hitting me like a ton of bricks this time?

It was because now I loved him. And that made the reality of
what he was doing even harder to swallow.

But wasn't it being the worst kind of hypocrite to get into a relationship with him, knowing exactly who and what he was, and now
to be disgusted by it? How could I expect him to change in such a
short period of time? It wasn't fair to him. It wasn't fair to me. It
wasn't fair to the relationship that we had only just started to build.

Yet as I stared after him, the sight of him selling pills to those
girls who grabbed at them greedily, willing to do just about anything for them, I couldn't see anything but the memory I had
never wanted to think about again.

◆

*I had exactly thirty minutes to get home and changed before meet-
ing a few friends at the diner downtown. I had a paper to write
that night and was already outlining it in my head.*

*I had stopped to talk to a few people in my English class, wait-
ing for the mad rush out of the parking lot to die down before I
headed to my car.*

Finally it was clear, and I walked out of the school by way of the side entrance that led past the football field. It was a bright, sunny day, so I slid my sunglasses down over my eyes.

I hurried underneath the bleachers, which served as a shortcut to the parking lot.

I heard a coughing, then a laugh I recognized all too well.

I veered back the way I came, curving around until I was approaching a pocket of bleachers tucked into the side of the building. It was dark back there, and it was a place the stoner kids liked to congregate between classes. You could smoke a joint or snort a line without getting busted. You would think the teachers would have gotten wind of the druggie hidey-hole by now, but it remained a safe place to engage in all kinds of nefarious behavior.

"I want another," I heard my baby sister demand, followed by the throaty chuckle of a guy who was clearly very pleased with himself.

"You know what I want first, Jay."

I peeked my head around a steel beam to see a small group of kids seated on the ground beneath the bleachers. A few were smoking cigarettes. One guy had a pipe and a lighter. A girl looked passed-out beside him, her head in his lap.

But that's not what caught my attention. Blake, my sister's loser boyfriend, dangled a baggie in front of Jayme. She laughed and tried to grab it from him. He pulled it just out of reach, making it a game.

For a second they looked like any other couple goofing around. How I wished that was all they were. But watching them, I knew a lot more was going on.

"I'm not doing that here. In front of everybody," Jayme said, casting a nervous look at her friends.

She was such a pretty girl, finally growing into her body. Her acne had begun to clear up, and she had lost a lot of the baby fat that had clung to her frame until recently, much to the detriment of her self-esteem.

"I don't care, Jay-Jay. You know what you have to do if you want any more. You're a greedy girl," Blake taunted, and there was something in his tone that made my skin crawl. I hated that guy. I hated how he treated Jayme. I hated how she defended him even when it was obvious what a jerk he was. Most of all, I hated that he was introducing my naïve sister to a world she should never have to know, one that I didn't know at the time would ultimately kill her.

Blake unbuckled his belt and pointed at his crotch. "No one sucks my dick like you do, baby," he crooned, as if that should be a compliment. No way would Jayme fall for that sleazy line of bullshit. I could tell she was uncomfortable.

So it was with complete and total shock that I saw her drop to her knees in front of him, her dress filthy from the dirt she took no notice of. She tilted her head up and opened her mouth. Blake laughed, knowing he was getting his way. He opened the bag and dropped two pills onto Jayme's tongue.

Then her hands were on his zipper, pulling it down, and Blake's hand went around to the back of her head, pushing her forward.

I looked away then, feeling sick. I stumbled away from the scene without intervening. I hadn't done a thing to stop my sister's degradation. I had walked away, wanting to forget I had seen anything at all.

And I never spoke to Jayme about it. I never offered any sisterly advice, explaining that no guy would ever respect her if she didn't have any respect for herself. I should have said those things to her.

But I never thought to until it was too late to say anything at all.

I left the disturbing scene behind me and hurried home, taking a shower and going out with my friends, trying to pretend I hadn't seen my sister barter a blow job for drugs from her shithead boyfriend.

And I spent years trying to forget that I had done nothing when it had mattered most.

✦

Looking at Maxx, I could only see Jayme and Blake and the sick, twisted joy on both of their faces as they got exactly what they wanted in the worst way possible.

I felt a flash of hatred so strong it took my breath away. It was at war with the love I felt just as strongly for the fucked-up man making a living by selling the shit that had killed my sister.

How could I love someone like that? How could I have become so enamored that I overlooked the fact that he stood for everything I should run far, far away from?

It was too much.

I couldn't handle it.

I pulled my phone out and called a cab.

Without a word to Maxx, I left.

I didn't want to see him. He terrified and disgusted me in equal measure.

Yet I loved him deeply all the same. And the love won out. My heart betrayed me again.

I told the cabdriver to take me back to Maxx's apartment.

I was such an idiot.

Feelings sucked.

chapter
twenty-seven

maxx

aubrey had left. One minute I was high as a kite, the next I was freaking the fuck out. I started looking for her in the crowd but couldn't find her. I searched for her red dress and blond hair. She should have been easy to spot. She was the most beautiful thing in the room.

I soon became frantic.

Because she was gone.

"Where's Aubrey?" I barked at Eric, grabbing his arm from across the bar.

Eric startled and tried to pull away from me. "Who?" he asked, his eyes darting around nervously. The buzzing in my head kicked into overdrive. The drugs hummed in my bloodstream, making me want to rage and tear shit apart.

I squeezed Eric's arm hard enough to crunch bone. "My fucking girl! Where is she?" I demanded, my vision becoming tinted with red the angrier I became.

"I don't know, man. I haven't seen her in a while. I swear!" Eric stammered. I lunged across the counter and grabbed hold of his shirt, wrenching him closer until I was within spitting distance.

"If you're fucking lying to me, I'll break your face," I seethed, baring my teeth in warning.

Eric squirmed in my grasp. "I'm not, X! I swear it! I haven't seen her!"

I released Eric's shirt and backed away. I pulled my cap off and ran a hand through my hair. Shit. She was gone.

My drugged-out brain was going into meltdown mode. I couldn't think about the situation rationally. I should never have gotten high when she was there and could see everything. And now she was missing, and I needed to find her before I lost my mind.

Soon I had completely lost touch with reality. I was smashing beer bottles, throwing bar stools, shoving people in my rampage.

"Aubrey!" I screamed at the top of my lungs. Everyone was giving me a wide berth as I destroyed everything around me.

And then someone had me in a headlock and was pulling me through the club. I struggled against the painful grip.

Suddenly I was outside and deposited on the ground. Marco punched me square in the jaw, and I fell backward into the gravel.

"Snap out of it, Maxx! Before Gash gets wind of your little tirade!" Marco snarled, flexing the hand he had just used to lay me out.

I rubbed at my face, working my jaw to make sure nothing was broken. "I can't find Aubrey," I explained, not caring how pathetic it sounded.

"Is that what's set you off?" Marco rolled his eyes and pulled out his cell phone, handing it to me. I looked at it, not registering what he was trying to say.

He threw it in my lap. "Call her, dipshit."

I picked up the phone with trembling fingers. Why hadn't I thought of that?

I could barely dial her number, I was shaking so badly. When I finally put the phone to my ear and listened to it ring, I wasn't sure I could handle the wait for her to answer. What if she had left me for good? What the hell was I going to do if she was finally done with me? I wouldn't be able to survive her leaving me.

"Hello?" Her voice sent a flood of relief through my body.

"Aubrey!" I let out in a rush.

"Maxx," she said. She sounded strange. Not upset . . . but *different*. But I wasn't interested in that right now. All I wanted to know was why she had left me.

"Where are you?" I asked, my heart in my throat as I tried to control my panic.

She sighed in my ear. "At your apartment."

"Why are you there?"

"I felt sick. I didn't want to *ruin* your night." There was that tone again. The one I should probably spend more time paying attention to.

"I'm coming home. I'll take care of you," I promised her.

"Okay," Aubrey said softly. We hung up after that, and I gave Marco his phone back. I got to my feet, a smile on my face. Marco arched an eyebrow at me and snorted.

"All better now?" he mocked. I punched him in the shoulder just hard enough for it to hurt. Call it a little payback.

"Oh yeah," I said, already going back into the club.

I told Aubrey I would come home. But I didn't go home. Not right away. I had a pocketful of pills I still had to sell, which Marco was sure to remind me of.

So I continued to sling the pills and made my money, selling them at double the price. Club kids were fucking stupid. They had too much of Mommy and Daddy's money and not enough brain cells. But it worked out well for me.

Many of my customers shared the joy, and I was able to get a nice, good high without dipping into the supply. Now that I knew Aubrey was safe, I could enjoy the rest of my night.

After a while, I completely forgot that I had told her I was on my way home.

Until I got there and found her waiting up for me. I was fucked-up and tired. I just wanted to sleep.

She was angry with me, I could tell. But the state I was in, I didn't care. She tried to talk to me, but I walked by her and went straight to my bedroom, where I promptly passed out.

✦

I woke up ten hours later, my body aching and sore and already in the throes of some heavy withdrawal, and Aubrey wasn't beside me. She was gone again, though this time she had left a note. I picked up a piece of paper from the pillow beside me and squinted in the late-afternoon light that filtered through my window. I scanned the contents, trying to make sense of it.

Aubrey had gone back to her place. She wasn't coming back tonight. She'd see me during the week.

Shit. I had really messed up.

I knew she was upset with me. And in the harsh light of sobriety, my body trembling, my stomach ready to heave, I just couldn't handle it. I needed her. I needed my girl, who made it all better.

Without a thought about what I was doing, I picked up the phone and called her. She answered right before it went to voice mail, as though she had been debating whether or not to pick up.

"Please come back," I cried, my voice breaking on a sob. I didn't allow her to say anything. I just cried into the phone, pleading with her to come back to me. I needed her so fucking badly. I ached. I hurt. I wanted more pills. But for the first time I was pretty sure that I wanted her more.

"I can't, Maxx," she said regretfully.

I wouldn't accept that. "Aubrey, please! I want to hold you. I just need to be with you right now. I'll come there if I have to," I said desperately. I would do whatever she wanted so long as I could touch her. Just touch her. I craved it.

Aubrey sighed, and I knew I had her. "I'll be there in a few minutes," she finally said, giving me exactly what I needed.

She arrived at my apartment fifteen minutes later, looking like the answer to all of my prayers, if I was a praying sort of guy. I pulled her to the couch and buried myself in her. And she gave herself to me just as she always did.

I was in too much emotional chaos to feel that there was a distance that hadn't been there before, that she was pulling away from me.

I was too thankful to have her naked body beneath me, her mouth on mine. I ignored everything else.

It wasn't until after we were finished, and she was making her excuses to leave, that I realized what was missing.

Her.

I had had her body for a time, but I didn't have her heart. And that made me wild.

Later that evening, after I had taken a few pills to even myself out and was feeling more in control, I decided to confront her. Aubrey had just walked into my apartment, and I watched as she dropped her purse on the table and came over to the couch where I was sitting.

She gave me a smile that seemed disingenuous. She didn't reach out to touch me like she normally did. She didn't lean in to kiss me. She sat beside me, a careful distance between us. Her altered behavior distressed me.

"What's going on with you, Aubrey? I feel like you're purposefully holding back from me," I said, trying not to sound as pathetic as I was feeling. I watched as a myriad of emotions flickered across her face. I grabbed her hand and lifted it to my lips, unable to hold myself back from touching her a moment longer.

She yanked her hand back, and I watched as anger settled over her features. She gave me her coldest stare. "Why should I give you everything when you give me nothing? When you're willing to stop the crap you do, then maybe I can trust you with all of me."

My mouth hung open in shock. Aubrey never talked to me like this. She never got angry and pissed. "What?" I asked as she got to her feet. It was then that I saw the tears in her eyes, and I was at a loss.

She leaned down and kissed my lips. "I care about you so much, Maxx," she said, making my heart clench violently in my chest.

She never said *I love you.* I had given her my heart, so why couldn't she give me hers? Why couldn't she tell me what I needed to hear? That she loved me? I felt alone in this torment of feeling. Her silence, her refusal to say those three little words, made me insecure. It made me doubt her.

It made me doubt *us.*

"Don't leave me," I begged. "I love you!" I was fighting dirty. I knew I was using those words as my weapon. But I didn't care. I'd use anything I could to make her stay. I needed her, now more than ever.

I started to cry. Ugly tears slid down my cheeks, and I watched as Aubrey's face softened. Maybe the tears would do it. Maybe they would make her stay. She wiped the wetness from my face, then turned her back on me. I sobbed more loudly as she picked up her purse from the table and opened the door.

She didn't turn to look at me. She refused to look at the tears, which were entirely her fault. "Get yourself together. Please." And then she left.

She abandoned me to my misery.

✦

I couldn't sleep. I had taken a few pills earlier and knew it was only a matter of time until they wore off.

I had tried calling Aubrey a dozen times since she had left me earlier in the evening, and she never picked up.

I was becoming desperate.

I was losing it.

I was losing *her*.

I was in a bad place. I couldn't see my way through.

Not able to toss and turn any longer, I threw on some clothes, laced up my boots, and grabbed my art supplies, throwing them in a large canvas sack.

I got in my car and started driving.

Given where my head was at, was it any surprise that I found myself outside Aubrey's apartment building at three o'clock in the morning?

Her street was empty. The air was cold and quiet. My breath puffed out from my mouth like fog.

The drugs should have made me mellow and relaxed. But things with Aubrey were making me anxious and restless.

I needed to get it out somehow.

I positioned the pots of paint on the sidewalk and grabbed my biggest brush. I popped open the top of the blue paint with a flat-head screwdriver and dipped my brush. Paint coated my freezing fingers as I swept the bristles in long, even strokes along the pavement.

I was frenzied while I worked. Focused. Manic.

I don't know how long I was out there. I didn't care that I could be discovered.

I just needed to paint.

I needed her to know what I was feeling.

How much I loved her.

How much she was breaking me.

When I was through, I dropped the brush and stood back, looking down.

Why couldn't I for once paint something that wasn't fucked-up?

I sagged to my knees in front of the portrait of my despair.

I had painted the broken shards of my face. My mouth was open and screaming. It was obvious it was me in the shattered glass.

And then there was Aubrey, with her long blond hair, sweeping me into a heap of dust, gathering my pieces as she prepared to dump them in the trash.

This was Maxx.

And this was X.

This was both of us, bled out on the sidewalk for Aubrey to see.

Maybe she would finally know how much I wanted to give her all of me. Even as I fought it, the desire was still there. I didn't want her to throw me away. I needed her to not give up on me.

And maybe one day I'd be able to give her everything she wanted.

✦

I had fallen asleep quickly after I had gotten home from my late-night painting excursion. I woke up a few hours later sick and achy, but with a clearer head than I had had for some time.

Aubrey had been right. I was fucking up everything. The club, Gash, the drugs, they were taking over. There was little room left for anything else. Let alone Aubrey.

But I couldn't let *her* go. The pills. The high. They felt too good. I had become too attached. How could I say good-bye to the one thing that kept me sane?

But I hated my need for it. I hated that when things got rough, that's what I turned to. I looked into Aubrey's eyes, and I saw myself as she did, a sad, pathetic excuse for a person.

But I couldn't give *her* up. My habit was my truest love. The one I couldn't live without.

Could I give up Aubrey?

No.

My obsessive painting last night should prove that.

I was in a bind. I couldn't do without either of the things vying for my love, my attention, my soul.

Yet my relationship with Aubrey wasn't the only thing falling apart.

I was spiraling. Worse than ever. I was losing the control I thought I was holding on to so tightly. My probation officer was breathing down my neck. It was costing me an arm and a leg to keep stocked with the herbal supplements I needed to fool the piss tests I was required to take every week.

That afternoon I was called into my academic adviser's office. Dr. Ramsey was a stuffy dude who had the bulbous red nose of an alcoholic. I had a good idea of exactly what he kept stashed in that locked drawer in his desk.

He sat me down and looked at me over the rim of his glasses. "You're failing everything, Maxx," he said in his nasally drone.

I knew I hadn't been doing that great, but I hadn't thought I was actually *failing*.

"Well, shit," I said, tapping my foot on the floor, already feeling antsy and agitated. I needed to get home. The pills I had taken before I had come to campus were already wearing off. I tried not to think about how it was starting to take more and more drugs to keep me on an even keel.

"That's one way of putting it," Dr. Ramsey said mildly, his brows furrowed in disapproval.

I knew he hated me. Just like I hated him. It was a match made in hell.

I took in the diplomas and certificates hanging on the wall. It was obvious Dr. Ramsey liked to show off, probably because he didn't have anything else going for him but his modicum of success. Guys like him bugged the crap out of me.

Dr. Ramsey crossed his hands on top of his desk and pursed his lips. "Maxx, are you aware that you will need to get an A on every single exam in order to pass with a D?" he asked in that condescending way of his that deserved a punch to the throat.

"Well, I am now," I told him dryly.

"And is that *okay* with you? To end up on academic probation with no chance of graduating? You'll be lucky to still have a place at Longwood after this semester," Dr. Ramsey remarked, curling his lip in disdain.

I was up to my eyeballs in disappointment. I sure as shit didn't need it from snot for brains with too many diplomas and no dick in his pants. I got to my feet, shoving my hands into my pockets.

"I hear ya, loud and clear, Dr. Ramsey. Thanks for the pep talk," I sneered, slamming out of his office without waiting for a comeback.

I left Dr. Ramsey's office fuming. Sure, I hadn't been as focused on school this past semester as I should have been. The club was taking up a lot of my time.

My failing grades had absolutely *nothing* to do with the tiny white pills that I was already obsessing about, the drugs that I couldn't wait to get home to.

I was in complete denial that I was about to lose everything.

As if my day didn't suck enough, my phone rang as I walked in the door of my apartment. I answered it, hearing my brother's enthusiastic voice on the other end.

"I'm applying to an art school in Philadelphia," Landon said excitedly. I barely heard him. I was searching through my drawer for the baggie I had put there the other night. Finally finding it, I shook out the pills I wanted.

Before I could take them, I registered what my brother had just said.

"You're what?" I asked, knowing that I should be more supportive, that I should be excited for him. But all I heard was the sound of more money. More money I would need in order to take care of him.

The noose around my neck tightened.

"Uh, yeah. My guidance counselor says I have a good shot at getting in. She wrote me a letter of recommendation. My SAT and ACT scores are really good, Maxx," Landon rambled on.

"How much does the school cost?" I asked, bursting Landon's bubble.

Landon was quiet for a while before answering. "I can get scholarships, Maxx. I can get a job. I'll make it work. You don't have to help me," he said, with more defensiveness than I had ever heard from him.

"You know I'll always help you out, Landon. I just wanted to know," I explained, and it was true. Even if it meant selling my fucking kidneys on eBay, Landon would go to school. Even if I had to drop out myself and become the biggest drug dealer on the East Coast, my baby brother would have his future.

"I don't want you to think you *have* to do anything, Maxx. I know you have it in your head that you need to take care of me. But I'm almost an adult. I'm not helpless. I can do this stuff on my own, you know," he told me firmly.

I never gave my brother enough credit for the man he was becoming. He was a fighter. He was a survivor. Just like me.

"Just let me worry about paying for it. You worry about getting your ass accepted," I said lightly, not admitting to the full-out panic the idea created.

Then we ended our conversation and I swallowed the pills.

And when I felt mellow enough to handle what needed to be done, I did the only thing I could think to do.

I called Gash.

✦

"I'm glad you called, X," Gash said, sitting in his spot behind his desk.

I propped my ankle over my knee and leaned back in the chair as though I didn't have a care in the world. Too bad I had way *too much* to care about. My life was one big, never-ending pile of fucking worry.

"I told you a few weeks back that I was expecting a shipment from Mexico. It just came in. This is grade-A shit, X. We're going to make a killing." Gash pulled three freezer bags out of his drawer and dropped them on his desk.

I picked one up and opened it, finding it filled with smaller baggies containing a fine, whitish-brown powder.

I looked up at my boss. "What is it?" I asked, sounding stupid. I knew what it was, I just wanted the confirmation.

Gash grinned. "Some of the best Black Pearl I have ever seen."

Shit, Gash was peddling heroin now.

Okay, so I was being a massive hypocrite, but I had my standards. Selling pills was one thing, but slinging fucking heroin was something else entirely. If I made that leap, I wasn't sure I could ever forgive myself.

There was something about the way heroin was taken. Snorted or injected. Needles gave me the heebie-jeebies, and snorting anything up your nose seemed like plain old stupid.

"I don't know, man," I said slowly, trying to think of an excuse so I wouldn't have to sell that stuff.

Gash frowned, obviously not liking my less-than-enthusiastic response.

"Do you understand how much money this could make me? Could make you? Are you a fucking moron?" he asked incredulously, looking at me as though I had been offered the Holy Grail and was turning it down.

"It's heroin, Gash. That shit is a bit too hard-core for me," I said lamely, knowing that I sounded like a complete pussy.

Gash leaned back in his chair and let out a loud laugh. He gripped his beer belly as though he feared splitting his gut. "Are you kidding me? A drug dealer with a conscience? Give me a break!" he wheezed between guffaws.

Fuck him!

I got to my feet. "Look, I'm not going to sell that shit. Find someone else," I said, heading to the door.

"I'd rethink that if I were you," Gash called out before I could leave.

I froze. His words were a threat.

"I know what you and Marco have been doing. You think I wouldn't notice the door coming up short almost every single weekend? I've been in this game longer than you've been alive, X."

I closed the door and sat back down. This asshole had me exactly where he wanted me.

"And I know you've got some sticky fingers when it comes to my drugs. But you've made the money, so I haven't begrudged you your fix. As long as it doesn't impact my business, I don't have a problem. But don't confuse my silence with ignorance. You have your uses, X. Just as Marco does. And you're going to sell my shit. And you're going to sell all of it." Gash wasn't open to an argument. He wouldn't take no for an answer.

I was stuck.

I needed the money.

I needed my drugs.

I needed each of those things more than I needed my self-respect.

And Gash was the one pulling all my strings.

I picked up the freezer bags and put them in my book bag.

"How long do I have?" I asked, my acquiescence making Gash very pleased with himself.

"Two weeks. Not a day more. You get ten percent like always. Make it work, X," he said, dismissing me.

I left his office, pounds of illegal drugs in my bag—and my soul up for grabs to the highest bidder.

◆

"Please come over," I found myself begging again. It had been days since I had seen Aubrey. She was making herself scarce. It was killing me.

The heroin sat like a lump of stone in my bedroom closet. The pills were quickly becoming not enough. The temptation to try *just a little* was getting harder and harder to ignore.

I needed Aubrey.

"I can't, Maxx. I have a lot of work to do," she said, making her millionth excuse of the week.

"Did you see the picture? The one I did outside your building?" I asked her. She hadn't mentioned it. It drove me crazy that she hadn't said a thing about my soul splattered in paint on her doorstep. I had really thought she'd get it. That she'd understand.

But it was like she didn't give a fuck.

I heard her take a deep breath. "Yes, I saw it," she said softly.

"Did you like it?" I needled, trying to get a reaction from her. Anything. I just needed *something*.

"It was beautiful, Maxx. They're all beautiful. But . . ."

"But?" I asked, my words becoming hard. She didn't like it. She hated it.

She hated *me*.

"It doesn't change anything," she said after a beat. And that hurt. A lot.

"Why don't you want to see me?" I asked, loathing the sound of my own voice. My love for this woman made me high. But it also brought me so fucking low. And it was in the lows that I felt like I couldn't drag my way out of the pit I found myself in.

I knew she had thought she could change me. She had gone into this relationship seeing me as a screwed-up addict who needed saving. And suddenly I couldn't help but feel like she didn't care about me for *me* but for the charity project she thought I was. And that pissed me off.

So I embraced the anger, because that was easier to handle than the fear that I was failing her completely. The idea that a girl like Aubrey could care about me, just as I was, felt almost blasphemous. Because she deserved better. And I was terrified the day had come when she had figured that out.

My hands were shaking and I was sweating. I felt the familiar sickness deep in my gut. I reached over to my bedside table and opened it, looking for the brown bottle I knew would be there.

"I do want to see you, Maxx," Aubrey said, and I could hear the lie.

"Then come over, just for a little while," I pleaded one last time.

I heard her sigh just as my hands closed around the bottle I was searching for. I shook it. It was empty.

Fuck me, it was empty.

I popped the top, thinking I must be imagining things, but there was nothing there.

I threw the bottle across the room. Aubrey was saying something on the other end of the phone, but I was no longer listening.

"Maxx?" she said when I didn't say anything. I was too busy ransacking my room, looking for anything to take the edge off. I had to have a pill around here somewhere.

"I've got to go," I said in a strangled whisper.

"What's wrong? Are you okay?" she asked, sounding concerned.

Oh, so now she wanted to play worried girlfriend? If she cared so much, she'd be here beside me, helping me when I needed her.

She was the only thing that could help.

But she wouldn't come. She was purposely staying away.

"That's fine, Aubrey. Stay the fuck away. See if I care," I barked petulantly. I know I sounded like an ass. But she was giving me no choice. I had to get off the phone. I had to stop thinking about her.

There was only one thing I could focus on right now.

Finding my drugs.

"Maxx, don't be like this. I just need some time . . ."

"Take all the time you need. I'm over it," I spat out, hanging up.

I dropped the phone onto the bed and crawled on my hands and knees to a pile of clothing on the floor. I destroyed my room in my search and couldn't find anything.

"Ahhh!" I screamed, curling up into a ball. My body was racked with the shakes. I felt the bile building up in the back of my throat.

My phone was ringing. I knew who it was.

Aubrey.

I reached out my hand, trying to grab it. I shouldn't have yelled at her. I should have told her what was wrong. Then she'd be here to help me.

I needed her so badly.

The phone went silent and didn't ring again.

She had given up. She wasn't calling back.

I looked over at my closet, knowing what was inside.

Maybe just this once.

No. If I went down that road I'd never be able to come back.

Come on, you know you want to.

It was taunting me now. It knew how weak I was.

Just one tiny little bump. Not much at all. You'll feel so much better.

Shit, I was hearing voices now.

I covered my ears with my hands, trying to block out the tempting voice ringing in my head.

"No!" I shouted, as though the bags of drugs hidden in the depths of my closet would hear me.

I uncurled my rigid body and dragged myself to my bed. Reaching up, I found my phone and brought it to my ear.

I wanted to call Aubrey. I needed to hear her voice. She'd get me through this. She was all I needed. She loved me. Her love was enough.

But instead, I called someone else.

The phone was ringing and then it connected.

One step closer to my salvation.

"Marco. I need you to bring me something."

chapter
twenty-eight

aubrey

I was trying to finish up my home-work. I had spent every day of the last week trying to get caught up.

After the disastrous night at the club with Maxx and staying up all night, only to have him show up at five in the morning high, I had made a hard decision. I had stayed up for a long time after he had passed out. He had never said a word to me. Nothing. It had hurt so badly. And I had cried for a long time after that. I had been completely depressed.

Our relationship was a mess. It wasn't getting any better. I was going to fall hard and fast with him to rock bottom.

I needed distance.

I hadn't been able to face his bleary eyes the next morning, so I made sure to leave before he woke up.

But then he had called me later, and I recognized the panic in his voice. He was in major withdrawal.

He had begged me to come over, and I had. I had never been able to say no to him, even when it was the best thing for me.

He had his drugs, and I had mine.

And mine was Maxx Demelo.

When I had arrived at his apartment, he seemed better, and I knew instantly he had used before I had gotten there. I wanted to cry. I wanted to scream. I want to smack the shit out of him for not caring enough about himself to stop.

But then he touched me, and even though I wanted to push him away, I didn't. I couldn't. My body craved him.

So I had let him take off my clothes and throw me on the couch, where he devoured me whole.

And while he thrust into me, my body wrapped around him, my heart began to break.

He was stuck in an endless cycle, and I was stuck in it with him.

This was going to ruin me.

This wasn't a story with a happy ending. Maxx and I weren't going to live that perfect life with the white picket fence.

The only life we could have together was ugly and messy and destructive.

And I knew without a doubt that it would kill us both.

I couldn't save him.

There was no changing the path he was on. He wouldn't let me. There were forces in his life that were more powerful than my love for him. The intensity of his feelings for me and mine for him just weren't enough. I wasn't sure they ever would be.

He was going over a very steep cliff, and if I didn't back away, he'd take me with him.

And I wouldn't do that to myself.

As much as I loved him, I couldn't turn a blind eye as he obliterated himself. I had sworn I wouldn't walk away, that I'd stand by him, no matter what. But those promises were made by a naïve fool.

I had stupidly thought that by helping Maxx, I'd be making up for the ways I hadn't helped Jayme. As though one life could replace the other.

It was absolutely ridiculous.

Maxx wasn't Jayme. He was his own brand of fucked-up, and he was so deep in his hell that the only way of being with him was to sink into it with him. He wasn't prepared to fight any sort of battle to get better. He wasn't willing to let me fight for him.

My issues about my sister were my own, and I had to find a way to forgive myself and move forward.

And watching the man I loved fall apart was not the way to do it.

But Maxx wouldn't let me go. He was persistent. He called me over and over again. Our conversations were always the same.

He *needed* me. He couldn't live his life without me. He loved me. Oh God, did he love me. He'd die if he couldn't be with me.

He'd cry. He'd beg. He'd scream. He'd yell. He had become my own personal devil, and I was terrified of him. And for him.

I almost caved so many times. I almost rushed over to his apartment to let him hold me. Maybe, just maybe, this time he'd hear me. He'd realize that he didn't need the drugs. That together we could get through anything.

I would almost have myself talked into it, and then the other Maxx would come out to play. And he'd become angry. He'd get nasty. And it was easy to deny the primal instinct to rush over and help him.

So I resisted. As painful as it was. I wanted him. My heart hurt from being away from him. In the short time I had known Maxx, he had become *essential*.

But I was doing this for *me*. I had to.

Then he stopped calling. He stopped coming to support group. Kristie talked about reporting his noncompliance to his probation officer. I never saw him on campus.

It was like he had disappeared.

I tried calling him, but he didn't answer. He *never* answered. He had disappeared—for good this time.

"Do you want some company at the library?" Renee asked me, poking her head into my bedroom. I was packing up my books and assortment of pens, about to head to campus to try to keep my mind off Maxx and what he was possibly doing.

As much as I knew staying away from him was the best thing for me, it didn't stop how maddening it was to be kept in the dark. The not knowing was going to drive me crazy.

Renee knew some of what was going on with Maxx. I had needed to confide in someone. But I hadn't been able to tell her everything. She admitted to not being very comfortable around him.

"He's hot as hell, Aubrey, and he's crazy about you, that's obvious," she had said.

"But . . . ," I prompted.

"But there's something in his eyes. They're so sad. But unbalanced. I've seen eyes like that before. Those are scary eyes to see," Renee had told me, and I couldn't deny it. Maxx did have sad eyes, and there *was* something unstable about him. I had seen that firsthand more times than I cared to think about.

As much as I appreciated the renewed confidences of our friendship, I still couldn't tell Renee everything. I couldn't tell her about watching Maxx sell drugs, or about knowing that every time we weren't together, he was using.

That was an ugliness that didn't need to be shared. It would be buried deep down in the pit of my heart.

What Renee did know was that my relationship with Maxx was in a really bad place and that I was hurting. And if there was anything my best friend understood, it was the pain only the man you loved could give you.

And I felt connected to Renee in a way I had never been before. We were linked by our love for men who could annihilate us.

"Sure, if you want to," I said, giving her a smile.

"Let me grab my stuff, and I'll meet you in the living room," Renee said, walking across the hall to her room.

The doorbell rang just as I finished packing up my things.

"I'll get it," I called out to Renee.

My heart started to beat in triple time. Maybe it was Maxx. God, I hoped it was Maxx.

I was pathetic.

The doorbell rang again and then again. Whoever it was didn't do patient very well.

"I'm coming!" I called out, hurrying to the door.

Please be Maxx.

It wasn't.

It was so much worse.

"What the hell are you doing here?" I asked angrily.

"Please, I just need to talk to her," Devon pleaded, his dark brown eyes ringed with black circles. His normally perfectly styled hair looked as though he hadn't washed it in days.

He was trying his best to look contrite and desperate. But I wouldn't be fooled. Devon Keeton was a manipulative snake.

"Get the hell out of here before I call the police!" I threatened Devon, before adding in a furious whisper, "I saw what you did to her, you piece of shit. If you think you're ever getting your hands on her again, you're more deluded than I thought."

Devon's face crumpled, and he cried big crocodile tears. "I didn't mean to hit her."

"So she just fell on your fist, then?" I asked, my voice dripping in sarcasm.

Devon shook his head. "I'll change. I swear it, Aubrey. Just let me see her. She won't take my phone calls. She won't answer my texts. I love her!" His voice rose, and I tried to get him to back away from the door so I could shut it in his lying face.

I didn't want Renee to see him. But it was too late.

"Devon?" she said from behind me. Devon shoved past me and

into the apartment. Renee cringed back, and I wanted to kick her ex-boyfriend's ass for putting that kind of fear in her.

I grabbed Devon's arm. "I said get out!" I yelled, yanking on him. He looked down at me, and the tears were gone. He was angry. Really, really angry.

"Get your fucking hands off me or I'll break your fingers," he warned in a deadly quiet voice.

Well, he'd just have to break my fingers then.

"Get out!" I screamed, hoping our neighbors would hear me and come see what the noise was about.

Renee had her back against the wall, but her face had softened. I couldn't believe it!

After everything he had done, she was looking at him like she actually missed him!

Devon was speaking to her, filling her ears with every line of romantic bullshit he knew she'd want to hear. His mouth was moving, but all I heard were the lies. To judge from the look on Renee's face, she was believing him. Or at least she wanted to.

I knew she still loved him. Why had she given her heart to someone who treated it so poorly? It was there, plain as day, on her face. Love. Heart-stopping, kill-you-slowly love.

My heart pounded in my chest as I watched them. The sight in front of me was so familiar that it took my breath away.

As Devon spoke, it was Maxx's words I heard. And it wasn't Renee I saw drinking in his pleading promises . . . it was *me*.

Our loves weren't so different, no matter how much I tried to convince myself that they were. They were equally destructive. Equally exhausting. And equally dysfunctional.

"Please, Renee. Just give me another chance," Devon begged, and Renee's eyes were filling with tears. Shit, she was going to cave.

She couldn't cave! If she gave in, then what was to stop me from doing the same? We needed to be strong. We had to do it together.

So I did the only thing I could, I screamed at the top of my lungs.

Devon turned on me, rage making him ugly.

"Shut up, you stupid bitch!" Devon roared, knocking me backward. His blow hit my shoulder, and I fell to the floor.

And finally Renee woke up. With trembling hands she pulled out her cell phone and held it up.

"Get out, Devon. *Never* come back here! We are done! We have been over for a long time! I never, *ever* want to see your sick, sorry face again! If you don't leave in the next thirty seconds, I'm calling the police. I'll get a restraining order. Your ass will be in so much trouble! And then what would Mommy and Daddy say about that?" she asked, her lips twisting in a smirk I had never seen her wear. Her shoulders were back and her chin lifted. I knew Devon terrified her, but she was standing strong. I had never been more proud of her.

Devon frowned, as though not sure he had heard her correctly. "Baby, you can't mean that. We belong together. I love you," he tried again.

Renee started to dial numbers and then was speaking into the phone.

"Yes, I'm being stalked, and he's here now. His name is Devon Keeton and he's my ex-boyfriend. I'm scared for my safety," Renee said into the phone.

Devon was furious. He looked ready to spit nails. With Renee still talking to the dispatch officer, he sprinted out the door.

I hastily closed the door behind him and locked it.

"He just left," Renee was saying into the phone. She sagged down the wall to sit on the floor.

"I don't think he'll come back. You don't need to send anyone. Okay. I will. Thank you."

She hung up the phone, and her head dropped in her hands. I put my arm around her shoulders.

"I've got to go down to the courthouse and file a preliminary restraining order. But maybe he won't do anything. Maybe he'll leave me alone now," Renee said, looking worn down but faintly hopeful.

"I'm not sure. But I think you should get one. For your own peace of mind," I told her.

Renee nodded, and we were quiet for a while. Then she looked at me, her face weary.

"Why do we do this to ourselves, Aubrey? Why do we give our hearts to men who crush them? I thought Devon was my prince. God, I thought he loved me. I'm such an idiot." She was sobbing, and I was crying with her. For her. For myself. For every shitty relationship that ended in tears.

"Love shouldn't feel like this," Renee said, sniffling through her tears. And she was right. This burning, aching pain deep in my chest shouldn't be what love feels like. It wasn't healthy. It wasn't right. And unfortunately, it just wouldn't go away.

I was a woman trapped.

"Come on, I'll go with you to the courthouse. Then I'll treat you to that chocolate cake you love from Caketopia," I offered gently.

Renee rubbed the tears from her cheeks and gave me a brave smile.

At least someone was learning from her mistakes before it was too late.

◆

After waiting with Renee to meet with the magistrate, I had stepped outside and, in a moment of weakness, tried to call Maxx again.

So much for my stern resolve.

But I couldn't help it. My keen sense of dread the longer he stayed off the radar wouldn't subside.

Of course he didn't answer.

I had tucked my phone into my pocket, and when Renee was done I had pretended that nothing was wrong. Afterward I had taken Renee to her favorite bakery next to the campus and started plying her with baked goods.

Renee hadn't cried. She hadn't wavered in her decision to get the restraining order.

She was downright amazing.

"Aren't you going to eat those?" Renee asked after polishing off her hot chocolate. I slid the plate toward her.

"Have at 'em," I said with the best smile I could muster.

My phone started ringing in my pocket, and just like every other time, my heart gave a thrill of hope that it would be Maxx on the other end.

And just like every other time in the past week, I was disappointed that it wasn't.

I was, however, surprised to see it was Kristie Hinkle, my support group co-facilitator.

"Who is it?" Renee asked, seeing the look on my face.

"My co-facilitator for group," I replied as the phone continued to ring.

"Well, shouldn't you answer it?" Renee urged.

I laughed a bit nervously and connected the call.

"Hello?"

"Hi, Aubrey. I'll make this quick. I need to meet with you. Today, if possible," she said, her tone brusque. We had already met for support group this week, so I couldn't think of any reason she had to meet with me so soon afterward.

"Uh, sure." I stumbled over my words.

"Good. I'm at my office downtown. Do you know where that is?" she asked. Her voice was cold, and I felt the tingling of alarm along the back of my neck.

"Yes. I think I do," I responded.

"Can you be here within the hour? I have a meeting later in the afternoon, but I need to talk with you first," she said.

"I can be there."

"See you then," Kristie said and then hung up.

I stared down at my phone for a moment.

"Is everything all right?" Renee asked, wiping her fingers on a napkin.

I gave her another smile, this one fake as hell. "Kristie wants to talk with me at her office in town. Are you okay to head back to the apartment by yourself?" I asked, hating to leave her so soon after the confrontation with Devon.

Renee waved me away. "I'll be fine. I'm going to go to the library for a while. Keep my mind busy."

I put my hand over hers. "I can call Kristie back and reschedule if you don't want to be alone," I offered, hoping she'd take me up on it. Instinctively, I knew that I wasn't going to like whatever Kristie wanted to discuss with me.

Renee tried to discreetly wipe away the tears that escaped from her eyes, but I had seen them. She was struggling, and I felt like the shittiest friend on the planet for leaving her right now.

"I'll meet up with you at the apartment later." Renee cleared her throat, bowing her head so I wouldn't see her now red-rimmed eyes.

"It's okay to cry over him. You loved him. It's only natural," I said gently.

Renee lifted her tear-filled eyes and gave me a watery smile.

"He doesn't deserve my tears, but God help me, I can't help but cry for him anyway." Renee sniffled, and I got up to give her a hug.

"I'll hurry back," I promised.

✦

Kristie's office was warm and cozy. She worked at the local community services board, which helped people with addictions and mental health issues living in the city. I had been waiting for only a few minutes when she opened her office door and ushered me inside.

Her walls were painted a golden yellow, her one window covered in a gauzy white curtain. She had several crystals and stained-glass pieces hanging on the glass, bouncing rainbows around the room.

The bookshelf was filled with books and framed photographs. Instead of clinical chairs, Kristie had a plush, red couch shoved against the far wall, complete with throw pillows.

Under any other circumstances, Kristie's office would have felt relaxing. But I could tell instantly from the way Kristie was looking at me that something was wrong.

"Have a seat, Aubrey," Kristie said, indicating the couch. I sat down, and instead of returning to her desk, Kristie sat down beside me.

I knew Kristie wasn't my biggest fan. Despite her positive reports to Dr. Lowell, I knew that after my verbal outburst earlier in the semester she was just biding her time until the group was finished so she could be rid of me. I had picked up on her wariness and underlying annoyance even as she attempted to feign professional support.

So I was surprised to see sympathy on her face. She was looking at me as though she felt sorry for me. Oh shit, what the hell was going on?

Kristie turned and pulled a framed picture off her desk. It was of her and a group of women. It was easy to tell from their dress that the picture was a decade or two old. Kristie was much younger in the photograph and had actually been very pretty.

"This was taken at my first job out of college. I worked as the services coordinator for a domestic-violence shelter back in Ohio. I loved that job. The women and children I worked with were unbelievable." Kristie put the picture back on her desk and then turned to me.

"I really struggled back then with my role there. I worked in an environment that served as the home for these people. They relied on me to provide for their basic needs: safety, food, shelter. It was easy to confuse work with friendship at times."

I didn't quite understand Kristie's need to take me on a walk down her memory lane. But her next words made it all too clear why I was there.

"Boundaries get blurred. Relationships form that shouldn't. It's easy to get confused. We come into this field because we care. We want to help. Sometimes we take that to a place we shouldn't."

This was about Maxx.

She knew.

I swallowed around the lump in my throat. I was having a hard time breathing. I felt like my world was starting to implode around me.

Kristie turned back to the picture. "I started to think of those women as my friends. But they weren't. They were clients. They were there because they had experienced an incredible trauma. They didn't understand boundaries. It was my job, as their counselor, to model them. And I had a hard time with that. How do you assert authority over women who view you as their friend?"

Kristie looked at me, her eyes blazing. "I had to ask one of the women to leave the shelter for not complying with the rules. She got understandably angry. But the worst part was when she looked at me and said *I thought you were my friend.* And that's when I knew I had screwed up. That I had allowed my personal feelings to get in the way of doing my job."

She scrutinized me closely. "Do you understand what I'm saying?" she asked me.

I swallowed again, my mouth dry.

"I'm . . . I'm not sure," I said awkwardly.

Kristie let out a huge sigh and got to her feet and went to sit behind her desk. It was obvious she was putting distance between us before she delivered the blow.

"I've been approached about something very upsetting. I was told that you were engaging in an inappropriate relationship with someone in the support group."

And the axe had fallen.

Kristie continued. "I have to take all allegations like this very seriously. So I did some digging, and it has become clear to me that you and Maxx Demelo are in fact seeing each other." She stopped, looking at me, as though waiting for my denial.

What was there to say? I had been busted. Just as I had feared I would one day be, though the "one day" came much sooner than I had anticipated.

"Well, Aubrey, what do you have to say about this?" Now she sounded like a grade-school teacher and I had been caught chewing gum in class. I hated feeling small, and Kristie Hinkle was making me feel very, very small.

I knew I had messed up. I had been taking a huge risk when I had gotten involved with Maxx. I had put everything on the line to be with him, and for what?

Look where our relationship was now. It was nonexistent because he had chosen drugs over me.

But I couldn't forget how much I loved him. How in those moments when we were together, with nothing between us but breath and skin, it was perfect. Seeing him with his brother, discovering who he was before drugs had come into his life, sledding with him in a place that was special to him, watching him cook me a badly burned dinner, these moments had shown me a passionate and complicated man. A man who was worth the effort.

I wouldn't apologize for following my heart for the first time in my life. For letting go of my obsessive need for control and to just *feel*.

For all the heartache, for everything Maxx had put me

through, I could *never* regret opening myself to him. I had been closed off for so long that I was slowly dying inside—until Maxx forced me to be someone that I had forgotten I could be.

I lifted my chin and looked Kristie in the eye. "What is there to say? That I was wrong? I think that's obvious. That I'm sorry? Well, I can't say that. Because I'm not. I wouldn't change a moment of being with Maxx, no matter what the consequences." I sounded steady and strong, and I was proud of myself, even as I faced the fallout from my choices.

Kristie's nostrils flared, and she looked taken aback. I could tell she hadn't been expecting my defiance.

She shuffled some papers on her desk, looking uncomfortable. "I have to report this to Dr. Lowell. You do understand that this means you could be put on academic suspension? Kicked out of the counseling program?" Kristie asked, looking at me as though I had lost it.

Because what person in her right mind would throw away everything for an unstable boy? Particularly when he was the last person she should bet her future on?

Love was insanity at its most beautiful—a madness of desperation and desire that made the most improbable choice possible.

"I understand," I replied simply.

Kristie stared at me for a beat, then seemed to come back to herself. "Well . . ." She cleared her throat and started again. "Well . . . I'm sure Dr. Lowell will be contacting you soon."

I nodded and got to my feet. "Thanks for the opportunity you've given me to learn from you, Kristie. I appreciate it even if it doesn't seem that way," I said, surprising her again.

She shook her head. "It's such a shame, Aubrey. You have so much potential. I hope it was worth it."

I left her office with her final words ringing in my ears.

Was it worth it?

chapter
twenty-nine

After leaving Kristie's office, I took my time heading back to campus. I was in shock. My entire life plan had been effectively decimated in the last thirty minutes.

Everything I had been working so hard for had been flushed down the toilet.

And all for a man who wouldn't pick up the goddamned phone.

I tried calling Maxx for the millionth time and again got his voice mail.

I was officially worried.

It had been a week since I had last heard from him. Since he had last told me he loved me and needed me.

I missed him.

With my head bowed down and my steps unhurried, I walked the two blocks back toward Longwood University.

I should have been devastated, but instead I was pissed. It was a misplaced emotion, but being angry made it easier to analyze what had become of my life.

Someone had ratted me out. And I had a good idea who it was.

Unfortunately for that person, I was boiling over by the time I reached campus and saw him immediately.

"Brooks!" I called out. He was walking down a path with Charlotte, the girl he had been with at Compulsion. I had seen them together around campus and wondered if they were dating now.

I couldn't care less about the state of his love life. I was feeling hurt and betrayed and ready to give him a piece of my mind.

He looked up and gave me a hesitant wave. Charlotte said something, and he nodded. I knew I was the topic of that particular conversation.

I hated to think that my onetime good friend was bitter enough to go behind my back and talk to Kristie. I didn't want to think it was true, that our friendship had deteriorated to such a degree. But he was the only person who had been aware of my relationship with Maxx and had been so vehement in his disapproval. Renee would never have done this. That left only Brooks.

Brooks stopped walking and waited for me to catch up. He said something to Charlotte, who gave me a troubled look before hurrying off.

He seemed tentative and unsure, with good reason. And when he got a look at my face, he knew I was mad. He just didn't realize how much.

"How could you?" I bit out.

Brooks frowned. "How could I what?" he asked, doing a good job of playing dumb.

"I had no idea you could be so callous. So cruel. I'm standing in front of you, Brooks, no need to put a knife in my back when I'm turned away. Do it where I can see you."

Brooks looked perplexed and a little worried. "I don't know what you're talking about, Aubrey."

I laughed hatefully. "God, I'm such a moron to think our friendship would stop you from betraying me. I should have known trying to be friends with a guy I had really bad sex with would only end in disaster."

Brooks flinched. "Why are you being like this?" he asked, and I tried to ignore the guilt I felt at seeing the pain in his eyes. But I was hurting. Because he couldn't keep his mouth shut.

"I know it was you who told Kristie. Don't try to deny it."

Brooks held his hands up. "Wait a second. Back up. Told Kristie what?"

I pointed my finger into his chest. "You told her about Maxx and me. Go ahead, lie to my face and say it wasn't you! Are you that freaking jealous that you needed to mess with my life?" I yelled, not caring that my tirade was getting us a lot of attention.

Brooks, however, cast an embarrassed look around and tried to shush me. "Keep it down, Aubrey. God, why don't you just announce to the entire campus your private business," he mumbled.

"Oh, so now you're worried about my privacy? Please, don't treat me like I'm stupid. Not after what you did!"

Even in the middle of my outburst, there was a part of me questioning why I was doing this. Was it really Brooks's fault that I was losing everything?

No.

Even if he had gone to Kristie and told her about my relationship with Maxx, I had made the choice to be with him in the first place.

Brooks laughed. "Are you serious?" he asked incredulously.

I glared at him. "I'm glad you think this is funny!" I scowled.

Brooks crossed his arms over his chest. "First of all, I didn't tell anyone anything, but given how much you've fucked up your life, I probably should have. It's what a *friend* would do," he said harshly.

I opened my mouth to hurl some more nastiness, but he kept going.

"And second, how dare you stand there and blame anyone but

yourself for the shit storm you've gotten yourself into. You"—he pointed at me—"made the choice to fuck around with the junkie. You"—he pointed at me again—"made the choice to not care about the consequences."

He took a deep breath and looked sad. "It was *you* who threw away our friendship. It was *you* who gave up on yourself." He walked around me, leaving me to stand there bewildered by the turn of our argument.

Brooks turned around just before he left. "Was it worth it?" he asked.

I had been asked that a lot lately.

Was it worth it?

Watching the man who had been one of my closest friends walk away from me and out of my life, I was beginning to wonder.

◆

I spent Friday night with Renee. We watched movies and ate junk food. I hadn't been able to tell her about what happened with Kristie. She was dealing with so much, no sense in adding more to her plate.

I was in the library most of Saturday, hoping schoolwork would keep my mind busy. For the first time in my life, it didn't work. I hadn't been able to concentrate. My thoughts were a jangled mess.

Finally, I gave up and returned home. Renee was asleep when I got back, so I thought I'd try to take a nap myself. But my mind wouldn't shut off. I kept replaying the events of the last twenty-four hours over and over again.

How did things get messed up so quickly?

Finally, not able to lie in my bed any longer, I got up. I checked on Renee, but she was still asleep, clearly exhausted from her own drama.

I went into the kitchen and, as quietly as possible, made myself some pasta. It was Saturday night, and I wondered if Maxx was at Compulsion. I had a brief thought of getting dressed and going there to find him. But I quickly dismissed that idea.

I parked myself on the couch and turned on the television, hoping mindless reality TV would be just what I needed.

And then around ten-thirty my phone rang. I was so engrossed in feeling sorry for myself that I startled at the sound.

I looked down at the screen, and my heart leaped into my throat.

It was Maxx.

"Hello?" I said.

"There you are," Maxx slurred, his words stringing together in a way that was barely understandable. I could hear the pounding of music in the background and knew he was at Compulsion.

"Why did you leave me?" Maxx sobbed into the phone, though it was hard for me to hear him. He sounded completely bombed out.

"Maxx, are you all right?" What a stupid question. He most certainly was *not* all right.

"I love you," he cried, his words garbled, and then I heard a loud smack over the thumping music.

"Maxx!" I yelled into the phone, but he didn't answer me.

The music continued to pound in my ear, but Maxx was gone.

"Maxx!" I screamed, and then I was cut off by the dial tone.

"You selfish fucking bastard!" I cried, immediately dialing his number.

It rang and rang and rang.

When his voice mail picked up, I hung up and tried again.

I called at least a half dozen more times before giving up.

Something was wrong. I recognized the sound of Maxx's voice when he was high, but this was something different. Something *more*. I couldn't stop thinking about how desolate he sounded. How lost.

Damn him!

I wrote a quick note to Renee, letting her know I'd be back in a bit, then grabbed my coat and keys with one destination in mind.

Compulsion.

Except I didn't know where it was.

My plan just kept getting better and better.

I needed to find Maxx's painting as quickly as possible.

I drove around campus, thinking it would be there. It wasn't. The whole time, I was becoming more and more anxious. I headed into the city, checking all the usual places. I tried to think about where Maxx would leave it. But trying to get into his mind was a difficult thing.

I was one panic attack away from calling the police and telling them to go to Compulsion to get Maxx. Right then I didn't care that he'd end up behind bars for possession. At least he'd be alive. Then I saw the group of people milling around the alleyway beside the movie theater.

I pulled into the parking lot and jumped out of my car. I ran across the street and elbowed my way through the small crowd.

This was it.

I should have known.

I should have realized he'd leave this at a place with significance to the people we had once been together.

The naïve, delusional people who were now long gone.

Painted along one side of the theater building was the picture of a man falling off the edge of a cliff onto a bed of knives. A woman, who I now recognized to be me, was standing above him. My face was a black circle, and my blond hair was turning into fingers tipped with bloodied talons.

The painting was the most depressing thing I had seen Maxx create. It made me want to cry.

It terrified me to think of what was going through his head in order for him to create this.

He had darkened my face. The deep psychological meaning of that wasn't lost on me.

It seemed as though he was trying to erase me from his heart, just as he had erased my face in the painting.

Pulling myself together, I wiped away the tears that had escaped from the corner of my eyes, and I searched the picture for the address I needed.

At the base of the cliff were the words *Wilby Street*. Numbers had been blended into the clouds. I pulled out a pen and wrote everything down on the back of my hand.

Once back in my car, I fiddled with my phone, pulling up my GPS, and put in the address. It was fifteen minutes away. I broke several traffic laws in my haste to get to the club.

I finally found the location, an old office complex on the outskirts of town in a run-down industrial park. Without bothering to get in line, I made my way to the front, where Marco stood with Randy, the scary bouncer.

"I need to get inside," I said, trying not to sound like a crazed lunatic. Randy barely spared me a glance.

"Then get in line like everyone else," he said gruffly.

"You don't understand. I'm looking for Maxx," I explained, hoping my attempt at name-dropping would work.

Randy looked at me, but there was no recognition of the name. "I don't care who you're looking for. You still have to get in the back of the line."

I looked over at Marco, but he wasn't paying us any attention. He was too busy flirting with a couple of underage-looking girls in tight skirts.

"Marco!" I called out.

"Look, girlie, you need to move, now," Randy warned.

"I know him!" I told him, pointing at Marco.

Randy rolled his eyes. "You're not the first one, sweetheart. Now get the fuck out of here!"

I lunged past Randy, who tried to grab me. "Marco!" I yelled again. Randy wrapped a beefy hand around my upper arm and yanked me backward.

Marco turned around at the commotion and finally saw me. But my heart dropped at the blank look on his face. He didn't know who I was.

"Marco, it's me, Aubrey!" I called out.

"You need to leave now, you're not getting in here," Randy growled, yanking me hard by the arm. Ouch, that would leave a mark.

"Hold on, man. I think I know this chick," Marco said.

"Dude, you know a lot of chicks," Randy stated, and not at all nicely.

"Seriously, hang on a second." Marco looked at me closely.

"I'm Maxx's girlfriend," I explained and was relieved to see understanding dawn on his metal-studded face.

"Right! I knew you looked familiar. Let her go, Randy. She's X's girl," Marco said, grabbing my other hand and putting a stamp on the back.

I should have thought to use his *other* name. But I didn't know X. I didn't think I ever would.

Randy loosened his hand around my upper arm, and my fingers started to tingle as blood rushed back. "Sorry, I didn't know," Randy mumbled, giving me a small push forward.

I rubbed my arm where he had grabbed me, wincing at the pain there.

"I had no idea you were coming tonight. Maxx didn't say anything," Marco said, leaving his post and walking me through the door.

Marco grinned, his lips stretching and exposing a tongue ring I hadn't noticed the last time I had seen him. "And just so you know, nobody around here calls him Maxx. That's why Randy didn't know who you were talking about," Marco explained.

"Do you know where he is?" I asked Marco, my teeth already rattling from the music that blasted just behind the door.

Marco shook his head. "I've been out here all night. I don't usually see him until just before closing."

Crap.

"Thanks, Marco. I appreciate your help back there," I said sincerely. Maybe Marco wasn't such a bad guy, even if he did look like a tattoo experiment gone wrong.

"Sure thing, Aubrey," Marco said, clasping my shoulder before returning to the entryway.

I took a deep breath and walked inside the club. It looked like chaos. Normally I found the craziness appealing.

Not tonight.

Tonight, I hated it. I saw it as ugly and sordid, its darkness hiding secrets and ruin. I wanted to leave.

But not without Maxx.

I started to push through the throngs of people dancing to the frenetic beat, straining up on my tiptoes in my search for Maxx.

No, not Maxx. Here, in this world, he was X.

I was pushed and jostled as the music reached its pinnacle. A mosh pit had started, and if I didn't get away from it, I was certain I would lose a tooth or two.

I could see the bar against the back wall, and that's where I headed. I recognized the bartender Maxx had called Eric.

I waved him down, and I knew instantly that he recognized me from when I was here before with Maxx. When he came to my end of the bar, I asked him if he knew where X was. It felt weird to call him that. It rolled oddly off my tongue, a stranger's name. But I knew that I was looking for a person I didn't know at all.

"I saw him over there a while ago. But I'm sure he's around. He never goes far, so just hang around and he'll find you." Eric grinned, winking at me.

I headed in the direction Eric had indicated. A door on the far side of the room led to a narrow hallway that held the bathrooms. If anyone was down there, I couldn't tell. It was too dark.

"Maxx, where are you?" I murmured to myself. The door to the men's bathroom opened and shut behind me, and I heard a couple of guys laughing as they walked by.

"Fucking junkies," one was saying.

Instinct took over, and I just *knew*.

I hurried into the men's bathroom. It was a row of four stalls, all of them shut. But the last one was propped open by a figure I would recognize anywhere.

"Maxx!" I yelled, running to him. I fell to my knees beside him, not caring about the piss and the filth on the floor. The bathroom smelled rank, making me gag. But it was nothing compared to the nausea I felt when I got a good look at Maxx, sagged over on the tiles.

He was on his side, his face pressed into the floor. His left arm was bare and stretched out beside him with a thin white strip of plastic tied tightly, just above the elbow, causing the vein to be exposed.

I knew exactly what Maxx had been doing. Anyone who had ever watched HBO or a bad health video in high school would be able to figure it out. I patted around on the ground next to Maxx's limp body until I found the empty syringe.

I sprang into action. I immediately loosened the plastic around his arm and threw it on the floor. Then I leaned in close to make sure he was still breathing. His breaths were slow and shallow, and when I felt his pulse it was thready. I wasn't sure how much he had taken.

I knew that a heroin overdose could involve depressed respiratory functioning. If a person took enough, eventually their lungs stopped working, and they'd suffocate.

"What the hell, Maxx?" I asked, knowing he was way past answering. I tried lifting him up, but he was too heavy to move. I rolled him over so he lay flat on his back.

He didn't make a sound. I laid my ear against his chest, listening to the strained beat of his heart. My tears soaked his shirt, and I turned and buried my face in the fabric, screaming to a man who couldn't hear me.

The door of the bathroom swung open, and a few guys came in. They noticed me on the floor with Maxx and chuckled.

"Sorry to interrupt," they said, turning to the urinals and taking a piss, unconcerned. They didn't see what was really going on. The sight was most likely not unusual at a place like Compulsion.

When the men left, I tried to get Maxx to wake up. I yelled in his ear. I smacked his face. I shook him hard enough to bang his head against the floor. Nothing worked. He wouldn't wake up. And when his breath started to rattle in his chest and his lips began to tinge blue, I knew I needed to get him to a hospital.

I hurried to the door of the restroom and locked it, not wanting anyone to come in. I got out my phone and dialed 911.

And then I watched Maxx's breathing slow down until his chest wasn't moving at all.

chapter
thirty

aubrey

I had given Maxx CPR while I waited for the paramedics. His skin had grown cold as I pounded away at his chest. I breathed into his mouth, wishing he would start breathing on his own.

He would for a little while, then he would stop, and I'd start CPR all over again.

The EMTs showed up with the police, who promptly shut the club down. I heard screaming and yelling, but I was too busy trying to keep Maxx alive.

I was exhausted by the time the paramedics rushed into the bathroom and took over resuscitation. One of the EMTs asked if I wanted to ride with Maxx in the ambulance to the hospital, but I said I'd go in my own car.

And I did. I went and waited in the emergency room. I waited until Landon and David showed up and were ushered into the back, neither realizing I was there.

I waited after the doors to the triage unit swung open and the shrill code blue wailed out into the ER. And I knew fear. I knew terror. I knew what it meant to feel your heart die.

I continued to wait while Maxx's life hung in the balance.

I watched Maxx's uncle leave the hospital hours later with Landon, who was sobbing. And I thought that was it. Maxx was gone.

Not able to sit there a moment longer, I asked the nurse about Maxx. When she asked who I was, I lied and said I was his sister.

The nurse eyed me skeptically but didn't call me out on my obviously false story. She clicked away at the computer before giving me the information I wanted.

"He's listed as in critical condition. But he's stable. They're beginning the detox process," she explained.

"Do you want to go back and see him?" she asked me.

I stepped away from the counter.

"No," I said, turning around and leaving the ER.

I drove home. When I got there, Renee was waiting up for me. And she wasn't alone.

"We've got company," Renee said, giving Brooks a fierce look.

Brooks got to his feet. "Hey," was all he said, and I lost it.

I just flipping lost it.

I rushed him and wrapped my arms around his waist, burying my head in his crisp, clean shirt, and sobbed.

Brooks stiffened the second I touched him, but as I started to shudder, my body going into spasms with the force of my cries, he slowly held me more firmly, his hand rubbing my back soothingly.

"What's wrong, Aubrey? What happened?" he asked over and over, but I couldn't speak. I couldn't say a word.

Renee joined us, and my two best friends held me while I fell apart.

When I was finished crying for Maxx, for myself, for the *us* that would never be, I fell into bed and slept. Thinking about what could have happened to Maxx if I hadn't gotten there in time was a pain I couldn't handle.

✦

I went to the hospital the next day and again claimed to be Maxx's sister. The nurse on duty didn't question me, and it was hard not to silently criticize their lack of security.

I was told to head down the hall and that Maxx's room number was 302. I followed the directions and found myself standing out in the hallway, unable to make myself go inside.

Maxx was sleeping; there were tubes and monitors everywhere. He was as white as a sheet, his blond curls lank and lifeless. Slowly I walked inside and sat down beside his bed.

I didn't take his hand. I didn't cry. I just stared at the man I loved with all my heart. He had been so willing to throw away what we had. And for what? This?

A nurse came bustling in, giving me a distracted smile. She checked the monitors and his IV.

"Is he going to be okay?" I asked her before she could leave.

"He's got a heck of a hard road ahead of him. He's been given naloxone through his IV overnight, which will put him into withdrawal. Once he's stable enough to be moved, he'll go to the detox unit. After that, the doctor will recommend a rehab program, but it will be up to him whether he goes or not," the nurse reported clinically.

"Okay, thanks," was all I could say.

"I'm guessing you're family, right?" the nurse asked, giving me a look that said she knew I was most definitely not family.

"Of course," I responded, my eyes flicking to Maxx, who still hadn't regained consciousness.

"Rehab is this young man's only chance. His heart stopped twice after he got here. His body is in bad shape. His organs were on the brink of shutdown. If he were my family, I'd do everything I could to make him go."

I nodded, my throat uncomfortably tight. The nurse turned her hard eyes on Maxx.

"Not everyone gets a second chance. Let's hope he takes

his," she said, her words clipped. She gave me a thin smile as she left.

I sat back in my chair, watching him sleep. I wish I could have been sure he'd make the right choice, that he'd go to rehab and get better. But I just didn't know.

There were two sides of Maxx that were completely at odds with each other. One side wanted a normal life. He wanted to go to school, take care of his brother, love me, and be happy. That's the side of Maxx that would undoubtedly make the right decision.

However, there was also the darker, more self-destructive side, which was selfish and miserable and needed the escape that only drugs could provide. And that side of Maxx would never do anything that would keep him away from the thing he loved above all else—his next high.

Needing to touch him, I reached out and took his limp hand in mine. I wanted to cry, but there weren't any tears left to fall.

So I sat there, holding his hand, knowing whatever road he'd take, he'd have to travel it alone.

✦

"Aubrey, please have a seat," Dr. Lowell said, closing her office door behind me. In the aftermath of Maxx's overdose, I had briefly forgotten about my day of reckoning.

Dr. Lowell looked older than I could ever remember seeing her.

"I never thought I'd be having this conversation with you, Aubrey. To say I'm sad and disappointed is a great understatement," Dr. Lowell began.

"You know I've spoken with Kristie Hinkle, and I know you are aware of what you have been accused of. Kristie tells me she has already spoken with you, and that you have admitted to engaging in an inappropriate relationship with a member of the support group you were co-facilitating. Is this correct?" she asked me, sounding weary.

I nodded. "Yes, it's true, Dr. Lowell." I wouldn't deny it. It was high time I accepted responsibly for my choices.

My mind wandered to Maxx, who was now most likely awake, lying in the hospital detox ward, probably wondering why I hadn't come to see him. He didn't know that I had been by his side most of the time he had been unconscious and that it was only when I knew he'd be okay that I'd found the strength to leave, knowing that he had to make his choices for himself.

And they could have nothing to do with me.

Dr. Lowell took off her glasses and rubbed her eyes. "I don't need to tell you how serious these accusations are. You have violated our ethical code of conduct. You have abused your role as facilitator and taken advantage of someone in a vulnerable position. This is the grossest kind of misconduct, Aubrey," Dr. Lowell stated, her voice hardening with her displeasure.

"I understand," was all I could say.

"I am going to have to begin a departmental investigation into your behavior. There will be a hearing where you will be able to speak on your own behalf. If you are found to have shown misconduct, as your own admission will surely prove, you will be put on disciplinary suspension. It will be up to the disciplinary council to decide whether you should be removed from the counseling program," Dr. Lowell explained.

I could only nod.

"You'll receive information in the mail regarding an investigative interview and the time of your hearing. You will get more information about the process when you have your interview. Do you have any questions?" Dr. Lowell asked, her eyes boring into mine.

"I have no questions," I said, resigned to my fate.

"You can go then. But just know I have never been so disappointed in a student. Your behavior is shocking and reflects poorly not only on yourself but on the entire department."

I had been dismissed.

I gathered my purse and left Dr. Lowell's office, head hung low.

My phone rang from inside my bag. I fished it out and looked at the screen, not recognizing the number.

"Aubrey," the voice breathed on the other end after I said hello.

"Maxx," I stated, easily recognizing his raspy tone.

I sat down heavily on a bench by the library, tucked into an alcove and shielded from view. My trembling hands had a difficult time holding on to the phone as I clutched it to my ear.

I had been both anticipating and dreading this moment. I had hoped Maxx would have used his time in the hospital to come to see where his life was heading. From the terse way he said my name, I knew that wasn't the case.

He was angry. And hurt. He felt betrayed and abandoned. It gutted me to think he was feeling all of those things because of me. But this was honestly the only way I could think of to help him. *And* to help me.

"Are you out of the hospital then?" I asked after an uncomfortable moment of silence.

"No. I'm still here. I've been in the detox ward for seventy-two hours, or so they tell me. They said I can go home tomorrow."

My heart twisted in my chest.

"You're not going to rehab?" I asked, already knowing the answers.

"I don't need to go to rehab to get better, Aubrey," Maxx said defensively.

"Maxx . . . ," I began, but he cut me off.

"I only need you," he said with such confidence that I knew in his mind those words were one hundred percent true.

"You almost died, Maxx! You used heroin. Injected it into your damned arm! Do you know I found you barely breathing on the bathroom floor? Your heart stopped! I had to do CPR! I have never been so terrified in my entire life!" I was yelling into the phone. I needed to calm down. But I was so frustrated with him and his complete and total denial.

Maxx was quiet for a time, and I hoped that maybe he'd listen.

"I'm sorry, Aubrey. I didn't mean for it to go that far. It was the only time I've ever used that shit. I didn't know what I was doing. It won't happen again." How easily he excused his behavior. He still didn't see the pattern he lived in.

"Maxx, the next time you might not wake up. The next time it could be too late. Because I won't be there." I had said it, the thing I knew I had to tell him but wished I didn't.

"Don't say that, Aubrey! Please!" I could tell he was crying. The tears started falling down my face as I heard the brokenness in his voice.

"I can't do this without you," he pleaded.

We cried together on the phone. I tucked my head down into my jacket, trying to get my breathing under control.

"Aubrey, I love you," he whispered, the words catching in his throat.

"I love *you*, Maxx," I choked out, my throat strangling the words as they erupted out of me. I heard Maxx's sharp intake of breath.

It was horrible timing. Here I was, finally telling him what he wanted so badly to hear, and it came when I was planning to leave him.

"You love me," he murmured, and I could hear the relief in his voice. I knew what he was thinking—that this made everything better, that I was giving in.

"I've waited so long for you to say that." I heard the catch in Maxx's voice. "So long." His words cracked and broke apart.

My tears, which I thought I was long past shedding, started falling in earnest.

"I've wanted to say it. I really have," I told him.

"Then why didn't you? Why wouldn't you tell me something so important?" he sobbed.

I scrubbed my face and rubbed away my tears. I felt the steel enter my spine as I prepared to tell him what needed to be said, the things I had been scared to share. But he had to hear them. There was no other choice to make.

"Because I knew something like this would happen, Maxx," I bit out angrily.

"Don't put your inability to communicate off on me! You didn't tell me because you like to fuck with my feelings! Because you like to torture me!" he yelled in my ear.

And then he was sobbing again. "I didn't mean that, Aubrey. I really didn't," he babbled.

"I can't trust you with my love, Maxx. Those words are precious. I wanted to know that when I gave them to you, you'd take care of them. You'd cherish them. You'd return my feelings as a healthy and whole person," I said earnestly.

Maxx took several shuddering breaths. "Then why tell me now? Why say you love me when it's obvious you're not sticking around? Because from where I'm sitting, that just makes you look heartless."

His words shook me, and I tried in vain to stop myself from crying again. "Because I want you to know what you're giving up by not going to rehab. I want you to see what I'm willing to give you. And I hope . . . I really hope that you'll want to fight for it—to fight for yourself!"

I swallowed thickly and prepared to deliver the final blow.

"I love you so much, Maxx. I do. And that's why I can't watch you kill yourself. I won't. And it's because I love you that I'm walking away," I said, my voice hoarse with emotion.

Maxx was silent for a long time, so long that I thought he had hung up.

"That's bullshit, Aubrey! If you loved me, you wouldn't leave me when I need you! Because I'll get better. I can do this. But only if you help me!" He was using emotional blackmail. He was sink-

ing to a low that I wasn't sure we could crawl out of. Our relationship was toxic. It was unhealthy. It was soul-defeating.

God, what had I been doing to myself?

And even still, when I logically knew how bad he was for me, I
wanted to run to him. I wanted his lies to be my truth. I wanted to
believe the false promises. I wanted to pretend he wasn't sick and
that his denial wouldn't destroy us both.

"That's not fair," I said finally, proud of how firm I sounded.

"What's not fair is you abandoning me when I need you! What
kind of selfish person are you? So this only works for you as long
as you're getting something out of it? Because I didn't hear about
any problems as long as you were flat on your fucking back with
your legs spread open," Maxx said nastily. I knew he was hurting,
that he was lashing out, but fuck him.

Seriously . . . *fuck . . . him.*

"Get your shit together, Maxx. And do it for yourself, and for
no one else. And then maybe I can learn to trust you again, trust
myself to be with you. Because this"—I paused for a moment—"is
wrong. This is unhealthy. And if you truly loved me, you'd see
that."

There, I had said my piece. What he chose to do with my
words was on him.

Maxx must have sensed my finality because I could hear him
start to cry again. "Don't leave me," he whispered.

I couldn't do this anymore. If I listened to him begging any
longer, all my conviction, all my strength, would evaporate, and I'd
crawl back to him, broken and bleeding.

"I've got to go. I hope you get better. I really do," I told him, my
throat closing up over the words.

And then I hung up before he could say anything else. For
good measure, I turned off my phone and dropped it into my bag.

My heart was wounded, but it wasn't destroyed. I would re-
cover from this, eventually. And I sincerely hoped that the day

would come when Maxx would come back to me, healthy and whole.

But I couldn't hinge my life on that. I had to go on.

And despite the emotional upheaval Maxx had unleashed on my life, I could never regret him. I hoped, in the future, when I looked back on our time together, I'd be able to look past the gut-twisting, heart-shattering wreckage and see everything that knowing him had done for me.

Because of *him* I had been opened to a side of myself I thought would never exist again.

Because of *him* I had learned to love with my whole heart.

Because of *him* I was stronger than I had ever been before.

I knew that in the next few weeks, when I was faced with the consequences of my choices, I would be sure that the path I took was the only one I could have traveled.

In the end—because of everything, rather than in spite of it— Maxx Demelo had been worth it.

Feeling a weight lift from my shoulders that I hadn't realized I'd been carrying, I headed home. And when I opened the door to find Renee curled up on the couch, watching TV, I knew, without a doubt, that I'd be okay.

Out of the ashes I would rise to become something better.

And I would find the strength to go wherever my road would lead.

epilogue

i stared down at the phone long after Aubrey ended the call. And long after there was nothing left but silence.

And all I loved, I loved alone.

Poe had been right. Loving was lonely.

I had really fucked up this time.

She had left me.

I should have known it was only a matter of time.

Aubrey Duncan was entirely too good for a screwup like me.

But she loved me.

Finally, she had told me the words I had waited so long to hear.

Even though she had given them to me as she had ripped out my heart, I was still happy to hear them.

But then I remembered her other words, and I knew we were over. And the decisiveness of that almost undid me completely.

And now I was stuck in this shithole I called a life.

Aubrey had given me a glimpse of something better. Something good. Something clean. And I had craved it so much, but ultimately I had destroyed it.

And now here I was, laid up in a hospital room, lucky to be alive.

When the doctor had come around and explained the detox process, he had encouraged me to continue with treatment by going to rehab.

I had dismissed the idea outright. I didn't need rehab. That shit was for junkies and losers.

I would be just fine. And I would do it on my own.

All I needed was Aubrey.

She'd help me. She'd get me through anything.

She was my savior.

But I didn't have Aubrey.

She had made it clear she *wouldn't* be there. That she couldn't help me.

That I had to *help myself.*

Shit. Now what was I going to do?

Landon had been by earlier with my uncle. Neither one of them said much. I had expected David to be a dick, so no big surprise. But I hadn't expected the stony silence from my kid brother.

It had ripped me in half to see an expression on his face I never thought I'd see.

Disappointment.

After Landon had left, I felt depressed. I was as low as I thought I could get.

I was wrong.

Because I had decided to call Aubrey.

I had been tormented with wondering why she hadn't come to the hospital to see me. I had no idea she had been the one who had found me at the club and essentially saved my life.

And now she was gone.

My chest ached with a pain I was all too familiar with.

Grief.

The night after talking to Aubrey I couldn't sleep. I tossed and

turned and thought about the ways I could have done things differently. What I could have said to make her stay.

And in the early hours of the morning, I was hit with a clarity
that comes only when you've lost everything.

So after forcing myself out of bed, I got dressed in the same
clothes I had been admitted in. They hung loosely on my hips. I
had lost weight in the week I had been in the hospital. Looking in
the mirror at my hollow cheeks and sallow skin, I barely recognized the man looking back at me.

I hated him.

"I have your release paperwork here. You just need to read
over everything and sign at the bottom," the doctor said, coming
into my room a short time later.

He held out the papers, waiting for me to take them.

This was the moment when I could change everything.

"Actually, I'd like to hear more about rehab."

acknowledgments

Sometimes the acknowledgments are the hardest part to write. But this time, they're the easiest . . .

This book is for the people who have supported me, no matter what. This is for my mother, who is no longer with me, but whose influence is still felt in every part of my life. She always told me to reach for the stars and to never give up until I could touch them. I didn't give up, Mom. And I never will . . .

For my dad and grandparents, who are my biggest fans. I love you all so very much, and I hope I always make you proud.

For Ian. You helped me brainstorm this incredible idea for a story. Something about clubbing and street art and addiction (and insisting I watch documentaries on Banksy) . . . and somewhere in our crazy stream-of-consciousness ramblings, *Lead Me Not* was created. You listened to me as I pieced it together, and you didn't grumble (too much) when I hid away in my writing cave to bleed this story out. Thank you for your endless patience. I said it in my first book and I say it again now . . . they're all for you . . .

For my daughter, who is old enough to be excited when Mommy is writing a new book, though she doesn't understand why she can't read it (when you're older, sweetheart). Thank you for being sparkly and pink and fabulous!

For my awesome agent, Michelle, who has listened to me freak out, explode, and lose it on numerous occasions. Thank you for always talking me off the ledge. You have loved Maxx and Aubrey from the start, and I'm so thankful for your endless cheerleading!

Thanks to Alex Lewis, my amazing editor at Gallery, who helped me mold this book into what it is. You had faith in this crazy, dark story, and I'm so thankful you took a chance on me. And thank you to the entire team at Gallery for believing in Maxx and Aubrey!

A super, humongous thank-you to Kristy Garbutt, my amazing PA and friend. Our chats and your encouragement have helped me in ways you don't even know. I'm so blessed to have you in my life!!!

Thank you to my lovely Bad Ass CPs: Tonya, Brittainy, Stacey, Amy, Claire, and Kelsie; you guys rock. It's awesome having six other authors whom I respect and admire so much and who are there to listen to me vent or just to make me laugh. Love you, ladies!

Thank you to all of the bloggers who have pimped my stories, spread the word, and been the hugest supports I could ever have imagined! There are too many of you to name—plus I'm scared to death I'd leave someone out—but to each of you who have shared my covers, talked about me on Facebook or Twitter, encouraged your fans to pick up my books, you all *rock*!

Thank you to my fantastic street team, Meredith's Maniacs! I'm so lucky to have you guys. Your endless pimping and enthusiasm for my books is what keeps me going.

And finally, thank you to my readers! Words can't express how much each and every one of you means to me. Every day I wake up and can't quite believe that I'm living my dream. And that's because of you!

Look for the continuation of

Maxx and Aubrey's story in 2015:

follow me back

Turn the page for a preview. . . .

chapter
one

aubrey

three months earlier

"Miss Duncan, you have been asked here today to discuss the allegations that have been lodged against you in regards to your behavior toward a member of the support group you had been co-facilitating. These allegations describe a personal and inappropriate relationship that is a clear violation of our ethical codes of conduct."

I looked steadily at the three people who sat at the table in front of me. I picked at the skin around my fingernails and tried not to fidget in my seat.

My day of reckoning was here.

I was nervous. I'd be an idiot if I wasn't. This was possibly the end of all of my dreams and aspirations. Three years of hard work crumbling around me.

But losing my place in the Longwood University counseling program wasn't what had kept me awake at night for the past two weeks. That wasn't the thing that had my insides twisted into knots and had tears drying on my cheeks. Seeing the future I had worked so hard for fading in front of me wasn't the explanation either. Nor was the breakdown of friendships that I was trying so hard to rectify.

My state of emotional upheaval could be attributed to only one thing, one pivotal moment that had shredded my soul and threatened to unravel me.

It was saying good-bye to Maxx Demelo. Choosing my sanity over his pain. Leaving him when he needed me the most.

My guilt was a wild thing inside me that at times seemed out of control. I hated myself for hanging up the phone after telling him I loved him. For effectively pulling away and out of his life.

Even if it was our dysfunctional love that had almost ruined me.

But I wasn't down for the count yet. It was time to pull up my big-girl pant- ies and face the consequences of my disastrous choices head on. It was my only option now that I had lost the person I had thrown everything away for.

Dr. Lowell, my academic advisor, sat beside two of her university col- leagues. She was looking staunchly down at the paper in her hands. Her mouth was pinched and her brow was furrowed. She was upset and dis- appointed with me.

And she had every right to be. I had been her most promising student. I had a perfect 4.0 average. I had been on the fast track to a great career as a substance-abuse counselor. I had taken my future seriously.

Until the day Maxx had walked into the support group and blown my life apart.

Now when she looked at me, all she saw was a screw-up. It sucked.

"We have read over your written statement, and it seems you aren't denying the allegations. Is that correct, Miss Duncan?" Dr. Jamison, the head of the counseling department, asked, pursing his mouth. He looked at me over the tops of his wire-rimmed glasses, condemnation written all over his face. Obviously he had already made up his mind about me. And his conclusion wasn't favorable.

I sat up straight and squared my shoulders. I took a deep breath and readied myself. Because all I could do was be completely truthful. I was long overdue for a healthy dose of honesty. I had lived with my head in the sand for entirely too long. Denial had gotten me nowhere.

"That's correct, Dr. Jamison. I admit to engaging in an inappropriate relationship with a member of the substance-abuse support group. As I wrote in my statement, I was aware that my actions were a violation of the code of conduct, and I accept any and all disciplinary action." I was proud of the fact that my voice never wavered. I didn't cry. I didn't whimper and plead. I would take my punishment, whatever it may be.

Dr. Jamison seemed taken aback by my honesty. It was clear he had ex- pected me to deny the charges. Or to play the ignorant-student card: *But, sir, I didn't know sleeping with a client was a bad idea!*

I wasn't an idiot; I had just made some stupid decisions. But I wasn't going to make ridiculous excuses now. And that was one thing out of this huge, life-sucking mess I had created that I could be proud of.

Dr. Jamison looked at Professor Bradley—a slight woman with obviously dyed brown hair and a nasty habit of mixing plaids with stripes—and said something under his breath. He then turned to Dr. Lowell, who nodded, her hands clenched on the table in front of her. They talked quietly amongst themselves while I fiddled with a piece of string hanging from the hem of my skirt.

I looked at the clock on the wall. It was a little after one. I had been in this chair, sitting in front of my judge and jury, for only half an hour.

But it felt like forever.

I knew that my friends Renee Alston and Brooks Hamlin were waiting for me out in the hallway. Brooks would be pacing the floor while Renee twisted her hands in her lap. I could practically feel their anxiety through the walls.

Anxiety I should have been feeling as well if it weren't for the giant lump in my gut and the shards of a broken heart piercing my chest.

It had been fifteen days since I had spoken to Maxx Demelo. Fifteen days since I had told him I couldn't stay and watch him destroy himself as he fell deeper and deeper into an addiction that I had tried to save him from. Fifteen days since he had almost died and I had left him anyway.

I had convinced myself that I had done the right thing. That standing by his side while he slowly lost himself to the dependence that controlled his entire world would destroy me. That I couldn't watch him make the same bad choices that had taken the life of my sister, Jayme, all those years ago.

I wouldn't enable him. I wouldn't hide from who he was either. And Maxx had to learn to stand on his feet without me holding him up.

It was the only way.

Even if I had to fight every instinct that made me want to run back to him. Despite the fact that I cried myself to sleep each night as I ached for the man I should never have fallen in love with in the first place.

"Aubrey." Dr. Lowell's voice brought me out of my suffocating self-pity. I blinked and tried to refocus on my situation.

"Dr. Jamison, Professor Bradley, and I all agree that you have behaved in a manner that is both unprofessional and inappropriate. Your actions have had a negative impact not only on your reputation within this department but on this department's reputation in the community."

I swallowed thickly, but I never looked away from the narrowed eyes of my favorite teacher.

"However . . ." Dr. Lowell began, and my heart skipped a beat at the slight change in her tone. A sliver of something other than displeasure laced her words.

"Given that you have admitted having the relationship and that you have taken responsibility for your actions, we have decided to place you on probation. While we cannot overstate how serious this offense is, it doesn't negate the years of hard work you have put into this program. However, your volunteer hours will be stripped, and you will have to begin your clinical hours again next year, which could impact your graduation next spring."

Dr. Lowell glanced back down at the paper in her hands, as though looking at me was too difficult.

My mouth gaped open. The shock made it hard for me to breathe. I had expected to be kicked out on my proverbial ass. I definitely had not counted on any kind of leniency.

"You will have absolutely no direct counseling interaction. You will complete extra course work on ethical boundaries. You will be required to meet with both Dr. Jamison and myself once a week to evaluate your progress. Each of these things will be mandatory if you wish to remain in the counseling program. And I don't think I need to tell you that any sort of contact with Maxx Demelo will be strictly prohibited while he is considered a therapeutic client."

That definitely wouldn't be a problem. But I couldn't say that. I could only nod, words being insufficient.

Dr. Lowell removed her glasses and folded them slowly, laying them on the table. Dr. Jamison was making notes, and Professor Bradley seemed to be counting down the time until the end of this uncomfortable hearing.

"Aubrey, I don't need to tell you again how your actions have put this department in a precarious position. It has strained relations with the community service board, which has been our partner in providing services to our campus community for over fifteen years. But that doesn't change the fact that you are a smart, capable young woman. A smart, capable young woman who made a horrible mistake. One that could have ended your career before it began." Dr. Lowell pursed her lips again.

"I hope you take this clemency for what it is: a second chance to prove to us, to the department, and more importantly to yourself that you can put aside your personal feelings and act in a manner that is both professional and appropriate."

"I will, Dr. Lowell. I promise," I let out in a rush, the relief almost crippling.

Dr. Lowell's eyes bored into mine and I wanted to look away. But I didn't. I had brought this upon myself.

"We will send you an official letter with the panel's decision in writing. The letter will also define the requirements of your probation and spell out what will be expected of you. Do you have any questions, Miss Duncan?" Dr. Jamison asked.

"No, sir," I said, hoping I wouldn't pass out. I just wanted to make it through these last few minutes and get out of there.

Dr. Jamison nodded, and just like that, I was dismissed. I quickly gathered my purse and hurried out into the hallway.

Brooks, as I had suspected, was pacing, and Renee was chewing on her thumbnail. Both looked up as I opened the door.

Renee got to her feet and rushed over. "What happened?" she asked, sounding almost as frantic as I felt.

Still in a daze, I looked from her to Brooks.

Renee gave me a little shake. "Damn it, Aubrey, what the hell happened?" my best friend and roommate demanded.

"Probation. They put me on probation," I answered, the words sounding dry and brittle.

"They didn't kick you out? You just got probation?" Brooks asked incredulously.

I let out a shrill, almost manic laugh. "They didn't kick me out. I have to meet with Dr. Lowell and Dr. Jamison once a week. And I have to take extra classes on professional boundaries and ethics. And of course, I won't be allowed direct client contact for a while. But yeah, I'm still in the program."

Brooks shook his head. "Unbelievable. You're damn lucky, Aubrey. Maybe now you'll realize how freaking stupid you were," he chastised.

Renee glared at him. "Now is not the time for the obnoxious Brooks Hamlin version of I-told-you-so," she growled, her voice full of venom.

Brooks's mouth pressed into a thin line, but he kept all further comments to himself.

"He's right, Renee. I've gotten off lightly," I said as we exited the psychology building. Renee had her arm looped through mine, a much-needed sign of solidarity.

Brooks walked a few steps behind us. He wasn't saying anything, but I could feel his tension. Things with Brooks had been decidedly strained for weeks. Our friendship had deteriorated after he'd discovered my relationship with Maxx. He had been understandably disapproving. At the time I had been infuriated by his censure, convinced that even though what I was doing would be construed as wrong by anyone else, for me—and for Maxx—it was perfectly right.

But I hadn't been able to escape the truth: that I had built a relationship with a man who was hell-bent on self-destructing. He had pulled me into his messy world of drugs and emptiness, and I had almost lost myself there. I had allowed myself to be blinded by my desire to help him, to save him, and I had ignored the blatant red flags waving in my face.

Because Maxx's secrets weren't the sort that just went away. They were the kind that could destroy you. And they almost had.

Our unhealthy love had impacted everything: school, my friendships, my self-respect. And in the end, Maxx had almost died and I had come perilously close to losing everything.

Now here I was, standing in the aftermath, trying to figure out how to put all of the pieces back together.

But I would. Because there was no other option.

It didn't change the fact that even though I had made the decision to remove him from my life, Maxx haunted my every thought. The shadow of him was everywhere. I wasn't sure I could ever truly shake him.

I looked over at my best friend and realized that one good thing had come out of all of this ugliness: Our friendship was stronger than ever. We had a connection that hadn't been there before. Because if anyone could understand how difficult it was to move past a destructive relationship, it was Renee. Like me, she was trying to rebuild a life that had gone dangerously off-track as a result of her love for the wrong man.

Brooks reached out and grabbed ahold of my arm, pulling me to a stop. "Hey, I'm sorry. I didn't mean to be a dick back there," he apologized, bowing his head slightly.

I wasn't surprised by Brooks's apology. He was a good guy who always did the right thing—even when it meant standing beside me as I made some really shitty choices. He had been angry with me over the Maxx situation, and I hadn't been sure our friendship would survive it.

But when I'd needed him, he'd been there, whether I deserved his support or not.

"You were only saying the truth, Brooks. You don't need to apologize," I said.

Brooks took my hand and gave it a squeeze. "I know you're beating yourself up enough without needing to hear my preachy judgments," he admonished himself.

I gave him a small smile and then extracted my fingers from his and tucked them into my pockets. His touch felt strange. Not exactly wrong, but not exactly right, either.

Not when my skin still remembered the feel of hands that I missed more desperately than I should.

"Thanks. That means a lot," I said sincerely.

"If you're okay, I've got to head to my study group. I can come by later . . . if you want," Brooks suggested. His hesitation was obvious, as though he was not entirely sure he should even be making the offer.

I forced my hand out of its hiding spot in my jacket pocket and took his again, feeling the need to give him some reassurance.

"Of course I want you to come over. But only if you bring the new Nicholas Sparks movie," I teased, trying for some normalcy in our otherwise abnormal situation. As I looked up at Brooks, his dark hair falling into his eyes, I wondered if things between us would ever be easy again. This odd discomfort made me edgy.

Brooks held on to my hand, his skin lingering on mine for a moment. My stomach twisted, my heart recoiled, and I immediately took a step back. Something that looked a lot like disappointment flickered in Brooks's eyes.

And I knew then that things would never be as they were. Not until I was able to eradicate the giant, Maxx-shaped elephant that sat heavily on the center of my chest. Even though I had made my choice where Maxx was concerned, he still invaded and conquered me completely.

Brooks gave me a lopsided grin that was more than a little forced. "You got it," he said, hoisting his book bag up over his shoulder.

He looked at my silent roommate. "See ya, Renee," Brooks said offhand-edly as he turned to walk away.

I let out a sigh and pulled my scarf tighter around my neck to ward off the late-afternoon chill. I was tired of the achy cold. I felt it from the inside out and longed to be warm again.

But I wasn't sure that was possible.

Renee walked beside me, her chin tucked into the collar of her jacket. "It'll get better, Aubrey. I promise. This is your second chance. Your time for something *more*."

Her reassurances fed a hungry place inside of me. I hoped she was right. I was desperate for that something better.

I can be so much more for you. I want to be everything you could ever want.

It had been only a matter of weeks since Maxx had said those words and given me his heart. Only weeks since he had made promises he hadn't been able to keep. It was such a short amount of time for my entire life to change.

But it *had* changed. And now all I could do was accept it and move on.

If only it were that simple.

My eyes were drawn to the brick wall that ran along the edge of the quad. Once-vibrant colors had faded, but I could still see the painting of a woman walking off a cliff, the word *Compulsion* woven into her familiar blond hair.

It was a small piece of the complicated man who continued to own me.

The tiny, intricate X's dotted throughout the picture seemed to scream at me, taunting me with their presence.

Even when he was gone, Maxx was everywhere.

His art. His love. His chaos.

I couldn't escape him.

And I was terrified that in the darkest recesses of my heart I didn't want to.